Robert Lassen was born in Oxford and raised in Cheshire ~~ ¹
spent 18 years as an officer in the UK
from service, he lives in Germany
their two children. He is the author
of novels, about a secretive wartime l
organisation using borderline supern
against the Nazis. He was also one of
writers for Sony Online Entertainme.. ₃ *Everquest Next* game
project. For more information on Robert Lassen and his books,
as well as free stories and fan content, please visit his website
at www.robertlassen.com.

C000217296

First published in by Silvertail Books in 2024
www.silvertailbooks.com

978-1-913727-38-3

OPERATION AFTERLIGHT

Robert Lassen

SILVERTAIL BOOKS • *London*

For Guy, Vera, John and Wilhelm, gone but not forgotten
And for Dad, gone before you could read this

Prologue

"Fireball, skipper. Four o'clock high."

Ignoring the sudden assault of nausea and the lurch of his pulse, Wing Commander Andrew Durban kept his de Havilland Mosquito straight and level and peered up into the darkness. It didn't matter that there was nothing in his navigator's tone to show concern. Ninety-three missions over Occupied Europe had carved all unnecessary emotions from Clive Lampeter's voice, until only calm detachment remained. After sharing twenty-nine of those missions by his side, though, Durban had learned to pay attention on the rare occasions the navigator spoke.

He saw it instantly.

At high altitude over Germany, the night sky had been well lit by moon and stars. Now, below the clouds, the cloying black of the rain-strewn night stressed the incandescent glow beyond the spinning props of the Mosquito's starboard engine. For a few moments, the fireball seemed to hang in the air while its light blazed violently on the underside of the shifting grey expanse brought in by the strong front from the North Sea.

It faded as if on a switch. Darkness returned, sinister and intense.

Durban tore his eyes from the few lingering tendrils of flame and focused on the Mosquito's controls. Rain slashed against the flat, armoured windscreen. It made it hard to see the dull smudge of the ground below. Harder still to pick out the dim landing lights ahead, their red glow partly shielded to mask them from unwanted observation.

The altimeter read three hundred feet. A little high this close to the runway. One hand automatically corrected for the mistake. The other reached for the lever that lowered the landing gear.

The words of their afternoon briefing rang clear in his mind.

Eight-hundred and seventeen bombers. Nearly five thousand airmen. Number Four Group to attack the synthetic oil plant at Kamen. Number Five Group to target the Dortmund-Ems canal.

Weather poor, with increased chance of misidentification and friendly fire.

Durban glanced to their right again. The blanket of the night had suffocated the last embers of the distant inferno.

A dozen things could destroy a bomber this close to safety. He'd heard stories of damaged aircraft nursed back against the odds to within touching distance of home before spreading flames incinerated the crew. Tired pilots made mistakes, descending too early, clipping a power line or dashing themselves against the flank of a mist shrouded hill. Sometimes a bomb clung too stubbornly to the bomb bay over the target only to detonate hours later, needing only a millisecond to turn both machine and its young crew into ten thousand smoking fragments.

Any good aviator knew they weren't safe until they shut the aircraft down and walked away. So many ways for the war to claim more lives. It didn't have to be a fighter.

A blinding flash ripped apart the darkness above them, and Durban's headphones exploded into life.

"Scram, skipper," Lampeter said, calmly repeating the panicked call of the distant radio operator. The same order that was resounding in the ears of every RAF aviator in the skies over eastern England.

A few thousand feet above them, Durban glimpsed a shark-like shape silhouetted against the new glare of a burning four-engined bomber. Then it was gone, its carnage wrought.

The red landing lights ahead of them blinked and faded to nothing.

'Scram' meant enemy night fighters in the area. *Abort landing. Divert to an airfield further west and south, out of enemy range.*

Durban frowned. A few years ago, scram orders were common, but not anymore. With the Luftwaffe reduced to a shadow of its prime and with Mosquito intruders like his own aircraft hunting them above their airfields, the enemy could barely operate in Germany's skies, let alone over Britain.

He increased power and retracted the undercarriage, feeling the aircraft's instant response through the control column. As always, the wooden airframe around him felt more like an extension of his body than a separate entity, but he still made the changes carefully. The twin Merlin engines and fabulous design left the de Havilland Mosquito all but untouchable for speed and handling at altitude, but at low level, low speed, buffeted by rain and wind? A new pilot could find himself horribly bent out of shape. He had lost friends that way.

He had lost friends every way imaginable these last four years.

"There's another," Lampeter muttered, pointing to a third distant glow, this time to their north. "How many of the bastards are out there?"

"Enough to ruin our evening." The landing gear thudded into place. Two tiny lights on the instrument panel flickered from the gear down position to up, and Durban felt the air flowing smoother around them without the drag of the undercarriage doors. "How far to our divert?"

Lampeter glanced at his chart. "Forty miles. Heading two-two-zero. Fuel state is good."

"Roger." Durban decided in a moment. No hesitation. He pushed the black-handled throttles open all the way. The

3

Mosquito seemed to leap forward, gathering speed even as he pulled back on the controls and climbed towards the cloud. He felt the navigator shift in his seat to look at him and knew exactly what was going through the man's mind.

"Might as well keep low, skipper," Lampeter said after a few seconds. "By the time we get to altitude, you'll be descending again."

Durban nodded. "Turn your radar back on."

Another pause. "We don't have fuel for that."

"You said our fuel state is good."

"Good for getting to our divert. Not for hunting German night fighters." Another pause, this one shorter but more painful. "Sir."

Durban winced. Despite their rank difference, Lampeter hadn't called him sir in the cockpit for over a year. They had too much respect for each other's abilities to need such courtesies. That the Flight Lieutenant did so now meant he didn't just disapprove of Durban's decision. He was furious.

"Hunting German night fighters is what we do," Durban said coldly. More than that, it was their *duty*. He flicked the gun master switch on the starboard instrument panel back from safe to armed. "Stay alert. There's more than one out there."

Lampeter turned his attention to the Mark VIII radar set in the aircraft's nose.

Keeping the Mosquito in a steady climb, Durban stifled a curse. His friend was only being sensible.

They had been circling over Germany before the first bombers even crossed the Channel, waiting for the night fighters. Their assigned mission was complete, their fuel tanks close to empty. He was tired, which would dull his reflexes and hamper his eyesight. Across England, fresh pilots in Mosquitoes like his own would be airborne now, ready to find whatever night fighter force the Luftwaffe had strung together and drive it back over the sea in bloody disarray.

The smart move was to let others handle it, and to head for their divert airfield while they still could.

And yet... in the time it took for reinforcements to arrive, the Luftwaffe would cause carnage among the vulnerable bomber crews. He'd already seen three bombers go down, their crews surviving the hostile skies over Germany only to be slaughtered above England. Tired or not, he couldn't hang back as it became four or more. If they could protect even one bomber, that meant seven or more lives saved. He had the best aircraft in the world. He had a brilliant navigator and radar operator next to him. Together, they outclassed anything the Luftwaffe had.

How could they put their own safety first, and leave others to face the danger?

"I've got something," Lampeter said. The navigator's gloved hands drifted over the controls of the radar set. His face showed no emotion in the faint light from the CRT radar screen. "Seven miles, straight ahead. Probably one of ours. Too big a return for a fighter."

"Keep looking," Durban said. He nudged the controls, banking the Mosquito into a gentle turn and remembering the briefing. The first bombers were supposed to land about midnight; the attackers had hit them rather than any stragglers. Most of the bomber force was still to the east, returning over France or the Low Countries.

The damned Germans had been waiting for them.

They must have come in low, staying under the weather the whole way across the North Sea to avoid British radar detection. Dangerous work. Brave pilots. He might have found time to admire them if he wasn't so busy trying to kill them.

"Two signals." Excitement laced itself around Lampeter's words, breathless and earnest. "Six miles. Keep this course."

"Ours again?"

"One of them. The other is moving too fast. Turn five degrees to port."

Durban stared into the darkness. It achieved little. "Anything on *Serrate*?"

"Not yet. He might be afraid to use his radar."

"Or he's already found a target and switched it off."

Serrate had been a fabulous gift for the Mosquito night fighter community from the electronic warfare boffins. It allowed them to home in on the radar emissions from their Luftwaffe counterparts. As always, the Germans learned fast and kept their radar off as long as they could. Tonight, in a bomber-filled sky, the attackers might not need radar at all.

The cloud closed like drapes around the cockpit. "Altitude?"

"A little above us but descending, I think. Four miles. They are cutting across our nose."

"I'm going to swing out and bring us behind them. Get ready to reacquire."

"Roger. What's our fuel state, skipper?"

Durban ignored the question. Lampeter wouldn't have liked the answer. Instead, he climbed to starboard for a few seconds, then rolled the Mosquito into a descending turn to port. Too fast, he told himself. Breaking radar contact was always risky, and it took as much luck as skill to reacquire. He glanced again at the fuel gauge. If they didn't find the target again immediately, they would head for the divert airfield.

Lampeter gave a grunt of appreciation. "Got them. Dead ahead, one mile."

The clouds parted, and Durban's hands tensed on the controls as tracers ripped through the sky. Away from them, he realised, but any relief dissipated as he saw their impact. Showering sparks became a sheet of flame, spreading mercilessly along the wing of the distant British bomber. He saw two engines next to each other, props still spinning despite the fire engulfing them.

That meant a Lancaster, or possibly a Halifax. Even a B-17 from the jamming specialists from 100 Group, but it didn't matter.

What mattered was the twin-engined shape that stood stark against the backdrop of the stricken bomber.

"Night fighter," Durban yelled in triumph, pushing the throttles hard against the gate, willing the Mosquito to more speed. "Visual intercept."

Lampeter abandoned his radar set and peered out. "Ju-88G," he said.

"You always had better eyes than me," Durban said, the tension between them evaporating.

The doomed bomber fell away as flames engulfed the fuselage, and Durban's momentary sense of success disappeared with it. It was a Lancaster, an aircraft notoriously hard to bail out from. Not that the crew would have time. They were simply too low. Even as he watched, the wing broke free of the aircraft, and the bomber's slow dive became an uncontrolled tumble as the Ju-88G turned away.

Eyes watering, bile burning at his throat, Durban banked the Mosquito to follow, while his gloved fingers adjusted the target size and distance on his Mk II reflector gunsight. Second by second, staying slightly below their target, they closed in on the oblivious German night fighter.

It was too late to save that bomber. He told himself that what he did now, he did to protect others. It was a lie. Durban watched the Junkers Ju-88G drift from side to side, its nose searching the sky with its mass of radar antennae like a foul predatory insect, and knew the truth. This was about vengeance. Nothing else.

He pulled back on the controls. The night fighter filled his gunsight. His pulse receded in his ears, a sense of calm washing over him. With practiced ease, he adjusted the lower flywheel on his gunsight to match the sixty-six-foot wingspan of the

German aircraft. His breath stabilised. Keeping the target in the centre of the reticle, he tweaked the upper flywheel until the wings filled the rangefinder ring.

Only then did he squeeze the trigger.

The combined recoil of the four belly-mounted 20mm Hispano cannon shuddered through the Mosquito's wooden fuselage. The first few rounds missed. The rest did not.

Heavy armour-piercing shells smashed into the centre of the Ju-88G's fuselage, ripping upwards through the grey-painted underside to shred control cables, electrical wiring, and human flesh with equal ease. The Perspex canopy broke apart, shedding fragments and viscera into the night air. Incongruously, the aircraft flew on, the props on its undamaged engines still turning and carrying it on through the night air, regardless of the horrors that had befallen its crew.

Then, with awful suddenness, the fuselage behind the ravaged cockpit collapsed in on itself. The Ju-88G flipped upside down and plummeted to earth, leaving only a thin wisp of smoke hanging in the air.

"That's number seven," Durban said, unable to hold the words in even though they were unnecessary. They both knew how many German aircraft they had destroyed in their year together.

As always, he kept his mind focused on the simple count of machines removed from the field of play, and not on the ten to twenty-one lives they had ended by their actions. He felt only the thrill of the successful hunt in his quickened breathing and his tingling skin. The sickening guilt would come later, after they landed safely.

"Fuel state critical," Lampeter intoned.

If they landed safely.

Durban tore his gaze from the tumbling wreckage of the Junkers and stared at the instrument panel. The climb and the pursuit of the Ju-88G had burned through their remaining fuel with alarming alacrity. They were deep into reserves now. Somewhere below them was their home station, with others dotted around it. This entire region of England was a mass of wartime airfields. In daylight, he would have backed himself to find somewhere to land, even if he had to glide the aircraft to safety. Now, with airfields blacked out because of the scram order and visibility wrecked by low cloud?

His eyes met Lampeter's. The navigator said nothing. He didn't need to.

Behind the navigator's head, bright lights like giant fireflies filled the sky, seeming to hover in the air before rushing past and vanishing into the darkness beyond.

Adrenaline hit Durban with the force of a kick to the chest.

They had flown straight and level for too long, too focused on their dwindling fuel to remember the more immediate perils. Another night fighter, drawn by the flames, had found the Mosquito unwary and vulnerable. If they turned sharply enough, they had a chance to evade it. A weak pilot could overshoot and lose them in the dark. A good night fighter pilot would expect a turn, be waiting for it.

Durban wrenched the controls and hurled the Mosquito into a fast break to port.

A roar filled the cockpit.

The night fighter pilot was good.

Wood splintered, sending thin slivers into the skin of Durban's neck. The instrument panel seemed to come apart, dials shattering or disappearing altogether. He felt something hot splash across his face, only to cool instantly as the howling gale from the fractured canopy rushed past him. The Mosquito's controls bucked in his hands, trying to tear loose of his grip. With desperate strength, he kept hold, kept the aircraft in a descending corkscrew turn even as the airframe groaned in protest, threatening to come apart.

The dark smudge of the ground spun dizzily below them. Above them, a familiar shape hung black against the cloud before it vanished from sight.

Too familiar. "That's one of ours," he shouted, furious with his fellow pilot. Furious with himself. He had known other Mosquitoes would fill the sky looking for German night fighters, not expecting to find one of theirs in the way. Lampeter knew it too.

Durban turned to apologise. And realised it didn't matter.

The navigator slumped in what remained of his seat. Most of his right side had gone, his ribs exposed and glistening beneath the tattered stump of his arm, torn away along with half his head. From beneath the broken lens of his goggles, Lampeter's remaining eye sat open.

No life there.

Only accusation.

The Mosquito shook. Lampeter's body collapsed forward, held in place by his straps. His ravaged head lolled down, swinging in time with the aircraft's wild shaking.

Durban hit the rudder, fought the controls. Despite the damage, despite the protests of the airframe, despite everything the Mosquito rushed to obey him. Wrestling the aircraft out of its dive, he scanned the ground below. The altimeter was gone, obliterated among the ragged new holes in the instrument panel, but through the rain that now streamed down his goggles, he picked out the shape of a narrow bridge over a canal. Four hundred feet, perhaps lower.

He switched to radio channel B, thumbed his Receive/Transmit switch and put out a distress call. The radio showed no obvious damage. The static that filled his headset suggested otherwise.

He checked both wings. No fire there, no light to draw their attacker back. A small mercy. The other Mosquito had likely chalked them up as a kill and moved on. Gun camera footage might reveal the pilot's mistake, but Durban doubted it. Idly, he wondered if he knew the crew who would claim a kill for their intercept of a "German night fighter" while elsewhere the casualty roll would list Wing Commander Andrew Durban and Flight Lieutenant Clive Lampeter as "killed in action, likely night fighter," and no one would ever wonder why there was only one wreck.

The thought brought anger. And anger brought strength.

Durban shifted his weight in his seat and put out another distress call. He heard no response, but that didn't mean they wouldn't hear his desperate voice and turn on their emergency landing lights.

With a bang and a pained wheeze, the starboard engine belched smoke. Possibly a stray round had clipped it, the damage taking time to manifest. Or perhaps shrapnel had severed a fuel line.

The cause was irrelevant, and he'd flown a Mosquito on one engine before. He reached for the two buttons at the top of the control console. He ignored the blood glistening on them as he pressed the right one, feathered the props, hit the cut-out button and silenced the damaged engine.

Ahead of them, somewhere, was an airfield. It didn't matter which. It didn't even matter if his landing gear worked. He just needed some flat ground. Somewhere to put the Mosquito down before it came apart.

Above him, many miles away, there was another flash, another RAF heavy bomber meeting its violent end amidst a sky filled with prowling night fighters, German and British. He ignored it, just as he ignored the dead friend in the seat next to him.

His eyes focused only ahead.

Lights appeared in the rain-swept darkness.

Chapter One

Norfolk, day, 10 March

Dougie Jeffries whooped as the two Mosquitoes roared overhead. "There they go, Johnny," he cried, pressing his face against the window. "Look at those beauties!"

Wearing the expressions of men who had seen it all before, the guards swung the gates open to let the bus in. "Welcome to RAF Charney Breach," one of them called, his words almost lost in the fading roar of Merlin engines and the lesser grumble of the vehicle's motor.

Johnny Grant gave his friend a smile. It was hard not to feel happy around Jeffries. The man had been living his dream since the moment he arrived from Australia. Since he first put on his RAF uniform, even. This, arriving at their first operational station, was just the latest milestone in one huge adventure. They sat forward in their seats as the bus crawled past the guards in a cloud of diesel fumes.

"It's brilliant," Jeffries grinned. "Look, there's another three." He pointed out across the grassy expanse of the airfield at a row of parked aircraft. "Did I mention how lucky we are to be going straight to Mosquitoes?"

Grant laughed. "Just once or twice, yeah." And the rest. They had flown many aircraft in training, first in Canada, then in England, but the Mosquito was special. Grant had known it at their conversion unit, but this was different. This was a front-line squadron, and a famous one.

He'd always expected to end up with a heavy bomber unit or some transport unit, never daring to dream that he would get Mosquitoes. The aircraft was a legend, up there with the Spitfire for reputation. All wood construction, twin Merlin 25 V12 engines that made it quicker than just about anything in the sky, lightweight yet able to carry a four thousand pound high-explosive "Cookie" to Berlin and back. That was the same bombload as a Yank Flying Fortress, but the Mosquito did it faster and higher and with two crewmen instead of ten.

The instructors who had done their time on heavy bombers said none of that was important. What mattered was the loss rate, the lowest of any frontline aircraft in the RAF.

Every new pilot and navigator in the RAF dreamed of a tour on Mosquitoes. Not all of them made their enthusiasm so overt as Jeffries. His round face beamed with growing delight at every new scene that unfolded beyond their vehicle's dirty windows.

The bus came to a halt outside a long, low building. Jeffries bounded out, barely remembering to grab his bags. Grant thanked the driver before stepping down onto the road. He inhaled deeply, smelling the familiar airfield scents of cut grass and aviation fuel, all drenched in acrid diesel fumes as the bus pulled noisily away.

A slight, somewhat weasel-faced young man walked towards them, wearing an expression of weary resignation. His shoulders bore the rank tabs of a Flying Officer, only one rank higher than them. "Are you the new boys?"

"Yes, sir," Jeffries said. "Dougie Jeffries and Johnny Grant, reporting from the Operational Training Unit."

"Aren't you just the cutest little nippers?" The man snorted in derision. "I'm Finny. Grab your bags and follow me, and don't dawdle. I'll show you to your rooms."

The man's accent made him sound like Jeffries. Grant couldn't tell one region of Australia from another. "How long have you been with 465 Squadron, sir?"

A sigh. "Stop calling me sir. It's Finny. And two years, if you must know."

"You were here for the Amiens raid?"

"Of course. And the Aarhus attack."

Jeffries whistled in admiration. Finny couldn't quite keep the satisfaction from his face at the younger man's reaction, but then his scowl returned. "The squadron was a proper elite, then. Not like now."

Grant exchanged a look with Jeffries, who appeared equally puzzled. "What do you mean?"

"You used to need a full tour to come here," Finny said. "Today they send us kids straight from training."

"Like us, you mean?"

"Yeah," Finny said, looking up at Grant with a furious stare. "Like you." Motioning them to follow, he walked to the edge of the road, stopping to let a silver Alvis convertible cruise past. "And as for that one..." He thrust his chin towards the Alvis as it slowed and came to a halt in front of a low building with the RAF Ensign fluttering in the wind above it.

"Nice car," Jeffries said. "Who is it?"

As Grant watched, a slim man of average height stepped from the car, adjusted his uniform and covered his boyish brown hair with his hat. The ribbon at shoulders and wrists marked him as a Wing Commander. "Is that the Squadron Commander?"

Finny muttered a curse and nodded. "Andy Durban, whoever he is."

"Andrew Durban? The Pathfinders chap who got the third bar on his Distinguished Flying Cross last year?"

"Maybe." Finny suddenly looked slightly less sure of himself.

"Our instructors talked about him all the time. I thought he was on night intruders?"

"He was. He just got here yesterday. Already settling in like he owns the place."

Jeffries frowned. "Well, doesn't he?"

"Shut up." Finny set off away from the HQ building. The new

men struggled with their heavy bags, trying to keep pace. "My mate Barto has been running this squadron for the past two months and doing a bloody good job of it. Then this Pom shows up and takes over without so much as a thank you."

"You've lost me," Grant said. He felt a growing dislike for this man already. "What's a Pom?"

"Pommie," Jeffries said. "English. A Brit. Always whingeing."

"Ah." Grant nodded, hoping they would think he knew what the hell they were talking about. "Right. Is that the only reason you don't like him, Finny?"

"Of course not," Finny said. "He also got himself shot down last week."

Grant turned again to Jeffries, but even his friend couldn't explain that. "I don't understand. Is that bad?"

"What squadron wants a boss with that kind of luck? Got himself shot up, had to crash land. Worst of all, his navigator bought it." Finny shuddered. "Bastard didn't have the courtesy to cop it with his buddy. They sent him to the hospital, and I hear they planned to delay his arrival. Instead, he insists on turning up on time so that my mate Barto could lose his job sooner than he had to." The man sniffed as he led them between two prefabricated buildings.

"You don't get that many DFCs for nothing," Grant mused. "Sounds like a good boss to have when we're on ops."

"What would you know about it, squirt?" Finny looked even more rodent-like when annoyed, Grant decided. "Besides, it's not like we're going to do many ops now."

"What do you mean?"

"Why do you think they send us the likes of you, with not a single op between you? War's done, boys. Our Army and the Yanks are racing Uncle Joe Stalin to Berlin, and the Luftwaffe can hardly find the fuel to get airborne. The worst thing likely to happen this week is another noise complaint from Matlock's

Farm. All the good missions are done. Nothing you do will make the blindest bit of difference. Here." He stopped at a metal door held open by a piece of scrap wood, reached into his pocket and gave them a key each, shoving it into their hands. "This is your block. The dinner hall and the bar are in the main building. You'll work it out."

Leaving them standing, stunned, Finny strode away, but slowed as he reached the corner of the next block. "You're not here to win the war, children. You're just here to survive it. Try not to get killed for no bloody point, eh?" With a sardonic laugh, he disappeared from sight.

"Welcome to Charney Breach," Grant murmured.

Jeffries laughed and punched his friend on the arm. Smiling, they grabbed their bags and headed into the cool darkness of their new home.

Chapter Two

Flossenbürg Concentration Camp, night, 10 March

The guards kept their faces impassive as they saluted him, but Stahl still sensed their fear.

And revelled in it.

Waiting impatiently for a young SS soldier to open the double doors at the entrance to the block, he strode down the corridor beyond. The thud of his boots on the tiled floors echoed from the walls. A balding officer stood waiting. The man was already sweating in his Obersturmbannführer's uniform, but at the sight of Stahl, he blanched.

Stahl removed one glove and reached into his own uniform, drawing out his papers. "Good evening," he said, shoving the papers towards the man. "I am—"

"I know who you are, Herr Stahl." The man's voice wavered, high and tremulous.

Stahl felt a familiar thrill. They were the same rank, but this man still cowered. After six years of war, few in the SS had not heard of Obersturmbannführer Jan Stahl. Or his reputation.

"My name is Koegel," the officer continued. "I am Commandant here. It is indeed an honour to host you. Quarters have been prepared."

Stahl silenced him with a wave. "I return to Berlin before morning. Where is he?"

"He? You mean Admiral Canaris?"

"Of course, Canaris. Do you think I would drive all the way from Prinz Albrecht Strasse to speak to some student protestor or Polish partisan?" He stepped closer to Koegel, close enough that their noses almost touched. The commandant was not a small man. He had probably twenty pounds and two inches on Stahl, and he was on his own ground, in the centre of his own empire. Flossenbürg wasn't nearly the largest of the concentration camps, but between the main area and the sub-camps, this man still gave orders to four thousand guards and held the lives of forty thousand prisoners in his hands.

Koegel took a half step back.

"Are you a fool, Koegel?"

"No, Herr Stahl."

"Are you loyal to the Reich, Koegel?"

A slight moan escaped the commandant's lips. His breath smelled of stale bread and schnapps. "I am loyal, Herr Stahl."

Stahl smiled. "Take me to Canaris."

Koegel nodded and spun on his heel, almost overbalancing in his haste to break their eye contact. Shouting orders to his guards, he led the way deeper into the sprawling prison complex. They passed cell after cell. Some rang with the whimpers of prisoners tormented beyond hope or dignity. Others stood silent, with only the thick miasma of human waste and terror to tell of the broken occupants within.

Four guards met them at a heavy steel door, their jackboots slamming onto the floor in perfect unison as they came to attention.

"You must understand, we were not expecting you," Koegel said, wringing his hands. "Otherwise, I would have ordered him cleaned up. The smell is..."

"He is a traitor," Stahl said. "Let him wallow in his own filth."

Koegel nodded to the guards, and they unlocked the door before stepping back. The commandant froze with his fingers around the door handle. His lips barely moved, his words only a mumble. "Herr Stahl, forgive me, but I am under strict orders to allow no visitors without prior authorisation."

"Rightly so," Stahl said. "Perhaps you wish to call Himmler himself and ask him?"

Koegel swallowed. His head twitched, side to side.

"A smart move," Stahl said. "Open the door." He waited while the commandant swung the heavy steel portal wide and stumbled back out of the way. "You may leave, Koegel. Have my Mercedes fuelled and waiting for me at the front of the building. This will not take long."

After the harsh electric lights of the corridor, Stahl's eyes needed a few moments to adjust to the semi-darkness of the cell. The stench he ignored. He had smelt worse things, like bloated corpses clustered in ditches under a blistering sun, bowels opening as traitors hanged or slowly bled out on iron butcher hooks. Since the foiling of von Stauffenberg's July plot, it had been one execution after another.

No, the smell didn't bother him. He only cared about the man who had avoided execution. For now.

"You look well, Admiral."

With pained slowness, the occupant of the cell rose from his hard concrete bed and shuffled forward. Stahl smiled, letting the guards see the contempt and amusement on his face. Admiral Wilhelm Canaris looked twenty years older than he had on the day when Stahl had arrested him, a mere eight months earlier. His neat white hair was mostly gone, reduced to a few wisps rising from a scab-covered scalp. The familiar face was almost unrecognisable, cheeks hollowed yet swollen with bruises. His cheap grey prisoner overalls hung loose on his emaciated frame.

"Good evening, Stahl," Canaris said. Even his voice had reduced to a shadow, a hiss of air from between blood encrusted lips. It seemed almost impossible that this man had spent a decade in command of the Abwehr, first in peace and then in war. Or that this dishevelled, broken creature had shaped and overseen German Military Intelligence for years, right until the day Stahl had exposed his betrayal of the Führer. Only the eyes were the same. As piercing and intelligent as the day they had first met, a lifetime away from this foul cell.

Pity welled up in Stahl, unfamiliar and unhelpful. Somehow, he kept his face impassive and his voice even.

He swung his hand in an airy gesture around the room, taking in the rough, stained woollen blanket and the almost overflowing toilet bucket. "I see you have made yourself at home." An amused snort came from a guard watching from the doorway. Stahl wondered if the man had ever seen combat or faced anything more dangerous than chained prisoners. "This place suits you, Admiral. If it were up to me, they would have shot you with Claus von Stauffenberg. Or perhaps not. Shooting would have been too quick. Strangled, like his brother."

"What do you want, Stahl?" The voice was weak, but without a trace of fear. An impressive old man, Stahl thought. But then, he had always known that.

"You know they revived him?" Stahl smirked. "Berthold von Stauffenberg, I mean. They strangled him to the point of death, then revived him. Many times. How must he have felt, to know death so many times? I am told the Führer loved the films they made of the executions. He watched them often. Perhaps, one day, he will enjoy yours?"

Canaris did not respond. One guard still wore a half-smile, but now it seemed sickly and unconvincing. The others looked pale and uncomfortable. None of them laughed. Not anymore. Stahl's reputation proceeded him wherever he went, but he knew that hearing the whispered stories about Obersturmbannführer Jan Stahl and being in his presence were two very different things.

"For reasons of his own," Stahl continued, "the Führer still wants you alive. It would appear he thinks you may still have more to share about your contacts with the British. I have assured him I have uncovered every detail of your tawdry little treachery. Most of your intermediaries and contacts are long since dead." He touched the pistol at his waist. "I eliminated many of them myself. I would love to do the same for you, but alas, orders are orders."

Still, Canaris said nothing. The eyes stared without blinking. Stahl felt their power, undimmed since that first time they had spoken, back in 1941 in the Admiral's office.

He felt the need to be honest with the man, as always. He forced the urge down. Honesty now wouldn't help either of them.

"As for why I am here," Stahl said, "I merely wanted to look at you. I fear I will not get another chance. The Führer's patience is not unlimited, and soon you will face the end." He stepped a little closer, his eyes on the old man's. "When that day comes," he said softly, "I pray you get what you deserve."

That much, at least, was true.

The slightest hint of a smile crossed the Admiral's face, and he gave a tiny nod. Then the smile faded, replaced by an expression Stahl knew well. Business-like cunning. The quality that had made Canaris such a respected spymaster, allowing him to serve Germany for years while secretly working with the British and helping to mastermind the military resistance to Hitler. "The Russians will be here soon."

Stahl scoffed. "We will yet turn the Bolsheviks back. And if not, you will be dead long before you see them." He breathed deeply despite the stench, took a last look at the Admiral's face, and headed towards the door.

"Germany's *Götterdämmerung* is at hand."

Stahl froze. Slowly, he turned back. "What did you say?"

"*Götterdämmerung*," Canaris repeated. "It is real, Jan. It is coming."

He stared at the Admiral for a few seconds more, watching

the way those bright eyes pulsed with urgency. Something churned in his gut, a feral sensation he hadn't felt in years. Fear. It took all his SS training and discipline to manufacture a mocking laugh. Something to fool the audience. "You have seen too many of Wagner's operas, old fool," he said, feigning amusement. He motioned to the guards to clear a path.

"Jan?"

"What?"

"Tell my family that I love them," Canaris said.

For a long heartbeat, the Admiral's eyes held Stahl's gaze, the way they had so many times in the years they had worked together. When they had been friends. Before Stahl had exposed the old man's betrayal, setting Canaris on the path that left him here. Frail. Fading. Waiting to die.

"You can tell them yourself, traitor." Stahl spat on the floor. "I will send them to join you in Hell."

He brushed past the guards, ignoring their salutes and the horrified looks on their bloodless faces. These men were among the most callous the Reich could muster, yet even they cowered in his presence. Somehow, it didn't bring him as much pleasure now.

The cell door slammed in his wake.

He didn't look back.

Koegel was nowhere to be seen, probably hiding, but the idiot had at least arranged for Stahl's black Mercedes to be waiting with its engine idling. Stahl was hungry and exhausted after the long drive from Berlin, but nothing could have persuaded him to wait another minute longer in this dismal place. Not after seeing the Admiral's eyes. Passing between the rows of barracks, each crammed beyond capacity with political prisoners, he waited impatiently for the soldiers at the main guardroom to open the gate, and then sped up onto the road beyond.

The road here wound tortuously through the pretty vistas of

the Fichtel Mountains, and Stahl took every corner as quickly as he dared. The squeal of the car's tires filled the air between the low peaks. Thirty minutes of driving and he reached the fast, straight road that had brought him here a few short hours earlier from the HQ *Sicherheitsdienst des Reichsführers-SS*, the Security Service of the SS in the Prinz Albrecht Strasse in the capital. For a few seconds he sat, engine idling, staring at the sign. It pointed right to Leipzig, and thence to Berlin. Himmler would expect his report.

He put the car in gear. And turned left.

Chapter Three

Andrew Durban lit another cigarette and stared out of the window.

RAF Charney Breach could have been any of the dozens of new RAF stations hurriedly built as the war progressed. Assorted hangars, low accommodation huts, a control tower that seemed relatively tall by comparison. Durban had seen so many airfields, and after a while, they all looked the same. At least the HQ building was modern and brick-built, though it had other drawbacks. It was only a single storey, and in the absence of proper Officers' or Sergeants' Messes it housed the dining room and bar. He didn't approve of that. Durban liked to drink with his men, but he also knew that a commander needed to keep a distance sometimes. Chatter and laughter just outside his door was an irritation he could do without.

From his simple office, he could see across the road outside to the parade square. A group of aircrew, in their shirt sleeves despite the lingering chill in the morning air, had hastily requisitioned it as a football pitch. Beyond, he saw the taxiways and the hardstanding where groups of engineers were busily working on their aircraft. He counted a dozen Mosquitoes, all FB Mark VIs with capacity for two 500lb bombs, and each a thing of beauty.

Each intact, not a twisted smoking wreck.

He found his hands shaking again and took a deep drag on the cigarette.

There was a knock, and the door opened almost immediately. Durban didn't recognise the Squadron Leader who entered.

Stocky like a rugby player, square-faced with dark hair, natural good looks distorted by an abomination of a moustache. The man stared for a second, as if disappointed not to find the office empty. "You wanted to see me, sir?"

"You must be Barton," Durban said.

"That's right."

"I expected you half an hour ago."

"Messenger must have got lost," Barton said, his accent thickly Aussie. Beneath the gnarled moustache, one lip curled in what was half a sneer, half a challenge. "Sir," he added, making it sound more an insult than an honorific.

Durban sighed and closed the file on his desk. Reading it had made him half-expect this moment. By any account, Don Barton was an exceptional pilot, but he was also a man who broke rules and caused problems. Beloved by his men, loathed by his superiors. Durban knew the sort. Barton was an excellent flight commander. He had done a more than adequate job as acting CO, too, but he hadn't made friends at higher HQ in the process. Now that he was a mere flight commander again, whatever chip was on his shoulder was only likely to grow.

"You're Australian, Barton?"

"What gave it away?"

Durban ignored that. "Whereabouts are you from?"

Barton stared. "Have you ever been to Australia, sir?"

"I haven't had the pleasure."

"Then what does it matter where I'm from?"

Durban returned the man's stare. Held it for a few seconds. Watched with satisfaction as the Australian blinked and broke first. "Tell me about the squadron," he ordered.

Barton shrugged. "They're good lads."

"You're an Article XV squadron, yes? Mostly Australian?"

"We're supposed to be." Barton sniffed. "We're lucky if even half of us come from Oz, though. The rest are all sorts. Brits,

Canadians, Kiwis, Rhodesians, an Irishman, even a Black fella from the Caribbean."

"Do you try to pair together pilots and navigators from the same nations?"

"Where we can, but it's more important to make sure the crew has some experience. We don't always have options. A lot of the experienced ones are dead, or have gone off to training jobs, which isn't much better if you ask me. Too many kids here by half. As for the leadership..."

"Yes? What of it?"

Barton thrust his chin out. Not a rugby player, Durban thought. A bare-knuckle boxer. "Nothing," Barton said. "You'd just think that an Australian squadron would have an Aussie boss."

"You're not an Australian squadron, Barton," Durban said. "You're an RAF squadron." He smiled to soften the statement. "And an excellent one, from what I hear. You did a damned good job keeping it together these last few months."

"Fat lot of good it did me."

The roar of twin Merlin engines filled the air, and Durban couldn't help but look. An engine test, he saw. The football game continued unabated, though the Merlins drowned out the shouting of players for now.

Barton coughed. "What's your background, then? Flying, I mean. I don't care what poncy public school you went to."

Durban finished his cigarette before drawing another and pushing the pack towards Barton. The Australian, he noted, wasn't so proud as to turn down the offer. "Six months of Beaufighters at the tail end of the Blitz. Then onto Mosquitoes. Pathfinders."

"Full tour?"

"Two," Durban said, enjoying the impressed look that the Australian tried and failed to hide. "Then a tour back on intruders."

"Four tours." A stream of cigarette smoke slid from Barton's mouth and rose to the office's low ceiling. For a moment, he almost smiled, but then the scowl returned with shocking speed. "All medium and high-altitude stuff, then."

"That's right. Does that matter?"

Barton shrugged. "Not to me. But Jerry and the ground might disagree. 465 Squadron is a specialist low-level unit."

"I'm well aware of it."

"You want to tell me, sir, why they put a fella with no low-level experience in charge instead of me?" Barton folded his arms. Above them, eyes darker than the moustache stared out in disgust.

"They must have had their reasons," Durban said. He left that hanging there. Saw the Australian's anger fade to confusion, then return to anger as he realised the implied suggestion of unworthiness. Durban doubted anyone had taken the effort to judge the Australian or found him wanting. More likely, the sprawling bureaucracy of the wartime RAF had simply looked at the man's rank and seniority and replaced him on procedural grounds, not merit. But the Australian clearly didn't like him, and Durban was finding it harder by the moment not to return the favour.

He stood up. The room felt suddenly small and airless. "Walk with me," he ordered, and without waiting for a response, grabbed his hat and threw open the office door.

With Barton trailing, he left the HQ building by the front door, giving a cheery greeting to a group of young airmen and returning their enthusiastic salutes. Ahead, the engine test had now become an air test. As he watched, a puff of smoke rose from the Mosquito's port engine. The engineers pulled the chocks from in front of the wheels, and the aircraft lurched forward onto the taxiway and turned towards the end of the runway.

"Who is that?" Durban pointed.

Barton glanced at the taxying aircraft. "Looks like Charlie Broadley. His Mossie was playing up yesterday."

"Is he any good?"

"Of course," Barton said. "He's from Victoria."

"Like you?"

Barton scowled, realising that he had given something away.

"Tell him to sort out his throttle control," Durban said. "I've seen carts pulled by donkeys that lurched less than he did."

"He's got a dozen low-level operations under his belt," Barton sneered. "That's a dozen more than some. He's one of our best."

"And he could be better," Durban said calmly. "If he can't use his throttles smoothly on the ground, what happens when he tries to land on one engine with a shattered left aileron?"

Barton sniffed but said nothing.

"Look out!"

Durban's head snapped to the side at the warning shout. He glimpsed something dark brown flying towards his face and shifted his weight on instinct. The thing passed within millimetres of his head, sailing past before bouncing twice on the road and rolling into the side of the HQ.

Barton chuckled. "Welcome to 465 Squadron, sir."

Durban watched a young Black man run towards them. The West Indian that Barton had mentioned, no doubt. The man's eyes opened even wider as he got closer. "Shit," he said. "Shit, shit, shit. You're the new CO."

"I am."

"And I almost hit you with a football."

"You did."

"Good job you're a navigator and not a pilot, Grant," Barton said. "Or I'd be telling you to improve your shooting next time."

"Shit," the young navigator blurted once more. "It won't happen again. And sorry for all the swearing, sir."

"Oi, Grant," someone called from the field. "Are you going to get the sodding ball or what?"

"Um. Permission to be excused, sir?"

Durban nodded. With a final apologetic smile, the man spun and ran across the road, barely avoiding being mown down by a fuel truck. "Got it," he said, lifting the heavy leather ball above his head like he'd won a prize. Several of the footballers clapped. From the look of unbridled joy on the navigator's face, he didn't hear the sarcasm in the applause.

"This is what we've had to deal with," Barton said with a grimace. "There was a time we had our pick of the best aircrew. All volunteers, all experienced. Now the training system spits out kids like Grant and sends them straight our way. No wonder morale is in the khazi." The Australian sniffed loudly. "In any case, it's your problem now, sir. You're welcome."

"I'll be needing a navigator, Barton," Durban said, raising his voice as the taxiing Mosquito sped up along the new concrete of the runway before rising effortlessly into the sky. He watched it clear the trees at the end of the runway and dwindle from sight before he realised he was holding his breath. He put his hands behind his back, one holding the other tight, feeling the shaking of his fingers. "How many do you have who haven't paired up with a pilot yet?"

"Just the two new lads." Barton pointed at the group of footballers. One of them, young and red-haired, controlled a dropping football beautifully and turned, sprinting past two older aircrew and leaving them stumbling in his wake. "That's Dougie Jeffries," he said. "Good lad. Played soccer for Queensland. Cricket, too. Second XI."

"What were his scores like, coming out of training?"

"How would I know? I haven't read his report."

"I have," Durban said. "And the other?"

"You just met him," Barton said, laughing as the young man

he had called Grant, sprinting to get open, took a body check from a big Rhodesian and tumbled winded to the ground. "That one is going to be a waste of space, I reckon."

Durban frowned. He watched as Grant leapt to his feet and dusted himself off. He could tell the impact had hurt, but Grant concealed any pain beneath a broad grin and ran gingerly onward. "Do you have a problem with West Indians, Barton?"

"Not particularly."

"You just have a problem with anyone who isn't Australian?"

Barton gave him a sideways look. He said nothing, but the edges of his mouth quirked with the ghost of a smirk.

With a triumphant yell, Grant met Jeffries' cross and poked the ball past the goalkeeper's despairing dive and between the folded blue service jumpers that passed for goalposts. He wheeled away in glee.

"Barton?"

"Hmm?"

"Ask Grant to join us, would you?"

Barton paused, looking confused, then turned to the football pitch. "Grant!" The single word echoed between the buildings.

"If I'd wanted someone to shout," Durban observed mildly, "I could have done it myself."

Sweating a little from his exertions and with grass stains on his shirt, Grant ran over to join them. His obvious nervousness wasn't quite enough to obliterate all traces of his grin, but it was close. "Sorry, sir," he stammered.

Durban raised an eyebrow. "For what?"

"I thought..." The young man pointed at the pitch. "You know, the goal..."

"Was worth celebrating. It was a good goal. Are you a good navigator?"

"Sir?" Grant's eyes flickered between the two senior officers.

"Answer the new boss, Grant," Barton growled.

"Well, sir, it's just I don't know how to. It's not my call to make, is it?"

The rest of the players had now stopped and were watching intently. Durban lowered his voice. It wasn't their business. "I've read your training reports, Grant, so I know what your instructors think. I'm asking what you think. So, again, are you a good navigator?"

"Yes, sir."

"Better than Jeffries?"

A pause. Grant glanced at the group of men with guilty eyes, but his voice stayed firm. "Yes, sir."

Barton coughed and covered his hand with his mouth, not quite concealing his mocking smile.

"That's good enough for me," Durban said. "Congratulations, Grant. You're now my navigator."

"Sir?"

Durban opened his mouth to speak again, but Barton interrupted. "You got much low-level experience, Grant?"

"Um, no, sir."

"Pity," Barton said. "But don't worry," he added, glancing at Durban. "Apparently, it's not required anymore."

Grant shifted nervously. "What do I need to do, sir?"

"Right now, you need to get back to your game. They are all waiting for you. Oh, and Grant? Watch out for that big chap. I believe he plans to put you on your backside again."

"He'll have to catch me first, sir." Grant ran to rejoin his colleagues.

"You're making a mistake not going with Jeffries," Barton said after a few seconds.

"Maybe," Durban said. "But if you'd read their reports, you'd know that Jeffries is prone to navigation errors under pressure. Grant isn't. He also topped his class in low-level bombing accuracy."

"That's training. Real world is different. I've seen plenty of boys arrive with great training reports, only to fall apart the first time they get shot at." Barton snorted. "It's your choice. Charlie Broadley's navigator is on leave. He'll be more than happy with Jeffries as a replacement. It hardly matters anyway, does it?"

"Meaning?"

"The war is nearly over. It's not like we're going to get any major low-level ops now." Barton paused. He mostly kept his gaze fixed on Grant, but just for a moment, he looked at Durban with eyes that pulsed with contempt. "It won't matter that Group choose to send us unqualified people."

"You don't know me very well," Durban said. This time, he did not bother to lower his voice. "So let me give you some insights. I didn't request this posting. You got a raw deal not being allowed to keep command, and I don't expect you to like it."

"Good to know."

"But I do expect you to keep your whining to yourself." Durban saw Barton flinch, heard the cold in his own voice. Ruthless. Unrecognisable from a few short years ago. "This is my squadron now. You're a key part of it. You're a leader, and I need you. But if you cross me or try to turn the men against me, you'll be gone from here so fast your Prime Minister will need to send a search party. Do you understand me, Squadron Leader Barton?"

From beneath thick eyebrows, Barton stared at him with baleful eyes. Durban didn't care. It didn't matter if Barton liked him or not.

It only mattered that he did his job.

"Yes, sir," Barton said.

"Splendid. I will address the squadron in the main briefing room at thirteen hundred hours. All aircrew to attend. I'll trust you to make the arrangements." He let his mouth curl into a thin smile. "Don't let the messenger get lost this time." Ignoring the looks from the football players, Durban turned and headed for his office.

He was halfway there before he realised his hands were no longer shaking.

Chapter Four

Bavaria, 11 March

The night was mild, and Stahl kept the roof down. Even with the wind ruffling his jet-black hair, his deep exhaustion made every mile a constant battle to stay awake. He skirted Munich to the north and west, telling himself he couldn't smell the fires from the terrible crematoriums at Dachau on the breeze. Twice, he stopped to refuel, his uniform being enough to secure him a precious ration of petrol without needing to show his paperwork or, crucially, having to sign his name. Berlin expected him back. They didn't need to know where he'd been, and his reputation ensured few would question him.

He didn't need the map that lay in the passenger footwell. Not here. Familiar names emerged from the pre-dawn darkness in the light of his lowered headlights, to vanish again in his wake as he sped southwest.

Mindelheim. Mimmingen. Leutkirch im Allgäu.

The first glow of dawn appeared in his rear-view mirrors, accelerating, trying to overtake him.

Somewhere beyond his sight to the south stood the house where he had grown up, nestled among the wooded peaks on the Austrian border. He remembered the sight of the clear blue waters of the Forggensee, glittering in the sunlight below the porch of his family's home, and fought the urge to take an exit and head there now. His father had been among the first in his village to embrace Hitler's rise. His mother had taken her sons to watch the brownshirts march. He had seen the pride in her eyes when he, her eldest son, had driven past her in 1938 at the head of his SS company, heading for the border to join the two proud nations of Germany and Austria into one Reich.

Would any of them truly understand what he had become?

He kept heading southwest, keeping the motor at four thousand RPM and damn the wasted fuel. Skirting the eastern edge of the Bodensee, which others called Lake Constance, he left the main road to take a winding country lane that crossed the unmarked former Austrian border that he himself had helped erase from the map. The road continued to climb.

The sun was high in the sky and burning his neck when he finally slowed.

Two checkpoints stood separated by a hundred metres of waist high grass and several thick clusters of barbed wire. The road was narrow here, with trees pressing close, so the border crossing didn't require any bunkers or heavy defences. Instead, there was only a small cabin with a steep sloping roof in the local style, and a single covered sentry box next to the red and white striped pole that barred the road. Across the way, where the road weaved through the wire, he saw another building, a little larger but otherwise near identical. They could have been two neighbouring buildings in any Bavarian village. Only the flags separated them. The distant building flew the white cross on a red field of Switzerland. The nearer one was also red, but with a white circle, and at its heart stood the same *Hakenkreuz*, the Swastika, that adorned his own arm and the banners on his staff car.

He brought the Mercedes to a halt fifty metres short of the guard post and put his hat on, then took the map from the footwell and dropped it on the passenger seat. A guard, pink-cheeked, emerged from the sentry post. Shielding his eyes against the glare of the sun, the young soldier beckoned him to approach.

Stahl raised one hand in acknowledgement. With his other,

careful to keep it below the protective cover of the dashboard, he slipped his Luger from the holster at his waist and slid it under the folded map.

The guard's mouth dropped open when he saw the rank and uniform of the approaching driver. Hastily, he threw up a salute. The old salute, that of the Army. Stahl waited for him to realise his mistake. They had banned that salute in the aftermath of the von Stauffenberg plot.

Hastily, the soldier transformed it into a Nazi salute. "Sorry, sir. Old habits."

Stahl returned the salute, the movement pattern ingrained in him after eight years in the SS. "A bad habit. One that could get you into trouble. See that you do not insult the Führer so again, you understand?"

"Yes, sir." The soldier swallowed.

He looked so young, Stahl thought. He could barely have finished basic training before the rules changed. Possibly even Hitlerjugend, playing at wearing a man's uniform.

Two more soldiers emerged from the cabin, not much older than the first. They stared at the car, clearly impressed, before noting the uniform and stiffening in concern. The senior man, himself a mere Sturmmann and no older than nineteen, braced himself before taking charge. "Good morning, Herr Obersturmbannführer. May I ask your destination today?"

"Switzerland," Stahl said shortly. "Anything beyond that is the business of the Reich Security Main Office. Here are my papers."

The Sturmmann took them with a trembling hand. Behind him, the other two guards looked longingly at the door of their cabin, maybe even the safety of the woods beyond, but they held their posts. Both carried early issue Kar98k carbines, slung from their shoulders and looking none too well cared for. Stahl doubted that such a backwater border post received priority of weapons any more than it did priority of recruits. The Sturmmann himself was unarmed, his weapon evidently left inside the cabin.

Across the border, he saw four Swiss soldiers standing with cigarettes, wondering what manner of bigwig was waiting to enter. Or, perhaps, they too were more impressed by the car.

The Sturmmann glanced at the papers. "My apologies, Herr Obersturmbannführer. We have so few visitors here. Most diplomatic traffic crosses further north."

Stahl frowned. "That is precisely why my orders stated to take this route."

"Of course, sir, of course." The man's gaze shifted to the passenger seat.

Stahl felt his gut lurch, but a quick sideways glance showed the pistol completely obscured beneath the map. The soldier's gaze moved on, taking in the leather interior.

"Well?"

"Sir?"

"My papers," Stahl snapped. "They are in order, yes?"

"Yes, sir."

Relief flooded through Stahl, but he kept it from his face, kept the icy disapproval in his voice. He reached out a hand. "Then open this gate so that I may proceed. Unless you care to be the one to explain to Berlin why you delayed me?"

"Of course, sir." The Sturmmann half-extended the papers, then drew them back. "My apologies again, Herr Obersturmbannführer. If you will be patient one moment more, I must just make a note of your crossing."

Panic. Quick rising. Debilitating. He crushed it down. "A note?"

"For the records, sir. I must record all traffic."

"That does not apply to me."

The Sturmmann's mouth twitched, and the colour drained

from his face, but he stood his ground. A brave man, Stahl noted.

Such a pity.

"Very well," Stahl said. "Rules are rules." He motioned to the two junior soldiers, who had returned to their covetous appreciation of the Mercedes. "This is a lovely spot," he said. "Is it just the three of you on duty?"

"Yes, sir. We don't need more. Few people cross here."

"It is very isolated," Stahl agreed. "I wonder if I have taken the wrong road somewhere. Could you help me with some directions?"

"Of course, Herr Obersturmbannführer."

"Thank you," he said, and reached for the map.

The man's eyes followed the fluttering paper as Stahl raised it. They all did.

That made it easier.

Rising in his seat, Stahl shot the Sturmmann in the throat, the hollow-point bullet splitting the windpipe before ripping muscles and tendons away from the neck, exposing the spinal column. The man stumbled back, arms flailing. Twisting, Stahl sent a bullet through the head of the young guard before he had the chance to even understand what was happening. The third guard was quicker to react. He almost got his rifle off his shoulder before the third and fourth Luger bullets hit him in the chest and he collapsed to the floor.

Calmly folding the map, Stahl stepped out of the car. The two junior men were clearly dead, but Stahl put a round in each of their heads to be sure. The Sturmmann lay twitching on the dirt by the car, arms splayed out. A spreading pool of blood haloed his head, while his eyes stared at Stahl and his mouth moved in silent question.

"I am sorry," Stahl said, and pulled the trigger a seventh time.

Across the barbed wire, he saw the Swiss soldiers looking at him, their mouths hanging open in shock. Slowly, making sure they could see, Stahl removed the magazine from the Luger, ejected the final unused round from the chamber, and dropped all three separately into the back seat of the Mercedes. Stepping over the still form of the Sturmmann, he raised the heavy wooden checkpoint barrier. Then he climbed back into the driver's seat.

His breathing had already returned to normal, he noted absently. Killing rarely bothered him for long.

Keeping both hands visible on the wheel and his eyes on the four men with their raised rifles, he drove at walking pace across the gap and came to a halt at the Swiss barrier. At their shouted commands, he turned off the engine. Climbed slowly out. Sank to his knees on the Swiss dirt. Felt the cold steel of a Mannlicher M1895 barrel press against his temple.

"You had better call the most senior officer you know, gentlemen," Stahl said. "This will take some explaining."

Chapter Five

"You know," the Wing Commander said, "I've always found England prettiest from three thousand feet."

Grant looked through the Perspex of the Mosquito's cockpit at the patchwork of fields and small villages that spread out beneath them and off the wingtips. So different to home, he thought. Everywhere he looked he saw signs of life, tiny cars and buses wending their way along the tarmacked roads that crisscrossed the landscape, the white smoke of a distant train rising in a column before dissipating in the afternoon sunshine. He hadn't even seen a car until he was eight years old. The islanders had little use for them, and almost none could afford one. He hadn't seen a train at all until he boarded the one that would take him and three dozen other recruits to Canada and their waiting flight training school.

"Up here, everything seems so neat," Durban continued. "Any higher, you can't appreciate the details. Any lower, and you see the chaos and the clutter."

The Wing Commander seemed a nice man, Grant decided, and in a good mood. He thought back to the day before, marvelling at the apparent change. Then, addressing the squadron from the low raised stage at the front of the briefing room, Durban had been all business. Impressive, yes, with ample reserves of what Grant's instructors had labelled 'presence' but with little of the warmth that Grant had found in him when they had first spoken. Some officers found it hard to relax and be themselves around their subordinates. Perhaps Durban could only do so when one almost struck him with a football.

He glanced at his map. Below and behind them, the Upper Thames meandered through the pleasant countryside towards the distant smoky smudge that marked London. Off their nose to the left, the ground sloped steadily upward into the low rolling hills of the Cotswolds.

Durban turned his head and smiled. "Where are we, Grant?"

"Well, sir—"

The world spun vertiginously.

Grant felt the straps of his harness scrape across his uniform tunic as gravity flung him around in his seat. Scrabbling for something to grip, he saw the ground below blurring past the wingtip. His map slid from his lap into the footwell. He fumbled for it, only to see it slide out of reach as Durban threw the aircraft into a hard bank the other way.

Nausea flooded through him as his fingers seized on a corner of paper.

The world stopped spinning as Durban brought the aircraft level. The pilot's eyes tightened, as if in pain, but it didn't show in his voice. "How many hours do you have?"

Grant swallowed back the vomit that rose, acrid and foul, in the back of his throat. The aircraft might have stopped its tumble through the sky, but his stomach hadn't yet caught up. "Sir?"

Durban kept his eyes on the world ahead, his tone easy and conversational. No sign that they had ever deviated from gentle forward progress. "How many flying hours as a navigator?"

"Um." Grant pulled the map from the floor. The aerobatics had left it crumpled. He tried to straighten it, his gloves proving more hindrance than help, while his mind scrambled to remember the contents of the logbooks in his room. "One hundred and thirty hours of day flying, sir. Forty-five hours at night."

"And the minimum to qualify for ops is still one hundred and twenty-seven day, forty-four night?"

"One hundred and twenty-seven and a half, sir."

"Where are we, Grant?" The tone echoed the earlier question as closely as the words.

Grant dragged the map into shape and tried to orientate it to the compass and the surrounding ground. He blinked as his eyes struggled to focus. The urban area to their east had to be Oxford, and he could see a Whitley glider tug getting airborne from RAF Brize Norton. That meant the cluster of houses alongside the narrowing Thames below their port engine should be Lechlade. Should.

Durban waited. Watching.

Grant took a deep breath. "I think—"

Durban slammed the controls forward.

Grant felt his body rise in his seat with the negative G-forces, held in place only by the loose straps on his shoulders. He struggled to hold both map and his breakfast down.

The earth below rushed to meet them, and for three terrified seconds Grant wondered if Durban planned to steer the Mosquito headlong into the fields that filled the windscreen. Instead, the Wing Commander pulled back on the controls, racing headlong barely higher than the trees up a low valley and towards the rising ground. They skirted the edge of a tiny village, the pretty stone buildings seeming to flash by mere feet beyond the wingtip. A group of schoolchildren interrupted their play to wave frantically as they flew past. Their teacher ducked, so low did the Mosquito seem.

This time, Durban winced, one hand shifting to touch his ribs before resuming a steady grip on the controls. "Give me a course for home," he said calmly, climbing slightly to avoid the trees that lined a road ahead.

Grabbing the map again, Grant twisted from side to side, looking for something familiar to help restore his equilibrium. At this altitude, there were few landmarks. Even those zipped past them in moments, gone almost before he could register the sight. This was nothing like medium altitude navigation. One-quarter inch to a mile maps became almost worthless at this height and speed. "I'm not sure I can, sir."

"I'm hit." His voice was ice cold, as emotionless as a steel bayonet. "I'm bleeding out. Unless you can get me home by the fastest route possible, we're both dead. You'd damn well better be able to work out a course. Go."

Grant forced his mind to ignore the speed with which the world was ripping past their wingtips. He'd done this before. He was good at this. Taking the map in one hand, he checked his compass, glanced at his watch. Familiar calculations ran through his head. Too quickly. He slowed them down, just enough to make sense.

Rushing means mistakes.

Slow equals fast.

Beyond the spinning props of the port engine, he saw the steel rails and wooden sleepers of the railway line from Oxford to Worcester. If that small town was Charlbury...

"Zero eight four," Grant said.

Durban didn't take his eyes off the ground ahead. "You're sure?"

"Yes, sir."

For two more seconds, Durban kept the aircraft barely above the ground. Then, with a nod, he pulled the aircraft into a steep banking climb towards the scattered cloud above and onto the bearing for home. "Tighten your straps," he said. Other than required radio calls, he didn't speak again for the rest of the flight, just a short grunt of approval when Charney Breach appeared off the nose without further corrections.

Grant turned to look out of the window, mostly to hide his own sigh of relief. It gave him a chance to see his new home from the air properly, with none of the thin mist that had obscured the view when they took off that morning. His first impression was underwhelming. It looked like almost any other RAF airfield he'd seen, bigger than a few, smaller than most. It stood isolated among dull fields, estranged from the nation it sought to protect. They flew close to a single farm, just to the right of the final approach. Presumably Matlock's Farm, the one Finny had mentioned. A cottage, two barns with roofs covered with patch-work repairs, a stone wall around them, a dirty cobblestone driveway leading to the narrow lane that ran perpendicular to the airfield's outer fencing. Nothing special.

Durban glanced at the farm, sighed, then returned his focus to the runway.

A vehicle was waiting for them in the late afternoon warmth, and they drove back to the dispersal building in silence. It was only when the vehicle dropped them off that Grant's resolve collapsed. "I'm sorry, sir."

"I've seen worse," Durban said. "I have three rules. Always know where we are, always know where we're going, and never get so lost in your map that you stop keeping a watch out for enemy fighters. Can you do that, Grant?"

"Yes, sir."

"Splendid. Now go get some food."

Grant braced to attention. "I'll be better next time, sir."

"I don't doubt it," Durban said, and headed off towards the HQ.

The food didn't taste great. No surprise there. Grant had barely enjoyed a single meal since he left the Caribbean. Overcooked. Undercooked. Over salted. Under seasoned. At some point, the RAF had inflicted every culinary indignity known to humanity upon him and his fellow recruits. By those standards, today's stodge was no worse than average.

"There he is," Jeffries said, his tray clattering on the table as he sat opposite. "The chosen one. How did you get on?"

"Not good," Grant said. "I'm pretty sure the boss is going to sack me." Quickly, he outlined the events of the flight, though he left out the pain that had shown on Durban's face. He had probably imagined it.

"You got this, mate," Jeffries assured him. "You were the best on our entire course. Other than me, of course," he added with an impish grin. "Sorry you got stuck with the miserable bighead Pom. I'm lucky. Charlie Broadley hardly had me do any of that rubbish. We just did some basic navigation stuff, then he goofed off a bit. I can't wait to do it for real. Great pilot, great bloke."

He smiled over at the nearby table where Broadley, Barton, and two other pilots sat. Grant couldn't help noticing that Broadley didn't acknowledge the gesture.

A WAAF admin clerk walked in, cleared her throat, and announced that there would be a briefing at seventeen hundred. Grumbling, the aircrew hurried to finish their plates before streaming down the corridor to the auditorium. Durban was already there, along with some of the Ops staff. The Wing Commander stood patiently waiting until they had all filed in and taken their seats.

"I hope you've all had an excellent dinner," he said, smiling tolerantly at the mumbles of derision that followed. "Orders have just come in. We're joining a Main Force raid tonight. Bomber Command is hitting Dortmund. This is a big effort, chaps. Eleven hundred aircraft."

"With that many," Barton said, "why do they need us?" A couple of others murmured their agreement.

"Do you have something better to do this evening? 465 Squadron hasn't flown a mission in two weeks." Durban ran his eyes over the crowd, and the grumbling faded to nothing. "Another squadron dropped out and we're taking their place. Our target is the main railway station and engine sheds. This will give us a chance to dust off the cobwebs before something more suitable comes along. We'll be above the flak until our dive on the target and I imagine any fighters will go after the heavies, so there shouldn't be much out there to concern us. That said, while the Luftwaffe night fighter force isn't what it used to be, they can still cause trouble."

Grant thought he saw a flicker of emotion cross the Wing Commander's face. It was gone in an instant.

"You all heard what happened last week," Durban continued. "We lost twenty-five aircraft within sight of their airfields. The Jerries suffered badly too, and I doubt they can mount an intruder push that big again, but stay alert all the way home. No careless errors. This should be a milk run. If anyone manages to get themselves killed, I'll be most put out with them." A titter of nervous laughter ran through the crowd as the Wing Commander handed over to the Ops Officer to run through the details of timings, formations and weather.

Jeffries leaned close to Grant. "Our first op, a juicy target, and it isn't even that far to fly. How brilliant is this?"

"Yeah," Grant lied. "Brilliant."

Somehow, he made it to the end of the meeting, despite the sweat that gathered on his temples and neck. He didn't make it much further, though.

Five minutes after the Wing Commander dismissed them, Grant stared at the remains of his meal floating in the toilet bowl, felt the seat shaking in his grip, and knew it wasn't brilliant at all.

Chapter Six

Sarah Lane took a sip of lukewarm tea and opened the next file. Only three sheets of typed paper. That brought the day's total to nearly one hundred and twenty pages of dense text. Not bad for a Monday.

Outside, beyond the brick walls, the sound of traffic rumbling past on Baker Street continued unabated, mingling with the clack of typewriters and their chatting operators. It was a wonder she ever got anything done here with all the noise, but she counted herself lucky. At least she had half an office. Few had even a shared workspace to call their own. Space was always in short supply at Special Operations Executive, though things had become a little better since the liberation of France had freed up some of the 'F' Section desks. And with her colleague absent for the week on some rare home leave, she had spread her files over his desk, too.

Not that she had found much. 'X' Section had always received less reporting and funding than 'F' Section. Things had been worse since the July coup failed. The Gestapo and the *Inland SD* had reacted with all their characteristic brutality, rounding up anyone even vaguely suspected of anti-Nazi sentiment in Germany and Austria. Thousands were tried and murdered on trumped-up charges and with little regard for process or evidence. Some had genuinely worked for 'X' Section. Most were just bystanders or ordinary citizens.

She glanced up, feeling a little sick as always. On the wall, a board of photographs and note cards, each carefully affixed with its own brass pin, marked the roll call of those of her agents still missing. She didn't need to look. Not really.

She knew all of their faces as well as she knew her own.

There was one more photo there, too. Bigger than the rest. Not an agent. An enemy. Blond hair. Blue eyes. More than one colleague had commented on the man's good looks, the sharp cheekbones, the thin lips that curled at the edges into the beginnings of an arrogant smile. She remembered how the appreciation vanished from the faces of those same colleagues when she told them who the man was. Thin pieces of string led from the man's face to thirty of the smaller photographs. She suspected there should be more.

Though she had seen it only once, in darkness, through eyes near-blinded by panicked tears, she knew that face best of all.

Finishing the tea with a grimace, she turned back to the report. Straight away, she could tell it was three pages of nothing. The source was a low-level bureaucrat in a Thuringia chemical company who had seen an opportunity to mix genuine antipathy for Hitler with the chance to turn a profit by selling secrets. He rarely had much to add.

She read it anyway. That was her job, after all. A page of rail movements to begin with. It used to be three or more pages, but the German rail system was suffering just as much as the rest of the Reich from the relentless assault of Allied air power. Most of the rest was gossip, little titbits from the factory canteen or casual conversations with senior management. The parts that could have been true weren't very interesting, and the interesting parts were clearly not true.

Sighing, Lane was about to close the file when she saw the single word.

Götterdämmerung.

She stared at it in silence for a long time.

Standing, she walked over to the filing cabinet and unlocked it. Calm contemplation of the contents became a frantic search. She found one file she was looking for, then two. A third had slipped to the back of a drawer. Slamming the cabinet shut and securing it, she dug through the files that covered her colleague's desk until she found the last one she wanted and rifled through dozens of pages.

The word fairly sprang from the page.

Götterdämmerung.

Lane reached for the telephone, but her fingers froze before they could touch the handset. With a sharp exhalation of breath, she grabbed the four files together, tucked them under her arm, and headed for the door.

She took the stairs up, trying not to run, passing a steady stream of people heading downstairs as their shifts ended. Most smiled, and some offered cheery greetings. A few simply looked at Lane with indifference or thinly veiled dislike. They were normally older hands, the ones who had been here since the beginning. The ones who remembered her arrival.

As she climbed further, she found herself alone except for the thud of her sensible issue shoes on the steps. The WAAF uniform she wore might have been a fiction, as she had never spent a day on an RAF station, in uniform or otherwise, but it had advantages beyond just the comfortable shoes. Most of the girls working in SOE HQ spent half their lives worrying about what to wear and the latest fashions. Lane didn't envy them that choice, or the burden that came with it. Most importantly, the WAAF Squadron Officer rank tabs on her shoulders, the equal of an RAF Squadron Leader, gave her some credibility with the military types.

Even if they could never quite see the uniform without first seeing the woman inside it.

She passed through a heavy wooden door, passed down the corridor beyond, and knocked on a door. Pushing it open, she smiled at the woman within. "Hi, Mary."

"Miss Lane," Mary said, beaming. She'd gone for yellow today,

Lane noted, with a floral hair clip to match. She looked awfully attractive, which was unfortunately the main reason her boss had picked her. "Squadron Officer Lane," Mary said, blushing. "Sorry."

"That's fine, Mary. Is the Colonel ready for me?"

Mary frowned and looked at her notes. "I'm sorry. I wasn't expecting you today."

Lane kept her face even. "Oh, that's my fault," she said. "He told me to let you know, and I'm afraid I simply forgot. Would you mind awfully not telling him? You know how grumpy he gets when he feels let down."

Mary winked. "Of course, Miss Lane. We girls have got to stick together. He's not busy. Please go on through. I'll bring some tea."

It wasn't easy lying to Mary, but it had to be done. Lane had been trying to arrange an audience for two weeks. The man always had some excuse.

This time, she couldn't afford to wait.

"When is he next in with the Joint Intelligence Committee?"

"Let me check." Mary opened her notebook. "Wednesday morning," she said. "Assuming he gets up in time. He missed it the other week, you know."

"Oh, I heard," Lane said. Giving Mary a grateful smile, she knocked on the interior door. Without waiting, she entered the office beyond.

Colonel James Dennison gave a disapproving grunt and closed the newspaper that lay across the large desk in front of him. As always, he wore his thinning hair neatly to the side, pomade helping to conceal the traces of grey spreading from the temples. Unlike Lane, he wore civilian clothes. Between his MC at Dunkirk and four years in SOE, he had all the credibility he needed and more. Secrets were Dennison's business, and he was good at finding them out. And keeping them, Lane thought.

Especially his own. "I don't believe we had an appointment today, Lane," he said.

"I'm sorry, James. It couldn't wait."

"It never can," he said with a sigh. "What is it today? Another crazy Nazi plot?"

"I'm not sure."

"Not a great start. I take it Mary said she'd bring you tea?"

"Of course. This isn't my first time."

"No, it's not." He sniffed. "Go on, then. You can have five minutes of my time."

"Fifteen."

"Ten. And you've already wasted one minute of it." He pointed at the first file she placed on his desk, thicker than the rest combined. "That looks ominous. I think I'd better have a smoke. Here, try these." He offered her a thin cigarette from a silver regimental cigarillo box, then lit it for her.

She inhaled deeply. "Parisian?"

A nod. "I was there last month for a meeting with Eisenhower's staff, before they moved to Reims."

"They're not very good, James."

"Well, *Silver Tree*, you should have brought your own." He seemed proud of his own cleverness. It was not his only fault. Not even the worst.

Exhaling, she opened the first file. "*Werwolf*," she said, ignoring his groan just as she ignored his use of the nickname that only he found amusing. She had long since stopped letting it bother her. "Last summer, Himmler gave an order for special SS units to be assembled to resist our advance. Stay behind forces, if you will, hitting our rear areas, conducting small unit raids and assassinations. The man in charge of them is an SS Obergruppenführer by the name of Hans-Adolf Prützmann. Here." Turning the file around, she pushed Dennison a full-page photo of a shaven headed officer with oddly reptilian eyes.

"Prützmann learned his trade studying the Partisan campaigns in northern Russia and the Baltic nations. He put them down, too. Murdered thousands."

"So far, so Nazi." Dennison yawned. "What was it Goebbels said? Something about fanatics keeping us up at night?"

"The enemy will be taken in the rear by the fanatical population," Lane quoted, "which will ceaselessly worry him, tie down strong forces and allow him no rest or exploitation of any possible success."

"Hmm. I said it in fewer words."

"Except," Lane said, "I don't think he was talking about *Werwolf*. My sources indicate *Werwolf* is a military unit, closer to our Commandos or SAS than partisans."

"All the better," Dennison said. "That will make it harder for them to vanish into the local population."

"While giving them access to better training and weaponry."

"Perhaps." The Colonel coughed, and a cloud of acrid smoke spilled from his mouth. "Damn it, these things really are awful. Bloody French."

Lane pushed aside the *Werwolf* file and reached for another. "Here. Look."

"A visitor log." Dennison peered at the page. "How fascinating."

"This is the visitor log for an underground pharmaceutical facility outside Hildesheim."

"Which is where?"

"Just south of Hanover. Look at the seventh name on the list."

With a theatrical yawn, the Colonel leaned closer. "Hans-Adolf Prützmann," he read.

"Why would the head of *Werwolf*, preparing to conduct operations behind our lines, feel the need to visit an obscure laboratory in Lower Saxony?"

He shrugged. "Perhaps he ran low on aspirin, or he's got a

morphine addiction like Goering. Or his sister works there. Who cares?"

There was a knock at the door, and Mary entered and placed two steaming cups of tea on the desk.

"Thank you, Mary," Dennison said. "Off you go now."

Smiling at Lane, Mary left, with Dennison watching her each step of the way. The Colonel waited until the door closed behind her, then gave his smouldering cigarette a rueful look and stubbed it out. Without asking, Lane took another and lit this one herself. She didn't mind the taste. It reminded her of happier days, before the war.

"You've got to admit, Lane," Dennison said, leaning back in his chair, "this is thin stuff. No wonder you didn't call to make a proper appointment."

"Do you blame me? I've been trying to brief you on this for weeks. Here." She gave him the third file and pointed.

"*Götterdämmerung*," he read. "The final part of the Ring Cycle, and the best if you ask me. I didn't know you were a Richard Wagner fan, Lane. That surprises me, given your heritage..." He tailed off, flicking his fingers in an airy but indeterminate gesture.

She ignored the comment and laid open the fourth file. "Here it is again," she said, pointing. "On a trans-shipping manifest for chemical rail wagons in Thüringen. This one came in today."

"Your ten minutes is nearly up," Dennison said wearily. "Would you care to get to whatever point you think you're making?"

"*Werwolf*. Prützmann. A pharmaceutical laboratory in Hildesheim, and a chemical factory near Weimar. This word *Götterdämmerung*, coming up over and over."

"So?"

She stared at him. "If the day should ever come when we must go, if some day we are compelled to leave the scene of history, we will slam the door so hard that the universe will shake and mankind will stand back in stupefaction."

"Hitler?"

"Goebbels."

"You know the man is a professional liar, don't you? That sort of nonsense is pure propaganda. Or else he was talking about the V1 and V2 or even the bloody V3, and we dealt with those all well enough, didn't we?"

"What if it's more than that?"

"It's not," he said firmly, closing the file and handing it back to her.

She stared at him. Not blinking. Just watching. It had the desired effect. It always did.

Even as a child, people had talked about her eyes. The more polite ones used words like "enigmatic." They were in a minority. Icy. Intimidating. That's what they really meant. She didn't care what people thought of her eyes, no more than she cared what they thought of her family, or blood, or her rise as a woman from the typing pool to Deputy Chief of 'X' Section.

All that mattered was that they did what she needed them to.

"Fine," Dennison snapped. "Get together all the evidence you can and bring it to me. I'll push it up the chain."

"At the JIC," she said. "On Wednesday."

"Put it all together in a briefing note, and I'll see what I can do. Now, if you'll excuse me, Silver Tree, your time is well and truly up. I have other business to attend to." He reached for his newspaper.

Lane stood to attention, then reached for the files. The picture of Hans-Adolf Prützmann slid free, and for a moment seemed to stare at her with cold mocking from those odd, pitiless eyes. She covered his face with the other papers and closed the file, piling it with the others before placing them under her arm.

"Sarah?"

She stopped halfway to the door. "Yes, sir?"

At least he had the courtesy to lower his newspaper. "No one has done more for this section than you," he said. "I know that more than anyone. You were my secretary, after all. You've come a long way since then, and you have truly been invaluable. But you seem tired. Why don't you take a few days off? Head to Brighton or Margate for some sea air?"

"Thank you," she said, "but I'm fine."

"Very well. I offered. Seeing as you're going to still be in town, at least come for a drink with me tonight at my club. They don't normally allow ladies, but as my guest..."

He already knew her answer, of course. He'd heard it often enough. She could have admired his tenacity, if only he'd applied it to his work instead. "I can't," she said, patting the files under her arm. "I have work to do."

"Of course. Perhaps some other time."

"Perhaps," she said, not meaning it. She turned and walked from the room, feeling his eyes on her the whole way.

After slamming the door of her office, she put the files on her desk and lit one of her own cigarettes. For a long time, she stared at her filing cabinet. Then she put in a requisition order for more files from the central registry and went to work.

Götterdämmerung was out there.

All she had to do was find it.

Chapter Seven

Above Germany, 12 March

Durban didn't need two tours in Pathfinders to find the target. He barely needed a navigator. All he needed was the vast glow that had, until recently, been the city of Dortmund.

"Jesus," Grant muttered next to him.

From twenty-eight thousand feet, the light of the waning crescent moon cast its dull glow across near-endless sheets of white cloud, broken intermittently by thinner patches through which the brighter, roiling light of the dying city rose. Below them, Durban could make out shadow after shadow of heavy bombers, powering across Europe in a concentrated stream of hate and destruction. Lancasters, hundreds of them. Halifaxes, too, even a few other squadrons of Mosquitoes. He'd long since lost count. This was the biggest raid he had ever seen, and he had seen too many. Maybe the biggest of the war. One by one, the lumbering behemoths disgorged their individual thousands of pounds of payload through the clouds into the city below. Incendiaries, to start a thousand fires that would, if the gods of devastation smiled this night, merge into a single firestorm like the one that had ravaged Hamburg. High explosive, to rupture buildings and streets, and to destroy the water mains that the firefighters needed to lessen the destruction.

As a junior pilot, Durban had hunted German bombers over London and seen the destruction they wrought on the city. He had known even then that this would only be the start. They have sown the wind, Churchill had said. Searching the skies near London night after night, scoring his first two kills, Durban had marvelled at the flames reflecting from the waters of the Thames and wondered how humanity could do this to itself.

This, below him, was so far beyond what he had seen back then that he struggled to comprehend it, even as he watched it unfolding.

Germany had truly reaped the whirlwind.

"One minute to the first aiming point," Grant said. He looked utterly nauseated. Durban hoped it was airsickness. At the very least, he needed Grant to control his squeamishness long enough to see them to the target.

Giving the younger man a nod, Durban twisted in his seat to look behind them. 465 Squadron remained with him. He could only see the first couple of aircraft, vague in the darkness, but he knew the others would be close, concealed in the depths of the night. Fourteen of the squadron's eighteen aircraft, with Barton leading A Flight and the Kiwi Kittinger leading B Flight. He felt a moment of relief. For low-level specialists like 465, this kind of navigation should be straightforward, but you never knew the measure of a new unit until you'd seen it in combat.

Not that this really counted as combat, he thought. Not compared to the bad days in 1942 and 1943, when a bomber crew's life expectancy was measured in single digits of missions. Despite his lofty vantage point, he'd seen only one Lancaster hit and burn before spiralling out of sight below the cloud. Flak, most likely, bursting above the clouds in little flowering puffs of orange and grey that might have been lovely if they weren't so deadly.

Germany was beaten, but no one had told the flak crews. Cued by the latest gun-laying radar, they continued to hurl their 88mm high explosive defiance into the skies.

"Mark," Grant said. "Heading three-four-five. One minute to second aiming point."

Durban shivered. He told himself it was the cold inside the

cockpit, the heater unable to fully cope with the indicated outside air temperature of minus sixty Fahrenheit. He knew better, of course. No matter how many times he had been in this position, he had never grown used to it.

Brushing the rudder to correct course, he checked his radio was set to channel A, then thumbed his R/T transmit switch. "Colt Leader to all callsigns," he said, hearing a slight crackle of reverberation in his headset. "Fifty seconds to second aiming point. Prepare to descend on my signal."

No one replied. They didn't need to. They knew their roles. It was the first time anyone had broken radio silence since crossing the Channel coast.

Forty-five seconds later, he gave the word and put the Mosquito into a shallow dive.

This was the dangerous moment.

From experience and the spread of the fires, Durban could see that the Pathfinders who had preceded the raid had marked a position close to the centre of the city with their Target Indicator flares. The first arriving bombers had doubtless dropped their bombloads close to this point, but with each subsequent wave there had been a slight creeping of the fire-struck area as some bombers dropped on the fires started by their predecessors, not the TI flares. It was a phenomenon as old as the bomber campaign, and Durban knew that despite all the new techniques and technologies – electronic bombing aids like Gee, H2S and Oboe, specially trained Pathfinder crews, even a very experienced crew flying as Master Bomber – it was a phenomenon that could never be fully erased.

All of which meant that, he saw with one practiced sweep of his gaze, the vast majority of the bombs had fallen on the centre and south of the city. Their target area stood on the northern edge of the city, right where the wall of flaming chaos faltered.

They could have dropped their bombloads from high altitude,

of course, but while the Mosquito squadron they had replaced tonight flew the unarmed bomber variant, with four thousand pounds of explosives in their bay, the FB Mk VI could only manage two 500lb bombs in the rear of the shortened bomb bay. The four 20mm Hispano cannon took up the rest of the space beneath the aircraft. With no air intercept radar to take up space like in his old NF Mk XVIII night fighter, the FB VI also found room for four .303" machine guns in the nose, fired electro-pneumatically by a push switch on the control column. Durban didn't expect to need them. Tonight, it was all about the bomb load.

One thousand pounds of high explosive per Mosquito scattered amidst the tens of thousands of tons raining down from the heavies would hardly make a difference. That same thousand pounds placed directly on the railway station by fifteen Mosquitoes one after the other could achieve plenty. Most importantly, it would give the squadron, and its commander, some valuable training. But it meant going beneath the cloud, into the teeth of the flak. If they were especially unlucky, it meant flying below that same stream of bombs dropping from on high, and Durban had seen more than once what happened when a fragile airframe found itself in the path of half a ton of fused and ready HE.

The cloud loomed ahead and their airspeed crept up as he kept the Mosquito in the pre-briefed dive. Throttling back, he watched the slow spin of the altimeter. He hoped he'd calculated their angle correctly. Too steep, and they risked damaging their airframes. Too shallow would leave them too high over the target. Their bombing would be less accurate, and worse, the gunners would find it much easier to track them. Durban expected the flak to focus on the easier heavy bomber targets, but the speed of their descent would add further protection if the gunners tried their luck.

Grant murmured something, barely audible over the engines and the whistle of air past the wings.

"Speak up," Durban said shortly.

"Thirty seconds to release point," Grant said, his voice louder this time but still tremulous.

Durban reached down with his right hand for the bomb door lever but didn't pull it yet. He kept his hands steady on the controls as they reached the cloud layer and it obliterated the view ahead. For several seconds, they flew alone in a world of swirling grey and white, but already he could see a growing glow ahead, increasing with intensity with each second of their quickening descent.

Then the cloud parted. He heard Grant's sharp intake of breath and blinked against the hellish glare of a city in the throes of immolation.

The possibility of picking out any individual landmark from the smoking wreckage below seemed remote, but he tried anyway. Beyond the outer edge of the fires just to the left of the diving Mosquito's nose, arcing away between the grasping beams of two anti-aircraft searchlights, he could just make out the thin black lines of the canal docks and the Dortmund-Ems canal itself heading northwest. That put the station directly ahead of them. Grant's navigation had been perfect. Now to see if his timekeeping was its equal.

"Ten seconds," Grant said.

Durban pulled the lever in his right hand. The aircraft shuddered in protest as the bomb doors fell open into the slipstream. He kept his thumb poised over the bomb release, waiting for what seemed an eternity while the burning city grew larger, the aircraft shook, and he wondered whether Grant had forgotten what came next.

"Mark," Grant said, his voice clear and firm and loud.

"Bombs gone," Durban said into his R/T, feeling the aircraft rise, buoyant without its deadly payload. He pulled the

Mosquito into a banking turn to port, still descending, accelerating as he closed the bomb doors and pushed the throttles forward. Behind him, the other Mosquitoes would release their own bombs, hopefully onto the same spot as his own. Not that he could know whether he'd struck the target. That was one for the battle damage assessment teams over the next few days, when reconnaissance photos became available. The priority now was to get clear of the target area before the flak crews found them.

A moment later, and he knew that it was too late for that.

The two massive beams of light swung their way with shocking speed. Durban saw a distant flash and heard the faint crump of the first anti-aircraft shell. A puff of smoke hung in the air off their nose before disappearing past the left wingtip. A marker shell, to help the gunners get their range. More followed, while the questing searchlights groped in the sky. If they found something, both searchlights would quickly cone it and keep it illuminated while every gun in the city turned like a hunting pack on the exposed prey.

The Mosquito gave a violent lurch as a shell erupted directly ahead. Even with his oxygen mask covering his face, Durban smelt the sour stench of cordite as they passed through what had, just a second earlier, been an expanding cloud of red-hot shrapnel. Then they were clear, leaving the searchlights sweeping across the base of the cloud, still forlornly searching for the attackers that had simply dived too fast and too steep for their beams to catch.

Durban glanced at Grant, pleased to see that he wasn't watching the fires but was instead scanning the sky for night fighters. He tapped the young man's knee. "Good job."

"Thank you, sir." Grant's eyes still seemed a little too wide, but his breathing was calm. He'd tightened his straps properly this time, Durban noted.

"Fancy giving me a course for home?"

A smile. Forced. Somewhat sickly. "Yes, of course." Grant checked compass and map with surprising speed. "Two-eight-five for thirty minutes."

"Remember to pick us a course that avoids any other flak concentrations, won't you, Grant?"

"Already done, sir."

Behind them, the dying city faded from sight, though the glow on the horizon lingered longer.

Dawn was still several hours away when they landed at RAF Charney Breach. Grant's course had brought them home ahead of the rest of the squadron, Durban noted with satisfaction. Shutting the aircraft down, he followed the navigator down the crew ladder, but did not walk straight to the waiting transport. Instead, he stood beneath the wing of his aircraft and watched the second Mosquito land. "You did well," he said simply, his eyes on the sky.

"Are you ok, sir?"

"I'm fine, Grant. Just watching the boys home." He zipped his jacket fully to the top against the cold night air. "It's a tradition of mine since my first days on Pathfinders. Silly superstition, really, but I can't help thinking if I'm not watching them home safely, who is?"

"That doesn't sound silly at all to me, sir."

Together they stood in the cool night air and counted aircraft in until fourteen more were safely on the airfield, with their crews streaming to the debrief. It was only when Durban followed them back that he learned that the missing crew were Charlie Broadley and Dougie Jeffries.

Chapter Eight

Zurich, 13 March

The café, a bustling place bedecked with pretty tablecloths and prettier Swiss students enjoying coffee and milkshakes, stood on the banks of the Limmat. From his comfy seat with his back to the wall and his eyes on the windows, Stahl could watch the traffic crossing the Münsterbrücke and admire the looming shape of the Grossmünster with its twin-towered twelfth-century splendour. As a young officer in the *Ausland-SD* he had spent many hours here, working but happy, watching the exiled German dissidents they had tasked him to monitor hold court and espouse their anti-Hitler views. Nostalgia was not why he had picked this place, though. Sometimes his orders had called for more than just watching and, more than once, he had used his knowledge of the city streets to the west and north to stalk a target or avoid the police when the work was done.

If today's meeting did not go well, he might need that knowledge again.

He sipped his Kaffe-crème and looked down at the remnants of his Gipfeli. He hadn't realised how hungry he was, but then he hadn't eaten a meaningful meal since leaving Berlin. The Swiss border guards hadn't fed him before they passed him on with typical efficiency to the police, who had likewise neglected his needs while they took a little longer to bring in the well-groomed gentlemen from the *Bureau Ha*. Normally, Stahl didn't like people to know too much about him, but in this case, it had worked to his favour. Hans Hausamann may have only established the Swiss national intelligence agency at the outset of war, but he ran it with excellent sources and clockwork precision. Best of all, Hausamann owed Stahl a favour, and had let him make a phone call to the British Embassy in Bern.

Right on time, their man was crossing the Münsterbrücke and making his way to the front of the café, pausing only to hold the door with a smile for two giggling students who clearly found much to appreciate in his tousled blond hair and rangy form. The attraction was mutual, with the man admiring their departing shapes before striding across the room with pantherish grace.

"Hello, Stahl," he said, placing his briefcase on the floor and adjusting his chair so that his back wasn't to the window before sitting. "It's been a long time."

"Yes," Stahl agreed. Not for the first time, he wished that someone had returned his Luger. By now, it was likely buried in a mass of triplicate paperwork in some Swiss militia armoury. "Too long, Anders."

"I see you've brought a friend." The killer he knew only as Major Anders settled into his seat and gave a nod to a thick-set man sitting on the far side of the room, pretending to read a novel.

"Not my friend," Stahl said as the man coloured and stiffly returned the nod. "The Bureau Ha may have let me leave their custody, but they aren't quite ready to allow me to wander the streets without a babysitter. Your own people took me a little longer to spot." He waved at the seemingly married couple sharing a dessert a few tables away.

Anders laughed. "*Guten Appetit,*" he called to them. "The best I could find at short notice, I'm afraid," he told Stahl. "Switzerland isn't exactly a priority for British Intelligence anymore, not with the war winding down. The focus is already shifting to Moscow, Prague and Warsaw. How's the coffee?" Without waiting for a response, he summoned the waiter and, in fluent French, ordered two more Kaffe-crème and four more croissants.

"The Swiss Germans call them *Gipfeli*," Stahl observed mildly as the waiter hurried away.

"My French is better than my German," Anders replied in perfect German. "How is the Admiral?"

"Doomed," Stahl said simply.

Anders nodded. "There was some talk of offering a swap deal for Hess. Senior leadership decided that if Hitler knew just how close Canaris had become to us, it might have made things worse for him."

"Worse?" Stahl grimaced. "It cannot get much worse. They will never let the Russians liberate him. It is only the Führer's belief that Canaris has more insights into British plans that keeps him alive. If he only knew how completely you have abandoned him..."

"The war is winding down," Anders repeated bluntly. "The British Government no longer sees much value in Canaris. It happens to us all in time."

"I hope when your time comes," Stahl said darkly in Danish, "they are a little less callous."

"I guess we'll find out," Anders said. Major Anders, son of a noble Danish family, turned merchant navy sailor and adventurer. When Germany had conquered his homeland, he had stayed with his crew until they reached Liverpool, then ditched them and joined the British Commandos. A dozen clandestine raids and a Military Cross later, he had earned a bloody reputation and the attention of both British Intelligence and the Abwehr, who gave him the rare honour of a file of his own.

Anders had not changed a bit since Admiral Canaris had shown Stahl that first photograph back in 1943. They had met four times these last two years, always clandestinely, always at the behest of Canaris. If anything, Anders looked younger every time. The strains and terrors of war seemed to have no more effect on that youthful, open face than the blood he spilled for the British Government.

"Here," the Dane said, passing a small brown envelope across the table. "You will want this back."

From inside, Stahl drew out his wallet, confiscated by the Swiss intelligence officers. His ID remained, but his money had gone. Border crossing tax, he thought wryly. It mattered not. Reichsmarks were worth little outside Germany. All he really cared about was the small photograph that he found within, creased but intact. He stared at her slim face for a few seconds, as beautiful as ever, wondering if others saw the same sadness in her eyes that he did.

"You never mentioned a wife, Stahl."

"My sister, Isobel," Stahl said shortly. "Who are you representing today, Anders? MI6? MI5? SOE?"

Anders shrugged. "Perhaps I'm just here to enjoy coffee and a pastry with an old friend."

"You know," Stahl said, taking his fresh coffee from the waiter, "Canaris always said that the worst part of trying to deal with the British is that you never knew who you were actually dealing with."

"A wise man," Anders said. "How did you find the border crossing?"

"Distressing."

The Dane's brow twitched. "Well, I have arranged a more pleasant route out. Swissair hasn't been able to operate at all since August, but I've arranged a Hudson to take us first to Paris, then onto England tomorrow. Tonight, we'll share a drink on the Champs-Élysées again." He paused, regarding Stahl with the same smile on his face, only now it sat below cold eyes, all bonhomie gone. "Assuming, of course, what you have to share is worth the airfare."

"It is."

"Good," Anders said. He winked. "Now enjoy your coffee while we wait for the car."

They didn't make small talk. Neither man was the type. Their ride was late, which gave Stahl a chance to order a slice of *Aprikosenkuchen* that partly filled the gnawing void in his stomach.

A black Citroen soon arrived. Leaving francs for the bill, Anders led the way outside. The 'married couple' followed, looking suitably embarrassed, and kept close behind until Stahl sat safely in the Citroen's rear. Anders went around the other side, taking his seat with the briefcase in his lap and both hands on the lid.

"Let's go," he told the driver, a big man with a more muscular frame than his apparent employment would warrant.

"To the airfield?" The driver regarded Stahl in his rear-view mirror with suspicion. His accent was British. London, Stahl judged. East End, most likely.

"For now," Anders said.

They pulled away into traffic, turning left over the Quaibrücke and speeding up under the tram wires on Rämistrasse until they passed the University. "It all seems very normal," Stahl remarked. "Really no different to how it was in 1939. You could believe there was no war at all."

"There isn't," Anders said. "Not here. One of the many benefits of neutrality."

Stahl remembered the files Canaris had shown him. Switzerland might have stayed neutral, but they were hardly innocent bystanders. "I am sure they will profit from the experience nonetheless."

"Of course," Anders said. "Now, tell me a story. Why are you here? I'm guessing by the three dead Germans on the border that this isn't exactly a diplomatic mission. The German Embassy was furious about that. They demanded to know who Switzerland had let in."

"What did they tell them?"

"Not the truth, that's for sure. Hans Hausamann may be an opportunist, but he won't spill any secrets he doesn't have to. As far as your compatriots in Berne are concerned, an escaped PoW killed the guards, then died in a car crash while evading police arrest."

"And they believed that?"

"Does it sound any more unlikely than the top assassin in the SS turning traitor?"

"I am not a traitor," Stahl snapped.

"Patriot, then," Anders said, amused. "But I'm still waiting."

Stahl considered the briefcase on the Dane's lap, the way the man's huge hands remained on it at all times. He had no doubts it contained a pistol. Or a knife. Anders was equally adept with either. If his visitor's story did not satisfy the Dane, he was surely under orders to resolve the issue quietly as well as quickly. Stahl figured he was getting on that plane either way; only his condition was open to debate. Britain wouldn't risk upsetting the Swiss government with unexplained bodies on Swiss soil, not when a slight deviation from their flight path would take them over the convenient depths of the Mediterranean.

"What does the word *Götterdämmerung* mean to you, Major?"

"Not a lot."

"It is the final part of Wagner's Der Ring des Nibelungen, his four-opera cycle."

"Do I strike you as an opera fan?"

Stahl ignored that. "The word itself is a literal translation of Ragnarök, the old Viking myth of the fall of the Gods. The end of the world."

"I have to say, Stahl," Anders said, tapping his fingers on the briefcase lid, "you're not filling me with confidence that this trip was worth my time." The driver's eyes flickered between the two of them, and almost imperceptibly, the car slowed.

"You do not believe that," Stahl said. "If you did, you would not have flown here on that Hudson when you heard of my arrest. So perhaps you and your hired thug driver stop should stop trying to make me nervous, and try listening?"

Anders stared a moment and then laughed. "I told you," he said, punching the driver on the shoulder. "I bloody told you, didn't I? Damn, Stahl, I have missed you. Sorry. Tell me about *Götterdämmerung.*" He settled back in his seat, beaming tolerantly.

The smile did not last long. Not once Stahl began talking. By the time he stopped, so had the talk of an overnight hotel in Paris.

London would not wait that long.

Chapter Nine

London, 14 March

Someone had once told Sarah Lane that an officer in uniform should never run. Regardless of the conditions, even under direct enemy fire, a good officer never ran.

Well, she bloody did. Especially when such an important summons arrived so late.

Ignoring Mary's despairing protests as the younger woman struggled to keep up with her, Lane weaved through the office workers and off-duty soldiers milling around the entrance to Charing Cross Underground station and raced along the Strand. Mary! What had she been thinking, waiting this long to knock on her door? Why couldn't she have sent a message, or called her landlady? SOE had the number. Mrs Rose was always so irritatingly proud that she had a telephone, but the one time it might have been useful, Mary had come halfway across London to deliver the message in person, leaving Lane only a few minutes to dress and no time to breakfast before running for the Tube.

She slowed slightly to watch for traffic coming up Northumberland Avenue. From his lofty perch, the statue of Charles I in the centre of the roundabout seemed to regard her with faint approbation. It wasn't Mary's fault, Lane reminded herself. After all, calling on an open line to invite someone to a Joint Intelligence Committee meeting wasn't exactly the done thing. No, this was Dennison's fault. He'd barely agreed to even bring up the subject of *Götterdämmerung* in the JIC. He certainly hadn't warned her that her presence might be required.

A little out of breath, she slowed enough for Mary to catch her as she passed through the shadow of Admiralty Arch.

There were two guards at the entrance to Carlton Terrace, rifles slung, faces wary. "Squadron Officer Lane," she said, showing her ID.

"They were expecting you a little earlier, Ma'am," one said. "Please make your way straight up. Just you," he added, shifting his body to cut Mary off from the door.

"I'll see you later, Mary," Lane said.

"Wait, Miss Lane." Mary fumbled in her purse and produced a crumpled white handkerchief. "For your face," she explained, pressing it into Lane's hands and giving them an affectionate squeeze. "You're looking a little warm."

"Thank you."

"Good luck," Mary said brightly, but Lane was already through the open door. She had only been here a few times, and Dennison never allowed her into the conference room, but at least she knew the way. She took the steps two at a time, nodded to the soldier standing outside the room, and raised her hand to knock on the door. Beyond it, she heard the muffled drone of a man's voice.

Wait, she thought. Compose yourself. She took a few deep breaths, willing her pulse to slow, feeling the sweat on her back beneath her warm woollen uniform. Taking the handkerchief, ignoring the smell of Mary's perfume on it, she dabbed at her neck and temples. The soldier pretended not to notice.

She knocked on the door and opened it.

The room fell silent. The speaker, who she recognised as Sir David Petrie of the Security Service, turned from his presentation to regard her. She felt a little jolt of surprise at his presence. Sir David normally sent a representative. His audience, all middle-aged men lining each side of the long, polished conference table, regarded her with blank faces. She recognised a handful of them

72

instantly, noting that the head of SIS was also here. Most unusual. There were three uniformed military types from the War Office, Admiralty and Air Ministry, accompanied by a handful of aides and bag carriers. She knew she had met the senior RAF officer in the room, a Group Captain, equivalent to a British Army full Colonel. He worked for the Directorate of Intelligence (Research), the cover name for the department within the Air Ministry that handled the hush-hush special operations that the RAF had occasionally undertaken on behalf of SOE and MI6. They had crossed paths in the build-up to both the Amiens prison raid in February 1944 and the Aarhus raid on Halloween. Frustrating, that she couldn't remember his name, but she'd worked with so many military men since the war began that they had blended into one another.

Colonel Dennison sat at the foot of the table, fiddling with an expensive-looking fountain pen while his face suggested he wasn't sure if he was annoyed that she was late or simply that she had arrived at all. Looking away from him, still furious, her gaze paused on a sturdy civilian she didn't recognise but who, for some reason, kept his hat on indoors.

Most shocking of all, she saw Lord Wolmer sitting close to the top of the table. Roundell Palmer, third Earl of Selbourne, known as "Top Wolmer" to friends and political rivals alike. The Minister of Economic Warfare. The man who "owned" SOE, and her ultimate boss. His face was not blank at all, though she wished it was. Behind him, a large clock showed just how late she was.

Glowering, Lord Wolmer shot a look at Dennison.

With colour flooding to his cheeks, the colonel pushed out the empty chair next to him and gestured sharply for Lane to sit.

"My apologies, Sir David," she said, taking her seat.

"No matter." Powerfully built with rugged features, the Scotsman had a reputation for being kindly. Judging from the

73

expressions on the faces of the others, he was the only one feeling so inclined.

Without meeting Dennison's eyes, she sat back in her chair, smoothing her skirt beneath the table and wondering why so many senior people had come today.

Sir David picked up where he had left off. The Security Service had arrested a German agent trying to work with organised crime groups in the dockyards area. With remarkable ease, Sir David said wryly, adding that German espionage efforts within the UK itself had been somewhere between amateurish and embarrassing for several years. The absorption of the Abwehr by the RHSA following the exposure of Canaris had only hastened the process.

Lord Wolmer cleared his throat. "And what can MI5 tell us about *Werwolf*?"

Lane sat bolt upright at the name.

Sir David shook his head. "Almost nothing, sadly. Most of the double agents we have captured and turned had already left Germany long before the Nazis started any proper planning for their defeat. The more recent ones, like the chap in the East End, just weren't in the know. Whatever the SS are planning, they are keeping their cards close to their chest."

"Rather." Lord Wolmer turned to the civilian in the hat. "What about your department, Quiet? Anything to add?"

"I think," the man in the hat said, the voice drifting from the shadows beneath the brim, "it would be better to delay until Major Anders arrives."

Wolmer frowned. "Not to second guess you, Quiet, but are you sure this...*guest* he's bringing is worth the risk we're taking? After all, whatever his track record, he's not exactly someone we would normally give top level security clearances to."

"I'm sure," the man replied, pausing, "that he won't be allowed to embarrass us."

A silence descended on the room, broken only by the ticking of the large clock on the wall.

"Well," Wolmer said, "let's hope he at least has something worth the wait, because as of now, this committee seems to have very little light to shed on this business. Colonel Dennison, does your own guest have anything to add?"

The Colonel squirmed in his seat. "Possibly. Just some minor points."

The Minister gestured him for silence. "Miss Lane, isn't it?"

She nodded. She saw the RAF Group Captain frown at the Minister's ignoring of her WAAF rank, but she had long since given up expecting people, especially civilians, to take her uniform seriously.

"The floor is yours, Miss Lane," Lord Wolmer said. "We're all excited to hear what you have to say." He paused. "However belatedly."

"Yes, sir." She looked at Dennison, more in hope than expectation that he might have thought to bring some briefing notes or materials. From his vacant look, she saw instantly that it had never even occurred to him. No matter. She had read every report, every cited source, a dozen times. She knew everything she needed to know.

She left her boss to play with his pen and turned her attention to the decision-makers.

"The first thing to note about *Werwolf*," she began, "is that its value is likely more in the propaganda sphere than any concrete military advantage. Goebbels is busy telling the world that every pure Aryan-blooded German man, woman and child will die before accepting surrender, but that is not true."

"Easy to say from here," the Brigadier from the War Office said. "But that will hardly help if my tank crews find schoolgirls in braids running under their tracks with an artillery shell strapped to their chest."

"I don't believe they will, sir," she said firmly. "Germany isn't Japan. Yes, there are some fanatics who think Hitler is a living God, but they are the exceptions, not the rule. For most, everything suggests survival is the priority. Germany might not be quite ready to fully abandon Hitler, even now, but the average citizen certainly isn't lining up to die for him."

"Is that all it is, then?" Sir David raised an eyebrow. "Propaganda?"

"Not quite, sir. There is a fake *Werwolf*, the one Goebbels is pushing, and a real one. The latter is a military operation, more akin to our SAS or SBS. Ambushes. Assassinations. Special Forces raids on bridges and isolated HQs. Messing with road signs and sowing confusion, like we saw in the Ardennes offensive a few months ago. That's what we should plan against for the occupation, not suicide attacks by children."

"That's certainly easier to cope with," the Brigadier said. "It's nice to know we don't need to be too worried."

"I wouldn't say that," Lane said. Dennison gave her a warning look. She ignored it. "I'm more concerned about a project called *Götterdämmerung*."

"Which is?"

"I don't know, sir."

A tremor of laughter rippled along the table. Lane didn't join in. She felt anger rising and placed her hands flat on the table to stop them clenching into fists.

"Forgive my colleagues, Miss Lane," Sir David said, frowning at the nearest men. "But you'll agree that isn't an enlightening start."

"I don't know exactly what it is," Lane said. "All I know is that it is important. My section deals with Germany and Austria, as you know. We don't get the quantity of reporting we used to before the July 1944 crackdown, but I still have an extensive web of agents sending updates night and day. The German resistance might not be as widespread or photogenic as the French one, but it is there. Priests. Students. Disaffected soldiers. Criminals, motivated by money. Even some Nazis who know they have lost the war but think that a swift conquest by the Western Allies is better than falling into Soviet hands."

"Which it is," Sir David said.

"The point is, this network is widespread and diffuse, and most of them share no contacts or common ground with the rest. Which makes it more concerning for me that this word *Götterdämmerung* keeps coming up."

"The Twilight of the Gods," the man in the hat murmured.

Lane glanced at him. He said nothing more.

"So far," she continued, "I have been able to discern it is linked to *Werwolf*, but separate. Whatever the operation is, it seems to report to SS High Command, possibly directly to Himmler himself. There is a network of scientists and medical research facilities involved. One report even suggests that the SS have requisitioned a U-Boat, though I can't yet determine why."

The Commodore from the Admiralty raised a hand. "What about chemical weapons? A modified U-Boat surfacing at night and firing chemical shells from its desk gun could spread panic up and down the east coast of England."

"Unlikely," the Minister said. "Hitler has had the entire war to choose to use chemical weapons. He hasn't used them for the same reason we haven't. And like us, it's not because he doesn't have them available. They just aren't very useful. Why wait until now, when his ability to reach us is at its lowest? He must know we'd retaliate with a thousand times the potency."

"Hitler's erratic, Minister," the Commodore insisted. "We shouldn't rule out chemical warfare."

"Or biological," Lane said quietly.

"Not a chance," the Brigadier said. "We all read the reporting from the Biological Warfare Intelligence Committee. We'd have known if there was any widespread attempt to use biological weapons. Besides, these things are horribly difficult to employ without your own side suffering just as badly. Once that genie is out of the lamp, it's awfully hard to stuff the bugger back in."

"If Squadron Officer Lane can provide some more details on these facilities," the RAF Group Captain from DI(R) said, "we can arrange some aerial shots courtesy of the photo-reconnaissance chaps. They might not tell us much, but it is worth a try. Please send the locations across."

"Will do, sir," Lane assured him.

There was a knock, resounding at almost the same moment that the door flew wide open. Two men entered.

The first, Lane saw, was tall. Broad-shouldered. A strong jaw, offset by ears that stuck out a little too fully from beneath his green beret. He seemed to be half-smiling, standing framed in the doorway for a moment as if inviting everyone to note the time and manner of his arrival. He wore the uniform and insignia of a British Army major, possibly tailored to better show off the powerful frame beneath. On his upper arm, she saw the Tactical Recognition Flash for Combined Arms operations.

"Good morning, gentlemen," he said. He walked towards the table. Stalked, Lane corrected herself. Every step seemed perfectly controlled and loaded with menacing intent. Like a tiger. "Sorry to keep you waiting. I'm Major Anders, Second Commando Brigade."

"We know who you are," the Brigadier said, jumping from his seat and shaking the newcomer's hand. "Jolly good show in Norway, and congratulations on your MC. Well deserved."

"Thank you, sir," Anders said, clearly not even slightly surprised at the praise.

"If the Army is quite finished being star-struck," Lord Wolmer said to a chorus of chuckles, "perhaps we can resume our meeting? Take a seat, Major."

Anders lowered himself gracefully into a chair. So completely had he absorbed her attention, and that of the entire room, that Lane had forgotten his companion. Still enjoying the Brigadier's obvious embarrassment, her gaze fell on the newcomer.

Recognition struck her as hard as a blow.

The air seemed to be torn from her lungs. Her hands shook in the sudden onset of violent, unreasoning terror. Waves of brutal cold seemed to run down her skin, her blood choking up in her veins as if might stop altogether. She felt her lips tremble, her mouth dry and her tongue swollen as bile and nausea bubbled in the back of her throat.

Anders announced the newcomer's name. Lane didn't hear it over her own pulse. She didn't need to. She had read it in a hundred reports, heard it from the lips of a dozen agents. Over and over, she had seen the name next to a picture of a dead agent, among the stark, unemotional words that sought to describe their last hours of freedom. Of life.

His photograph hung on her office wall.

For two years, his face had haunted her dreams.

The man took a seat next to Anders. Opposite her. Pressing her lips together to stop any sound escaping, she fought the unreasoning pressure to empty her bladder on the seat and the expensive carpet below. She tried to force herself back in her chair. To shrink.

Like Anders, the man exuded predatory danger, but that was where the resemblance ended. Where Anders had the size, power and grace of a big cat, this one was something else entirely. A snake, perhaps. Slim. Wiry. Deadly.

Lane stared, and now the man seemed to notice her. With deep-set eyes of infinite coldness, he regarded her without emotion. Then the corner of his mouth quirked in the slightest hint of a smile.

He recognised her, too.

Her resolve snapped.

For two years, she had fallen asleep every night in the near-certain knowledge that one day, SS Obersturmbannführer Jan Stahl would come for her. The way he had come for her agents in Berlin, in Copenhagen, in Kiel and Vienna and Salzburg. The way he had come for her that spring day in Paris, when she had escaped while so many others hadn't.

But he wouldn't take her. Not like this.

Snatching the silver pen from Dennison's sweating hand, she launched herself across the table.

She almost got him. The pen arced in the light as it descended, its point glistening with a single drop of ink. Aiming for one reptilian eye, the way the SOE instructors had shown her when they taught her to fight dirty. Through the eye socket, into the brain. Except Stahl was already moving. He shifted his weight back so that the point missed his eye, brushed his cheek as her momentum failed her, drove its point into the meat of his thigh instead. Stahl's brow twitched, and the smile grew.

Then the room exploded into confused pandemonium while grasping hands seized her and pulled her back into her chair.

"What the hell is the meaning of this?" The Minister was on his feet, cheeks red. She suspected his anger was less about the disruption, more that it was one of his people who was the cause.

"He's a murderer," she near-screamed. "He killed my people. Hunted them down!"

"For God's sake, be silent, woman. Dennison?"

"I'm sorry, sir," Dennison stammered as the soldier from outside rushed in, his pistol drawn and eyes wide at the sight. "The pressure of the job—"

"Damn the pressure, you fool," Lord Wolmer roared. "Get her out of here!"

Dennison nodded and grabbed her arm, hard. The Naval officer took the other side, looking horrified to be asked to play any role in this. Together, they lifted her up out of her chair.

"Have a care, chaps," Sir David Leslie said. "Be gentle. As for you," he added towards the young guard, "put that silly pistol away, please."

"I've seen nothing like it in all my days," the Minister roared. "Someone is losing their career over this, you hear me?"

Pushing the chair aside, the two men handed her over to the guard. Holstering his pistol, he looked at her in confusion. He probably had no clue what had happened, Lane thought. She could barely explain it herself. Three years of ceaseless work to get to this point. So many late nights. So many tears, when no one was there to see and when the faces of her agents were all that filled her vision.

All of it, thrown away in a single moment of blind, unreasoning terror.

"Gentlemen," she heard a voice say. Soft. Barely louder than the continuing grumbling of the audience as they retook their seats. But it silenced the room in an instant.

The guard stopped, allowing her the space to turn, to look back. Not at the speaker, still sat in his chair while everyone else milled on their feet. She wasn't ready for that. Not yet.

The Minister broke the silence first. "You have something to add, Mister Stahl?"

"I do," Stahl said. He looked at each of them, then turned to regard Lane. The smile was gone. There was no emotion at all in that gaze. She felt all strength draining from her legs and was grateful for the guard's firm hand still clutching her arm below the elbow to steady her. With his eyes still on her face, Stahl reached down and pulled the pen from his leg. "I would like to request that Sarah Lane remain in the room."

"Impossible," the Minister spluttered. "After what she did to you—"

"No harm was done," Stahl said, rising and sliding the pen across the table to Dennison. A small stain was forming on the German's thigh. Lane couldn't tell if it was ink or blood. "And I believe she will be of great value to our discussion."

Lord Wolmer looked back and forth between the German and Lane, then glanced at the man in the hat, who gave a slight nod. "Very well," the Minister said, throwing his hands up. "But keep that woman in line, for God's sake."

One by one, they took their seats, until only Stahl remained standing.

"Let me tell you," he said, "about *Götterdämmerung*."

Chapter Ten

Norfolk, 14 March

Grant wasn't sure whose idea it was that sent the aircrews running for their cars. Finny's, probably. The rat-faced Aussie seemed to be at the heart of everything on the squadron, for better and worse. But the haze and rain sweeping in off the Wash appeared to be missing them, there was no flying planned while the engineers serviced the fifteen Mosquitoes after their night's exertions, and they were all young men and thus already bored. With no agreed plan or even coordination, they all piled into the assorted Austins, Humbers and others outside, cramped shoulder to shoulder because there weren't technically enough seats to go around. Few junior pilots and navigators could afford to buy and run a car, and others simply didn't bother. Those that did made certain to specify what should happen to their vehicle in the all too likely event that their need for it should abruptly and permanently end.

A New Zealander pilot introduced himself as Kittens and offered a space in his ageing Austin Seven. Grant did not know what the man's real name was, only that he was the acting commander of B Flight. His navigator, Sisterson, and their two other passengers made room with smiles and good grace. The suspension creaked beneath their weight and the exhaust left a greasy pall of smoke hanging in the air when the car loudly set off, but somehow it got them there, dragging its cargo along the narrow, hedge-lined back roads before struggling to keep pace with a convoy of Army lorries on the main road that led into Staverton.

The sign at the edge of the town said Staverton-Saint-Mary, but the aircrews simply called it Stav. It was their preferred off-base drinking place, not that they had much choice. From the air, Grant had already seen that it was the only notable settlement within several miles of Charney Breach, but for tiny clusters of houses and the many isolated farms that dotted the flat landscape stretching from the North Sea in the east to the Fens in the west. From ground-level, it was even more featureless. The town itself seemed nice, though, with stone houses built in the local style. Overlooking a neatly maintained cricket pitch stood a fine church which was likely a few hundred years older than anything he'd set eyes on growing up in the Caribbean or training in Canada.

The other cars had already arrived and stood in various stages of abandonment in the town square. Kittens parked smartly in the shadow of a white Victorian clock tower, and they made their way across the cobbled square as a group. A few locals waved at them, and a couple of children in neat school uniforms threw up mock salutes. Kittens shouted a greeting as he returned it, but the kids were already looking past him, mouths open as they stared. They've never seen a Black man before, Grant realised, but the stares seemed full of wonder, not malice. Within seconds, both children grinned and waved to him before running off down a side street.

"Friendly town," Grant said.

"Yes," Kittens agreed. "The locals don't seem to mind too much when we get rowdy. Well, they rarely call the police, at least."

"That's sweet of them."

"I suppose some of the younger men resent that the local girls love a man in uniform."

"Do you have a girlfriend, Kittens?"

"A nurse." A wistful look passed over the New Zealander's face. "Not a local, though. A few of the lads have girlfriends in town, but I wouldn't recommend it."

"Why not?"

"Well," Kittens said, looking a lot older than his twenty-two years, "it's a very small town. There have been a lot of boys pass through 465 Squadron, and only a few local girls. Even if you are lucky enough to attract the eye of one of the pretty ones, you may not be the first to do so. And marrying one is a big no-no."

"Why?"

"Because every time the rest of us come down here for a drink, we'll have to see another widow."

Grant stumbled, but Kittens didn't seem to notice and led the way towards the pub. Peals of laughter drifted out from inside. The sign hanging above the door said The King's Refuge. It showed a bearded man with a lopsided crown cowering in the shadows while a black-hooded figure with an axe lurked behind.

"Charles the First," Kittens said, following Grant's gaze. "Legend says he spent a night here before he went into hiding at Downham Market. After the Battle of Naseby," he added, seeing Grant's confusion. "Don't they teach you Caribbean boys about the English Civil War?"

"Funnily enough, no."

"I'm teasing you, Johnny," the New Zealander laughed. "I only know about it from books, and I doubt our Aussie colleagues know even that much. They consider reading a form of devil worship. Let's just say hiding out didn't help old Charles much. Come on, the beer's getting warm."

A well-natured cheer went up as they entered. Grant was certain they meant it for Kittens, not him. A couple of pilots made unflattering remarks about the Austin Seven, expressing surprise it had made it. Grant saw a gap at the bar and waited until a middle-aged woman with blueish-grey hair bustled up to him, wiping her palms on her apron.

"Hello, love," she said. "My name's May, and this is my place. Welcome to RAF Charney Breach. Not too cold for you, is it?"

"It's always too cold, May," he said. "You don't seem surprised to see someone like me."

"We've had all sorts here, love," she said. "Black, Czech, Polish, a few Indian boys, even a charming French gentleman. Though he only came once, God rest his soul. What can I get you?"

"Five pints, please."

"The good stuff?"

"I'm sure it's all good, May," Grant said.

"Well, aren't you a sweetheart?" She winked and began filling the first pint mug from a tap that seemed to require substantial pumping. Kittens gave him a thumbs up.

"Here you go," May said, pushing five sloshing glasses towards him and taking his money. "Thanks, love. Enjoy yourself. And do me a favour, will you?"

"What's that, May?"

"Promise you'll come and have a drink with us the day the war ends, yes?"

"Of course." He sipped his beer. It was terrible, like every other pint he'd had in Britain.

May ran her eyes over the assembled aircrew. "You hear that, lads?" She had a very loud voice, Grant noted admiringly. She would have done brilliantly on a drill square. "I want to see all of you in here when the war is over, yes? That includes you, Finny. You tell that Barto to stop working you all so hard."

"Barto's not in charge anymore," Finny said.

"What? Which silly sod made that decision? You give me a name. I'll sort him out." Laughter filled the air, and a couple of pilots clapped. May's smile faded. "I'm serious. All of you."

"Don't worry," Kittens said, "it won't be long now."

"That's what they say, love." May gave Grant his change and, spotting a glowering local at the other end of the bar, hurried off to serve him.

Kittens took his pint from Grant with a grateful smile. "May's a star," he said, nodding his head in the landlady's direction. "Like a mother hen sometimes. God knows what she'll make of the new boss. Might peck his eyes out, I fear."

"Let's hope," Finny said, jostling Grant's shoulder as he joined their conversation. "What's it like flying with the knob, Grant?"

"Fine." He thought of the practice flight, of his body being hurled against the straps while he fumbled for the map. Durban's voice. Calm. Ruthless. Then he thought of that same voice, praising him after the night's raid. "I mean, he's distant. He is the boss, after all." He saw Finny's expression darken at that. The Australian's obvious annoyance pleased him. "He's good, though. He knows his stuff."

"We all know our stuff," Finny said. "That's why it's an elite squadron. Or was, anyway." Still grumbling under his breath, he wandered off to join another group.

Kittens watched him go. "What's his problem? Apart from being an Aussie, I mean?"

"I don't understand, Kittens," Grant said. "Aren't Aussies and Kiwis the same thing?"

"I'd call that fighting talk," Kittens said, "if you hadn't just bought me a pint. Cheers." They clinked glasses.

The pub door swung open and in walked Barton, with three other crewmen behind him. "Nice of you lot to wait for me," he roared. He pointed at Finny. "Especially you, you little rodent. Next time we're over Germany, I'm letting you walk back."

"You couldn't find your way home without me, boss," Finny laughed. "Besides, I bought you a pint, didn't I?"

"I should bloody think so. Where is it?"

"I drank it. You were late, weren't you?"

As the glowering Barton walked past, Kittens tapped him on the arm. "Don?"

"Don't touch the uniform. It's impossible to get Kiwi out of this material." Barton smiled. "What's on your mind, mate?"

"Have you heard anything about Broadley and Jeffries?"

"No."

"Nothing from any of the other stations?"

"I've tried them all," Barton said wearily. "Of course, they could have diverted somewhere further north, or dropped into one of the forward airfields in France, but it's impossible to get hold of them. It's only been twelve hours. Be patient. Jeffries is your mate, isn't he, Grant? Are you doing alright?"

An image of Dougie's smiling face flashed across Grant's mind. Two years they had been friends, since the first day of flight training in Canada. It hadn't been easy for any of them, but as one of only half a dozen Caribbean lads on his course intake, and the only one who made it onto Mosquitoes, it had been harder on Grant than most. There had been times he had thought about giving up, but Dougie had always been there to cheer him up and cheer him on.

"I'm fine, sir," he lied.

"Good," Barton said. "Now get out of the way so I can reach the bar before Finny drinks my next pint, too."

One pint soon became four while a massive Rhodesian called Hick banged out a tune on the piano in the corner. At least half of the drivers probably weren't in a suitable state for driving by the time they headed back to the airfield. Kittens was fine, his car being simply too slow to crash, but one pilot arrived outside the accommodation block to hoots of derision and with a suspicious quantity of torn grass in his front bumper.

Barton leapt out of his Hillman Minx. Grant had seen him drink at least six pints, with no apparent effect. "What's for dinner?"

"Nothing good," someone said.

"The usual, then."

A car horn sounded, and the assembled aircrew scrambled out of the road, laughing like naughty schoolchildren. Grant saw a staff car drive past them and pull up in front of the HQ. Immediately, like he'd been waiting, Durban emerged from the building and walked out to meet the new arrivals.

Four people emerged from the vehicle, three men and a woman. Grant didn't recognise any of them, though he recognised the woman's uniform as WAAF. One man wore a civilian suit, a little ill-fitting. Another carried a briefcase and wore a green beret above an Army uniform. Grant couldn't quite identify the rank of the last, the oldest, but he had more lace on his RAF uniformed shoulders and more "scrambled egg" gold braid on his hat than Grant had ever seen.

"Who is that?"

Kittens leaned closer. "That's bad news. AVM Embry. Air Officer Commanding, Two Group."

"The big boss," Barton said, seeing Grant's blank stare. "Not a bad bloke for a Pom. Smart, too. Married an Aussie girl."

Durban saluted and shook hands with each visitor.

"Why is he here, Kittens?"

"Well, now, that's the bad news, Johnny. We haven't seen Embry since the Aarhus raid, back in October." Kittens sniffed. "He could be here for an inspection, I suppose."

"Not likely," Barton said.

Pleasantries complete, the group headed for the HQ building. For an instant, Grant's eyes met Durban's. He saw no emotion in the Wing Commander's gaze.

"That man only shows up when something big is brewing," Barton added. "Look at his car. No flags showing. Whatever he has come for, he isn't advertising that he's here."

Grant watched as the group disappeared into the building. "When will we find out?"

"The last minute. As usual." Barton fixed Grant with a stare. "You'll let us know if old Big Head Durban lets anything slip, won't you?"

Grant felt his hands becoming sweaty. They were all looking at him. The CO's navigator. Their own personal spy into the mind of their boss. "Of course, sir."

"Good lad. Come on. The food won't be any better if we let it get cold."

Chapter Eleven

Norfolk, 14 March

"I'm sorry, sir," Durban said, clearing a space on his desk before clasping his hands behind his back. "It's a bit too small in here for all of us, but it's the best I can do. Unless you want to move to the main Ops room?"

"Here will be fine, Andy." Air Vice Marshal Sir Basil Embry motioned to the big man in the commando uniform to lock the door, then closed the single window. The chatter of the aircrew outside dwindled. "The fewer people know about this, the better. Right now, it's the five of us and almost no one else. Let's keep it that way, shall we?"

"Of course, sir." With all of them crammed together and the evening unseasonably warm, the little office would feel positively claustrophobic soon. The civilian leaned against the wall, eyes hooded, fingers loosely interlinked in front of his chest. The commando noted his position, then edged sideways, placing himself between the civilian and the woman while keeping his eyes on the door.

"Squadron Officer Lane here is from Special Operations Executive," Embry said. "She'll handle the briefing. You've worked with SOE before, Andy?"

"I haven't had the pleasure, sir."

"It's rarely a pleasure," Embry said. "SOE only call me when they have something particularly awkward they need doing. You know about the raid on the prison at Amiens?"

"Of course, sir."

"That was theirs. The strike on the Gestapo headquarters at Aarhus, too. Fair play to them, SOE does lay on some fun stuff. I treated myself and flew on that one."

91

"I heard, sir," Durban said blandly. Embry was a legend, popular with his crews, brave to a fault, and more than happy to adopt a pseudonym to join his beloved airmen on a raid from time to time. Durban wasn't sure he would want an AVM in his formation, even one who was keeping quiet and wearing the uniform and name tags of *Wing Commander Smith*. But if he had to, Embry would be the one.

Embry adjusted his neat side parting before turning to the woman. "Over to you, Sarah," he said. "Smoke if you want to. Same for all of you."

"Thank you, sir." The woman drew out a Senior Service cigarette and held it between two thin fingers. Durban offered her a light, and their eyes met as she leaned towards the flame. She glanced down at the lighter, only for a moment, but he knew she had seen the slight tremble of his hands that he had tried to conceal. He guessed she was in her mid-thirties, maybe ten years older than him, several inches taller. Her neatly pulled back hair framed a face that, while severe, had a certain handsomeness to it.

Most of all, Durban noted the eyes. Cool. Professional. Steely.

With a nod, she drew back and took a deep drag on the cigarette, then opened her leather attaché case and placed the contents on the desk.

Durban saw the colour of the files. All at least Top Secret, some marked with additional caveats he had never seen. "I'm not sure I'm cleared for this level, sir," he said.

"You are now," Embry said.

"Wing Commander Durban," the woman from SOE began, "I shall do my best to make this quick. As you know, the war is nearly over. Hitler and his inner circle might publicly expect a miraculous turnaround, but behind the scenes, the SS are preparing for the next stage. So far, we've identified two major components of this plan. The first is a special forces operation known as *Werwolf*, but that doesn't concern us. We know the second only as *Götterdämmerung*."

From a file, she drew several glossy photographs, which showed a picturesque stone church surrounded by trees and low bushes. She pushed the first in front of him. "These are from photo-reconnaissance runs over northern and eastern Germany. It's hard to tell, but the photographic interpreters at Medmenham believe this one shows the concealed entrance to a laboratory, built partly underneath church grounds just outside the town of Hildesheim. This is one of several sites we have linked to *Götterdämmerung*." She reached for the second photo.

Durban glanced at it. "Uelzen?"

"You know your Luftwaffe airfields," she said.

"I know to avoid them," Durban said. "Uelzen sits right on the flight path to Berlin. I've met their night fighters more times than I'd like."

"It's not just night fighters." She moved one long finger across the image to a large hangar. Next to it stood a series of protective revetments, each big enough for a single aircraft. They appeared heavily fortified with sandbags, with the entire area enclosed within a barbed wire perimeter. Durban counted four 20mm flak positions near the revetments alone, not to mention the rest of the heavy defences that surrounded any German airfield.

Lane pointed to the familiar shapes in each revetment. "These may look like ordinary night fighters, but they aren't."

"What are they?"

"Unknown. All we can say for sure is that they lack radar, ergo they aren't night fighters. The SS has requisitioned and occupied this area. They don't allow regular Luftwaffe personnel anywhere near it."

"Gotter..." His mouth stumbled over the unfamiliar word.

"*Götterdämmerung*," she corrected. "Yes. Though for what

purpose, we don't know. There is one other target." She reached for a third file.

"I think that's all the Wing Commander needs for now," Embry said. "Major Anders has other business to attend to in London and elsewhere, but Squadron Officer Lane and Mister Stahl will keep you in the loop. You can take them into your strictest confidence. Yes, Mister Stahl is a German, and Lane is not…" He paused for a moment, looking at her, as if mulling his words before deciding against them. "Try not to let that throw you off, Andy," he continued. "They will be in touch in the next few days with more details." He made a gesture, and Lane packed away her briefing materials. Embry looked around the room, frowning at the pall of smoke that hung above the table. "You can crack a window now."

Durban didn't move. "I'm sorry, sir. You still haven't actually explained our role in this."

"Well, I thought it would be obvious, man. You're going to blow them up. First the lab at Hildesheim, then that special hangar at Uelzen, then whatever else Lane and Stahl tell you to drop an egg on. Until then, get your crews practicing their low-level skills and their bombing. You, too. You don't have much experience of that kind of work."

"You're not the first to mention it, sir," Durban said. "What about regular operations?"

"Rescinded. I have placed you at the complete disposal of the Joint Intelligence Committee as part of Operation AFTERLIGHT."

"AFTERLIGHT, sir?"

"Damned silly name, if you ask me," Embry grumbled. "It means twilight, or a meditation on the past, or some rubbish like that."

"I'm familiar with the word, sir."

"Good for you. I had to ask my wife to explain it. Is everyone ready? I'd like to get back at a decent hour. Margaret is hosting a bridge foursome this evening, and she sometimes lets me play a rubber or two. She never lets me win, of course."

Durban hesitated. Outside the window, the gathered men had long since dissipated, but the sight of Grant still weighed on his mind. "Sir," he said as Embry headed for the door. "Are you sure we're the right unit for this?"

"Of course. 465 Squadron is one of the best in the Wing, possibly the entire RAF. You're the experts."

"We were the experts," Durban said. "465 hasn't flown a proper low-level operation since Aarhus. Many of the experienced crews have already gone, and I've got a lot of youngsters who have never been shot at. I have no doubts they will do their best, but perhaps 464 Squadron in France or the New Zealanders from 487 might be more suitable?"

Embry stared at him. They all did. At least the big Danish commando was polite enough to feign sympathy.

"Are you ok, Andy?" The AVM kept his voice noticeably, horribly soft, but his vivid blue eyes stared with piercing intent.

"I'm fine, sir."

"Because I heard about that Gisela business last week. You probably should still be in the hospital, and no one would blame you if—"

"I'm fine, sir," Durban interrupted. He knew what the AVM was suggesting. Even if Embry was too good a commander to mean anything by it, Durban still felt his fists clench with anger. At least it stopped the shaking for a moment. "We'll get the job done."

"Good man," Embry said, clapping Durban on the shoulder. Durban was grateful the senior man turned away as he did so. It meant he didn't see the wince on Durban's face as pain tore through his body. "I have complete faith in you." He sounded like he meant it, too, Durban noted, which meant he was also too good a commander to let his doubts show in public. "Remember," the AVM said as he reached the door. "Lots of low-level practice and get that bombing accuracy right. I don't want you missing, or the SS cockroaches will scurry into their holes. Who knows if we'll get a second chance?"

"You will not," the German said, following Embry and the Dane from the room.

Only Lane delayed, turning to give Durban a half-smile as she zipped up her bag. "Thanks for the light," she said.

"Any time."

"I guess we'll see you soon."

"I'll look forward to it."

She paused a moment more, as if about to speak again. Instead, she picked up her case.

Cracking the window open, Durban watched as the woman hurried to catch up with the others. She didn't glance back before she closed the car door. He waited only until the car began moving before slumping back in his chair and quickly pouring himself a whisky. A few moments later and the last sound of the staff car's engine had faded, leaving only the rattle of the glass in his hand against the wooden desktop.

Chapter Twelve

Everyone knew something was up. Embry's visit, the focus on low-level flying, the twice-daily visits to the bombing range at Holbeach Marsh. As Durban's navigator, they all expected Grant to know more than everybody else. Grant wasn't sure they believed him when he said he didn't.

Maybe that was why they had left him to eat lunch alone. There were other plausible reasons, of course, why every table except his own had half a dozen men sat at it. He wouldn't have minded so much if the food had been better, but he had long since grown tired of pushing spam and over-boiled potatoes around his plate.

The Operations Officer, Flight Lieutenant Wright, walked into the room. Grant realised he didn't know the man's first name. Tall, angular and with an odd, upright walk, everyone simply knew him as Bony. "Excuse me, gentlemen," he began.

No one paid him much attention.

"I have some news about Flight Lieutenant Broadley," Bony persisted, and the hubbub of conversation ceased in an instant.

Finny half-rose from his seat next to the equally expectant Barton. "Is he back?"

The Ops Officer shook his head. "They found Broadley's Mosquito this morning on a sandbank close to Aberdeen. The fuel tanks were empty. The crew's bodies have been recovered."

Barton swore. The Ops Officer paled and hurried from the room.

"Bloody new navigator," Finny spat. "Ran Charlie out of fuel. Didn't he, Grant?"

They were all staring at him, Grant realised. Not one of them had anything in their eyes except contempt.

Except one. "Grant wasn't there, Finny," Kittens said. "And there are a dozen other ways it might have happened."

"Like what? Enemy fire? Bony would have told us that. No, this is a case of new boy, old mistake. I told everybody this would happen, didn't I?" Finny looked around, his eyes wild. "I told you that all this new blood would land us in trouble, didn't I?"

There were nods and mutters of agreement, though not from everyone. Several other aircrew seemed unhappy. Grant guessed that anyone who had been here less time than Finny counted as new in the little man's view.

The door opened, and Durban walked in, his hair still unruly from wearing his helmet. The room fell silent. "I've just heard about Broadley and Jeffries," he said. "I'm sorry. They were good men."

Barton frowned. "What would you know about them?" If he made an effort to keep his voice low, it wasn't enough.

Durban didn't blink as he made his way across the room.

"Watch out, sir," Finny said. "You need to be careful with these new navigators."

Still refusing to dignify the comments with a response, Durban deliberately made his way to Grant's table and pulled up the seat opposite. Out of his eyeline, Finny smirked.

Durban pointed. "How's the food?"

"Beautiful," Grant said, pushing the plate and its contents to the side.

"I can tell." Durban made no move to get any of his own.

"What's next, sir?" Barton, one table along, pushed back his chair. "We off to scare some more seals at Holbeach this afternoon? Or is there a treetop we haven't shaved off yet?"

"Not today," Durban said, ignoring the indistinct murmur of approval that followed Barton's comments. "The engineers tell me they need a few hours to service everything, so I've cancelled flying for the rest of the day."

"Great," Finny said, clapping his hands. "Down to the King's Refuge it is."

"Not quite." Durban looked directly at Barton. "You play cricket, don't you?"

"Of course, mate," Barton grinned. "We all do. The Australians, at least."

"Good. I've spoken to the vicar in Staverton. It's a bit early in the year for cricket, but he's had a word with his groundskeeper and said we can borrow the pitch for the afternoon."

Barton laughed. "What's everyone else going to do?"

"They will be with me. Australia versus the rest of the world. You and me as captains."

Finny spluttered over his drink, a stream of tea running down his chin. "You kidding? It will be over in ten minutes."

"I like confidence in a navigator," Durban said. "Don't you, Barton? How about a wager? If your team wins, I'll let you decide tomorrow's training program."

"I like the sound of that. Done." Barton rose from his seat.

"And if I win..." Durban said.

"You won't."

"You keep your mouth shut for twenty-four hours. If you can." Absolute silence.

"Done," Barton said, then laughed. "You're crazy, sir." Oddly, it didn't sound like an insult.

Barely pausing long enough to change out of uniform, the entire squadron headed for Staverton. At Durban's suggestion, Grant rode with him in the open-topped silver Alvis, which the Wing Commander handled with the same calm skill that had been obvious in the Mosquito's cockpit. Barton was already waiting, decked out in cricket whites. Several Aussies had dressed the same, but no one else.

"I see he's brought his own kit," Durban mused as they parked, watching the Aussie lifting a bat from the boot of his Hillman and twirling it in one gloved hand.

"I don't mean to overstep, sir," Grant said, "but are you sure this is a good idea?"

"I'm absolutely sure it's not," Durban said. "But it will be fun. Come on. Let's say hello to the vicar."

While Durban exchanged pleasantries with the churchman and thanked him for the loan of the pitch, Grant called in the rest of the non-Australians and gathered them in a huddle. There were only nine, including Durban. Not a good start. "Who has played before?"

Four hands went up. Not getting better.

"Any bowlers?"

"I spin a little," Kittens said. "But I'm not very good."

"Anyone else?"

Nothing. Just some nervous shuffles.

"Right," Grant said. "Kittens, you and I will open the bowling. The rest of you stand where the boss tells you to stand, catch the ball if you can, try not to let it hit you in the face. It hurts."

Kittens nodded. "What about you, Johnny? You played before?"

"A little. Let's hope the boss has, too."

The two captains strode out into the middle of the field, waited for the vicar to toss a coin, then shook hands, holding the grip a little longer than necessary. When Durban came back over, his face gave almost nothing away. Behind him, Barton was shouting instructions while his teammates fanned out across the pitch. With far more players than the eleven he needed, he motioned the rest of the Aussies to the sides.

"We lost the toss," Durban said, pulling on pads. "Barton's asked us to bat first."

"We don't have a lot of talent here, sir," Grant warned. "Half the boys don't even know how to hold a bat."

"That's easily fixed. Mark Kittinger and I will open. You come in at number eleven. Or number nine, I suppose. Try to show the boys which way the bat goes as best you can, alright?"

Grant pointed to the additional Aussies, who had parked themselves on the wooden benches in the shadow beneath the square church tower. "If we ask nicely, maybe Squadron Leader Barton would let us have some of his spares?"

"Don't want them, don't need them. Come on, Kittinger. Stick with me and don't give your wicket away."

"I don't have a bloody clue what's going on," a Welsh pilot said as they watched Durban and Kittens walk out to the crease where Barton stood, waiting to bowl the first delivery.

"Join the club, Chapple," Grant said.

Swinging his arms in big circles, Barton paced out his mark on the slightly damp ground, jogged on the spot, and came charging in for the first ball of the game.

A bouncer. Fast. Spitting off the pitch with venom, racing towards Durban's face. The Englishman swayed back, barely more than a hand's breadth, and the ball whistled past the wicketkeeper's gloves and raced away to the boundary rope.

Barton roared and stared at Durban. He received only a calm half-smile back.

"Four byes," Grant called to the Aussie selected to track the scoring.

"I know how to keep score, mate." The man spat on the ground, then scribbled in his notebook.

"Four byes," Chapple repeated. "What does that mean?"

"Four points for us."

"Only four you'll get," the scorer muttered darkly.

The man wasn't quite right, though it soon seemed to Grant that the prediction wouldn't be a million miles off. Durban, looking unflustered despite the speed and hostility of the bowling, hit the next ball for two, blocked out a few and took a single off the last to keep the strike while Finny took over the bowling. Kittens didn't face a ball until the third over, when he managed a streaky four before his middle stump span through the air, uprooted by a yorker from Barton that was simply too fast for him. Grant hastily explained basic batting technique to each new batsman, then sent them out only to see them traipse back minutes or sometimes seconds later, their wicket gone, looking chastened, horror-struck or just plain terrified. Desveaux and Johansen, the inseparable Canadian crew of Bravo Two, were out for first ball ducks in consecutive deliveries. Tucker, a young navigator from Kent, took a short ball to the shoulder, and spent a few minutes rubbing it and suggesting he was too hurt to continue until his Australian pilot ordered him to stay on. He was out next ball, nicking a Finny delivery to the closest fielder.

Chapple went in at number eight. The Welshman hid his fear well. "Any last pointers?" It sounded like the desperate plea of a condemned man.

"Yeah," Grant said. "Duck the short ball, watch out for the slower one at your pads. You don't want to be out LBW, do you?"

"LB what?"

"Leg before wicket. It's when…" Grant waved him away. "Never mind."

Chapple lasted two balls. Grant hadn't even finished putting his own pads on when the Aussies started calling impatiently for him. The Welshman walked sullenly past, muttering unintelligible curses under his breath as he dropped his bat at Grant's feet.

Grant turned to the nearby Aussies. "What's the score?"

"You're losing, mate."

"We'll see. What's the score?"

"Fifty-three," one said. "Your mate Durban has forty-three. Some lad called *extras* is the second highest scorer with six." They both laughed.

Grant ignored them. Picking up the bat, he walked out, flicking his heels to loosen his muscles and swinging the bat from side to side. Durban met him halfway. "Still not a good idea, sir," Grant said.

"Actually, it's going rather better than I expected," Durban said. "Can you hold up an end?"

"I can try."

"Good. It is definitely too early in the year for cricket, so the pitch isn't very good. Let's give ourselves something to bowl at, Johnny. Don't take any risks. Only play when you have to."

Barton and Finny had both taken a well-earned break, so the first ball Grant faced was from a tall Aussie Flying Officer by the name of Johnson. It was, predictably, a bouncer, but Johnson lacked the true pace and venom of Barton. Grant hooked it away to the boundary for four.

"That works, too," Durban said.

A few more balls, and Grant felt his muscles relax. He hadn't held a bat in three years, but it surprised him how quickly it all came back to him. Double figures came quickly, while at the other end Durban passed fifty without overt celebration and accumulated runs with steady grace. At every opportunity, they would seek quick runs between the wickets. If the batsman hit it ahead of him, it was his call to run or not. If it went behind or square of the batsman, he had to trust the non-striker's judgement. Either way, there was no hesitation. Each trusted the other.

Suddenly, with no time seeming to pass, fifty-three had become one hundred and three.

"Right, I've had enough of this," Barton said, bringing himself back on to bowl. "Fun's over, gents." With a wicked grin, he took his mark and came sprinting in towards Durban, his face red with exertion and anger.

The ball was short, but this time it didn't rear up like the others. Instead, in a puff of disturbed earth, it kept lower, surprising Durban and slamming into his ribs. The Wing Commander gave a grunt, dropped his bat, and walked off to the side, wincing while the ball ran forgotten to the nearest fielder.

Barton kept running, stopping just short of Durban. "You alright, boss?"

"I've had worse."

The Australian gave a brief nod, though any hint of approval or respect vanished almost instantly from his face. "That was a loosener," he said, loudly. "Next one will be quicker!" His teammates cheered that, but there was also a ripple of grudging applause when Durban retrieved his bat and took up his guard again.

They didn't applaud and certainly didn't cheer when the next ball sailed into the bushes by the church. No bounce. Six runs. Better still, it gave the batsmen a chance to catch their breath while Barton stood with his hands on his hips and six cursing Aussies searched through thorns and mud for the ball.

The fun didn't last, of course. It never could. Ten minutes later, and to his annoyance, Grant mistimed a pull shot to give Barton his fifth wicket. The Aussie players gathered around their captain to congratulate him, although a couple took the time to shake Durban's hand first. One hundred and thirty-six runs total, with Durban left stranded on ninety-eight not out.

"It's not enough," Grant told him as they walked off.

"We'll see," Durban said. "Are you nicely warmed up?"

"I haven't bowled in three years, skipper."

"Don't worry, Johnny. It's like crashing a bike. You never forget how."

Grant took a new ball, enjoying the familiar weight and the touch of leather and seams in his hand. As the opening Aussie batsmen walked to the crease, the fielders spread out, watching as Durban called instructions from the wicket-keeper's position and pointed out their places. They were still too few, of course. That left a lot of gaps, and Grant had little faith that more than a couple of them could catch.

So he took them out of the equation.

His first delivery, eighty-five miles an hour, blew off the cobwebs of three years, slammed into Durban's keeping gloves with a satisfying thud, and left Finny hopping about the crease in stunned confusion. His second, quicker, clipped the top of the Australian's off-stump and sent him stumbling off the pitch, swearing loudly.

On the edge of the pitch, he saw Barton in animated conversation with the vicar. "He seems angry about something," Grant observed.

"He'll be bloody furious in a few minutes," Durban said. "Have at them, Johnny."

And he did. Two more batsmen fell for ducks. Another went for a lucky single. At the other end, Kittens turned out to be a half-decent spinner, and two shell-shocked Aussies got themselves caught out playing ambitious shots, desperately trying to score some runs before they had to face the express pace of Grant again.

Barton brought himself in at number seven and proved a capable tail-end batsman. Just not quite capable enough. He made a gritty fourteen before he was out, plumb LBW to a Grant slower ball but still willing to howl protests at the unfortunate spare Australian pilot officer acting as umpire.

Forty-seven all out.

Back aching from all the congratulatory slaps on it, Grant jogged over to join Durban.

Barton threw down his gloves and stormed towards them. "I thought it odd that the vicar seemed to know you so well. You didn't tell me you opened the batting for Middlesex before the war."

"You should always do some research before you challenge an opponent," Durban said. There was no mocking in his voice. The tone was one of absolute seriousness. "If you had, you'd have known all about me. You might also have heard about Johnny Grant, who took eight for eleven for a Barbados Governor's XI before he volunteered for the RAF."

Barton snorted. "My Mum always said I was a fool. I hate proving the old bag right." He shook Grant's hand. Then, after a moment's hesitation, he shook Durban's. Behind him, the Australian team had formed a line and were busily shaking hands and congratulating their rest of the world counterparts.

"For the record, Don," Durban said, "what would your training program have looked like if you'd won?"

Barton shrugged. "Low-level training, and probably a run up to the range at Holbeach. I'm a fool, but I'm not stupid. Whatever we're training for, it's hardly likely to be easy, is it? So, we train, and we get better, and then we go to work."

"Bollocks to this," Finny said, sticking his hands in his pockets. "I'm not shaking their hands. Bloody cheats."

"Flying Officer Finnegan!" Barton's roar echoed from the church wall, loud enough to make the vicar jump. "You will shake every one of their bloody hands and twice if they want you to! Do you understand me?"

"Yes, sir," Finny mumbled.

"Sorry about the noise, vicar," Barton called. "As for me, boys, these will be the last words you hear from my mouth until this time tomorrow."

Chapter Thirteen

Norfolk, 17 March

Barton didn't stay quiet for long, of course. Not once the beers started flowing in the King's Refuge. Handshakes became pats on the back, then toasts. Within scant minutes, the whole squadron was drinking as one, and the reminiscing about the game seemed to gloss over any mention of who had won or lost. A bloody good afternoon, as Johnson put it, and not even Finny disagreed with that.

Broadley and Jeffries went unmentioned. Not forgotten, but already fading into the past. A squadron had to have a short memory if it was to go on.

Durban put some money behind the bar, checked that Barton was happy to give Grant a lift back, and then left them to it. He drove alone, and quickly. In the tumult in the pub, with the beers flowing and May holding court like she had taken the final wicket herself, few noticed that he hadn't touched a drop. He never did when he was driving or flying. Even this last year, when the shaking had been getting worse than ever, he'd stuck to that rule.

It was already getting dark when he left the pub, and the rain that had been threatening all day arrived as he passed through the front gates. He parked near his room in the accommodation block, wrestled the protective rain cover into place, and walked through the increasing fury of the spring storm to his office. He had work to do. Much as he didn't want to go near it, especially after the tiny victory of the afternoon, no one else was going to do it for him.

He wouldn't have let them, even if they had offered.

After checking he was alone in the building, he closed his office window blinds and locked the door before pouring himself a whisky. Laying down a piece of personalised headed letter paper, he reached for the pen his father had given him the day that he graduated from the RAF College at Cranwell. A long time ago, it seemed. He had lost count of the times he had used that pen for this exact task. It should have become easier with time. It hadn't. Just got harder with every letter.

Dear Mr. and Mrs. Broadley, he wrote. And stopped.

First mistake. He couldn't remember if Charlie Broadley had two living parents, or if his mother was a widow, or if they had divorced. He opened his desk drawer and checked the man's file, delivered at his request late that morning by Bony Wright. Both parents alive and still married. Happily, he assumed, unless the news had already reached them in Australia. At least his letter wouldn't beat the telegram to them, and he didn't have to be the one to break the news that their only son and heir was dead, his body shattered in the crushing embrace of a crashed Mosquito.

A vision of a different Mosquito's cockpit flashed across his sight.

He downed his whisky. It burned, good and hot at the back of his throat, sending little explosions of sweat to burst at his temples and neck. He turned back to the letter. *It is with deep regret that I must inform you of the death of your son Charles in combat.* He let the pen drop from his fingers. It clattered from the desk and fell to the carpet. Stupid. They would already know that from the telegram. That's if they hadn't felt the moment of his death from ten thousand miles away, as some swore could happen. Durban had never believed such things. Now he wasn't so sure.

And in their grief, would they want to be lied to? Charlie Broadley wasn't dead because some German night fighter pilot was great at his job. Nor had he died because he got unlucky with the random slings and arrows of flak or engine failure. No. Charlie Broadley was dead because his navigator messed up and left them roaming the night sky, terror growing, until the fuel ran out and their time with it.

It was worse than that, too. Charlie Broadley died because Durban had chosen Grant to be his navigator. He'd doomed Broadley to a pointless death the moment he'd left him to pair up with Dougie Jeffries.

Not pointless, he corrected himself. At least, no more pointless than the rest.

Hearing a sound, Durban stopped and listened. Nothing. Just a patrol passing by, or a careless engineer in one of the distant, half-lit hangars. He was alone.

It was one of the fundamental realities of command. He could have his entire squadron in the room, a senior HQ on the telephone, printed and detailed orders in his hand, but in the end, he made the decisions. Only him.

Decisions that could mean success or failure. Life or death. Like which navigator would fly with which pilot.

Reaching for the fallen pen, he gasped as pain plucked at his side. Gingerly, he pulled up the shirt, wincing as he felt scabs tear away with the material. Where the cricket ball had struck him, the skin was already turning mottled black. Combined with the half-healed lacerations from the crash, it made for a dismal sight.

He let the shirt drop, not caring that the reopened wounds would soon discolour it, and reached for more whisky. It was good stuff. Expensive. It deserved a more appreciative audience, but right now it tasted like water. The liquid trembled in the bottle as he held it. Odd, how his hands shook so badly now, but stayed solid as the White Cliffs when he held the controls of his Mosquito.

He poured a double, then added more.

Screwing up the letter, he threw it in the wastepaper bin. It nestled among the half-dozen attempts he had made this morning, when he'd first heard.

Jeffries, he thought. Perhaps Jeffries would be easier. The lad, he remembered, was an orphan. Raised by a maiden aunt. He had to check her name.

Dear Mrs. O'Keefe. I was your son's commanding officer for the last few days of his brief life. I wish to tell you he died doing his duty to the best of his abilities.

And maybe that was right. The report from the training school said that Jeffries was generally sound but made mistakes. He had got them to the target just fine. Maybe that was the best he could do, and Charlie Broadley had never been destined to come home.

Yes, it wasn't a lie. But it wasn't the truth, either.

But the truth is that he killed himself, and took an expert pilot with him, and it should have been me in the cockpit with him, watching the ground rushing up to meet us...

He pushed the letter aside, not even seeing it anymore. He heard the thud as his whisky glass hit the floor, but it vanished in the squeal of tortured metal as the damaged undercarriage gave way and the Mosquito slammed into the runway, filling the night behind with sparks. The urgent stink of burning fuel and rubber and wood filled his nostrils. Clive Lampeter's body brushed against his as he scrambled past the navigator to the emergency exit hatch, feeling those dead fingers clutching at his overalls, ripping a single startled sob from his lips.

He was alone, he told himself. It didn't matter.

Alone.

Reaching for another glass, he let the tears come.

Chapter Fourteen

Above England, 18 March

The night's rain still hung in the air as they climbed out of Charney Breach, giving a vibrant sheen to the patchwork of fields two thousand feet below. Behind them, thick cloud spread unbroken to the sea and beyond to Europe, but in the west a stiff breeze had torn wide swathes from the grey, giving the spring sun leave to tease the earth with the hope of better weather to come.

"Oxford, please," Durban said simply. They were almost the first words he had spoken all day. The Wing Commander had briefed them all that morning, putting Barton and Kittinger in charge of the day's training, and even as they tracked west, the rest of the squadron were getting airborne in their two flights for another day of low-level bombing practice. There had been a few muted grumbles in the briefing room, but A Flight's commander had silenced them with just a tightening of the lips below his moustache.

Grant checked his maps, then gave both a heading and a time estimation. At first, he'd felt worried that Durban was angry with him, but there was no malice in the silence. Instead, the pilot seemed perfectly content simply to enjoy the flight, turning his head from time to time or craning to look down past the spinning props at a passing village or train. As they drew nearer to Oxford, Grant felt a small thrill of satisfaction that his course would take them almost directly over the old and distinguished University buildings at its heart.

"I wanted to thank you, sir," Grant said. "For sticking up for me yesterday in the Mess."

Durban gave a nod, so slight that it might just have resulted from a slight buffeting of the airframe. He corrected only slightly during the last mile of their approach, bringing them directly over the High Street and Carfax Tower, banking the Mosquito to look down as he did. "Castle Combe next," he said. "Low level."

"Yes, sir." Again, Grant plotted a course, adding a couple of waypoints to avoid high ground. Durban took them down to barely one hundred feet, and lower where the ground allowed it, following the course of the sparkling waters of the Thames for a few miles before breaking away. This low, Grant couldn't rely on many landmarks. Instead, he concentrated on his timings, noting the impact on their course of each minor change Durban made, seemingly on a whim, to take them over some village or pub or pond. This meant more course corrections, and Grant kept them coming as often as needed.

Durban noted each change of heading and timing with a nod, but said nothing.

Grant made his final calculation, then considered Durban's calm face. Something wasn't quite right. The Wing Commander seemed happy enough. Serene, even, controlling the Mosquito with smooth inputs, his face emotionless but for the slightest hint of a smile. But there had to be a reason he had left others in charge of training, and why the rest of the squadron had gone one way while their lone Mosquito went another.

They climbed a little on approach to Castle Combe, and Durban flew a circuit of the town that allowed a better look at the stone buildings that straddled the Bybrook, ripped straight from the pages of some medieval saga. Sometimes, just sometimes, England really was beautiful. Nothing could stop Grant feeling homesick for Barbados, especially when the English weather set in on the flat, featureless terrain that surrounded most RAF airfields, but there were definitely places that made it easier to bear. This entire part of the country was a delight on a day like this, with the sun illuminating some sights while leaving others wreathed in early morning fog, shadowed in mystery.

"Thank you," Durban said when the slow circuit was complete. "Cornwall, next. Kynance Cove."

Grant's stomach lurched, and he knew it wasn't the dip of the controls that sent them lower again, racing down the slopes of the Cotswolds towards the distant southwest. They had plenty of fuel for the trip, but Cornwall wasn't on any of their previous training routes, nor did it make sense as a waypoint on the way to somewhere else. It was a long way from anything.

He reeled off a course and took a long breath. "Sir? Is this a test?"

"What do you mean?"

"Because I know Jeffries messed up, and he and I were friends."

"It's not a test," Durban said.

"If you think I need more practice, or—"

"I have complete faith in you, Johnny."

"Then why this crazy route, sir?"

Durban gave him a sharp look, and Grant knew that he'd overstepped. They flew in silence for another mile, still low, passing over a small tractor. The farmer gave them a cheery wave. At least, Grant thought it was cheery. It might have been an angry shake of the fist. They really were very low.

"Not a test," Durban said softly. "Today, I just wanted to fly."

They climbed to fifteen hundred feet as the south coast appeared ahead. Off their port wingtip, the sun glimmered on barrage balloons and the hulls of Royal Navy warships in the great docks at Devonport, but Grant's course had already steered them clear of the anti-aircraft positions there. German air attacks might have dwindled almost to nothing, but it made no sense to give a gunner the chance to make a terrible mistake. Leaving the docks behind, they flew on until Durban made a sharp left turn, bringing them eastbound just above the sea, with the cliffs to their left.

Grant sat bolt upright as a small bay appeared, the sand beautifully white, starkly contrasting with dark green and red serpentine shades in the rocks and islands that rose from it. Most of all, he stared at the water, clear and blue and glittering. He hadn't seen water that colour in three years. "It's like being home," he gasped.

"Kynance Cove," Durban said. "There's nowhere else quite like it. My parents would bring me here as a child. My sisters and I would play on the sand, dare each other to go out to the little islands that you can only see at low tide, then race the sea back in. I'd always stay that bit too long to make sure I won." He smiled. "Because I'd get so wet and cold, my parents would let me have extra ice cream. They never worked out that was part of the victory."

In seconds, the cove dwindled behind them. Durban didn't look back. "Ok, Johnny. Take us home. Quickest route. After lunch, we'll join the afternoon push to the bombing range."

"Yes, sir." Grant hesitated, but curiosity beat back caution. "Did you grow up in Oxford, sir?"

"Castle Combe," Durban said. "I went to Oxford University."

He said nothing more, and Grant asked no more questions. He didn't need to. They completed the rest of the flight in silence, straight and level with no real training value, but then the day's business hadn't been about training. No.

It had been about saying goodbye.

It was only after they landed that another thought struck Grant, one that turned a pleasant morning into a thing of horror, and his fond approval of the Wing Commander to terror.

If Durban was saying goodbye, it was because he wasn't sure he was coming home.

And wherever he expected to go that was so dangerous, Grant would be sat right next to him.

Chapter Fifteen

Norfolk, 21 March

Durban met her outside the HQ and opened her car door for her. A gentleman, or at least well-schooled enough to pretend to be. The young Wing Commander looked more tired than she remembered him, and Lane told him so as she followed him to his office.

"There's lots to do," he said. "We've been flying three or more sorties a day, navigation, bombing. Low-level flying is physically exhausting, especially at night, but I think we're getting better. You can hang your coat there." He pointed to a hook on the back of the door.

"Thank you." She took off the coat gratefully. The sheepskin-lined collar really was a bit much for this weather, even though the last few days had seemed more like they were returning to winter rather than springing forward. The little white flowers on the windowsill at least brightened the room with a touch of the changing seasons. "Very pretty."

"One of the WAAF clerks from the air traffic control tower brought them over. They help to blot out the smell of aviation fuel."

They did, too. She had no interest in flowers and did not know what type they were, but they filled the air with a delightful fragrance. She couldn't help but detect another faint scent under it, though. Like spilled whisky. She ignored it, just as she ignored the little paroxysm of jealousy at the thought of how long it had been since anyone brought her flowers. "Will they be ready? The squadron, I mean?"

"I hope so." Durban took a seat behind his desk, offering her one opposite him. "Their navigation skills are up to speed. Bombing accuracy is still a little down from where I'd like it to be, but I can practically guarantee that three out of every four aircraft will hit the target. We normally fly with twelve aircraft, but I have enough crews to push to sixteen by getting the reserve aircraft fully airworthy. That will take time, though."

"It shouldn't be necessary," Lane said. "Not for the first target." Her chair was comfortable. From the way Durban shifted his position, she guessed his seat didn't share that quality. That meant he'd likely switched them in anticipation of her arrival. Perhaps he genuinely was a gentleman. She met so few in her line of work.

"It's still the Hildesheim lab first, then? Do we know when?"

"Tomorrow."

A pause, a single beat between Durban's lips opening and the words coming. "Not a problem. What's your role in this?"

"You obviously don't work with SOE very often," she said coolly.

He seemed unfazed, his calm gaze on her. "If you can't tell me, I understand. I won't insist, even if I could. But you're clearly important to this whole thing." He shrugged. "I'm asking about you, rather than the mission. Consider me intrigued."

"Intrigued? Where I come from, we'd call that nosy."

"And where do you come from?"

"We'd call that nosy, too."

He laughed. "Fair enough. Do you mind if I guess? About your role, not where you're from. It's obvious," he continued without pause, "that you are the expert on this subject. AVM Embry deferred to you, which he doesn't do for the Chief of the Air Staff himself, and that Commando Major seemed there purely to provide muscle. So that leaves you and the German chap. Stahl?"

She nodded.

"Is he coming?"

"Not yet."

"You don't seem cut up over that. Given how that commando put himself between the two of you, it's clear you're not friends. You work together, but you're not happy about it."

And that, Lane thought, was the understatement of the year. "Wing Commander Durban," she said deliberately, "I'm thinking you are one of those English gentlemen who is too clever by half."

"Clever is rarely a word used about me," Durban said. "But I know that when you find yourself in a hole, you stop digging. As an apology, can I get you a cup of tea?"

"I'd much rather have a tour of the squadron. Particularly the aircraft."

His eyebrow twitched in surprise, she noted, but he hid it well. "Of course."

She followed him into the mid-afternoon grey, crossing the road and heading towards the hangars while he pointed out the various components that went into the establishment and running of a front-line squadron. It was impressively complex, but irrelevant. She had precious little interest in the intricacies of air traffic control, and none in where the men spent their time when they weren't flying. But, because Durban seemed nice and because she admired his enthusiasm, she asked polite questions and made the right noises until he brought her at last to the one thing she did care about.

The aircraft. The machines that would destroy *Götterdämmerung*.

"This is the Mosquito," he said, leading her into a hangar where the aircraft stood, proud and solitary, with its tail down and chin raised. It was bigger than she'd expected, with the cockpit towering over them above four huge gun barrels that seemed to peer out with lethal menace. From the two long engines, the propellors reached down almost to the concrete floor.

"You have sixteen of these?"

"Total, yes. This one is mine." He put his hand on the underside of the fuselage, resting it there while he looked up at the aircraft. "Geoffrey de Havilland's finest creation. They called him crazy when he designed it, but not anymore. Here. Feel this."

She thought of saying no. It wasn't what the aircraft was that interested her; it was what it could do. Despite herself, she reached out and touched the dark green skin of the aircraft. It felt warmer than she'd expected. "That's not metal."

"Wood," Durban said. "She's built of wood. English ash, Alaska spruce, Canadian birch and fir, even balsa from Ecuador."

Lane couldn't quite bring herself to use the female pronoun. It was a machine, nothing more. "Doesn't that make it flimsy?"

"Not the way they build her. No more so than aluminium, and it's not like a German twenty-millimetre shell cares what it hits. It will make a right mess either way. But wood makes her light, and a joy to fly. Two Merlin engines, same as you'd find in a Spitfire. Together they make her fast, faster than any German night fighter, as fast as most of their day fighters, especially once you've dropped your bombs. Heavier armament, too." He walked along the side of the aircraft, his fingertips caressing the underside. "She's beautiful, isn't she?"

A wave of embarrassment flooded over her as she laughed, then covered her mouth with her hand. She was blushing. She hadn't done that in years. "I'm sorry," she said, seeing the confused look on his boyish face. "It's just that you describe this aircraft like another man might talk about a woman."

He gave a little snort. "Well, she is the only lady in my life right now. And I don't think she'll mind the flattery."

"No wife to get jealous?"

He shook his head. "This country has enough widows already."

Matter of fact. He might have been talking about airspeed performance figures or fuel load, not the looming likelihood of his own death.

He beckoned her closer, kneeling to point at the panels beneath the aircraft's belly.

"There's the internal bay," he said. "The bomber variants can carry more bombs, but we have enough to let the Hun know we were there and still strafe secondary targets or tussle with fighters."

The momentary chill she had felt at the offhand fatalism of his widow remark vanished, replaced by professional interest. This was why she was here. "What types of bombs?"

"High explosive, mostly."

"The bunker at Hildesheim is underground. Can you get to it with HE?"

"Certainly," he said. "As long as it's not too deep. We set a delay on the fuse so that the weapon has time to burrow into the ground a little before it detonates. How far down is this bunker?"

She thought back to the engineering report provided by one of her agents last year. The last report the man had ever sent. The SS had got him the next day, shot him in the head as he tried to evade arrest. Shot dead in front of his own family.

Her sources told her it was Stahl who had pulled the trigger.

She realised Durban was looking up at her, and she took a second to remember his question. Another second, to compose herself. "Not deep," she said, wondering if he heard the catch in her voice. "It's mainly for concealment rather than protection. Probably four to six feet."

"Easy. If you were talking about deep bunkers, proper ones,

you would need something bigger, like a Lancaster with the Tallboy that Barnes Wallis came up with. Earthquake bombs," he added. "They are twenty times the size of the ones we can drop, but that would be overkill for Hildesheim."

"What about fire?"

"Incendiaries, you mean? We can carry those. No good against a bunker, though."

She felt a little tightening in her chest and realised she was holding her breath. What she was about to ask skirted close to giving away things that this man wasn't cleared to know. Not yet. He'd already proved dangerously clever. She needed to know the answer, though. She couldn't be sure, but by the time this was over, a lot could depend on it. "I'm not talking about starting a fire," she said carefully. "I'm thinking more if you had to destroy something by fire. Completely. Quickly. So that nothing escaped, and the only thing left was ash."

He rubbed at his eyes. They were the eyes of a tired old man, she thought, incongruous in that youthful face. The moment passed, though. Careful to avoid cracking his head on the fuselage, he picked a path under the engines and stood by her side, both looking at the Mosquito.

"I'm not sure," he said. "We could try napalm, I suppose."

She frowned. "What's that?"

"Something new. The Americans came up with it a few years back. I've never used it, but I know Mosquitoes have dropped it in France. We can carry it right enough, but I'll have to ask Group to deliver some. I wouldn't want to use it without practicing first."

"But what is it?"

"Think of it like a bomb full of petrol and glue," he said, grimacing. "The petrol ignites when the bomb goes off, creating a fireball in an instant. I read somewhere that we're talking about nearly two thousand degrees Fahrenheit. That will suck the oxygen right out of the air. Anything that isn't destroyed by the fireball finds that the gelling agent sticks to it, and it keeps burning much longer than petrol alone would. Are you ok?"

Lane nodded. Her mouth tasted sour, and she wanted to spit to clear the excess saliva. Unclean. That was the word. It wasn't just the thought of what she might have to order. The worst part was the little thrill of triumph she'd felt when she'd realised this napalm stuff was everything she had hoped for. "These things we do to each other."

He nodded. "The war will be over soon," he said. For a moment his hand lifted, moving towards her arm, but then it dropped back by his side. "Being able to look at ourselves in the mirror might take longer."

She found a smile for him from somewhere, grateful that she didn't cry easily. "Thank you for showing me your Mosquito," she said, forcing levity into her voice. "You make a lovely couple."

"Thank you. We couldn't be happier." Suddenly, Durban chuckled. "Come on," he said. "Let's head back before I try to talk you into going for a flight with me."

Together, they walked back from the hangar. They passed several young airmen – they were all young – and Durban returned their salutes, greeting each by name. A few gave her an odd look, as if trying to work out whether her uniform was real or a fancy-dress costume. She doubted they saw many WAAF officers here.

"Hey, boss," came an Australian voice from one of a group of aircrew stood smoking behind a small building, "when are you giving us a rematch?"

"When the war is over, Steve," Durban called back.

"When will that be?"

"When you pull your finger out and win it, chap."

The men laughed and went back to their cigarettes.

"You seem to enjoy your job, Wing Commander Durban," she said.

"Please call me Andy," he said. "It has its moments, I'll admit. You'll stay the night?"

It took an instant to take in what she'd heard. Another instant more and she stumbled, felt the blood rushing to her cheek, imagined that the aircrew were all staring at her. She looked at Durban and saw his own face reddening.

"Sorry," he stammered. "Poor word choice. What I mean is that AVM Embry said you'd be remaining at Charney Breach until after the first AFTERLIGHT raid was complete."

Despite herself, she laughed. That was twice in a few brief minutes. It felt good. Like it had been too long. "Yes," she said. "If you don't object."

"Of course not. I've had a room prepared. Come on, I'll show you."

She followed but couldn't resist a look back at the distant hangar and the aircraft inside. Beyond it, more Mosquitoes stood in the open. To her eyes, they had purpose and symmetry, but not beauty, no matter what Durban said. In less than twenty-four hours, she knew, they would leave here and fly east on the strength of her word.

It wouldn't be the first time she had sent people into danger. She could only hope that, unlike those she had sent before, the young men enjoying a smoke and a laugh over the road would come back.

Chapter Sixteen

London, 21 March

"*Unglaublich*," Stahl muttered, turning to yet another page of detailed insights into SS business. "Where did you say you got this reporting?"

"He didn't," Anders said, before Colonel Dennison could answer. "Nor will he. Further questions would be unwelcome, Jan. Just keep reading before I need to put it all away."

Stahl rubbed his chin, eyes sliding down the page so quickly that he almost couldn't keep track of the words, so keen was his brain to learn all it could. It really was unbelievable. It could only have come from Signals Intelligence, intercepted German communications, but he was familiar with the Enigma encoding device and knew that it was unbreakable. And yet, here was the evidence, printed and proud on the page in front of him. Even at the height of the Abwehr's success and prestige, Canaris had always admitted that British Intelligence outclassed his own department, but this? It seemed like they knew everything.

Well. Not quite everything.

On one page, he found a complete list – names, ranks, service numbers, even dates of birth – of the twelve experienced pilots recently reassigned to a new training flight at Uelzen, an airfield that had never previously had a training presence, particularly not one with six operational Dornier Do-217s. On the next, he found details of an order sent to the Commander of the Fourth U-Boat Flotilla at Stettin by SS Obergruppenführer Hans-Adolf Prützmann requisitioning U-78, a Type VIIC submarine, for unspecified "special duties." He did not yet know why Prützmann needed a submarine, though he had heard talk in the SS that several senior officers and politicians had purchased land in South America. They would need a way to get there.

What he had not found was confirmation of the two things that Sarah Lane hadn't been able to work out, and that Canaris himself had never known for sure. What *Götterdämmerung* was and, crucially, where it was.

So, he kept looking. Searching through page after page, everything Anders had found that contained Prützmann's name or any reference to U-78 or Uelzen. At some point he must have downed a third cup of tea because someone produced a fourth; he did not remember tasting any of them. He found references to prisoner transfers and concentration camps, grateful that they contained the names of the men who would hang for it. He discovered things that sounded exciting, like modified artillery shells, and others that really did not, like replacement ovens and sheep quotas.

But still not what he needed.

"That's two hours," Anders said, yawning.

"I need more time."

"Time's up." The Dane reached across and began placing the papers back in their covering folders.

Stahl swore. Three days running, he had found nothing. It was bad enough with the regular files they had given him, but these new reports that Anders had brought in a locked briefcase today had proved doubly frustrating. For hours he had felt like he was on the verge of a breakthrough, that something was just evading his understanding, but it all vanished the moment Anders took the reports away. Canaris would have solved it, he knew. But there was nothing about Flossenbürg in there either, no news of Canaris at all. "When can I look at them again? Tomorrow?"

"Don't count on it," Anders said. "Do you know how many strings my boss had to pull just to get you temporary access?"

"I've certainly never seen them," Dennison sniffed from behind the shade of his newspaper.

Stahl sat back in his seat, interlocking his fingers behind his head, listening to the mocking tick of the clock on the wall and grateful that the ever-present paper kept him from having to look at Dennison. The man annoyed him. Stahl's colleagues at the Reich Security Main Office had not rated Dennison at all and had been shocked to hear of his promotion a few months ago. He was clever, they said, but also thought he knew better than everyone else, which made him stupid. Just as basic errors by SOE's F Section had delivered dozens of their agents into the hands of the Parisian SS *Sicherheitsdienst* HQ at 84 Avenue Foch, so had Dennison's follies revealed the identities of many in Germany. Sometimes, if he was lucky, Stahl would hear early that the Reich's security apparatus was closing in on an agent, giving him the chance to find the poor bastard before anyone else did. If he was unlucky, he received a call when the SD or the Gestapo were already on their way. Too late.

He wondered if Dennison knew. He must suspect. Whether he cared was something else.

And then there was the woman. The SD had known all about her, too. It was the closest he had ever seen to respect coming from any of them. "This would be easier," he said to no one but the ceiling, "if Sarah Lane would work with me instead of looking like she would kill me at any opportunity."

"I'm sorry," Dennison said. "She's always been a rather difficult woman."

"No," Stahl snapped. Dennison blanched. Anders raised an eyebrow but said nothing. "Do not cheapen her with an apology." He brought his voice back under control and looked back at the ceiling. "I would want to kill me too, if I knew what she thinks she knows."

"All the same," Dennison said, huffing, "she needs to get her emotions under control and do her job. I've explained that you have been working for us for two years now, and that all these stories about you killing her agents are obviously mistaken."

Stahl sighed. He leaned forward, putting his elbows on the desk, and beckoned Dennison closer. "Listen carefully, you arrogant buffoon." His lips curled with pleasure as he saw the shock in the Colonel's eyes. "I have not worked a moment for you. Everything I have done, I did for Germany. A better Germany, without war, without Nazism. Sarah Lane is correct. I do have the blood of her agents on my hands. And if they had dropped you into Europe and revealed your name to me, I would have shot you the same way I shot them."

Dennison fell back in his chair, mouth fluttering, looking at Anders. Not in outrage. In a silent plea for protection.

Anders shook his head. "I think you've had too much tea, Jan."

"Did you ever wonder what happened to those agents you betrayed with your incompetence, Colonel?" It was not anger that drove Stahl's words, at least not anger at Dennison. "The lucky ones died by my hand. The unlucky? Tortured, stripped of their secrets and their dignity. Some may still be in SS hands now. The rest went to the camps and saw first-hand the crimes that will shame Germany for a thousand years, before they took their turns in the crematoriums..."

The words died on his lips.

"I think, Major Anders," Dennison said softly, "that I'd like you and your guest to leave my office now."

"Shut up," Stahl said. "Anders, show me those files again."

"Sorry," Anders said, nodding to the clock. "You know the rules. Seventeen hundred, the files get locked away. I need to return them this evening."

Stahl was out of his seat and moving before he even thought about it. He wasn't sure he could have stayed in the seat a moment more if he had tried. Adrenaline flooded his system. Ignoring Dennison's involuntary whimper at the speed of his movement, he reached the clock in two paces before pushing its fingers with one hand. "There," he said. "Sixteen fifty-eight. I have two minutes, Anders."

"That's not how it works, Jan."

"Two minutes. That is all. Then you can burn the damned things."

Anders sighed. "You saw nothing, Colonel." He opened the case and dropped the files on the desk. "You've got ninety seconds."

Stahl only needed sixty before he stabbed his finger down in triumph. "There."

"Sheep allocations?" Dennison, curiosity overcoming fear, had moved around the desk for a better look and stood peering over Stahl's shoulder.

"A cancelled sheep allocation," Stahl said. "This is a public health laboratory in the suburbs of Königsberg. It specialises in the prevention of bacterial disease among farm animals. Particularly important during wartime. Germany is slowly starving and cannot afford to lose flocks to blackleg. I suspect when we look back through Sarah Lane's reports, we will find they have been receiving a dozen new sheep every few months. In August 1944 they stop. Why?"

"Perhaps they lost their taste for lamb," Anders observed dryly.

"Here." Stahl grabbed a second sheet. "This is the same laboratory. October 1944. Six prisoners requisitioned for duties at this facility. That is not unusual. Slave labour has been the backbone of the Reich's production for several years. But in November, nine more arrived by bus. December, another fourteen. January, twenty-seven. This is not a big facility, and there are no accommodation areas, no dining areas. They could not house or use that many prisoners if they wanted to, yet they keep demanding more at an increasing rate. And all while the Soviets are cutting off East Prussia and isolating the city. They keep working. More and more new prisoners."

Dennison stared. A fleck of spittle glistened on his lower lip as it hung open.

Anders stayed silent. Two minutes had long passed, but he made no move to take the papers away. Their eyes met. The Dane knew what it meant. But there was one last piece to play.

"Here," Stahl said. He fell into his chair, legs no longer able to hold his weight. Something foul was in his mouth, choking him. He barely swallowed it. "The replacement oven," he rasped. He could not look at the paper now. He did not need to. He knew every word. Wished he did not. "I should have seen it before. It is not for cooking. It is the kind I have seen in the extermination camps. Why risk disease and waste time digging ten thousand graves a day when you can simply turn the dead to ash?"

"It's inhuman," Dennison said.

"It is logical," Stahl said. "The logic of the SS. The same logic that will send them all to Hell. But right now, it is a clue. *Götterdämmerung* is in Königsberg. That is where they are testing it. And whatever it is, it is killing people every day."

Chapter Seventeen

Norfolk, 21 March

To her surprise, accepting Durban's invitation to join him for dinner came naturally. Leaving her overnight bag in her room, Lane followed him, still in uniform, to the dining room. He apologised profusely for the simplicity of her accommodations, and again for not having the time to leave the HQ to take her to a restaurant.

"You know, you can only apologise so many times," she said.

"You'd be surprised. I still think I have one or two apologies left in me." He leaned back while a kitchen steward placed two plates in front of them. "I'm saving one for the food you're about to eat."

"I'm sure it will be better than anything Mrs Rose would have prepared for us." Which it was, she quickly discovered, if not by much.

"Mrs Rose? Your housekeeper?"

"Landlady," she said. "Am I to assume you've never cooked a meal in your life, Andy?"

"Alas, it is one of a long list of things I am terrible at." Durban looked with dismay at the meal in front of him. "Lord knows what I'll do after the war. Flying is the only thing I've ever been any good at."

The table Durban had chosen was apart from the others, but it proved an unnecessary gesture. It seemed most of the rest of the squadron had received better offers, because only a few other men came in for dinner. Lane saw their surreptitious glances. "I'm guessing you don't have many women eating in here?"

"You mean me personally?" He smiled. "Don't worry if they stare. They know something is going on, they just don't know what. I'm sure the rumours have been going around constantly since you showed up with Embry."

"And you haven't tried to quash them?"

"Why would I? The more you try to quash a rumour, the faster it grows. Besides, they know better than to talk away from the airfield. This squadron has done jobs like this before."

There has never been a job like this, she thought. "What about you? Have you done this before?"

"Not at all," he admitted. "That's why I'm enjoying it so much."

They talked through dinner. In truth, Durban did most of the talking, partly because she peppered him with personal questions, and partly because he was too polite to ask her any in return. About the only thing they truly had in common was that they were both unmarried. She learned he was twenty-five years old, eleven years her junior. Middle-class parents and three sisters. Oxford University. Extensive service career. A long list of decorations, including a DFC and an almost unheard of three bars, though those she had only read about. She imagined he would never consider bringing them up himself, no matter how much she asked. Self-effacing, then. In short, quintessentially British.

Everything she wasn't.

She also learned that he had a charming voice, and she surprised herself again when she agreed to walk with him while he visited the Ops Room, the Senior Engineering Officer, the Armaments Officer and the ATC personnel, checking in that everything was ok. He introduced her each time as Squadron Officer Lane from Group HQ, giving them nothing to suggest her visit was important or that tomorrow was anything out of the usual. No sign of any stress or nervousness at all.

But she still remembered seeing his fingers shake when he'd started to reach out to comfort her in the hangar.

It was close to nine o'clock when he was done with his rounds and meetings. Oddly, she'd enjoyed herself, even if she had learned little other than that a squadron really was much more than just the aircrew and their machines. But it had been a long day. Four hours with Stahl and Anders, comparing notes, sifting reports like they had every day since the German had walked, uninvited and unwanted, into her life. Four hours that felt like a month. Then the three-hour drive to Norfolk, where the fresh air should have invigorated her, but just left her exhausted. Her room might have been simple, but it didn't matter. She needed to sleep.

They reached her door, and she put her hand on the cold metal handle.

"Would you like a drink?"

"Yes," she replied, almost before he'd finished the question.

"I keep the best whisky in my office," he said. "But the stuff in my room is good too, and the chairs are much comfier."

"Your room it is," she said.

She followed him two doors down. His room wasn't much bigger than her own, but he had done his best to make it seem like a home. A rug on the floor, a nice-looking lamp, a couple of expensively framed landscapes on the wall. The bed was bigger than hers, she noted idly, though made with the same rigorous attention to straight lines and general neatness as hers. Two chairs stood by a round coffee table with an expensive looking crystal ashtray. Durban walked over to the wardrobe and took a bottle and two glasses from the shelf above the ranks of ironed blue shirts.

"No ice, I'm afraid," he said, motioning her to sit. "Sorry."

"Stop apologising," she said. "It's too British for words."

He poured two glasses and pushed one towards her. Reaching into his jacket pocket, he pulled out a packet of cigarettes and offered her one.

"Senior Service," she said. "Did you get them especially because you knew I was coming?"

"Of course not." He lit it for her and dropped the packet on the table.

"You're a terrible liar. I should know. I do it for a living."

He picked up his glass. "What should we drink to? Lying?"

She laughed.

"AFTERLIGHT?"

"No, thank you," she said. "And not to victory or country or the King either."

"In that case," he said, lifting his glass to hers, "here's to whisky."

"Perfect." And it was. Speyside, she guessed. Not too much peat, just the right amount of smokiness.

"You know," he said after a few moments, "that's twice you've talked about the British like they were an alien species. And it was obvious Embry was going to say something about you the other day in my office."

"Is there a question in there?"

"If you don't mind."

"But I do, Andy." She sat back in her chair, regarding him across her glass. He looked back without embarrassment. Sighing, she downed her whisky and let him pour her another. "Embry talks too much," she said. "Most men do. He was going to say that I am not a British citizen."

"Really? I thought SOE insisted on such things."

"They do. Normally. But they took me on as a secretary because of my background, and after that, as I proved useful, it was convenient for them to overlook any paperwork issues. My mother was British, but I was born in Poznań."

"Poland?"

"Yes. Now. When I was born, it was called Posen, and it was in Germany."

His head tilted slightly to the side as he watched her in silence. Other than that, he hid his surprise well.

"I was born Sarah Silberbaum," she said, hesitantly. Even within SOE, few knew it, and only Dennison ever brought it up. Silver Tree, he called her, knowing she hated the translation. "My grandfather was a Polish Jew. My father spent his whole life trying to claim he wasn't. He made a fortune in timber, lost it all, made another fortune in shipping. I grew up in big houses with servants one year, living on the charity of friends the next. I spoke English with my mother, German with my father, Polish with my friends. My father knew people, you understand? Local magistrates. Politicians. Ambassadors. Which meant I knew them. I think that's what SOE hoped I could bring them. But much as my father tried to pretend otherwise, once the Nazis came along, a family with a name like ours would not stay friends with politicians for much longer."

"You fled to England?"

"Via Paris," Lane said. "When we eventually arrived in London, I registered under my mother's maiden name, Lane. Without the war, they would probably have given me a British passport there and then. With it... well, I'm rather afraid they saw me as a German. If SOE hadn't knocked on my door, who knows where I'd be now?" She grunted. "I'm not sure it could have been worse."

Her glass was empty, she saw. She didn't realise she had finished it again. Their fingers brushed as Durban took it from her and refilled it. "Who is Stahl, Sarah?"

She fumbled for the cigarette packet and the lighter. She drew the soothing smoke deep into her lungs, hunching forward, letting her eyes fall shut. "When I was in Paris, I learned French. It was a mistake. It meant that when F Section unexpectedly needed a woman to be landed outside Paris to approach a high-ranking German officer about possibly defecting, they chose me."

She still remembered the crunch of the leaves underfoot in

the little clearing, the smell of half-burned aviation fuel as the Lysander that had flown her from England took off and disappeared back into the night sky. The torchlights winking in the darkness as her contacts came out of the shadows to meet her. The sudden glare of headlights and the angry shouts as the Germans sprang their ambush.

"Stahl was waiting." It took all her strength to force the words out. "The Gestapo and the rest of the SS would try to arrest you," she continued, aware that her voice cracked with every syllable. "Take you alive. That wasn't Stahl's way. He's a hunter. He could track almost anyone. Any clue, the tiniest mistake, and he would have you. But every good hunt has to end with a kill. Like he killed my contacts that night. Like he would have killed me, except I got lucky. He stopped to search the bodies, and that gave me time to run and to hide."

"And now he's here."

She heard Durban's voice, but didn't see him. She kept her eyes screwed tightly closed. "They tell me he's been working for us for the last three years. Working to bring down the regime. Canaris converted him, they say, turned him from a die-hard Nazi. Maybe it's true. All I know is that I have sent one hundred and thirteen agents on their way, a handful to France, most to Germany or Austria. Stahl killed at least thirty himself, most of them during those three years he was supposedly on our side. A few are still out there, each sending back their reports, hoping that it won't be their last and that they will give us something worth their sacrifice. The rest? I don't know."

She opened her eyes at last, realising they were still dry, despite everything.

"I need you to understand this, Andy." There were words waiting in her throat, words that she knew she should keep to herself. As she stared at his face, though, something about Andrew Durban demanded her honesty. "I'd kill him."

His eyes widened slightly, one eyebrow quivering. No other reaction.

"Stahl," she said. "I'd kill him if I could get away with it." She took a deep shuddering breath, letting the half-finished cigarette drop into the ashtray. "Possibly even if I couldn't. I would go quietly with the police afterwards. Life imprisonment would be so much better than what he gave my agents."

His eyes never leaving her own, he reached across the table. His hand closed on hers. "I understand," he said simply.

For what seemed a long time, they sat there, silent. Then she coughed, slid her hand free of his grip, and slumped back in her chair. She'd thought herself exhausted before. She'd been badly mistaken.

"I'd prefer you didn't go to prison," he said. "If it's all the same to you."

"I'll try," she promised.

"Especially not before we've finished the job." Durban flinched at his own words. "I'm sorry," he said quickly. "A poor attempt at lightening the mood."

"There you are," she said, "apologising again." She covered her mouth and yawned. She could see the confusion on his face, wondering how she could revert to such emotionless coolness so quickly. It wasn't a mystery to her; after all, she'd had plenty of practice. "I think it's long beyond time I got some sleep," she said. "Tomorrow will be another long day. Do you mind if I take these?" Without waiting for an answer, she scooped up the cigarettes, then quickly refilled her glass and picked that up too.

"Sarah?"

She stopped at the door. "Yes?"

"Your agents didn't die in vain."

"We'll see," she said. "Goodnight, Wing Commander Durban."

"Goodnight, Squadron Officer Lane."

Chapter Eighteen

Norfolk, 22 March

The briefing room buzzed with anticipation, despite the very early start and more than a few bleary faces. That AVM Sir Basil Embry had joined Wing Commander Durban on stage only added to the effect.

"Told you," Grant overheard Finny say to a colleague. "This is big."

"You might have told us that before we started drinking, Finny," came the grumpy reply.

Kittens leaned in close to Grant's shoulder. "Who do you think the ladies are, Johnny?"

"No idea," Grant said. It wasn't entirely true, as he'd seen the older of the two women before, most recently being given the tour of the station by the boss the previous afternoon, but he didn't know why either of them were there. The younger woman, freckled and with red hair pulled neatly back in a bun, wore the uniform of a Section Officer, the WAAF equivalent of his own Flying Officer rank. He hoped she felt more confident and experienced than he did, surrounded by three dozen men for whom this type of briefing was old hat.

Although, he saw as he scanned the rows of seats on either side of him, their experience didn't obliterate the anxiety from their excited expressions.

There was another man on stage, too, a wiry civilian who had arrived that morning with Embry. Grant had seen him before too, the evening this business began. No one had introduced him, but he held himself with a military bearing and the rumour was he was a German. Grant didn't doubt it. The man certainly had the right amount of arrogance in the haughty expression with which he regarded the assembled aircrew.

At a nod from Embry, the Station Warrant Officer called for the room to take their seats, then made his way to the exit. Grant glimpsed two armed RAF policemen outside the door as it swung closed. Bony took his place next to a large overhead projector.

Embry stood. Walking past a table covered in a thick cloth, he took his place at the centre of the stage like a man used to being there. "I know what you're going to ask, gentlemen, so save your breath. No, I'm not flying with you today." He smiled at the obvious disappointment and the handful of theatrical boos. "And if you've seen this morning's newspaper headlines, you can guess why."

Mosquitos wreck Gestapo lair, at least one had read. Twenty-four hours earlier, the rest of the Wing had obliterated the German secret police headquarters in the Danish capital, Copenhagen, in a stunning display of precision bombing. The papers didn't mention the presence of a Wing Commander Smith on the raid, but one look at the twinkle in Embry's eyes was all that was needed to confirm it.

"But I did want to see you on your way," Embry continued. "You're all smart boys, and no doubt you've worked out by now that something unusual is going on. Listen carefully. This briefing stays within these walls. That includes today, tomorrow, and on your death beds. If I read a word of this in your memoirs, I will personally force-feed you the damned manuscript. Understood?"

"Yes, sir," the audience mumbled in unison.

"Good. Wing Commander Durban, the floor is yours."

Durban nodded and took his place. Though much younger than Embry, he had that same air of confidence, like the stage belonged to him. He just didn't seem to enjoy it as much, like briefing and command itself was a required chore before taking to the air and getting the job done.

"We'll be going to Hildesheim today," he began, motioning to Bony. A map appeared on the screen at the back of the stage, showing the location and the planned routing. "As those of you who can read a watch will have worked out, this will be a daylight raid." He paused at the murmurs of surprise and consternation. "We all remember when German fighter defences were so ferocious that even a Mosquito was taking an enormous risk tangling with them. Luckily, those days are past. Most of the fighter units have withdrawn further east or simply don't have the fuel. We won't be alone, either. There will be several RAF and USAAF fighter squadrons operating over the area, and there will be a distraction too. Two hundred and eighty Lancasters will hit the rail yards and the town itself shortly after our strike run."

A second image appeared on the screen, a far more detailed map. At the top of the image, Grant saw the urban sprawl of Hildesheim and the railway. A black square with a cross stood out to the southeast of the town, ringed in an ink circle.

"The Lancasters will plaster HE and incendiaries all over the shop, but our target requires rather more precision." He pulled back the sheet covering the table to reveal a model, with a church standing about twelve inches tall among detailed grass and trees. The men leaned forward as one. "Don't worry if you can't see it; you'll have time to walk around it after the briefing. Section Officer Beverley Gerrard has come down from the Central Interpretation Unit at RAF Medmenham to give us more details. Bev?"

"Thank you, sir," Gerrard said. She almost seemed to bound to the middle of the stage. No lack of confidence there, Grant thought. Someone wolf-whistled from the back of the room, and a couple of men laughed.

If the young Section Officer had heard, she gave no sign. She nodded to Bony. He brought up the next image, an aerial close-up of a church and its lush grounds. "The target facility is underground," she said, pointing to the image, "extending from a concealed entrance here about one hundred feet back along the western edge of the church, and about one hundred and fifty feet out here. The main research area is in the centre, with offices and decontamination facilities along the north and west sides."

Finny stuck up a hand. "I see nothing. The target is under that field there?"

"Yes," she said. "Underground."

"Or it could just be a field, love."

Durban started to rise from his chair, but Gerrard simply stared at the Australian. "Yes," she said. "We started with the same assumption. The whole point of a concealed entrance is to make it hard for us to find it, but we had the intelligence briefings from SOE and Mister Stahl to work from. First, we tasked a photo-reconnaissance Spitfire to get stereo pair images of the site. I imagine you're all familiar with stereoscopy and three-dimensional imagery analysis..." – it was abundantly clear to Grant from the confused faces they were not – "...so I won't bore you with the details. Suffice to say, the ground there may look flat, but it actually rises slightly. We didn't have access to many historical images of the target area, but we found pictures of the church in a tourist guidebook from the 'Thirties. No sign of any rise in the ground. Flight Lieutenant Wright?"

Bony brought up the next image, a close-up of the field itself.

"We also had a bit of luck," Gerrard said, "because it had been raining a lot in the days ahead of the Spitfire PR pass. That allowed us to determine that multiple vehicles had clearly driven to this point by these bushes, likely for loading and unloading at a concealed entrance."

Grant stared at the image, but he saw nothing clear about it. It didn't matter. Gerrard's confidence in her professional skill was infectious. He hoped that one day he might appear half as credible as she did.

"The last piece of the puzzle is the one that will probably most interest you, gentlemen. Could you bring up the final image, please? As you can tell, we zoomed this one out a little. I assess each of these three circled areas to be a flak emplacement, likely twenty-millimetre Flakvierling Thirty-Eight's semi-concealed under camouflage netting. They provide a triangle of defensive fire against any incoming attacker. And that concludes my briefing, pending questions."

For a full fifteen seconds, the assembled aircrew sat in absolute silence, their eyes fixed on the circled smudges. Grant didn't need to have faced such guns to know their reputation. His instructors had warned all of them often enough. Training had burned the technical specifications into his mind.

Shells tipped with a high explosive or incendiary warhead to rip apart a fuselage or set it ablaze.

One hundred and eighty rounds per minute.

Each travelling at nearly three thousand feet per second.

Deadly out to two thousand four hundred yards.

The Mosquito could outrun most fighters and could fly above the effective range of heavy guns, but at low-level, the four-barrelled 20mm guns were king.

Finny's hand shot up. "Section Officer Gerrard?"

"Yes, sir?"

"How would you like to become Section Officer Finnegan?"

Gerrard sighed. "Any better questions?"

"Thank you, Beverley," Embry said, rising. "Squadron Leader Barton?"

"Yes, sir?"

"Find out who whistled and give him a bloody good kick up

the arse. I want the disrespectful toerag wincing in his cockpit seat."

"I've been warming up my foot for the last five minutes, sir."

"Good." Embry turned back to the throng. "Now, remember, just because you aren't likely to see many fighters doesn't mean this is going to be a piece of cake. That church clearly has sentimental value for the Jerries, given how many guns they've positioned around it." A few chuckles rippled through the crowd. "Keep low, drop your bombs on target, and get the hell out of it. Wing Commander Durban, any last remarks?"

"I think you covered it all, sir," Durban drawled.

"I think so too. You're all dismissed. Except you, Finnegan. You and I need to have a little chat about manners."

Chapter Nineteen

Norfolk, 22 March

Durban stared down at the model. The detail was exquisite, every bush and tree lovingly hand-painted. He couldn't help but admire the time and craftsmanship that had gone into making it, but that wasn't why it held his attention. The combination of the model and the image still on the screen was allowing him to compose a plan of attack. Risky, but if it worked, the rest of the squadron would have an easy ride.

Deep down, though, he knew that wasn't the only reason he loitered while the aircrew filed out.

Embry knew it, too. Having sent Finny scurrying from the room white-faced, he made his way over and stood by Durban's side. "Something on your mind, Andy?" He kept his voice very low. Behind him, Lane and Gerrard sat talking. Stahl stood apart, arms crossed, face expressionless.

"I looked at the Bomber Command orders for today's raid, sir," Durban said. "They call for an unusually high concentration of incendiaries for a raid that is supposedly targeting the railway yards."

"Is that so?"

"Our target might be right on the edge of town, but once those fires start, there's a good chance that they will reach the church, too."

Embry nodded. "What of it?"

"The Lancasters are going to do a wonderful job of concealing the fact that we deliberately targeted this laboratory. The SS might even think it was an accident. Collateral damage."

"Let's hope."

"Is Hildesheim being struck to conceal our tracks?" The words burst from his lips before he could stop them, torn from his lungs. "The war is nearly over. Are we destroying that town and killing all those people on the off-chance that it gives us a fraction more secrecy?"

He realised he had spoken louder than intended. His eyes met Lane's. Section Officer Gerrard had left, leaving only Lane and Stahl in the room. Both watched him. Lane's gaze pulsed with questions, but also warmth. Stahl's? Durban couldn't tell. The German might as well have been a mannequin, his eyes dark and lifeless.

"I don't know," Embry said. "That's the truth. Listen, Andy. We have only given you the most basic details of AFTERLIGHT. Hell, even I only know a little more. This business, this *Götterdämmerung* or whatever they want to call it, is bigger than you know. DI(R) have been calling me every hour, the Joint Intelligence Committee is spooked, and even the Prime Minister is being given daily updates. Whatever the Jerries are planning, we need to put a stop to it at all costs."

"I understand that, sir."

Embry steered him further away from the others. "I've said this before, and you shot me down. Hear me now. You weren't my choice for this job. If it was up to me, you'd be off on an instructor tour right now. Better still, on long-term leave. God knows you've earned it, especially after Gisela. You said yourself you have very little low-level experience, and these are dangerous targets. You've flown more sorties in harm's way than just about anyone I know, and there's only so many times you can go back to that well."

It took Durban a few moments to realise what Embry meant. He felt his cheeks redden as waves of heat pulsed through his body. His body tensed, every muscle quivering. Embry still talked, but Durban barely heard the words. Out of the corner of his eye, he saw Lane take a hesitant step towards them.

And still Stahl watched.

"How dare you," Durban grated, interrupting but not caring. "How bloody dare you, sir."

"Excuse me?"

"Four tours, sir." He spat the words out. "Have you ever seen me hesitate? Have you ever known me to be anything other than the first to attack and the last man over the target? If you want to sack me, go ahead, but don't lie to yourself that you're doing me a favour. I'll take a court martial before I take that from you or anyone else."

The blood had drained from Embry's face. His lips twitched as if trying to find words.

Well, Durban thought, you've done it now.

Career over.

Get ready to be grounded.

Lane was next to him now, he realised, blinking rapidly, her lips pursed. Her hand rested on his sleeve. He wondered if she knew it was there.

"Wing Commander Durban," Embry said, the words slow-paced, as deliberate as a court statement under oath. "It appears I owe you an apology."

"Sir?"

The AVM rubbed at his neck. Hard. His hands shook with his own anger, but he kept it from his voice. "I certainly did not mean to imply..." He let out a sharp breath and stood straight. "The squadron is yours. I know you'll lead it well. Mister Stahl, Squadron Officer Lane, you are welcome to join me in the Ops Room to observe the mission." Without a further word, he strode from the briefing room. Stahl's gaze fixed on Durban. Unreadable. Then, without a word, he followed the AVM.

Lane's long fingers still rested on Durban's arm. Only now did she appear to notice, almost snatching her hand away. "Let's talk when you get back," she said.

"I'd like that," he said, waiting until she left his sight before taking a deep, shuddering breath and freeing it in a single explosive blast. Then he set off to find Grant, marvelling at how close his flying career had come to ending and trying to ignore the clamouring voice in his head that wished it had.

Chapter Twenty

Above Germany, 22 March

Grant had never seen so many bombers before. Even now, with the formation dwindling behind them as the Mosquitoes sped towards their target, they seemed to fill the sky like a distant flock of huge, dark birds. Their wings left faint contrails that glowed in the early afternoon sunshine. The smaller shapes of dozens of escort fighters lurked above them, poised to drop with lethal grace onto any German fighter foolish enough to challenge the vast air armada.

None had.

Grant adjusted his smoked goggles. They took the edge off the sun's brightness but could not stop its rays from turning the expansive Perspex cockpit into a greenhouse.

An errant drop of sweat stung his eyes. He blinked.

Without the suspense that darkness brought, that constant nagging fear that something was lurking just out of sight, the scene felt unreal. Off the nose to the left, a smudge of urban sprawl on the horizon broke the monotony of the North German plain stretched below them. Hanover. Gratitude fluttered in his chest. Their flight path mercifully kept him from seeing the miles of shattered factories and fire-gutted homes that were the legacy of so many Bomber Command raids. Of course, that wasn't why his map told him to avoid it. Hanover might be all but dead, but flak still clustered heavily around the corpse.

The city served a purpose, though, as a good final aiming point for their descent towards Hildesheim. There, the flak should not be heavy at all, except around an isolated church on the southeast side.

"Thirty seconds," he said.

To his left, in the pilot's seat, Durban nodded and thumbed his R/T switch. "Colt Leader to all callsigns. Attack plan Delta."

No response came. None needed. Behind their right wingtip, Barton's Mosquito peeled away in a steep dive to the southeast, the other seven Mosquitoes of A Flight following. The plan was simple. A Flight's job was to hit the laboratory itself, attacking at low level from the shallow hills to the south, six minutes after the first attack began. By then, Durban had briefed them, the flak would be suppressed or distracted, leaving Barton a clear and unopposed run at the target.

That still left the small matter of the suppressing and distracting.

"Ready?" Without waiting for an answer, Durban pushed forward on the controls.

The earth seemed to float upwards until it filled the windscreen. Even with the throttles at minimum, the whistling of air past the nose grew louder. The green expanse of the landscape began to break apart, individual trees and buildings emerging from the amorphous mass, reaching towards them. No flak yet.

Grant checked their six. No enemy fighters, either. Just the seven Mosquitoes of B Flight arcing down, slicing through the late spring air.

Durban pulled out of the dive at four hundred feet, then allowed the Mosquito to sink still lower. Ahead, a railway line and a road meandered through a low valley, the river that had carved it over centuries a thin band of blue alongside them. "Kittens, stay at fifteen hundred feet and loiter here. Mark the flak positions but engage only on my signal."

"Wilco, Colt Leader."

Suspicion writhed in Grant's guts. Attack plan Delta called for B Flight to race in at fifteen second intervals and strike the three flak positions that Section Officer Gerrard had highlighted. There had been nothing about the Squadron Commander going in alone.

Alone, but for the terrified navigator sat to his right.

Grant checked his map, comparing the lay of the land to the villages and streams flashing past beyond the Perspex. They were still about three miles short of the target, far less than a minute of flying at this speed. Just outside 20mm flak range. His stomach lurched as the Mosquito bobbled in a crosswind. Ahead, a line of trees on a low ridge obscured their view. Durban pulled back on the controls to bring them over the top.

The church, peaceful and alone among green fields and trees, came into sight. Which meant the flak dug in around the building could see the Mosquito, too.

Where at first Grant saw only the rapidly closing shape of the old stone building, suddenly the ground itself seemed to transform as tiny figures raced to pull aside camouflage netting. Ugly black shapes emerged from beneath, each pointing to the sky with four thin fingers. Directly off the nose, one crew wrestled their gun into position, faster than the rest. The tips of the barrels turned towards the onrushing aircraft. Each blinked, the muzzle flashes visible even in the sunlight.

Tracers sawed through the air on either side of them.

"Hold on," Durban said into the intercom. With a sharp wrench, he threw the Mosquito into a hard right turn which hid the guns from sight. That brought no sense of relief. It merely exposed the vulnerable belly of the aircraft to their fury. Barely three thuds of Grant's frenzied heartbeat and Durban shifted the controls again. Dived the Mosquito to barely fifty feet. Pulled it into a tight left bank.

Grant dragged his head back, agonised neck muscles protesting as he stared almost directly up through the cockpit roof. First one gun, then three spun in place to track their movement.

Shells poured out in long streams of glowing beads. The

Mosquito shuddered as one smashed a hole through the right wing. Grant heard a whimper. His own voice.

At this height, any damage to the flight surfaces meant instant death.

Durban's grip remained firm as iron on the controls. He guided the Mosquito around in a half-moon circuit to the east before pulling into a shallow climb. The guns continued to track them, firing more in hope than expectation now as the range increased. "Colt Leader to B Flight. Did you see them, Kittens?"

"Marked all three, sir."

"They're all yours. Start your attack run now."

Grant swallowed. Sour vomit burned his throat. The professional part of him wanted to congratulate the Wing Commander. By exposing their own aircraft, Durban had led the flak crews to reveal their positions, making them far easier targets for the onrushing B Flight. Grant could understand the logic in it. It didn't help him control the terror that left his body trembling. His eyes remained locked on the guns, waiting for them to come closer, daring them to creep into range again.

Sweat poured down his spine, soaking his shirt. Not the sun's fault. Not now.

"Stay alert," Durban said, levelling out at a thousand feet. "Shout if you see anything."

Grant nodded. No obvious admonishment in the Wing Commander's voice, but there didn't have to be. Too fixated on the flak, he had neglected to watch for fighters. He scanned the sky above and behind. Nothing but the near-cloudless azure expanse beyond the Perspex and the town of Hildesheim spreading out to the north, nestled at the foot of the low hills. The people there must have heard the crack of the Flakvierlings. Did they know what was coming for them, just a few minutes away now? Probably not. Night had brought terror to nearby Hanover so many times, but surely the daylight meant safety.

Continuing his scan, Grant's gaze drifted back to the church. So innocuous. Like they had picked the wrong building, despite the ferocity of the flak. Then the first Mosquito emerged from the valley beyond, two hundred feet above the railway line, racing at full throttle.

Still focused on Durban and Grant, the air defence crews reacted a second, a lifetime too late.

Beneath Kittinger's Mosquito, bomb doors dropped open. The aircraft swept past the first gun position. Two small objects tumbled down as it passed over the second. The gun crew kept firing until, after half a second's delay, five-hundred pounds of high explosive detonated either side of them. Grant glimpsed twisted metal hurled into the air, alongside smaller, less sturdy fragments. Then a rapidly spreading ball of smoke, dust and ejected soil and grass obliterated the gun position from sight. He couldn't be sure if the sudden buffeting of the aircraft was shockwave or simply a pocket of warmer air, but there was no mistaking the dull thuds of the detonations even above the roar of the two Merlin engines.

"Nicely done," Durban said.

The second Mosquito hurtled in. It seemed like an age had passed since Kittens had attacked, but Grant knew that was just a trick of the mind. Fifteen seconds, no more. The Mosquito struck the first flak position. Only one explosion this time. The second bomb must have been a dud. It didn't make an iota of difference. One was enough. As smoke bloomed, Grant saw enough to know that the blast had left the gun largely intact. The crew was a different matter.

The second Mosquito followed Kittinger's path, low and fast. It was almost clear when it suddenly lurched in the air, almost crabbing sideways before the clawing propellors regained their grip on the warm air and righted its course. Trailing fragments of shattered fuselage, it raced away to the east, chastened.

A faint puff of smoke hung in the air among thick bushes to the east of the church.

"There's a fourth gun position," Grant yelled, pointing.

"Seen," Durban said. He didn't radio it in, simply pulled on the controls and swung the nose towards the new threat.

The third B Flight Mosquito was already inbound. Grant felt a surge of relief as the flak crews focused their ire on it, but that emotion turned instantly to guilt. He pulled his eyes away from the vulnerable attacking Mosquito and back to the target position ahead.

He looked at Durban. Saw the concentration on the man's face. "Should I open the bomb doors?"

"No," Durban said. "Guns will do."

The flak position grew larger. Close enough now that Grant could see the individual men of the crew, expertly working their Flakvierling as they plotted to bring a Mosquito down.

The B Flight Mosquito. The wrong Mosquito.

Another second, and Durban depressed the firing stud.

Their airframe juddered. The enormous recoil of four 20mm cannon and four .303" machine guns arrested its momentum as sharply as if the pilot had somehow slammed on the brakes. Durban's first rounds fell just short, the cacophony of the firing guns finally alerting the brave gunners to their imminent doom.

Heads turned. One man threw out a hand. A last panicked attempt to hold a beast at bay.

Bullets, shells, and razor-sharp fragments shredded through human flesh. A soldier took a half-pound high-explosive shell full in the chest, his body virtually dissolving into red mist as the limbs fluttered uselessly from either side. Another collapsed, head and upper torso sawn away.

The eviscerated remains of the crew disappeared beneath their nose as they passed overhead.

Grant's stomach heaved. It took everything he had to keep his breakfast from exploding over the flight instruments ahead of him. The Mosquito trembled as a passing shockwave marked B Flight's destruction of the final Flakvierling. Then they were clear and climbing into the blue sky.

"Colt Leader to Bravo One, is that all of them?"

"Roger, Colt Leader." Kittens sounded almost bored. So calm. "Looks like a clean sweep."

"B Flight, clear to the west and loiter in case we need to reattack. Alpha One, are you in position?"

"Yep," Barton replied. "Is anything left for us to hit?"

"We don't get a bonus for bringing bombs home. Once you've dropped, break hard to port. Make sure you don't stray too near to Hildesheim. The Lancasters will be there any moment now."

"Yeah, we remember the brief. Out." The radio fell silent.

"What an obnoxious fellow," Durban said as the first A Flight Mosquito approached the target, flying slower now that Colt Leader had eliminated the flak as a planning factor.

Whatever Barton lacked in civility, he clearly possessed in skill. The first two 500lb bombs impacted in the dead-centre of the target area. They sent twin plumes of dirt into the air, their pre-set delayed fuses giving them time to burrow deep into the earth. Moments later, the ground itself heaved upwards, the grass sheath of the hidden laboratory splitting apart and great clods of mud spattering against the church walls.

"Bang on the money," Durban said. "Are you ok? Johnny?"

Grant opened his mouth to reply, but then his stomach bubbled again. He clamped his lips tightly shut. Partly it was the image of the butchered gun crew that clung to his retinas. Partly it was the thought of what high explosive and blast in the tight confines of the underground bunker would do to soft tissue and skin.

Mostly, it was knowing that Durban had deliberately drawn the enemy fire to them, putting Grant's own vulnerable body in the firing line to make it easier for the others. That it had worked, and that the aircraft of A Flight now struck the laboratory with impunity and clockwork ease, offered zero consolation. Yes, it had worked. This time.

He said nothing.

"For what it's worth," Durban said, "one hundred percent oxygen always does the trick for me."

Grant fumbled for his mask before gulping in a lungful of sweet, fresh air. The nausea subsided, his head clearing. The memory of the dying men faded, but still lingered.

Above the incessant growl of the engines, a thudding sound filled the cockpit. One, two, then dozens, then a constant rhythm. To the north, columns of smoke twisted their way into the sky above the town of Hildesheim, trying to reach the hundreds of dark silhouettes that filled the sky above.

Chapter Twenty-One

Norfolk, 23 March

Durban stared through his office window, idly turning his car keys between his fingers. Little stirred outside. Normally, Charney Breach was a hive of activity at this hour. Engineers working away, air tests, pilots enjoying the downtime that came with a limited flying schedule. Today, it seemed it wasn't just the low clouds that hung lazily over the base. He knew a good leader could inspire his command with his energy and enthusiasm. Was the opposite also true? His own body carried the same torpor he sensed outside, but then he'd only slept two or three hours at best. The rest of the night he had simply lain staring at the ceiling, trying in vain to look through it to the sky above.

He already knew the next target. Uelzen. The question was when, and not even Sarah Lane could tell him that.

A knock, and the door opened. He saw a tall figure reflected in the window's glass. "What is it, Bony?"

"Sorry to disturb, sir, but you said you wanted this as soon as it arrived." The Ops Officer passed him a large brown file cover.

"Thank you. Would you ask Squadron Officer Lane and Mister Stahl to join me, please?"

"Yes, sir."

Letting his car keys clatter to the desk, Durban opened the file. The trembling was back in his fingers. Something to keep an eye on, while preventing others doing the same. The Squadron Medical Officer might have something in his dispensary that would help. A trapped nerve, he thought. Nothing more. Opening the file, he sifted through the glossy enlargements until he found the photo he wanted. Two seconds told him everything he needed to know.

He sighed. He had thought it would be more satisfying.

Stahl walked in silently and took up his customary position with his back to the wall and his hands touching in front of his chest. Lane took a few minutes more. "Sorry, Andy," she said as she came in, fumbling the door shut behind her, ignoring Stahl altogether.

Durban felt an odd flutter in the pit of his stomach. She looked like she'd recently woken from an afternoon nap, her hair a little out of place, eyes a little bemused. It seemed he wasn't the only one who had slept badly.

Damn, it was good to see her.

"The battle damage assessment from Hildesheim has arrived," he said, motioning her to sit. "A PR Mosquito from 680 Squadron went over the town about four hours after we left. The images are a little obscured by smoke in places, but I think you'll agree they tell a story." He pushed the first one in front of them.

"You didn't damage the church." Lane smiled. "Somehow, that's comforting."

"I imagine there is some shrapnel in the stonework," Durban said, "but nothing it won't survive. As you can see, the main lab has been exposed here and here. This debris field spreading here was likely ejected by a bomb that landed in the centre of the lab after the first detonations tore away the overhead cover."

"What are those?" She pointed to two large rectangles near the bottom of the image.

"The doors," he said. "Blown outwards by the overpressure of the first bomb detonating inside the bunker. This area here looks like it has caved in. Any parts of the bunker not destroyed outright by the bombing were likely buried when the roof collapsed on top of it."

She nodded. "Any survivors?"

"Depends. Was there a night shift?"

"No," Stahl answered for her. "The scientists worked in a single team, fourteen-hour days."

"Only cleaners and administrative staff worked at night," Lane said. She crossed her arms and shifted her weight in her chair. She still didn't look at Stahl. Hadn't done so even once.

"There may have been a few personnel sick or on leave," Durban said, "but I think it's fair to say that the ones inside the building..." He let his voice tail off.

Stahl reached to the desk, and Lane jumped. The German didn't notice. Sifting through the images, he drew out the one that showed the widest view. An aerial view of the entire area from over thirty-thousand feet, no magnification. "Hildesheim?"

"Yes," Durban said, "the city itself. This area here is where the station and marshalling yards were. You can still see sections of intact track here and here. Remarkable when you consider the amount of cratering. This area here has been almost totally destroyed." He paused. Three churches had stood out on the pre-attack imagery. None were visible now.

"This is cloud?" Stahl pointed.

"Smoke. From incendiaries. This area here is mostly fire damage, very little blast. Large parts of the town are burning."

"Still?" Lane frowned. "Four hours after the attack?"

Durban shrugged. "The HE likely ruptured the water mains. The fire brigades would do what they could, but without water, and with the fires so widespread, it could have taken them all night to bring it under control."

Stahl's finger still rested on one part of the town, largely obscured by smoke but clear enough in places to show collapsed buildings, ruptured streets, an open area that might have been a park but now a wasteland pockmarked with craters. Wordless, he dragged his hand away, leaving a smudge on the image before his other hand half-threw the picture across the desk.

156

"If you will both forgive me," Stahl said, "I think I need some fresh air." He backed away, his gaze still transfixed on the image.

Durban heard the clatter of the German's heels in the corridor and the rush of air as he left the building through the front door. "What was that about?"

Lane didn't respond, only shook her head slightly as she stared at the door.

Chapter Twenty-Two

Norfolk, 23 March

Stahl walked for an hour, following the perimeter track around the outer limits of the base. He found no fresh air. Only the smell of aviation fuel that hung in the afternoon air, and the remembered stench of smoke and burning flesh.

The raid had been a complete success. That was something. Twenty-six scientists had worked there, as best he could tell. Most with families, though that did not upset him. Given what those men were working on, they had long since forfeited their human right to see their loved ones again. Perhaps they didn't even qualify as human anymore, but after six years of war, they weren't alone in that.

His gaze fixed on an isolated Mosquito. Three men fussed about it, apparently patching holes in the wooden fuselage. Stahl could see the descending sun through another, larger rent in the tail. Lane hadn't invited him to join her yesterday afternoon when she went out to count the sixteen Mosquitoes back home. He wouldn't have gone, anyway. Though content that the first element of *Götterdämmerung* had been destroyed, he had eaten nothing and slept poorly.

After what he had seen, it would be worse tonight.

His path back took him close to the Squadron Commander's office. The woman had left, but Durban still sat at his desk, pen in hand. The fool had his back to the window, oblivious. A few seconds was all it would take to walk up, put a single round in the back of the man's head, and vanish among the scattered buildings nearby where shadows had already pooled as the sun dropped.

158

Instead, he went looking for the Black man he often saw with Durban.

He found him in the dining room, laughing and joking with several other men. The table fell silent as he approached. Three of the men stared at him with distrust, a fourth with absolute hatred. Grant's eyes held only a question. He doubted the young man had ever known true hate. He would, with time.

"Can I help you, sir?"

"Call me Stahl. May we talk?"

"Of course." Grant excused himself and followed Stahl across the room. The other men watched. "Were you looking for the Wing Commander?"

"I have just left him," Stahl said. "He said to come and see you."

"Really?" The man visibly shrank. "Why?"

"I have been trapped on this airfield for two days now." True. "I have never been to England." Untrue. "And he said you would show me some of the local area."

Most definitely untrue.

"I thought we weren't supposed to leave the base right now," Grant said. "Until we find out what we're doing next. Do you mind if I check with him?"

"I do not mind," Stahl said, reaching into his pocket. "He is in his office. But he seems very busy. That is why I left him to be alone. He is... how do you say it? Stressed. I heard him shout at that poor man with the funny walk."

"The Ops Officer?" Grant ran his hand through his hair. "Bony did seem nervous when I saw him a few minutes ago. Mind you, he always does. Fine, I don't want to get shouted at. But there is one problem. We don't actually have a car."

"We do," Stahl said, opening his hand to reveal a set of car keys. It had been the easiest thing to palm them from the desk while the photographs distracted Durban and Lane. "I will drive."

Grant frowned.

"If you are anxious," Stahl said, "you can ask him to repeat his orders directly to you."

"Best not, I suppose," the young man mumbled after a long pause. He waved goodbye to his still staring colleagues and led the way out of the back doors of the building to where the Alvis sat parked. Stahl admired the silver bodywork before sliding into the driver's seat. The Alvis was smaller than the Mercedes he had left in the hands of the Swiss, but most things were. The leather seat was well-worn and cracked in places. Comfortable enough, though. A nice car, he thought, waiting for Grant to get into his own seat before starting the engine and reversing onto the road.

His earlier walk had given him a good understanding of the layout of the roads, and Stahl felt confident he could reach the gate without risking passing by Durban's window. He put the car into first gear and felt a surge of pleasure as the power built beneath his right foot.

"Other side of the road, sir," Grant said.

"Of course. I can see why Andrew speaks so highly of your navigation skills."

Grant beamed at that, and Stahl felt a momentary pang of guilt. He forced it away. After all, he was not lying for once, not really. Durban had said nothing, but Stahl knew enough of fighting men to know who they trusted, and Durban and Grant clearly trusted one another.

He wondered if the same would be true when Durban realised his keys had gone.

Chapter Twenty-Three

Lane knocked and waited, holding the briefcase loosely. It seemed heavier than the mere weight of the paper inside. She checked her watch, knocked again, and was about to leave when she heard the muffled voice.

"You sound exhausted, Andy," she said as she pushed open the door. "You look it, too."

"Thanks," Durban drawled from behind his desk.

"Were you asleep?"

"Sorry. No. Just concentrating." He motioned to the photographs in front of him, the same as this afternoon, now augmented by long sheets of numbers and acronyms. "Just trying to work out if we could have done it better."

"I'm not sure you could," she said, pulling up a chair and placing it next to his, so that they sat side by side. She wasn't sure he'd noticed, his eyes still fixed on the desk. "You destroyed the target, and you brought everyone back alive. You did everything right, Andy."

He started at her touch on his arm. "Yeah," he said. "You're probably right. I just feel like it could have been, I don't know, cleaner."

"This isn't that kind of war," Lane said sadly. She offered him the penultimate cigarette from the pack he had given to her, then took the other herself and lit both.

"You know," he said, looking at the ceiling as smoke trickled from his mouth, "in Pathfinders I saw a dozen Hildesheims. Bigger cities, bigger raids. I dropped target indicators over Hamburg the night of the firestorm. None of it truly bothered me before now. I didn't enjoy it, but it was the job. This feels different."

"The war is almost over," Lane said. He nodded. "But it's not over, Andy," she added. "There is still a job to do." She opened the briefcase.

"Is that what I think it is?"

"The next target." She took out several aerial photographs and a hand-drawn map of an airfield. "Here," she said. "Does it look familiar? The airfield at Uelzen. You can see the area marked out where the SS detachment took over."

"I remember it," Durban said. "I remember those revetments too."

"We've confirmed the aircraft are Dornier Do-217s. Six in total."

"Uelzen isn't close." He turned in his seat and stared at the planning map on his office wall. "We'll load up half the kites with rockets; they are lighter, which will buy us a few more miles, and they will give us more options. When do we attack?"

"I don't know."

Durban rubbed his eyes. "Well, the squadron is as ready as it will ever be. We could go as soon as tomorrow afternoon if you want us to."

"No," she said. "We need to wait."

"Why?"

"If we strike too soon, especially after Hildesheim, we risk alerting the SS that we know something. If they take *Götterdämmerung* underground, we've lost the game. It's already a risk going after the airfield."

"Then why bother?" At her sharp look, he spread his hands. "I'm serious. They are just aircraft, modified or not. It's been years since a Dornier could survive long enough to reach London. They are slow, we are fast. I'd be more worried if they had converted some of their new jets, but these old kites won't make it far."

"What if they don't need to?"

"Meaning?"

She paused, knowing she had already told him far too much. She lived in a world where "need to know" was more than a mantra. It was a tangible shadow hanging over everything. The intelligence reports that reached her desk could change the fates of nations, but each was as fragile as the cheap, thin paper it was printed on. One innocent yet careless breach of security, and the lifespan of the accrued knowledge became as short as that of the agent who provided it. She had lost too many agents that way, betrayed by a single wrong word. To arrest. Torture. The final bullet in the back of the skull.

And yet, the same secrecy that protected her agents put others in danger. She could sit and read these reports at her desk, warm and safe and sipping tea. Meanwhile, the pilots who would have to fly the mission, deep into the lethal heart of the enemy's homeland, learned the details of their target only a few hours before the mission.

It had never affected her before. But then, none of those men risking their lives had been Andy Durban.

His gaze flickered away from the photographs and fell on her. Expectant.

"A local girl who works as a cleaner for the Luftwaffe Officers' Mess at Uelzen drew this map for us," she said, feeling her cheeks warm. If Durban had to go, she needed him to have the longest possible time to prepare for it. "She saw engineers working on the bombers."

"Doing what to them?"

"The girl doesn't know, but she saw metal cylinders under the wings."

"Bombs?"

"Anna's seen bombs before. These are too fat. According to her, they look more like shiny metal Zeppelins, but with no tail fins.

163

She doesn't own a camera and couldn't get close enough to draw a sketch. She tried to talk her way closer, but the SS guards got suspicious and detained her. The Luftwaffe airfield commander had to vouch for her before they would let her go back to work."

"Poor thing must have been terrified," Durban said, rubbing his jaw. "Brave girl."

"They all are," Lane said. "Those that are still alive."

"We have no clue what the modifications are for?"

"No," she admitted. "But if the SS have gone to the effort, despite the age of the aircraft, they must know something we don't. When you attack, it should be at night. During the day, they sometimes fly in the local area. Mostly low-level passes over villages and towns. I don't want you arriving there only to find half the aircraft missing. Also, the building behind this hangar is the aircrew accommodation. At night, the pilots will be there." She took a breath. Her stomach roiled at the thought of violated security rules.

It is necessary, she told herself. If they are better prepared, the mission has a better chance to succeed. And we need it to succeed.

"Destroy the aircraft, kill the pilots," Durban said, turning to fully face her for the first time since she'd arrived. "The latter is easy enough, but those revetments look horribly solid." He smiled, without even a trace of humour. "We'll need more than the rockets. I guess I should order some napalm early."

"You don't need to give me the details," she said with a shudder. She realised that, while he focused on the map and photographs, on their mission, she had been watching his face since the moment she came in. The exhaustion in him seemed much more than just the shadows under his eyes that, while deep, did little to detract from his pleasant features. At worst, they just made him seem a little more of a match for her own age. "Andy?"

"Hmm?" He was back to staring at the photographs again, turning the image of the airfield first one way then the other, as if planning the perfect attack route.

"Do me a favour and go to bed early tonight?"

"I'll try." He yawned. "I have to write a letter tonight. I've put it off for too long."

His yawn triggered one of her own. "Stop that," she mumbled, pushing him playfully on the arm.

"Sorry," he said, smiling. "What about Stahl? Does he have anything to add?"

The name brought a wave of cold with it. Everything playful inside her shrivelled in an instant. "I don't know," she said. "I haven't seen him since..."

"Since he looked at Hildesheim."

"You saw it too?"

"Hard to miss," Durban said. "I don't know what he saw that we didn't, but it doesn't matter. He's not here for the good of his health. He has work to do, same as us. If we're discussing target planning, he should be here."

"He was supposed to be," she agreed.

"Perhaps you scared him off."

"I doubt it. Fear is an emotion. Stahl has none."

Durban stood abruptly and began policing up the photographs and other paperwork. "Come on," he said. "Let's secure these in the safe. Then we'll dig up Stahl from wherever he's hiding, wrap this up, and still have time for a drink afterwards."

She stayed seated, chin resting in one hand, looking up at him while he took the briefcase from her and began shovelling files into it. Tired or not, she felt the warmth coming from him. The energy. The dedication. His country had got lucky the day he joined the RAF, she thought. More than that, he made her feel warm, too. But there was something she'd been meaning to ask him.

"Who is Gisela?"

She blurted the words out before she could think them through. It wasn't jealousy that drove the question, of course. That was impossible. Mere curiosity. Asking questions was her job, and it was important that she understood this man who had become so important to her.

He looked startled. "Where did you hear that name?"

"Embry. He mentioned her twice." Professional curiosity, she told herself again. Nothing more.

To her surprise, Durban laughed. "You don't mean her, you mean it. Operation Gisela. Do you really want to know?"

"Why? Don't you want to tell?"

"There's not much to tell," he said. He fell silent for a second. The speed with which the levity slid from his face brought a twinge of regret. That odd, queasy feeling in the depths of her stomach? Guilt. She should not have asked the question.

The guilt passed. Losing out, as always, to her commitment to knowledge.

He took a deep breath, his eyes widening for a beat before his professional cool returned, the way it had when he showed her the Mosquito. "We have the Germans beaten," he began. "The fight between our bombers and their night fighters used to be evenly matched, but not anymore. Every night we fly more heavies, drop more bombs with better accuracy, and they can't kill enough of us anymore to make a difference. We know it. They know it. But what the Germans don't know is how to admit defeat. The stubborn bastards changed the game."

"How?"

"An aircraft is never more vulnerable than when it is taking off or landing," Durban said. "The Luftwaffe aren't stupid. God, I wish they were. They would love to hit our bombers on take-off, with a full load of bombs and fuel just waiting to go up like a Christmas tree. But they can't; we take off in daylight, with our air defences fully alert. No way could they get close, and it would be suicide to try. They used to make hay over the target, but these days, with our overwhelming numbers, with 100 Group jamming their radars and sending dozens of night intruders out looking for trade every time there is a raid, their odds aren't much better than suicide even on home turf."

She nodded. Her agents in Germany had said the same thing, talked about the fuel shortages, the horrifying loss rates for the Luftwaffe, the youths sent straight from flying schools to fly outdated aircraft against the overwhelming might of the Allied air forces. A brave people, the Germans.

Her people, she thought, however much she might pretend it wasn't true.

Had so much courage and integrity ever been so sickeningly abused, squandered in the service of such darkness? She wasn't religious – how could she be, after what had been done to those who followed the religion of her birth? – but she wished fervently that Hell was real, so that the Nazis could burn in it for eternity.

"What's a night intruder?" She said it before Durban could continue, knowing the answer but needing to distract herself from the thought of who else might join the Nazis in their damnation. After six years of bloody war, no one's hands were unstained. Hers, least of all.

"Me," Durban said. "In a radar-equipped Mosquito night fighter. Not alone, of course. For eleven months, I flew with the same navigator and radar operator. Clive Lampeter. My friend." There was a catch in his voice, the first chink in that infuriatingly British calm resolve of his. "As part of 100 Group, our job was to catch the Germans with their trousers down. As they got airborne," he added, possibly seeing the look on her face.

Certain English idioms still confused her, even after all these years. It was her third language, after all.

He looked away from her, staring at the wall. The shadows under his eyes darkened as his face turned from the light. "People think of air combat as somehow noble," he said. "Knights of the sky. It's rubbish, all of it. A man doesn't get seven kills by playing fair. He gets them by circling over enemy airfields at night, waiting for some scared boys to get airborne with dreams of protecting their country, and then hunting them down before the poor bastards even have time to get their landing gear up."

She let the silence hang for a good ten seconds. "Tell me about Gisela."

He nodded. Resumed, as if nothing had happened, tone dispassionate. A history lesson, nothing more. "The Luftwaffe did to us what we were doing to them. Instead of meeting us over the target, they would get us when we were landing. Getting a heavy bomber on the ground safely is never easy. After ten hours in the air, fuel running low, battle damaged over the target, possibly with dead or wounded onboard, it becomes a nightmare. Can you imagine it?"

She shook her head. She didn't want to.

"The night of 3 March," he said. "Our intelligence chaps put it all together afterwards. We sent over eight hundred bombers that night. Mission successful, lots of damage. Eight bombers lost over Germany. Less than one percent loss rate. We used to dream of figures that low. My 100 Group colleagues killed two of their night fighters over their bases. Clive and I didn't find any targets. I remember being disappointed that there weren't more German aircraft up. I felt like we'd missed out. Still, it all looked good. Another job well done. What we didn't know was that the Luftwaffe never intended to fight us over the target that night. They followed us home instead."

His hand shook. "Ju-88s. The only fighter the Germans had left with the range to pull it off. They came in low, below our radar coverage. No one expected them. Certainly not me." He glanced at her, then closed one hand over the other, tilting his body away from her to hide the motion.

"Even low on fuel, a bomber burns brightly. The first Clive and I knew was when they started lighting up the skies before dawn, like new-born stars. I don't know how many German night fighters there were. One hundred and fifty? You would think they were everywhere. Attacking bombers by the glow of the runway lighting, homing in on their navigation lights, hitting tired crews already thinking of supper and bed. I know how many they lost. Six over England. Clive and I got one of those. Best part of twenty if you include crash landings and bail outs over the Channel. I know how many we lost. Twenty-five, including my own. Seventy-nine men. Including Clive Lampeter." His voice sank to a whisper. "That one's on me."

"How do you mean?"

He turned back to her. To the sound of her voice, she corrected herself. Nothing in his eyes suggested he saw her. He was somewhere else.

"Clive wanted me to land. We were short on fuel, even shorter on options. Airfields were going dark across England, trying to deny the Germans easy targets. Clive's job was to get me home, and he'd done it twenty-nine times before. You'd think I would be smart enough to listen, but my job was to kill enemy fighters. I took us back into the fight. I got a Ju-88, too, only for one of our own side, another bloody Mosquito, to return the favour. Clive died instantly, leaving me to crash land alone."

"One of ours hit you?"

"Friendly fire," Durban said, a bitter chuckle escaping his throat.

"And yet you blame yourself?"

He snorted. "Of course. Who else would you blame? The other Mosquito? He was supposed to be there. I wasn't."

She didn't flinch at the anger in his voice. After all, it wasn't directed at her. "How many other men might have died if you hadn't got that Ju-88? You did your job."

"I ignored my navigator, and my arrogance got him killed."

"You did your job," she repeated. "Surely, you're too smart to blame yourself for that? The guilt comes because he died while you walked away, and that isn't fair."

He mumbled something.

"I'm sorry?"

"I didn't exactly walk away," he said.

"You were hurt?" She remembered the way he had winced when Embry had clapped him on the shoulder.

"Not badly. A broken rib, some bruising. A few stitches." He sounded like a man confessing to a crime, but still holding something back. Underplaying the damage. "They carried me on a stretcher and straight off to the hospital. Rather efficient of them, if I'm honest."

She frowned. "That was the third of March?"

"Morning of the fourth."

"Andy, the first time we met was the fourteenth."

"Well remembered."

"With injuries like that, you should still have been in the hospital."

"The doctors said much the same thing, yet here I am. I have a squadron to command."

"You have a job to do." She wondered if he heard it as affirmation or accusation. His face betrayed nothing. Truth was, she didn't know herself.

"Look," he said, rubbing his eyes as if to clear them, "I may have taken us a little off the subject there. What were we supposed to be doing now?"

"Finding Stahl." She forced a smile. "Then you said something about a drink."

"Right," he said, then paused. He swallowed. "Sod it. I need a drink more than I need Stahl. Let's get one in the bar. Better still, two. Then we'll dig him up. Does that sound ok?"

"It sounds good."

He sucked in a deep breath, grabbed his hat, and patted his trouser pockets. "Can you see my car keys anywhere?"

She shook her head.

"Never mind." He shrugged. "I'm sure they will turn up."

Chapter Twenty-Four

Norfolk, 23 March

With Grant waving to the dithering guards, they left the front gate and turned right onto the main road. Stahl genuinely wanted to see more of the local area, and he felt an immediate softening of the pressure on his chest the moment the airfield was behind them. The surrounding fences looked too much like those around Flossenbürg, and every glimpse of a Mosquito brought fresh memories of what he had seen below the smoke on the photographs of Hildesheim. Durban would be furious if he knew, but Stahl reckoned that, with luck, he could return the car with the Wing Commander none the wiser. Even if Durban noticed the lowering of the fuel needle, the man had no meaningful power over him.

"We have about an hour of daylight left," Grant said. "What do you want to see?"

"Show me something beautiful."

"Around here?" Grant laughed. "I'll try my best. It's all a lot like this, though."

"Flat?"

"You think this is flat? You should see where we trained to fly in Canada. Just like this, but fewer trees and villages, and it just went on forever, horizon to horizon. Boring as hell. Take a left up here."

"Boring can be beautiful," Stahl said. "I have not been bored since 1939." He slowed for the junction, waiting for three army lorries to pass before turning. "I grew up in the mountains of Bavaria, not like this at all. Your island home, it is beautiful?"

"Oh, yes," Grant sighed. "I didn't realise how amazing it was until I left. As a kid, I didn't appreciate things like the trees or the colour of the sea." His voice wavered as he spoke. "I was too busy wondering whether our Murr would find food for us to eat that day."

"You were poor?"

A shrug. "No more than the other children."

"You miss it. So why are you here, Grant? After all, you are..."

"Black, sir?"

"Not British."

"Same King," Grant sniffed.

"Is that it? King and country?" He put on his best British accent for the phrase.

"Not really." For a few seconds, Grant just stared out to the side at the Norfolk countryside, spreading away in all directions. "It's not just me. There must be five hundred of us in Bomber Command alone, counting all the islands. We're doing our bit, don't doubt that. But when the war is over, I'll be going home and doing my best to make sure Barbadians never have to fight in a British war again."

"You surprise me. A revolutionary?"

"A politician," Grant said. "There is already an independence movement at home. Once we have peace, the clamour will only get stronger. We need changes. I want to be part of that."

Stahl laughed. "You could be the first Prime Minister of the independent Barbados."

"Why not?" Grant fixed him with a furious gaze, and Stahl realised he had caused offence. The young man intrigued him. He had taken Grant for a youth, a child playing among men, but there was true strength in those flashing eyes. Perhaps if the young men of the Weimar Republic had been more like Grant, they would have fought back against Nazi ambitions instead of joining the Party in their droves.

"You do not wish to be ruled by the British Empire," Stahl said, "and yet you fight for it."

Now it was Grant's turn to laugh, a mirthless bark dragged from him. "Do you think life on the islands would be better under the Führer?"

"I know it would not. But Germany lost the war the day Hitler turned on Russia. We stopped posing a threat to your home long ago. So, I ask again. Why?"

"Because I don't like bullies," Grant snapped. "And because you don't make a better world by ignoring the horrors in this one."

Yes, Stahl told himself. More German youths like this one, and the Nazis and their whole twisted ideology would have been stillborn on the altar of forgotten history.

If he'd been more like Grant himself...

Ahead of them, stone buildings rose out of the deepening gloom beyond a narrow bridge. Stahl forced levity into his voice, even as his hands threatened to crush the steering wheel in his pained grip. "Thank you, Grant."

"Johnny."

"Thank you, Johnny Grant. This trip has been most illuminating. Perhaps I could buy you a drink in this lovely little town?"

"I think not. The Wing Commander would definitely not approve of that."

"This is a two-seat car, Johnny. And I am the only one in it with you." Their headlamps illuminated a square ahead, and the swinging sign above the door of a pub. "And as I am the driver," he added, "I think I insist."

Grant was not quite ready to give up. Not yet. "This isn't a good idea," he mumbled as Stahl parked.

"Nonsense." Stahl found his British accent again. "I speak perfect English. I assure you, I will not stand out." To his own

174

ears, at least, he sounded exactly like Andrew Durban. "And I would very much like to try this warm beer I have heard so much about."

"One drink. That's it."

The pub did not exactly fall silent as they walked in the door, but reputations were hard to earn in the SS, and Stahl could not have survived to garner his own without being able to read the danger in a changing mood. It didn't matter that he had only been in British pubs three times before, including one memorable occasion when he had eliminated a traitorous double-agent in the stinking toilets of an underground London tavern, cutting the man's throat before calmly washing his hands and leaving. He didn't need more experience than that. The warning signs of potential hostility and violence were universal.

Sweeping the room with a practiced gaze, he counted seventeen people. He dismissed four immediately. Older men and their wives. Of the rest, the six young men watching from the far end of the bar stood out. Farmers, he guessed, their hands calloused, the exposed skin of their thick forearms tanned despite the early season. He noted the way the two young women with them stared at Grant with wide, appreciative eyes. The navigator wore the only uniform in the pub.

The sensible move was to walk straight out.

He thought of the aerial photographs of Hildesheim.

He was not feeling sensible.

Grant swept past Stahl on his way to the bar, obviously oblivious to the atmosphere. Brave, but not too smart. He greeted the older woman behind the counter with a big smile. "Evening," Grant said. "Two pints of Best, please."

"We don't often see men in uniform on their own here, Johnny," the woman said. "Not on a locals' night. Who is your friend?"

"Sorry, May. This is…" He hesitated.

"John," Stahl said. "John Steel. It is a pleasure to meet you."

"I'm sure it is," May said, ignoring his offered hand. She made no move towards the long-handled beer pumps, either. "Look, Johnny, tonight isn't a good night."

"It's alright, May," one youth said, walking towards them. "We're always happy to see the brave boys from the RAF."

There was the hint of a slur in his words. Sunburnt skin at his temples. A long day in the field on an unseasonably warm afternoon, probably some dehydration, followed by several pints. Tipsy.

Belligerent.

"Are you a pilot, mate?" The youth ran his fingertip along the breast of Grant's uniform, picking at the wings of the aircrew brevet, pushing a little harder than necessary.

"Navigator," Grant said. The smile was still on his face, though a little forced now. He didn't back away, Stahl noted, even as the rest of the farmers moved closer.

"Isn't that just a passenger?" The man laughed at his own cleverness. A few others joined in. Stahl guessed the rest did not understand the joke. "Still get flying pay, though, I guess. Must be nice. Come on, May, why don't you pour us all a pint? Flyboy here can spare the money, I'm sure."

"I think the young man and his friend were just leaving," May said firmly.

"No, they're not," the farmer said. "That would be rude of them. Why don't we all have a drink together? Like the friends we are."

"Go ahead, May," Grant said. "Eight pints, and whatever the ladies want."

"Rum and lime, please," the first girl said.

Stahl leaned back against the bar and let his fingertips close together in front of his chest.

"Phil," the second girl said to the farmer, "can we just go back to our table?"

"Shut up," he hissed at her, then looked at Stahl. "What about you, mate? You a hero too?"

"Just a friend," Stahl said mildly, "enjoying the local scenery."

"I'll bet," the man said, leering, revealing teeth stained by tea, with a few missing altogether. "You like them a fair bit younger, don't you?"

The other men snickered. It took Stahl a moment longer to realise what that comment meant. Perhaps his English was not as good as he thought it was. It mattered little. Languages had never been his primary skill set.

There was still time to walk away, a small part of his brain told him. Buy the men some drinks, mutter a bland apology, walk out of the door and ignore the laughter behind. That would be the efficient option.

May began placing pints on the bar. "If you cause trouble in here, Philip Mugleston, you'll be looking for somewhere else to drink. And I'll be having words with your father."

Mugleston. Stahl was glad for a name.

The drinks were not well-poured. Rushed. A pity. He had been looking forward to an English pint, even if only to remind himself how much better the beer was in Bavaria.

"No trouble, May," Mugleston said. "Just a drink with our heroes." He grabbed a pint and took a deep swig before wiping his mouth with the back of one dirty hand. "Pay the woman," he said.

"These are on the house, Johnny."

"Rubbish, May. Johnny here can afford it, can't you? So go on then. Eight pints."

"And a rum and lime," the first girl added brightly.

The navigator did not move, and Stahl felt a sudden surge of admiration. The young man really did not like bullies. A truly impressive individual. If only he had known more men like Johnny Grant.

"I will get these, May," Stahl said. Familiar sensations flooded into his limbs. He welcomed them. Right now, he needed them. Needed the reminder that he still lived. He held up a thumb and one finger, then let the hand drop back in front of his chest. "Two pints, anyway. The little ones can pay their own way."

Now, at last, the room fell truly silent.

A couple of the farmers, the ones least blinded by drink, backed off. Not physically, but Stahl saw the retreat in their eyes, like a partial release of air from an overfilled balloon. The girls, too. Whatever they thought was happening, it had just stopped being fun for them.

The other men, less so.

"That's not very friendly, mate," Mugleston said. "All we wanted was to have a drink with you." He looked down at the half-finished pint in his hand.

This close, Stahl smelt the beer on his breath. Far more than one pint. He saw the telltale signs of tension in the farmer's body, the little glimpses of the mental script that the man was following, preparing himself, the same script that had roamed his stupid, overconfident brain since the moment Grant had opened the front door.

If he had been feeling more generous, Stahl might have thanked him. Images of Hildesheim fled his mind, driven out by the now. Flossenbürg. Paris. London. Vienna. The teenage soldiers on the Swiss border. All faded to nothing.

But Stahl wasn't feeling generous.

"Pay for my drink." Mugleston raised the pint glass to his lips. "Or I'll kick your fucking teeth out."

Chapter Twenty-Five

Durban felt a touch of surprise when he didn't find Stahl in the bar. It seemed like a good night to get drunk, but for now, he and Lane kept themselves to a single gin and tonic before resuming their search.

The German wasn't in his bedroom or the Mess Hall, either. Durban stuck his head through the doorway to the snooker room next, where Kittens and his navigator were inexpertly playing billiards. "Have either of you seen Stahl?"

"No, sir," Kittens said. "Not for at least an hour."

"Where? Here?"

"The Mess Hall. He was with Johnny."

"Johnny Grant?"

"Yes, sir. I think they were planning to go for a drive."

Durban frowned. "Ok. Thanks. That's odd," he said to Lane. "Grant doesn't even have a car. Follow me." He walked into the office of the Mess steward, apologised for the intrusion, lifted the telephone and dialled the guardroom.

"Hello, it's Wing Commander Durban. Has anyone left the base tonight?"

"Not since yourself, sir." He didn't recognise the voice, just another of the many corporals who checked his ID periodically.

"What?"

"Wait one," the corporal said. "I have the log here, sir. Eighteen-fifteen. Silver Alvis, driver in civilian clothing, Black officer in passenger seat."

"Why didn't you stop them? I gave orders no one was to be allowed to leave the base."

179

"We thought it was you and Grant, sir."

"Well, you thought wrong," Durban snapped. Hanging up, he looked at his watch. "They could be halfway to London by now."

"I doubt it," Lane said, her voice somewhere between soothing concern and wry amusement. "Johnny is a smart boy."

"It's not him I'm worried about."

"Hello, sir!" Flight Lieutenant Wright came striding down the corridor. "I've been looking all over for you."

"Not now, Bony," Durban said. "I'm a little busy."

"Sorry, sir. There is a woman on the telephone for you. She says it's urgent."

Durban stopped with his hand in the air, frozen in the act of brushing Bony away. He only knew one woman who might call him at Charney Breach, and she stood next to him. "Where?"

"My office, sir."

Almost at a sprint, Durban ran to the phone, lifted it, and listened in silence, feeling the blood draining from his face.

"I'll be right there." He dropped the phone. "Bony, get the SWO. Quickly."

"Andy?" Any amusement had gone from Lane's voice now. "What is it?"

"That was the landlady from the pub in Staverton," he said. "Stahl and Grant have been in a fight."

"My God. Are they ok?"

Durban nodded. "But others aren't. The police are on their way."

"If they arrest Stahl..."

"We need to get there before they do. And Stahl stole my car."

"We'll take mine. But I need to make a phone call first."

She began dialling, while another clatter of shoes announced the return of Bony Wright with the Station Warrant Officer.

"Thanks for coming, Mister Davis," Durban greeted him. "Who have you got sitting around who is good in a fight?"

"Other than me, sir?" WO Graham Davis didn't seem perturbed at all by the question. Shorter than Durban but heavier, with the build of an English bulldog and the voice of an executioner, he had a reputation for being a lovely man when he wasn't ruling by fear. "Let's see. Scouse Harbon is Duty NCO at the front gate. He's never found a face he didn't want to punch."

"Perfect. Call him and tell him to be ready. We'll pick him up in two minutes."

"Right you are, sir."

Durban smiled, despite the seething anger and growing horror that churned his guts. "Don't you even want to know where we're going?"

"I presume you'll tell me when we get there, sir."

"I couldn't get hold of Major Anders," Lane said, emerging from the office with her car keys in hand. "I left a message."

"He wouldn't get here in time, anyway," Durban said. "Are you happy to drive?"

She was more than happy to drive, he soon realised. She was far better at it than him. Her Humber wasn't a fast car, especially with the two heavies looming silently in the back seat, and its skinny wheels squealed in protest at every corner. Nevertheless, despite the darkness and the narrow lanes, it seemed only a few minutes before they screeched to a halt outside the King's Ransom.

Durban threw open his door. "We're too late."

Two police cars, their lights flashing, stood outside the entrance. A crowd had gathered outside, perhaps twenty strong. One constable was pacing in front of them, warning them to stay back, but it seemed a wasted effort to Durban. No one looked like they wanted to go inside. Instead, they stared transfixed at the doorway as if afraid of what might come out. Three more constables stood near to the door itself, one of them holding a bloody handkerchief to his nose, another breathing hoarsely with a hand clutching his ribs.

Nearby, trying to comfort two girls with tear-streaked faces, stood the navigator.

"Grant!" Durban pushed his way through the crowd, the others following. "What the hell is going on?"

"He knocked out Phil," one girl shrieked, fresh tears coursing down her face.

"Not me, sir," Grant said quickly. "Stahl."

Lane reached out to touch Grant's cheek, then pulled her hand back, looking at her fingertips. "You've got blood on you."

"It's not mine," Grant said. "Some local boys were causing trouble. Telling us to buy them drinks, poking fun at us. One started making threats."

"That's not how it happened," the girl whimpered.

"Yes, it is," her friend said. "Go on, Johnny."

"I don't know what happened, sir," Grant continued. "I mean, it was all so quick. Before I knew it, the first lad was on the floor spitting out teeth and broken glass. Then a couple of his mates had a go at Stahl. He was just so fast. It was like watching a ground lizard. I couldn't keep up. I punched one—"

"Best you keep that to yourself, sir," the SWO interjected.

"—but only because he took a swing at me first. By then, the others were all down and hurt. I told Stahl we should run, but he said he wasn't going anywhere, and he had the car keys." He froze. "We took your car, sir."

"I noticed," Durban said between gritted teeth. "We'll be having a long talk about that later. Did he kill anyone?"

Grant shook his head. "I don't think so. They are all still in there. If you listen carefully, you can hear them groaning. He wouldn't let the doctor near them, though. When the police arrived, he attacked them, too. That's when I thought I should probably come outside and wait for you."

"You should have done that before he punched the first man," Durban said.

"Glassed," the second girl corrected him. "He glassed him. Shoved his pint glass into his face. Made a horrible mess, didn't it?"

The first girl wailed.

"Enough," Durban said. "Get over there, Grant. Keep an eye on the young ladies for me and stay out of trouble. I'm going to speak to Stahl."

"Yes, sir. Come on, girls." He walked away, one arm around each set of thin shoulders.

Scouse Harbon, balding and wearing glasses that looked like he had repaired them a dozen times, started unbuttoning his jacket. Durban motioned him to stop. "Stay out here. You too, Mister Davis. If I need you, I'll call you." Checking on the policemen, who made no effort to talk him out of his plan, he picked his way to the front doors. He felt someone close behind him. "You too, Sarah."

"You're not my boss, Andy," she said.

"I'm asking you to stay out here. Please."

After a long pause, she nodded. "But if you start screaming, I'm coming in."

"I should hope so." He winked at her and stepped over the threshold.

The smell hit him first. Spilled beer, and the coppery tang of blood. A man lay on the floor at his feet, whimpering. His face was a ravaged mess below the nose, his head lolling back in a puddle of blood and scattered white pieces that could only be fragments of teeth. Each breath sent little gobbets of pink spit bubbling down his ruined cheeks.

A woman stood behind the counter. Grey-haired. Regarding him with cool detachment. "I suppose you're the new CO of 465 Squadron, then?"

"That's right. You must be May. You should step outside with the others."

"No one makes me leave my pub, Wing Commander. Especially not your friend there."

Durban nodded. He looked across the prostrate figures, some still, some groaning, to the man who sat against the back wall, his hands closed in front of him in some blood-stained mockery of a prayer. "Hello, Stahl."

"Your police are unarmed, Andrew Durban," he said. His shirt hung loose, ripped in two places, smeared with blood. A cut glistened below his right eye. His left was rapidly swelling shut. But the eyes themselves looked straight past Durban, at the men on the floor.

"There are more on the way," Durban said. "Want to tell me what happened?"

"Why are they not armed? The German police are. The French police are. Why not yours?"

"Our police don't really enjoy shooting people," Durban said. "Personally, I approve of that."

"German police would have shot me the moment they saw what I had done," Stahl said, his voice barely audible above the pained, wet coughs coming from the pub floor.

"Is that what you want, Stahl?"

No reply.

Durban stepped over a man lying spreadeagled on the floor, kneeling to check the man's throat. A pulse. Out cold, but alive. "What about *Götterdämmerung*?"

"What?"

"Let's assume you find a constable willing to shoot you. Or May does it herself. I wouldn't blame her, by the way. What then? How do we stop it?"

Stahl sniffed and dabbed at the blood under his eye. "Miss Lane will find a way."

"What if she doesn't?"

"What does it matter, Durban? I am going to prison tonight. Maybe for a long time."

"Then I'll come and visit you," Durban said. "Not because I like you. Because we need you."

"You do not know what I have done."

Durban laughed and looked around the room. "I think it's clear enough, don't you?"

"Not this," Stahl spat. "This is nothing. A few idiots. They will heal. I will not. Even Miss Lane does not know the depth of blood that drowns me."

"What's the German for melodrama, Stahl? Look, it's really very simple. You can come with me and we'll work this out somehow. Or you can stay here feeling sorry for yourself and let *Götterdämmerung* go ahead, and spend the rest of your miserable life whining about that, too. What's it to be?"

Stahl moved. Fast. One moment he was sitting, the next he was a foot in front of Durban, eyes burning with fury. Well, Durban thought, his body tensing in expectation of the blow that had to be coming, leaving Scouse and Davis outside had seemed like such a good idea.

"Go easy on Grant," Stahl said. "It is not his fault. He is a good man."

Durban swallowed. Stahl came no closer. Just stared. "Yes, he is."

"You, I am not so sure." The German's mouth twitched, and then he sighed. "Let us go, then."

Outside, Lane was waiting for them, ignoring the German as she threw her arms around Durban, hugging him quickly before stepping straight back. A tremor ran through the crowd at the sight of Stahl, but no one dared to say a word until a trembling constable had cuffed him. Even then, the threats of retribution rang hollow, and the crowd quickly dissipated, many following the local doctor inside to help the injured. As yet another police car raced into the square, Grant untangled himself from the pawing hands of the two girls and ran over to Stahl. "Are you hurt?"

"I am fine, Johnny," Stahl said. "Sorry I lied to you."

"It wasn't all lies." Grant shrugged. "You do speak English well." With a sad sigh, he stepped back out of the way to let the police and their captive through.

"You men, stop there," a voice called. From the newly arrived police car, a man stepped out. Durban didn't know police uniforms well, but he knew enough to see this was a very senior officer. "Is anyone dead?"

"No, sir," one of the policemen said. "A lot of hurt people, though."

"Never mind that. Is there a woman here named Sarah Lane?"

"Here, Chief Inspector," Lane said.

"Chaps, you might as well unlock his handcuffs," the officer said. "Well? Hurry," he snapped as they hesitated. "It appears that you have important friends, Miss Lane. Twenty minutes ago, I received a telephone call at my home. I won't say who it was from, but calls don't come from much higher save Buckingham Palace. It appears I am to release your friend, at least for now, on the questionable provision that he remains at RAF Charney Breach. Of course, I asked why." A sickly expression spread across his face. "They did not appreciate my question. Wing Commander Durban?"

"Yes?"

"I know where to find him when his day in court becomes due. Until then, I release this man into your custody. I recommend you do a better job of controlling him than you have so far."

Chapter Twenty-Six

Norfolk, 23 March

Stahl felt cold water rush over his hands, knowing that water alone could never remove the blood they bore.

The evidence of the evening's edification ran away down the sink easy enough, of course. It had barely had time to dry before Durban rushed him back to camp, a passenger in the Alvis this time rather than the driver, not a word exchanged as they raced along the country lanes. Stahl scrubbed between his fingers, wincing only slightly as he found a bloody gouge in the second knuckle of his right hand. With a brush of his left thumb, he dislodged a small sliver of tooth and watched it spin away into the drain.

That was his only real mistake, he thought. He should never have punched the third farmer in the mouth, but the man had rushed him before he had properly dealt with the second. Other than that, he had been as professional and thorough as always. There was satisfaction in that. The most troublesome part had been leaving them alive.

Two mistakes, he corrected himself. The second had been his failure to remember that British police did not carry firearms. Such a shame that Anders had not been there. The Dane would not have hesitated. He never did.

Drying his hands, he walked out into the corridor. Durban was waiting. Sarah Lane stood a few paces away, one hand on the door that led out of the HQ.

"My office," Durban said. "Now. I've sent the others away."

"I'll leave you to it, Andy," Lane said. "We'll talk tomorrow."

"Miss Lane?"

She stopped, the door ajar, staring at him.

"I would prefer that you stayed," Stahl said.

He knew her look. He'd seen it a thousand times, infinitely colder than the breeze that raced in from the night through the half-opened door.

Haunted. Hunted. But above all, that burning desire to kill him.

"Please," he said.

She looked at Durban and let the door slam shut at his nod.

There were only two chairs in Durban's office. The Wing Commander gave one to Lane and took the other himself, motioning Stahl to stand in front of them. Instead, Stahl rested his back against the cold wall. Keeping the threat to the front of him as always. The war had changed everything else, but not that.

"Talk," Durban said.

Stahl looked at them.

He could stay silent, he knew.

British Intelligence needed him. The intervention of that senior police officer to have him released was just the latest proof. Durban had earned some respect from him – he was smart and brave, and his men admired him – but he was ultimately just a tool to them, a delivery boy for weapons on target. He had no serious authority. Lane had some influence, but Dennison had made it clear that for all her proven competence, her reputation was suspect. She was a foreigner, a Jew no less, more obsessed with trying to locate her missing agents than doing the proper thing and sweeping SOE's mess under the carpet. Stahl disagreed. A few more people like Lane in positions of power and the war might have already been over. Still, it changed little. She could do nothing more damaging than hate him.

Stahl saw the look she exchanged with Durban. The faint sigh.

The shake of the head. As if his silence was all they had expected.

No. He didn't have to tell them anything.

But he wanted to.

"I was sixteen years old when I joined the Nazi Party," he said. He saw the surprise on Durban's face. Lane's face gave away nothing. "I was jobless, I was angry, like so many others. My father served on the Western Front at the Somme and Ypres. He raised me to believe we had never lost the war, that communists and Jews betrayed us. The economy lay in ruins while the Weimar socialists sat in Berlin and grew fat. Germany was dead around us, and the French and British feasted on the meat."

He could still remember the growling of his belly when his mother came home from the shops empty-handed. As a child then, he couldn't understand how hyper-inflation had doubled the price of a loaf of bread in the time it took her to get there, outstripping their meagre budget. He knew only hunger. He could never forget the look on his father's face, stripped of pride while he tried to sell his gallantry medals. There were no buyers, of course. Germany had too many men with medals, too few with money.

"I remember the first time I heard Hitler speak. I stood in a crowd with my father and ten thousand others, but it was like he was speaking directly to me. He had all the answers. More than that, he had questions. Was I with him? Was I with Germany? And I was. Completely. Hitler was Germany."

His eyes never leaving Stahl's face, Durban opened his desk drawer and drew out two glasses. A moment's hesitation, and he took a third, then reached for a bottle of whisky.

"I joined the SS in 1932. Nineteen years old. A foot soldier. When we took power, I cheered with my friends. I was a leader, the one who shouted the loudest, who pushed the boundaries even when my fellow SS hesitated. Not because I thought I

189

would gain from it, but because I believed it. Others saw, and they approved. I rose quickly. I was a street thug, but I was cunning. First, they transferred me to the SD. Counterintelligence. Then they made me an officer in time to lead men into Austria for the Anschluss." He sighed. "The day cancer took my father, three weeks before my unit marched into Poland, his last words were Heil Hitler, and I am proud of you, Jan."

Wordlessly, Durban rose and brought him a glass of whisky. Stahl gave only a nod of thanks, his mouth suddenly dry. The adoration in his father's eyes, even as the light faded for the last time. Otto Stahl had not died an evil man. He had only wanted what was best for his family, which meant turning a blind eye even when the crimes became so clear that nothing could obscure them. When they even stopped trying to hide them.

Would his father have changed if he had lived long enough to know what Stahl knew, to learn the truth about Dachau and Auschwitz and the Einsatzgruppen?

He took a sip of the whisky. It burned on his lips, but he tasted nothing but ash.

"In the SS," he croaked, "reputation is everything. Mine brought me to the attention of Heydrich, not long after the fall of Warsaw."

Durban frowned. "Why do I know that name?"

"SS-Obergruppenführer Reinhard Heydrich," Lane said. "SS-3, behind only Himmler and Hitler."

Stahl nodded. "I could do two things better than anyone. I could find traitors, and I could kill them. Heydrich saw my potential right away. I killed my first man for him precisely five years ago."

A vehicle drove past outside the office's shuttered windows. For an instant, Stahl thought it was thunder, the same thunder that had rippled across the Berlin sky that night. Stahl had uncovered that a Nazi Party official had been passing internal party memos to the British SIS. The traitor was not senior, but the evidence against the man was weak and a trial would be embarrassing. Heydrich did not tolerate embarrassment. Stahl had stalked his prey on the walk from his office, following the man along the banks of the Spree, closing the gap. Two hundred metres from the Hauptbahnhof where the official's train home awaited, Stahl saw his chance. No pedestrians, the rain and darkness blocking the view of the traffic from the Weidendammer Bridge.

It needed one blow, just one, the dagger sliding into the fleshy folds of the neck, sawing back and forth, opening the carotid. He held the choking man down with his knee while he stole his wallet, took the watch from the wrist while the hand pawed weakly at him. Then a quick shove to send the dying man into the river. Stahl had heard him thrash in the rain-lashed water, then nothing.

"It took me ten seconds," he told Durban. "The Berlin police investigated, but within two days they decreed it a street robbery. After that, I was Heydrich's favourite. I cannot tell you how many I killed for him." It was his first lie since he had started his story. He could count every single one. "Not just traitors. Foreign agents, dissidents who had gone overseas to rally support against Germany, industrialists who had wealth and influence but did not show the proper respect to the SS. Some were in Germany, but not all. Three in London. One in Madrid. Two in Lisbon. Wherever Heydrich sent me. His word was law, but I never questioned an order. Not once. Until the day he sent me to spy on Canaris."

Once again, the two listeners exchanged a look, and Stahl knew that the name Canaris meant something to them. They had been talking about him, he realised. He sniffed, irritated by their speculation. This was his story. They knew nothing of him. They knew nothing of Canaris.

"Heydrich hated how people referred to the Admiral as 'Germany's spymaster'." Stahl could still remember Heydrich's pouting, more dangerous than any other man's rage. "He hated that the Abwehr led as the premier intelligence agency, instead of his SD. But Canaris had been his friend once. For all his willingness to humiliate the Abwehr, he was reluctant to believe me when I told him my suspicion that Canaris was working with the Allies against Hitler. He refused to sanction an assassination, fearing for his own career if his part became known. Instead, he had me transferred as a liaison officer to Abwehr HQ. My cover role was to lead joint SD-Abwehr investigations as a representative of the SD. My true task was to find the proof that would allow Heydrich to crush his rival. I began my new role in September 1941. A few weeks later, Himmler promoted Heydrich and sent him to Prague as Acting Reichsprotektor of Bohemia and Moravia, but he and I communicated secretly until the day SOE killed him."

Durban raised an eyebrow. "Sarah?"

"It wasn't my operation." The words were the first she had spoken since they had entered the office. From her face, she clearly would have preferred to remain silent.

"You seem upset," Durban said. "If he was the number three in the SS, wasn't this a major success?"

Tight-lipped, looking straight ahead, she sipped her whisky.

"Miss Lane does not celebrate," Stahl said, "because after SOE's people killed Heydrich, his people killed over a thousand Czechs in reprisals. Even after death, Heydrich remained a murderer."

"And you worked for him," Lane snapped.

"I did." Exhaustion washed over Stahl. At last, he felt the desire to sit down, and wished there was a third chair. His legs felt weak. Hollow, like the muscles had wasted from within. He pressed himself further back, hoping the wall could support the unnatural weight that hung suspended over his entire body. "For a year, I tried to find the evidence against Canaris. He gave away nothing. The second year, he shared things with me, but not the evidence I needed. I read accounts of the concentration camps, the exterminations in the East, the corruption at the heart of the Nazi Party itself. Canaris forced nothing on me; he just left the information where I could find it. I followed his trail of breadcrumbs, and it led me to the truth."

His words died on his lips. The room shuddered and spun. He screwed his eyes shut and let the nausea wash over him, let it fade before opening his eyes and motioning the concerned Durban back to his seat.

"We can do this tomorrow," Durban said. "If you need to rest—"

"I need to talk. Please, sit. And listen." He knew he was speaking quicker now. It wasn't conscious. The words themselves wanted to be heard. "The day I read of the Wannsee Conference was the day my belief in Hitler died. Heydrich chaired it himself. Educated men, family men who knew the law and the Bible and philosophy, calmly discussing how to exterminate an entire race. This wasn't about the safety of the German people or raising the nation to glory after the darkness of the Weimar years. We had become the darkness. Canaris saw the change in me before I did. I was no longer the SD's man spying on Canaris. I was the Admiral's man in the SD."

Durban whistled. "When was this?"

"It took some time to know for sure. But by early 1943, we both knew it."

"You lie to yourself." Lane stood, the blood rushing to her cheeks. "You hunted my people long after that. Hunted me. You would have killed me, the way you killed them."

"You are right, Miss Lane. About almost everything. Why do you think I continued to kill your people, even after Canaris turned me against the Nazis?"

193

"Because you're a psychopath."

"No. Never that. I took pride in a job well done, but never pleasure. Answer me this. Would not the correct move have been to capture your agents? Question them? Find out what they knew, even turn them against you to capture more? Play SOE the way Josef Kieffer did 'F' Section in France? Yet, I didn't. I shot them. A single bullet in the head. Why?"

"Because Canaris knew their names." Durban looked sick. "He knew which agents were blown."

"*Genau*," Stahl shouted, stabbing his finger at the Wing Commander, watching how they both blinked in surprise at his sudden flaring anger. "Precisely." He forced his voice back under control. "Every time an SOE or SIS agent gave themselves away or was betrayed, Canaris found out. I was not the only one he had brought to his cause. He had contacts in the SS, the Gestapo, even the French police. As soon as suspicion descended on a British agent, or worse still one of his own, Canaris sent for me. Gave me everything I needed to make it seem like I had exposed them, and to get to them first. Once I did, I finished them. Cleanly."

"You murdered them," Lane said. "Captured, they still had a chance. They could have lived."

Stahl chuckled, forcing every ounce of his scorn and mockery into the sound, not caring that it wasn't aimed at her at all. "Now who is lying to themselves? Let me tell you what we both know. Sometimes I was too late, and the Nazis had already captured them. A few lucky ones escaped, or died trying to. The rest they took, tortured, and sent to the extermination camps. Most are already dead. Less than one in ten will survive the war. Some died knowing that, in their agonies, they had betrayed others to the same fate. I did not allow that. I pulled the trigger that set them free, and I gave my soul so that theirs might rest."

"How poetic," Lane sneered. "And now you're here."

"And now I'm here. Because Canaris gave me one last mission. He might be dead already. I hope to one day see his face again, but I know I shall not. His parting task for me was not to arrange his rescue, or even to grant him the clean death the Nazis will surely not. It was to destroy *Götterdämmerung* before I take my place in Hell."

His legs finally gave way beneath him, and he slid down to the floor until he sat on the carpet with the half-finished whisky in his hand, forgotten.

"I think," Durban said weakly, "that's enough for tonight." He stood, taking Lane's empty glass from her. She didn't seem to notice. Stahl felt her eyes locked on him the whole time. Durban ran his hand through his hair as he stood in the centre of the room, looking at the desk, then the carpet, then Stahl's slumped form. Finally, with a sigh, he walked over and reached for the glass in Stahl's hand.

"Wait," Stahl said. He had told them nearly everything, but this last one, he wished he could keep to himself. Not because it would upset them, but because saying it out loud meant accepting it as real. He snatched his glass back from Durban's outstretched fingers and downed the contents in a single hit.

"I said my family was proud of me. Mostly, they were. One was not. My sister. As children, we were close. Inseparable. It took the Nazis to drive us apart. I know she tried. Tried to fool herself that Hitler was a good man, that the things the Nazis did were justified, the same way we fooled ourselves. She couldn't do it. Three months after my father died, she left. No note. Nothing. All I had left was this."

He opened his wallet, passed the photograph inside to Durban.

"She's very beautiful," Durban said.

"Of course, for a man like me, finding her was easy. I located her when she moved north, kept track of her when she met her

195

husband, when they had their two wonderful girls. My nieces. I never had the courage to knock on her door, but part of me always hoped that I would get to meet them all one day when the war ended. That I could explain everything. Once I even went to the charming little house where she lived and watched her play with the girls in the local park. But they didn't see me."

He raised the glass to his lips, found it empty, and let it fall from his fingers.

"That house was in Hildesheim." The words echoed in his ears, the cold metal rattle of steel and finality. "That is the price paid to stop *Götterdämmerung*. Now, there is only one last bill to settle." The words faded to nothing on his lips, and he let his eyes close and his head fall back.

Silence descended, cold and complete, broken only by the clatter of Lane's footsteps and the slam of the door in her wake.

Chapter Twenty-Seven

Above Germany, 30 March

A strange thing, the moon.

Waxing gibbous, only two days from its full light, it was both ally and enemy. The glow, powerful enough to cast faint shadows from the Mosquito's wings onto patches of cirrus cloud, aided both navigation and targeting, though Durban knew from bitter experience that nothing could make either task easy.

He scanned the sky behind them for what seemed the thousandth time, his neck aching from the effort of constantly twisting in his seat. Certainly, the moon brought a serene beauty to the night sky and a near-magical sheen to the darkened fields and towns of northern Germany twenty-six thousand feet beneath their wings. And yet he would trade it for a dark night in an instant. Difficult enough already to avoid the radars of the Luftwaffe's night fighters, without giving them the extra help of a silhouette or a shimmer of reflected light on canopy or props.

At least it would help them pick out the barracks, and the six Dorniers in their protective revetments.

"Sir?"

Grant looked at him, and Durban realised he must have spoken aloud. "Nothing. Keep doing your checks."

Another bad sign. He was distracted. Poetic musings on the beauty of the night and mumbled vagaries about the target, when his focus needed to be solely on getting them there. They had been lucky so far. No flak. No sign of night fighters either, possibly because the forty-three Mosquitoes hitting Berlin as a diversion had drawn the defenders further east, or because at their height and speed the Luftwaffe pilots knew better than to waste their time. Even now, with the new jet fighters making their presence known, an undamaged Mosquito at altitude was almost impervious to German defences.

That, of course, would change when they descended for their attack on the airfield. Focus would be even more important then. Still, at least for the first time in days, he wasn't thinking about Sarah Lane.

"Time to target?"

"Four minutes," Grant said. Confident. Secure in his ability and his understanding of the map spread out on his thigh in the moonlight. Durban gave him a nod of approval, but the young man didn't see it, his gaze already returning to the gloom behind them. The moment he'd read his training report, Durban had believed that Grant had the talent; now, it seemed, the navigator believed it too.

"They are still with us," Grant added.

"I should bloody hope so." He hadn't been able to see them all, of course. Even the brightest moon couldn't hope to extend visibility that far. With every check, though, he caught comforting glimpses of the shapes of other Mosquitoes, their sleek contours sometimes tarnished by unfamiliar dark shapes. Half, including Durban's own aircraft, carried the RP-3 rockets. Three-inch in diameter, four under each wing, each with a sixty-pound explosive warhead. The rest carried a mixture of bombs and napalm. As he'd signalled to Sarah, he wanted options for every eventuality.

That's enough, he told himself. She had done her job. Three times she had contacted the squadron since the night she stormed out of his office, leaving the broken Stahl sitting on his carpet. Three signals, in writing, each dispassionate. Business-like. The way it should be.

Her last message gave the order to attack. Nothing more said.

Nothing more needed.

"One minute," Grant intoned.

Durban moved his gloved thumb and rested it on the R/T transmit switch. The strict radio silence observed so far meant he had heard no voice in his ears since taking off, save his own and Grant's occasional updates on the intercom. Nothing but the steady drone of the Merlin engines and the whisper of thin air passing by the cockpit.

"Thirty seconds."

He pressed the switch. "Bolo," he said, the prearranged codeword, just once. Then he rolled the Mosquito into a fast, spiralling dive, knowing that above and behind, the others would follow.

The profile had been Grant's idea. The sudden change in altitude would make it difficult for the network of German air defence radars and fighter control stations to keep a good track of them, if the defences had tracked them at all. Either way, the defenders would expect them to continue to Berlin or dogleg right to Erfurt, the second diversionary target. They wouldn't have planned for the possibility of a full squadron night attack on an obscure airfield in Northern Saxony that the Mosquitoes had already bypassed.

That was the theory, anyway.

Twenty-thousand feet. Durban felt the vibrations of the airframe through the controls, the Mosquito signalling its displeasure. Grant shot him a questioning look. Keeping one hand on the control column, he eased back slightly on the throttle with the other. "Don't want those rockets ripped off our wings, do we?"

"Best not, sir."

Fifteen-thousand feet. A Mosquito passed across the face of the moon, stark black against the glowing radiance. A ready victim for anyone who was looking up. If they could catch it.

Ten thousand.

"Cloud over the target," Grant said.

"I see it. Bugger."

For three hundred miles, the cloud had been scattered or absent. Now, looking west as they continued their rapid descent, Durban saw a smudge at ten miles, lingering over Uelzen at three thousand feet. Any relief that they would not be silhouetted against the moon lasted less than a second. Without the moonlight, the camouflaged blobs of the target revetments would be horribly difficult to spot, especially from a Mosquito flying at nearly four-hundred miles an hour only a few hundred feet from the ground.

There was a plan for dealing with cloud. He just didn't much care for it.

"Shall I open the bomb doors?" From Grant's tone, he wasn't best pleased either.

"No sense waiting, I suppose." He levelled out at a thousand feet. The others would keep going lower, but they wouldn't attack until he had paved the way. Ahead, the looming cloud bank seemed to cast a wall of deeper darkness below it, right over the target. The expanse of the airfield just stood out from the surrounding trees, the flat ground bisected by the unnatural straight line formed by the runway.

The aircraft twitched as the bomb doors dropped open.

Durban reached for the bomb selection switch. He ignored the gunsight and his payload of rockets. Their time would come.

No flak yet. That, too, would be coming. All too soon.

He pulled back and pressed the bomb release. "Flare gone."

For a second only, darkness endured. Then the night exploded with light far beyond the gentle glow of the moon.

Pathfinders called it *Sky Marking*. The name was well-chosen. Tumbling from the aircraft before being arrested by the opening parachute, the Target Indication flare burst into life. A new sun in the sky, it stripped the airfield of concealing shadows with the ferocious glow of two hundred and fifty thousand candlepower. Beneath them, the barracks, the runway, the perimeter fence, and the critical horseshoe shapes of the revetments were all laid bare in an instant. Durban saw it all.

But the flare worked both ways.

Grant yelled a warning. Unnecessary. Durban already had the bomb doors closed and the Mosquito racing for the deck.

Not quick enough.

The gunners were good. Even taken by surprise, squinting up into the sudden artificial daylight, they still picked him out in seconds. The first muzzle flashes seemed to appear at once. Four, five, maybe more 20mm guns. All sharing one target. No obvious glow of tracers – the flare saw to that – but Durban didn't need to see them to know they were there.

The aircraft rocked as black smoke flowered either side of them. A crack of splintering wood echoed in the tight confines of the cockpit.

Down, down, further down, close enough that the grasping branches of the trees at the perimeter of the airfield seemed ready to pluck them from the air. More rounds passed overhead, the Mosquito now too low and too distant for at least some of the anti-aircraft gun emplacements to track.

"I think you pissed them off, sir," Grant said.

"They will be even more upset in a minute."

On the distant side of the brightly lit airfield, the next Mosquito raced in. Full throttle. Too fast. The crew was lucky that the gunners, probably expecting only a single night intruder, still focused on Durban. The pilot, whoever he was, didn't take full advantage. Trailing smoke in their wake, eight rockets streaked from beneath his wings, sending lumps of dirt and grass wheeling into the air fifty or more yards short of the nearest revetment.

"Colt Leader to all callsigns, pick your targets properly," Durban snapped into his radio. "Take your time, use your sights and correct for the trajectory drop-off."

"Sorry, Colt Leader." A Welsh accent.

"Get yourself home, Chapple," Durban said as the now spent Mosquito raced into the darkness beyond the descending flare's radiance. "Everyone else, like we practiced."

The next Mosquito was already inbound. Ignoring the fingers of tracers heading its way, the pilot kept the aircraft perfectly level. Two rockets shot from under the wings. Two seconds to judge the fall, and then six more. The aircraft turned slightly, both to confuse the flak and to avoid the detonations of its own ordnance as five rockets slammed into the protective sandbags and earth around the aircraft. The sixth did the damage.

"Like that?"

"Yes. Thank you, Barto." Durban glanced at his watch. Only thirty seconds since the flare had ignited, but already the circle of radiance was shrinking rapidly. The 4.5-inch Skymarker burned for up to two minutes, but it wasn't burn time that was the problem here but its steady descent, the parachute unable to arrest it sufficiently.

Despite the now alert gunners and the sheer volume of cannon shells zipping through the sky above the airfield, the third and fourth Mosquito somehow made their runs unscathed. Sadly, their targets were similarly blessed. The rockets either missed or exploded uselessly against the revetments, their protective bulk taller and thicker than expected. Durban cursed. "All rocket armed callsigns, focus on the barracks. Kittens, put your napalm on the building once the rockets have done their work. Everyone else, focus on the aircraft. Torch them."

"Roger," Kittens replied curtly.

"One thousand feet is too low," Durban told Grant, as the

encroaching darkness overtook the barracks building before being briefly repelled by the flash of impacting rockets. "We'll need to drop the next flare higher."

Grant's eyes bulged behind his goggles. "The next one?"

Pulling the Mosquito into a climb, Durban looked across the airfield. Smoke billowed from the barracks building. Flames glowed in the upper windows. Still, the damage was negligible. Worse still, only one of the six Dorniers had been destroyed so far. Lane had made it clear that they would only get one shot at this. If they didn't get all the targets tonight, the rest would be gone by dawn. Maybe taking the whole of *Götterdämmerung* with them. That could not be tolerated.

"This isn't a good idea, sir," Grant said as they passed one thousand feet.

"Neither was volunteering for the RAF. But you're here now. Might as well enjoy it."

A whoosh and a crump, audible even over the screaming engines, drowned out Grant's response. A second Dornier disappeared, enveloped in an incandescent frenzy of petrol and glue. This time, Durban caught only the briefest impression of the Mosquito responsible before it disappeared into the night, pursued by a swarm of tracer and leaving a thin tendril of smoke in its wake.

The flare settled on the ground. It didn't sputter and die immediately. He'd seen Lancasters drop on far dimmer markers. But for precision strike, it was all but useless now. "All callsigns hold and wait for the next flare." Next to him, he saw Grant twitch in his seat. He couldn't blame him. They were at two thousand feet over a heavily defended and very alert airfield, and Grant's pilot and commander had just ordered away any other aircraft that might have drawn some fire away from them.

The navigator was right. This wasn't a good idea.

Durban watched the altimeter hit two thousand feet, opened the bomb doors himself, pushed aside another sudden thought of Lane, and released the second flare.

The guns turned on him instantly, but this time he didn't rush into the darkness. The view afforded by the igniting flare revealed the exposed topside of a Dornier. An easier shot in a dive than low and level. Far more dangerous, too, but the time for such considerations had long passed. He clicked the rocket salvo switch to *on*. "Resume attack," he barked into the radio, then threw the Mosquito into a sixty-degree dive.

The controls writhed in his hands. The world raced towards them. He felt the rockets strain against their mounts, on the verge of being ripped away in the slipstream and probably taking the wings with them, but then his finger was on the firing stud and the rockets were gone and streaming ahead of them. All eight at once. No ranging shot. No need.

He pulled back on the controls. Nothing happened, the flight surfaces barely responding.

You've left this too late, he told himself.

What a bloody stupid way to die.

The nose twitched.

He heard Grant groan. Or maybe it was the aircraft itself.

The Dornier exploded, the impact of at least three rockets sending huge chunks of fuselage cartwheeling over the collapsing walls of the shattered revetments.

The nose came up, slowly. Too slowly. Muscles screaming from the effort, he tried to wrench the controls into his chest, into his seat. The burning wreckage of the Dornier filled his vision. Beckoning.

And then it was below the nose, and the smell of burning fuel filled the cockpit, and his eyes blinked to clear the image of the flames from his sight.

"You're climbing again, sir. Keep the nose down."

204

"I can't see," Durban said. He blinked furiously. Mottled colours danced across his eyes.

"Nose down ten degrees. More. There. Hold her steady."

Durban took a deep breath. The night ahead resolved itself into darkness. His eyes watered. He had to restrain his hand from pulling off his goggles and dabbing at them. "Are you okay?"

"Fantastic, boss." Grant's grin seemed a little too wide. His eyes, wider still.

"Well played," Durban said. "Thank you. Did the flak follow us?"

"Are you joking, sir? I reckon they thought we'd crashed."

"Not this time, Johnny." He decided not to add that there was plenty of time left for that, and banked back towards the glowing sphere above the airfield.

"Aren't we heading home? We're out of rockets."

"Doesn't matter. The job needs completing."

The radio crackled into life. "Colt Leader, this is Bravo Four. Another Dornier down, but we're hit."

Durban thought he recognised the man's voice as Hartley, one of Barton's friends. The accent was Australian, the fear in each syllable universal. "Good work, Bravo Four. Can you make it home?"

"I reckon so. Might be a near-run thing, though. I think we're leaking fuel."

"Divert to a nearer airfield if you have to. Remember to broadcast and let them know you're coming. Good luck."

"You too, sir."

Durban kept them low, circling outside the flare's light but close enough to watch as another Mosquito came in fast and struck the damaged barracks with napalm. Kittens. Nothing wrong with his aim. Already leaking smoke and fire from several obvious rents in its walls, in an instant the building became a ferocious mass of flames. A funeral pyre for the specially trained pilots.

"Colt Leader to Bravo Leader, fine bowling. Do you have anyone left to strike?"

"Negative, Colt Leader. We're all done. All revetments struck."

"Sir!" Grant pointed across the airfield, away from the smoking building, towards the line of hangars away from the main strike route. "I think that's a Dornier."

It took Durban's eyes, still smarting from staring into the fires, several seconds to spot it. He knew instantly that the navigator was right. The aircraft stood alone on a concrete area outside the hangars, its distinctive shape long and spindly, almost insectoid. "Excellent spot. They must have moved it there for maintenance." He switched to the radio. "Colt Leader to all callsigns, does anyone have ordnance left? Napalm or rockets?"

No reply. Radio silence adopted once more as the Mosquitoes streamed back towards England, each alone in the moon-haunted darkness.

He looked again. In the last dying light of the flare, there was no sign of the specialised containers under the wings. The thought crossed his mind that this could be an ordinary night fighter, just a regular Luftwaffe aircraft assigned to Uelzen like dozens before it. But he couldn't take that chance.

"We'll have to take them ourselves," Durban said.

"Yes, sir," Grant intoned.

Rolling back in towards the target, Durban pushed the throttles forward. Perhaps the flak crews thought it was over. Perhaps they were reloading. It didn't matter. No one fired at them as they passed over the burning barracks. Two hundred feet below their wingtip, an amorphous figure stumbled out of the inferno, a small ambulatory flame detached from the greater mass that made it perhaps ten yards before collapsing on the ground.

That, perhaps, was the signal the gunners had been waiting for.

From all sides, tracers hurtled towards them. Durban heard a dull thud, like a leather belt slapping a drum. Grant gasped. Twenty-millimetre shells left glowing streaks in the air either side of the cockpit as he kept the Mosquito howling low over the airfield, letting the Dornier fill the gunsight before firing. Falling rounds stitched a path across the earth until they met the fuselage. Empty of fuel and stripped for engineering work, the aircraft didn't explode, but the fading light was enough for Durban to see it collapse as heavy shells shattered the undercarriage and sent sparks flying as they slammed into the port engine.

The controls bucked once more in his hands as a shell burst nearby, and then they were clear and out of range and racing westwards.

"That should do it," Durban said. "Time to plot us a good course for home, Johnny. The bastards might get that thing flying again if they had months, but they don't." Whatever the SS planned to do with *Götterdämmerung*, they would need to do it without their modified aircraft. Or their pilots, he thought with a grim half-smile of satisfaction.

With the airfield now ten miles or more behind and wreathed in darkness but for the glow of the burning barracks, Durban pulled the aircraft into a climb, then frowned as he watched the speed drop. Not a terrible reduction, but more than expected. "Power is down a touch." He glanced to his left. The port engine ran true, props blurring in the gloom. "The starboard engine may have copped a packet on that last run. Any sign of damage?" He checked the fuel gauge. Half a tank, despite their manoeuvring over the target. More than enough, and no sign of any leaks. The oil temperature and pressure indicators seemed normal. The controls still felt solid, the aircraft handling well despite the reduced climb rate, but something wasn't right.

Still no response from the navigator. He turned in irritation.

Grant was looking down at his gloved hand, tilting it first one way and then the other, eyes transfixed.

"Johnny, any sign of damage?"

A sharp intake of breath. "Sorry, sir," Grant mumbled. He turned to the side, away from Durban, to look back at the starboard engine. "It seems ok," he said after a few seconds, his head seeming to loll against the seat.

The clouds broke above them, and in the sudden moonlight, Durban saw the glistening moisture on the glove, dark against the leather. "Johnny? Are you hit?"

Grant sighed and stared at his hand again. "Yeah, boss," he breathed. "I think I am."

Keeping the aircraft climbing with one hand, Durban scanned the cockpit. No sign of any damage, no sound of air whistling through any fissure in the airframe. But there was little mistaking the dark patch spreading on the navigator's overalls, nor the ragged tears in the material of his yellow life preserver.

"How bad is it?" He regretted the question immediately.

"It doesn't feel great," Grant said. "Sorry."

"Ok, ok," Durban said. "You're going to be fine. I've seen men come back with far worse, and you'll have a nice scar to show the girls in Stav. Here's what you're going to do, Johnny. You're going to give me a course for the nearest divert airfield in the UK. Then you're going to take a field dressing from your pocket, find wherever they've pranged you, and shove that dressing in the hole."

Grant coughed. It sounded weak, but at least there was no whistle or creak from the lungs. "Bearing two-eighty," he said, without checking his map.

"Are you sure?"

"Of course," Grant said. "I'm a good navigator."

"That you are, Johnny."

They passed fifteen thousand feet, still climbing, Durban keeping the RPM as high as he dared. Grant fumbled for a field dressing and reached inside his overalls, shifting uncomfortably in his seat until he winced.

"I take it you found the spot?"

"One of them, sir. I could really use some morphine if you have it."

Durban shook his head. "Not yet. I need you to stay awake. Can you do that?"

"Is it an order, sir?"

"Yes."

"Then I can do it. But can I have a late start tomorrow, please?"

Durban smiled, despite himself. "Yes, you can. I promise." Behind the navigator, he saw an odd glow. It added the faintest halo to the young man's head. He felt a sudden chill. "Listen, Johnny, we're in a bit of a pickle here. I don't think you soaked up quite all the shrapnel. They hit the right engine. The exhaust flare shield's gone."

"Is that bad?"

"It's less than ideal. It's just a dim glow for now, but that thing is going to be a white-hot beacon soon. Every night fighter in western Europe will see it. I'd take us lower and worry about the flak instead, but I suspect you've had quite enough of flak for one night, right?"

"I just want to sleep," Grant mumbled.

"And you will. When we get home. Right now, I need you looking at your map. You knew where the main night fighter areas are, yes? Then rustle us up a route that avoids them."

Grant sniffed but sat up taller in his seat. His finger left a dark smudge on the map as he worked.

"Oh, and Johnny?" He checked behind them. Nothing there. Not even the familiar silhouette from another night, another cockpit. "Make sure your route avoids British night fighter bases too, ok?"

They flew on. The black of the night drew closer, darker still, bands of cirrus cloud obscuring the moon. Durban kept the Mosquito's path unpredictable, not letting it stay straight and level for too long. Changing course to clear the sky behind them and to take advantage of the concealment of cloud. Never straying too far from the headings that Grant gave him. At first, the navigator kept up a steady stream of instructions. With each passing minute, they became less common, the voice fading.

"We're getting near the coast," Durban warned him. "That flare shield is like a bloody flashlight now. I'm going to have to drop a little lower to hide in the cloud band over the Channel, but I need you to steer me through the main flak concentrations."

No response. He looked over. Grant slumped unmoving in his seat. The way Lampeter had.

He reached out and grabbed the navigator by the arm, hard.

"Jesus," Grant said. "That hurts. I'm here. I'm just resting."

"You were asleep. Turn your oxygen on full."

The navigator didn't move. Durban stretched across and did it for him, then nudged him again, more gently this time. Slowly, Grant's eyes focused. His eyes flickered to the map, and his hands seemed to gain new strength as he made further calculations. "Three five zero for four minutes," he said finally. "Then two nine five for twelve. That should see you straight to Charney Breach."

Durban frowned. "I told you to get us to the nearest divert. How much extra time have we taken to get home instead?"

"I don't think it will make much difference, boss," Grant said. "And you're a busy man. You need to be at work tomorrow. What happens if Sarah Lane calls and you aren't there?"

"I'm sure Squadron Officer Lane will be just fine if I'm not there, Johnny."

"She likes you."

"Turn your oxygen up further," Durban ordered. "You're getting delirious."

Grant nodded. The navigator's hand, Durban noted, barely had the strength left to work the oxygen controls, but it seemed to help. "This operation doesn't end tonight, does it, sir?"

"No, Clive," Durban said. "The job isn't done."

"Don't go without me, will you, boss?"

"We'll talk about that when you're back from the sick bay."

"You'd get lost without me."

"Ha. We'll be on the ground in fifteen minutes, and you'll be in an ambulance a minute after that. Save your strength for chatting up those nurses."

Grant fell silent for a few seconds. Durban felt the man's gaze on him.

"Sir?"

"Yes, Johnny?"

"Who is Clive?"

Durban shook his head to try to clear the fog from his mind. He hadn't realised how tired he was. Not just from tonight. From everything. "Clive Lampeter. He was my navigator before I came to 465."

"You lost him in the crash?"

"How do you know about the crash?"

Grant let his head rest back against his seat. "The boys were talking. Said you were lucky to walk away. That you should still be in the hospital."

"Rubbish." Durban checked the time and slowly pushed forward on the controls to begin their descent. Invisible through the cloud, the restless grey waters of the Channel lurked below, with the Norfolk coast tantalisingly close beyond. "I survived, didn't I?" He paused, letting his voice drop to a whisper, as if it was still possible to keep the truth concealed, like it might somehow change it. "Clive didn't."

It would hardly have mattered if he'd shouted it. Grant's eyes were closed, his mouth hanging open, his body bouncing limply as the Mosquito hit a pocket of turbulence.

"Johnny!"

Nothing.

Gripping the controls, Durban slammed the throttles all the way forward. The starboard engine whined in protest, a puff of smoke bursting from the glowing exhaust. Loyal to the end, the Mosquito surged forward, helped by a dive to gain yet more speed. A strip of scrubby beach flashed beneath him, the sand and fenlands beyond faintly visible in the first stirrings of the rising sun behind him. He was barely conscious of making the radio call to the tower at Charney Breach, warning them of his impending emergency landing, exhorting them to have an ambulance standing by. AFTERLIGHT, *Götterdämmerung*, even Sarah Lane, all faded away, until nothing remained but the urgent need to not fail Johnny Grant the way he had failed Clive Lampeter.

If it wasn't already too late.

Chapter Twenty-Eight

London, 5 April

"Hurry and take your seats, gentlemen." Lord Wolmer stared down the length of the polished tabletop, looking first at Stahl, then across the protective width of the table. The seating plan had not been an accident. "I trust, Miss Lane, that you will conduct yourself with more decorum today?"

"This is a room full of His Majesty's finest intelligence professionals, Top," Sir David Leslie said before Lane could respond. "I would recommend that you trust as little as possible."

A ripple of laughter passed around the conference room, the comment enough to even draw a half-smile from the Minister of Economic Warfare. Sir David was well liked, and the tension in the room had needed that little outlet. For six years, this mismatched group of uniformed services, foreign office, and civilian intelligence agencies had tried to put aside their own rivalries to focus on the common goal of defeating Hitler. Now, with victory seemingly a formality, all those rivalries had resurfaced in an unseemly scrabble for resources and influence in the new, post-war world.

But this war wasn't over yet.

Gradually, the amused hubbub faded. Only two men hadn't smiled. One was the civilian from the unidentified agency, his face still half concealed beneath the shadows of his hat. Lane guessed he never smiled. The other man was Stahl, his eyes dark pools beneath the sharp bone of his brow. Empty. Only the occasional blink betrayed any life in him at all.

As for Lane, she had never felt less like smiling.

Air Vice Marshal Sir Basil Embry cleared his throat. He was one of several men strategically placed between her and the German. Just in case. His dark blue uniform made Lane think of Durban, and that thought brought with it a stab of irritation. Not at Andy, of course. It wasn't his fault that memories of his face distracted her. She wished he was here now, if only so that she could have a more recent memory to replace the look of shock on his face the last time she had seen it. Over two weeks ago now. The night she had stormed out of his office.

Before Uelzen. Before a shell hit his aircraft. Before poor Grant...

At a nod from Lord Wolmer, Embry began his briefing. The raid on Uelzen had been a complete success, he told them. Photo reconnaissance had proved that the modified aircraft had been destroyed by fire. "You'll be pleased to hear, sir," the AVM wrapped up, "that all our aircraft returned to England, albeit with three badly damaged and several men wounded."

Lord Wolmer made an impatient gesture with his hand. "What about their pilots?"

"Immolated," the man in the hat said.

Embry took a few seconds as if trying to recall what that word meant, then nodded. "No survivors, my Lord."

"That's decent news at least," the Minister grumbled. "Not quite enough to make up for the other... well, we'll get to that. Miss Lane, you have an update for the group?"

"Yes, sir," she said. She adjusted the papers on the table in front of her. This time she had come prepared, wary of any further reliance on Dennison.

The Colonel hadn't even met her eyes when she had entered the room. He had merely shrunk tiredly back in his chair. Now he sat playing with his pen, until he saw her watching and hastily stuffed it in his jacket with a guilty look at Stahl.

"As you know, gentlemen," Lane began, dismissing Dennison

from her mind, "we recently traced the *Götterdämmerung* program to a laboratory just outside Königsberg, in East Prussia. It is likely that development there has been ongoing since at least the autumn of last year."

"The Soviets have got that place sewn up like a Christmas goose," the Brigadier grumbled from across the table. "They already have the rest of East Prussia under their control, and right now they have the Red Army artillery working day and night to pound Königsberg to hell."

"You mean what's left of it," Embry said. "Our heavies made a right old mess of the place back in August, too. Is the city completely cut off?"

"Completely," the Brigadier assured him.

"It's not," Lane said. "Sir."

Ignoring the outraged look on the Brigadier's face, she rose and walked to the huge, floor-to-ceiling map of Europe that dominated one side of the room. A sliver of spring morning grey snuck through the blinds on the opposite side, casting a weak shadow from her hand as she pointed. "The Russians have overrun most of the region, but the Germans have fought hard to keep this land bridge open." She ran her fingertip along the coast, down the narrow spit of land that separated the Vistula Lagoon from the Baltic Sea. "Here," she said. "The port of Pillau. My sources say that a few hundred thousand refugees have been herded onto ships here and moved to central and western Germany."

"Anything to escape the Soviets," Stahl said softly.

Irritated, she stared at him. He didn't meet her eyes. Just continued to stare into space.

"About three weeks ago," she continued, "an SS transport company in Pillau received orders to make two trips from the port to the site of the Königsberg laboratory. They departed Pillau empty and returned full."

"That could be anything," the Brigadier sniffed. "It doesn't have to be *Götterdämmerung*. For all you know, Miss Lane, they are moving unwanted furniture or extra toilet paper." He chuckled at his own joke.

"Quite so, sir," Lane said, ignoring his deliberate slight of the rank she bore on her RAF uniform. "But, right now, German army transportation is down to horses and carts. Even tank crews are begging for petrol. And yet this particular SS unit had permission to draw all the fuel they needed."

"Damned important toilet paper," someone muttered. No one laughed.

"They moved *Götterdämmerung* to Pillau," Lane said. "For all we know, they already loaded it onto a ship."

"No." Stahl shook his head. "It is not ready yet."

"How do you know?"

"Because the Baltic is not deep enough to hold the corpses if it was."

"Does it matter?" The Brigadier sneered at the German, then gave Lane a withering look of contempt. "In a few days, a week or two at most, the Russians will overrun Pillau and everything in it. Even if the Huns get the stuff onto a ship, we've destroyed their special planes. I think it's fair to say that our Soviet friends are about to solve our problem for us."

"No." The man in the hat tapped his finger once on the table. A sudden silence descended on the room. "We've only compounded one problem with another." He turned slowly to look at Lord Wolmer, the tilting of his head revealing more of the emotionless face beneath the hat's brim.

To Lane's shock, the Minister of Economic Warfare coloured. He made a movement in his seat that was as close to squirming as she could have imagined from him. "Don't give me that look, Quiet."

"Top," Sir David Petrie said, the single word sounding more

216

an admonishment than an affectionate nickname, "what did you do?"

"What did you expect me to do, eh?" Lord Wolmer sat upright in his chair, arms folded, chin thrust out in pugnacious defiance. "You've all spent weeks telling me how dangerous this thing is, how we must stop it at all costs. So, I made a call to some people who could take care of it for us."

"You told the Soviets." Stahl half-rose from his chair, his hands gripping the table. Lane saw his dead-eyed placidity disappear, and a light come to the assassin's eyes. Not a healthy light. Not life. Just an unreasoning animal instinct.

He was terrified.

What would it take to terrify a man like Stahl?

"Top?" Sir David's voice broke the sudden silence. "Is this true?"

"Don't be naïve, David," Lord Wolmer sneered. "Not one of you could tell me where it was, or how to destroy it, could you? Besides, they are supposed to be our bloody Allies."

The man in the hat kept his hooded gaze fixed on the Minister. "Are they?"

"Yes," Lord Wolmer snapped. "They are. I don't trust Soviet intentions for eastern Europe any more than you do, Quentin, but unlike you and Winston, I'm content to wait for one war to end before I start fighting the next."

It didn't surprise Lane that no one had much to add to that. The military men in the room seemed deeply uncomfortable, poised in their seats, hoping to be dismissed. Sir David's mouth twitched, betraying thoughts that found no spoken form. The man in the hat returned to his contemplation of the table's surface.

Her eyes met Stahl's. The fear remained, but now there was something else. An urgent pleading.

"Sir?" The word escaped her lips before she could rein it in.

217

Lord Wolmer gave an irritated sigh. "What?"

"Were the Russians able to destroy the Königsberg site before that SS company arrived?"

"We passed them the information on *Götterdämmerung* under the strictest confidence and with the guarantee that they would pulverise the site with artillery as soon as possible." The Minister paused. "I'm afraid the guarantee proved rather limited."

"You mean they accepted your invitation to take it for themselves?"

"Careful, woman. I'm growing tired of your impertinence."

"For God's sake, Top," Sir David said wearily, "this is far more important than your ego. Answer the question."

"Yes, David. They tried to take it. And they were too bloody late."

"They will try again," Stahl intoned. "They know it exists now."

Something in his tone made Lane start and turn to stare at him again.

He returned her gaze. How many of her people had looked into those cold, hateful blue eyes as he came for them, and seen only their death? Even as she thought it, though, her insides lurched and squirmed at the memory of what he had told Andy and her that night in the Wing Commander's office. Mercy, he had called it. Killing them to save them.

She swallowed. He still pulled the trigger. The why of it changed nothing.

Except everything.

The blood of her agents was still on Stahl's hands. But now that meant something different.

Stahl blinked. His angular cheekbones dipped as his head twitched in the slightest of nods, and understanding flooded through her.

"You know," Lane said, "don't you? You know what *Götterdämmerung* is."

"I suspected. Now I know. Because of your work."

"What?" Lord Wolmer rose from his chair. Disbelief and outrage competed to dominate his expression. "You should have told us a long time ago."

"Wrong," Stahl said. "You have already proved you cannot be trusted. I tell you now only because, once you know the truth, you will do anything to stop it."

"The truth," the Brigadier snorted. "I've been fighting Germans since I was eighteen years old, and I haven't meant a single one I would trust."

"Right now, sir," Lane said, "he's the only man here I do trust."

Outraged grumbles filled the air. Embry frowned. The Brigadier's face turned bright red, a vein springing to pulsing prominence at his temple. Colonel Dennison paled and shrank back, as if to distance himself as far as possible from the woman he had been stupid enough to invite before this august group.

A hint of a smile flickered on the face of the man in the hat.

"Silence, you bloody fools," Sir David shouted. "The only people I want to hear for the next five minutes are Stahl and Lane."

"David," Lord Wolmer warned, "this is my meeting."

"That silence includes you, Top. Go on, Stahl."

The German took a breath, perhaps the first in a minute or more. Slowly releasing his fingers from their death grip on the table, he rose to his full height and looked down the length of the table, his icy gaze passing over each man.

Such arrogance, Lane thought. This was the Stahl she knew, the man who had haunted her nightmares for two long years. Like a venomous snake beholding vermin. And just like a snake, he could kill any of them without blinking.

Then he turned to her, and his eyes softened. He walked towards her, past men who sat as still as wax effigies, his feet making no noise, as if he was gliding over the floor. Closer. When he spoke, she knew he was speaking to her alone.

"My farmer friends from Staverton St. Mary could tell you about Coxiellosis," he said. He stood barely a foot in front of her now. Close enough that she could feel the touch of his breath on her face. "Maybe they know it better as Q Fever. It is a disease of sheep and cattle. When it strikes, you must quarantine the herd. Stop it spreading. Sometimes it makes farmers sick, but they rarely die. In nature, it does not kill. That is where *Götterdämmerung* is different."

"They have made it worse?" She already knew the answer.

"Better," Stahl corrected. "Better at reproducing. Better at killing. Somehow, they have made it not just possible, but simple to spread between two people. Some it will kill in days, but others will make it weeks before they feel the symptoms. By then, they may have passed it to a hundred others. No quarantine can stop that."

"Don't be so sure, Stahl," Sir David said. "We've already prevented the aircraft from being able to reach us. I'm sure the Royal Navy can take care of any ships—"

"You do not understand, do you?" Stahl cut him short. He did not take his eyes from Lane's. "This is not about an attack on your precious England. It is not a last attempt to steal a victory."

"Hitler's going to release it on his own people," Lane said. "Isn't he?"

Stahl nodded. "One final atrocity. A judgement on the German *Volk* for failing him."

Lane drew a shuddering breath.

It all made sense now. Years of intelligence reporting. Months of poring over agent reports. Murdered prisoners. Ovens. The lab outside Hildesheim, the special bombers that had no hope of surviving outside German airspace. *Götterdämmerung*. The Twilight of the Gods.

It all came together now, so much worse than she could ever have imagined.

A chuckle broke the silence.

"I'm not certain, Brigadier," Sir David Petrie said, "that I see much cause for mirth."

"Well, I bloody do," the soldier said, mirth bubbling in his eyes. "Hitler's going to wipe out half of Germany and save the British Army a fortune in shells and bullets. Hell, if he does a good enough job, we might not need to go a third round with them in another twenty years!"

"Millions of my people will die," Stahl said. "And yet you laugh."

She knew the look in his eyes. The snake was back. The Brigadier saw it, too, his chuckles abruptly fading to nothing. Now, at last, the others in the room saw what she had always seen. SS Obersturmbannführer Jan Stahl. The assassin. The killer without equal.

Stahl's hand reached towards his pocket. Without thinking, she reached for his arm. Her fingers closed on corded muscle and bone. No soft flesh. No hint of warmth. She almost recoiled.

He turned to her, and she saw confusion in his eyes. Something else, too.

Guilt.

"Might I remind you, Brigadier," Sir David said, "that Germany has many borders? There are a few hundred million people in Europe that we have spent the last six years trying to liberate. I, for one, would rather not see them die alongside the Third Reich."

"Not to mention hundreds of thousands of British troops," Lane added, "who could soon return home with *Götterdämmerung* in their veins."

"Well said, Squadron Officer Lane," Sir David said. "I rather fear that we've been one step behind this whole time. How do we get ahead? Could your RAF heavy bombers do it?"

She shook her head. "Too imprecise. Damaging the facility might do nothing more than expose *Götterdämmerung* and release it early."

"Then what?"

"You need 465 Squadron," Stahl said.

"One squadron? Alone?"

"He's right," Embry said. "465 Squadron can hit the building itself."

"Bloody dangerous work," Sir David said. "Flak everywhere, and I can't imagine German fighters will let them just swoop in and hit it."

"Nor Soviet fighters," the man in the hat observed.

"They can do it," Lane said firmly. Durban's face sprung to her mind again, more vividly than ever. She remembered standing close to him, looking up at an aircraft. "We'll use napalm," she said, hearing his voice in her ears rather than her own. "Burn it. Set the surrounding air on fire. It must all be destroyed."

"The scientists, too," Stahl said. "If they escape, they can create it again." His eyes met Lane's again.

"The submarine," she whispered.

He nodded. "That's their way out."

"Then it's agreed," Sir David said. "465 Squadron will destroy the building. In the meantime, I want the Biological Warfare Intelligence Committee working on this Q Fever business. I want every expert in the UK who knows a damned thing about sheep diseases to be working on prevention and cure. If this thing gets loose, millions will die. Our duty is to make sure someone in Europe remains alive to bury them." He stood in silence for a moment, then turned hesitantly to the silent

Minister. "My Lord?"

"I couldn't have said it better myself, David," Lord Wolmer sighed. "I'll inform the PM. 465 Squadron will get the support they need if I have to fly a damned plane myself. Those of you who can help should do so to the utmost of your ability. Those who can't? Consider this a direct order to get down on your knees and pray for them. Squadron Officer Lane? How long will it take to locate the target building?"

"I..." She froze. All eyes were on her. Waiting for her answer. Just as 465 Squadron was waiting, ready to be thrown one last time against the maelstrom of defences that would meet any attempt to target *Götterdämmerung*. Cold, unreasoning horror crept over her skin, crushing her chest and churning her stomach as the thought hit her in waves. Of what she had committed the Squadron to. What she had committed Andy to.

And still they waited for her answer.

"I don't know," she said.

Silence filled the room. She saw the men look at each other, and the hopelessness in their eyes.

"None of my agents can help now," she said, feeling her hands tremble and powerless to stop them. "Not there. Most of East Prussia is in Soviet hands, the rest is chaos. I have no sources inside Pillau. I doubt more than a dozen men outside the city know the location, and the secrecy will be at its height, now that they are so close. There will be no more intercepts of signals, no more reports."

Somehow her knees hadn't buckled, but still she sank back into her chair.

"Then we've failed," Sir David said. "It's over."

Lane closed her eyes. At least, now, 465 Squadron wouldn't have to go. Andy could survive, if only until *Götterdämmerung* swept across the world.

"No," Stahl said. "The SS would know. The ones in the city."

Lane sat up in her chair. He was looking at her. Those dark eyes. There was life in them now. Fierce. Frightening.

She knew exactly what he meant to do.

Sir David looked up at the assassin, hardly a trace of weary hope left on his face. "And do we have an SS source in Pillau?"

"No," Stahl said. "Not yet."

Chapter Twenty-Nine

Norfolk, 6 April

The nightmare woke him, but it took the sight of the person by the bedside to draw a pained gasp from his lips.

"Bad dream, Grant?" Barton put down his newspaper and sat back in his chair.

"No, sir," Grant lied. It hadn't been as bad as some others. At least the aircraft hadn't caught fire this time, and the memory of the enclosing cockpit and the stink of cordite and smoke and his own blood was fading with merciful speed. Even the half-remembered dregs that remained, though, were enough to draw fresh needles of familiar pain from beneath the bandages around his torso. "How long have you been there?"

"Long enough to be bored of watching you sleep."

"You shouldn't do it, then."

"Don't feel too special. You're not the first wounded aircrew I've visited in this place. I brought you some tea."

Suddenly aware of the dryness of his mouth, Grant reached for it. His fingers brushed the cheap hospital mug, and he knew immediately it was empty. "Was it good?"

"It was cold," Barton said. "I'm sure a nurse will bring you some more. They all seem to like you. One even called you a hero." He sniffed. "I said I'd bring her a dictionary next time I visit."

"Oh," Grant said. "So there has to be a next time?"

"Ungrateful sod," Barton said, reaching for his newspaper again. "If you don't want to be visited in hospital, the answer is simple."

"Yeah, I know," Grant said. "Recover quickly."

"I was going to say just get killed next time, mate," Barton said. "Save us all some effort." He sighed, crunched up the newspaper, and threw it across the room into the wastepaper basket. "It doesn't make better reading the third time around."

Grant adjusted his position. The thin white sheets clung to the sweat from the nightmare, and the bed creaked and sagged with his movement. "I appreciate the gesture, Squadron Leader," he said formally. "It's nice to have a visitor. Not everyone has bothered."

Barton barked a harsh laugh. "Don't have a pity party, Grant, just because it's me sat here and not Durban."

"I wasn't." Grant marvelled at how he'd been raised not to lie and had now managed it twice in the first ninety seconds of being awake. His mother would not be best pleased. "I expect he's very busy."

"He is." Barton lowered his voice, looking at the handful of other occupied beds in the ward. As usual, most were asleep or too distracted by their own pain or recovery. The ward received a dozen visitors a day, and even an RAF Squadron Leader with wings on his chest warranted little attention. "Something big is coming up. He's got us flying twice a day, sometimes three times. Low-level, high-level, dive-bombing, air-to-air."

"And yet," Grant said, "you found time to come and watch me sleep. I'm honoured, by the way."

"Bloody right, you are." Barton tugged at the ragged edges of his moustache. "But between you and me, I didn't come here because I wanted your company."

"Oh. Suddenly I feel less honoured."

"Look," Barton said. "You might have noticed I don't like Durban. I don't much like you either, though at least you're not a Pom. But I'll say this for the smooth bastard. He's got the squadron running well. Better than ever. The men love him. And he's no coward."

226

"No, he's not," Grant said. The pain pulsed again, where the shrapnel had torn at flesh and muscle.

A spent shell, the surgeons had told him, shattered into fragments by the impact with the engine cowling and slowed by the wood of the fuselage. A little more metal, a touch more energy, another few inches up or down, and he'd have probably bled out. As it was, the wounds were healing well. With rest, he would be back to flying soon enough.

Though not too soon, they had assured him. The war would probably be over by the time he was certified fit to fly. Grant could still remember the thrill of relief that had passed through him.

And the shame that followed.

Further down the room, a heavily bandaged man gave an anguished moan, but didn't wake despite the afternoon sunlight pouring through the windows.

Barton gestured. "What happened to that poor sod?"

"Sergeant Laycock," Grant said. "Tail gunner. Pulled from his burning Lancaster. Not quickly enough, sadly, though he never complains. Brave man."

"You know," Barton said, "I've met a lot of brave men. No two were the same. I've met men who would go out night after night without a flicker of emotion, like it was just any other job. And," he added, glancing at Grant before turning his attention to the ceiling, "I've met lads who shat themselves before every mission. But they still went. You tell me which is the braver."

Grant opened his mouth to speak but changed the words before they could reach his lips. "Which one are you?"

Barton winked. "I'm one of the special ones. I'm too stupid to think I could ever get a scratch on me. Mind, three years of ops and no one's proved me wrong, so maybe I'm smarter than I look."

Grant chuckled, then coughed and waited for the sudden waves of agony to pass through him.

"The problem is," Barton added, "you stay in this game long enough, and it doesn't matter how brave you are. Sooner or later, everyone reaches their limit. Take your mate, the Wing Commander, for example."

"What do you mean?"

Barton frowned in surprise. "Aren't you navigators supposed to be observant? That man has been hurting since the day he arrived."

"He's not a coward," Grant said, feeling his cheeks redden.

"I already said that, didn't I? Keep up. Like I told you, everyone reaches their limit. Everyone. Unless they get killed first. Andy Durban didn't get those DFCs from a Christmas cracker, but he's flown more operational missions than anyone I've ever met. His last navigator died in the seat next to him, and you tried to pull off the same trick. Have you never seen the way his hands shake?"

"No. He gave no fear away." Except once, Grant thought suddenly. On their last sortie. When he had thought Grant was dying.

Barton snorted and shook his head. "God help Durban up there if he has to rely on you to spot anything."

Nurse Anita entered the ward, and the Australian fell silent. She checked on Laycock and the other men, then scowled at Barton before giving Grant a sweet smile and taking his temperature. Promising to come back to bring Grant a fresh cup of tea and some food, she tapped her watch with a pointed stare at the Squadron Leader and continued on her rounds.

Barton watched the pretty nurse walk away with obvious appreciation. "Can you believe Kittinger pulled that?" He shook his head. "The man must be packing artillery in his trousers."

"That's Kittens' girlfriend?"

"For six months now, at least. It doesn't seem fair, does it?"

"He never mentioned it, even when he came to see me."

"He's a private individual. Did you ask him? Well, there you go then," Barton said as Grant shook his head. "You also haven't asked who your replacement is."

"What?"

"As Durban's navigator."

"Oh." Grant hadn't even thought about that. It brought an odd twinge of jealousy. "Who was it? Finnegan?"

"Finny? No chance. That little toe rag has been with me since Australia. No way I'm giving him up, and Durban knows better than to ask. Which is just as well, because he's asked just about every bugger else."

"What do you mean?"

"That he's trialled every other navigator on the squadron. A few even got to go twice, but then he decides they aren't good enough and sends them packing. Apparently, mate, you're his Finny."

"I doubt it," Grant said. "If I was, he'd have visited. I know, I know. He's busy."

Barton laughed. "Not so busy that he doesn't ask for updates on you half-a-dozen times a day. Why do you think I came? I'm hoping if I tell him you're fine, he'll stop beating himself up about how you got here. You are fine, aren't you? I mean, you're going to be back flying soon?"

"The doctors said it could be weeks."

"We don't have weeks," Barton said. All humour faded from his voice. "Whatever this job is building up to, it's happening soon. Durban is one of the bravest men I've ever known, and he may well be the best squadron commander in the RAF, but I'm worried for him."

He rose from his chair. "And if you tell anyone I said that, you'll be back in here for months. Get better, Grant. Fast." He stared furiously down at the navigator for a few seconds, then stormed out of the room.

Grant closed his eyes and listened to the thud of the receding footsteps until they faded into the general indistinct murmur of hospital life. Somewhere beyond the window, he heard distant Merlin engines. He didn't look. He simply lay there, with his hands resting on the bandages around his midsection. They felt damp. Sweat. Not blood.

The sound of the engines grew louder, filling his ears with their roar, and he heard the clattering thud as the cannon shell slammed into them again.

With a gasp, he sat up, pain flooding through him.

"Sorry," Anita said, snatching her hand back from the mug she had just placed on the bedside table. "I didn't mean to wake you. Just bringing you some tea. Are you ok, love?"

Outside, the daylight was fading, and the sky was silent.

"No, Ma'am," Grant said. "I don't think I am."

Chapter Thirty

Bedfordshire, 9 April

No one spoke. Major Anders drove quickly, expertly, seemingly unfazed by the dark country road or the dim headlights that were all that blackout regulations permitted. Stahl sat next to him upfront, eyes hooded, unmoving. Somewhere between sleep and waking. Between life and death.

Lane sat alone in the shadows of the back seat, glad that she was just a passenger this time around. Now it was up to Stahl. Her work here was done. Most of it, anyway.

It was only when they got close to RAF Tempsford that she felt the pressure build on her chest.

The strip of land between the Great North Road and the main line from Kings Cross to Edinburgh seemed an odd location for the most secretive airfield in the United Kingdom. Occasionally, the police or security patrols picked up a suspicious person roaming the surroundings, and at least two had turned out to be bona fide German agents. Lane didn't know what had happened to them – whether they had been turned and become double agents or chosen the other option and hanged as spies – but it seemed clear they had not got word back to Germany. Tempsford and its two highly specialised RAF squadrons remained a well-kept secret. Even the locals who heard the hum of aero engines on moonlit nights had little idea that those aircraft were ferrying agents into occupied Europe.

Her agents.

Of course, it was a two-way process. They also brought agents home, their pilots landing their Lysanders and Hudsons in too-small clearings or lonely meadows lit for them by welcoming committees of resistance fighters. Dangerous work. A hastily lit flare path to guide the aircraft in, a mad dash by the agent to reach the aircraft as it turned ready to launch again, a scramble to close the door as the aircraft accelerated and hauled itself into the sky as their allies disappeared back into the darkness. Sometimes they cut it close and came back with holes in the fuselage from the rifle fire of some German patrol. Sometimes they didn't make it back at all, but plenty of agents did, with intelligence to report and stories of terrified heroics to tell.

Not her agents, though. Not one.

Still without speaking, Anders turned off the Great North Road and followed a country lane. He kept the speed down, though she doubted the closeness of the hedges on either side bothered him. Ahead, a barrier barred the road, and Anders drew to a halt as dark figures closed in on them. One tapped on the window and waited for Anders to open it before shining his flashlight on each of their faces. The soldier checked their identification, paused for a little longer on Stahl's, then gave a grunt. "Welcome to Gibraltar Farm, sir," he said, saluting and motioning to two companions to move the barrier aside. "Welcome back, Ma'am," he added with a smile to Lane.

She tried to reply, but her parched mouth betrayed her, leaving only a half-whisper to drift between her chewed lips.

"Farm?" Stahl's eyebrow twitched, the most emotion she'd seen from him in hours.

"You'll see," Anders said, but the German had already returned to his silent contemplation of the darkness beyond his window.

With the engine of the Morris sputtering slightly, they crossed one of the three runways that together formed a triangle, and followed a partly paved track. Just like her, Anders knew exactly where they were going. A few seconds more, and the bulk of a building loomed up from the night. In the daytime, it could pass for the sort of barn found at a thousand farms across England. Now, beneath the faint light of the waning crescent moon, the illusion was even more complete, but that's all it was. Illusion, like so much else in this war.

Anders switched off the engine and sat with his eyes on Stahl. "Time to go, my friend."

A nod. A soft intake of breath. Stahl opened his door and stepped out into the night, leaving Lane wondering if she would ever see more emotion from him than that.

Anders ushered the German into the lightless barn, then stood waiting for her.

She didn't move. Couldn't move. Just getting out of the car had taken every ounce of her willpower. She simply stood with one shaking hand still on the door handle, staring at the barn. Up close, she could see the hidden bricks beneath the gaps in the wood cladding. This was no barn, the name Gibraltar Farm at once both a cover story to foil foreign agents and a desperate effort to ignore reality. This was where they came. The agents. Their final stop before they boarded the aircraft and headed off into Europe.

Little wonder that the gate guard had recognised her. She had been here so many times. Too many times.

"Are you coming, Sarah?" If her hesitation embarrassed Anders, he kept it to himself. No emotion at all. She knew he had been here just as many times as her, but if the experience had let any demons loose on his soul, his face gave no sign.

"What are his chances, Anders?"

Anders grinned. "Any other man, I'd say the chances of successfully pulling this off were zero. Stahl? I'd give him ten percent. Twenty, if he's lucky. He's good, Sarah. Almost as good as me."

"I meant of surviving," she said.

The grin became a frown. "I don't understand the question."

Pull it together, she told herself. Move. Take control. Do your job, just like every other time.

This is what you do.

"Sorry to keep you waiting, Major," she sniffed, brushing past him and waiting impatiently for him to close the door before hitting the light switch. With a low hum and a click, the two electric bulbs sprang to life, illuminating the exposed brick interior with its thick wooden double shelves and the exposed beams of the high ceiling.

Stahl stood in the centre of the room, motionless as a statue and with the face to match.

"Ok." It amazed her how business-like she could make her voice sound despite the roiling chaos in her stomach. She'd always been able to do that in this place. Her agents were nervous enough already, she had told herself; perhaps her feigned confidence might give them confidence for real. She had never had the chance to ask any of them if it worked. "Let's get you ready, Stahl."

SOE had already laid the equipment she had requested out on the shelves, half a dozen items next to a large kitbag. She went straight to it, beckoning him to follow and then tapping her fingers on the shelf until he did so.

"Walther P38," she said, pointing to the pistol that lay on the counter next to four magazines. She did not pass the weapon to him, nor even touch it. "Standard SS issue."

"I know," Stahl said. He lifted the pistol, turning it one way, then the other, examining it. Somehow, it seemed to complete him, like he'd been less than whole without it. Satisfied, he put it down again and waited, his eyes on the counter or the wall, anywhere but her.

She swallowed. "Your papers," she said, handing him a leather file folder.

He flicked through them. "Obersturmbannführer Karl-Heinz Plendl," he read. "Will they pass?"

"They're good, Jan," Anders said. "We got the originals from a dead man in Holland last week, and our best forgers have worked on them. Unless documents issued in East Prussia are different, you'll be fine."

He nodded. "Uniform?"

"In the holdall," Lane said, pointing. "SS field uniform, plus a spare set. Tailored for you."

"He'll need a radio, too," Anders said. "To contact us when he locates the target building."

Lane shook her head. "Too obvious. It will be a dead giveaway if a patrol stops him. Besides, he won't be able to reach England from East Prussia. The range is too far."

"What do you suggest?"

"I've written callsigns and frequency details of the British Embassy in Stockholm for you. Learn them, then destroy the paper. Someone will monitor at all times. They will pass your message on, but you will need to gain access to a radio."

An RAF sergeant knocked on the door. Lane vaguely recognised him from previous visits. "Is there a Major Anders here? Telephone call for you in the Ops Room."

"Probably Quiet checking up on me," Anders said. "I'll only be a minute. Don't leave without saying goodbye, Jan." He winked and followed the NCO from the room, leaving Lane and Stahl alone with the empty silence of the barn.

Stahl sighed, slipped off his jacket, and unbuttoned his shirt.

"There's a place inside you can change."

"I would rather have it over with," he said. His breath hung in the unheated air of the barn as he slipped off the shirt, but he gave no signs of noticing the cold. The skin of his torso was pale, flesh pulled too tight over taut muscle and the sharp ridges of his ribs.

No scars that she could see, nor any markings at all, including under the arms. "No blood group tattoo."

235

"You are thinking of the Waffen SS." He reached for the folded uniform without looking at her. "They have their blood type tattooed for the medics in case they suffer wounds in combat. That is not my role."

"Too dangerous? But of course, you would choose easier prey." She regretted her mocking tone as soon as she spoke. Whatever Stahl had done, she had to see past it now. He was working with her now. More than that, his role was critical. If *Götterdämmerung* was to be stopped...

"My choice had nothing to do with it," Stahl said. "You do not waste a scalpel blade on cutting down a tree. The SS trained me for efficiency. A precision tool for specialised targets."

But even if they were on the same side now, that couldn't clean his slate altogether. Nothing could. "Like unarmed women?" The words tore their way free of her lips.

"Sometimes," he said. He pulled on a new uniform shirt, his attention on the buttons as he fastened them with slender fingers. "Unarmed men, too. Armed targets increase the chance of failure. I was too good to take such risks." His voice echoed in the room, as cold as the brick walls.

So many times, she had wondered how men like Stahl could do the things they did and remain sane. It was obvious, watching him, hearing the ice in his words. There was no feeling. This wasn't a man at all. It was as he said. A precision tool, executing his mission without compunction, without the weakness of emotion to cloud his actions or delay the simple pull of a finger on a trigger.

And yet, she had seen the horror in his eyes in Durban's office. Heard the anguish in his voice when he had talked of Hildesheim and what he had seen in the aerial photographs. The same photographs she had looked at and yet thought only of a job well done.

She turned away as he unbuckled his trousers, letting her eyes play over the well-remembered walls and shelves. This place had become so familiar to her these last few years. The drive down. The briefings. The delay for the aircraft to arrive, interminably long when waiting for one to make a dawn landing from France with a returning agent safely onboard, yet all too brief when sending her people into the darkness. Most familiar of all was this place, this barn, this gateway between safety and the nightmares of Occupied Europe. So many times, she had recounted the same last warnings, handing out weapons and equipment and advice in equal measure, while the agent about to depart for the first, second, possibly last time, stood and listened and pretended to be brave.

No, she corrected herself, feeling her teeth grind and her fingernails digging into her palms. They were brave. It was she who was the coward, working in her warm office, saying goodbye and then heading back to London while, time after time, they never came back at all.

Even now, it was Stahl who was going. Not her. Never her.

A gentle cough behind her. She sniffed, took a sharp breath and the briefest indulgent moment to compose herself, and turned.

"How do I look?"

SS Obersturmbannführer Jan Stahl had dressed, and despite the familiar surroundings and the comfort of knowing she was in the heart of England, surrounded by British soldiers, Lane still had to restrain a sudden, suffocating panic. "Like the devil," she whispered.

"Good." Stahl adjusted the collar. Lane's stomach lurched as she watched his fingers brush against the four squares and two horizontal bars of his rank on one side, the stylised lightning bolts on the other. The stylised runes of the SS. To her eyes, the ultimate symbol of hatred, more so than the Swastika itself. Many ordinary Germans had no choice which flag they fought under.

The men of the SS chose their own flag.

"You picked the size perfectly," Stahl said.

"You wear it well."

He smiled, a thin veneer of faked amusement beneath eyes deep with sorrow. "Perhaps. Or perhaps it wears me."

Enough, she told herself. Time was ticking. Out in the darkness beyond the walls, she heard a muffled cough and a low roar. An aero engine starting. As always, the sound brought a wave of nausea with it. "You'll be flying in on a No. 161 Squadron Lockheed Hudson," she said. "We've cleared a flight path for you across France and Switzerland. Your drop zone is fifty miles inside Bavaria, outside a small town called Oberammergau."

"I selected the location myself," Stahl reminded her gently.

"Of course. Sorry, Jan." Odd, that his first name should slip from her lips now. "You are sure you can find transportation from there to northern Germany?"

"That will be easy," he said. "SS rank still means something. The tough part is getting onto a ship into Pillau."

"If the Soviets haven't taken the city."

"If they have," he said softly, "it is already over."

He turned and took the pistol from the shelf, sliding it easily into the holster at his waist and securing it in place. She watched as he smoothly went through his final preparations, packing the second set of uniform into a holdall, placing the forged papers inside his field jacket. But for the hateful uniform, he could have been any of her agents. Just like them, he gave no overt sign of fear.

And, just like them, she would probably never see him again.

The door swung open, the cool night breeze bringing the sound of Twin Wasp radial engines.

"Ah, Anders," she said. "Right when you're needed, as always. Do you know where the parachutes are?" The question faded from her mind as she saw the look on his face.

"Stahl?"

The German turned. "I am ready, Anders. Do not tell me there is a change of plan."

The Dane shook his head. "That was London. We just got word from Germany. There's a capture or kill order out for you for treason. Issued by Himmler himself."

"I am honoured that Heinrich would take the time," Stahl said.

A sudden tightness descended on her chest, setting her innards quivering. "Anders, if the SS are hunting for him..."

"Sarah, the Reich is in chaos. Russian tanks are closing on Berlin, and the SS is putting out fires from the Oder to the Rhine. They won't have time to look for defectors, and even if they did, why would they think he would come back to Germany? There is every chance he makes it through."

"He's right," Stahl said. "It changes nothing. Where are the parachutes?"

"Jan, there's something else." Anders hesitated, his eyes briefly flickering back to Lane. "They executed Wilhelm Canaris today at Flossenbürg concentration camp. Our source said—"

Stahl held up one hand to cut him off. Motionless, he drew in a single breath that hissed and rattled in his throat. For a second, the reptilian eyes closed.

A second.

No more.

With machine-like efficiency, the eyes clicked open. "My parachute, Anders?"

Major Anders nodded. "On the aircraft. It's ready when you are."

"Then let us go," Stahl said.

She stopped him on the way to the door. She didn't mean to. Just found herself moving to cut him off. "Jan," she began, voice halting as she realised she had nothing else to say.

"*Selbstmitleid*," he said, softly.

She repeated the word. "Self-pity?"

"Andrew Durban asked me what the German word for melodrama is. I think this is what he was really asking. Tell him for me, please?"

"Of course," she mumbled.

He stepped around her, then halted and leaned close to her ear. Even now, despite everything, she flinched. "Sarah," he said, pretending not to notice, "tell Durban that when the time comes and I show him the building, don't hesitate."

"I'll tell him."

"And don't miss."

"He won't."

Anders called for Stahl again, and in another second he was gone, out into the night and the roaring of the waiting Hudson.

Lane didn't follow. She leaned back against the brickwork, ignoring the cold that seeped through her fur-lined leather flying jacket. There she stood, her mind as empty as her whole body felt, until the Hudson's engines reached a crescendo and quickly faded away into nothing. The sound made her think of Andy, but not of his face or the way he looked at her and how much she missed him. It made her think of their differences. Andy always needed to see his aircraft come home. But she could never watch her agents leave.

Not even this last one.

Chapter Thirty-One

Norfolk, 10 April

Durban pushed the paper away and let his father's pen drop onto the desk.

This should have been the easiest letter of them all to write. No research into personnel files needed, no handwringing over how best to address it or what flowery, misleading phrases to use to soften the blow. And yet, instead, it continued to elude him. He had got no further than the addressee line. The delights of the spring morning outside provided no inspiration, nor could the sunlight streaming through his office window do anything to dispel the gloom that seemed to hang within it.

A knock at the door. Two knocks, then one, oddly tremulous, barely audible above the sound of a Mosquito engine test outside Hangar Six, half a mile away. "What is it, Bony?"

"Signal from HQ, sir," Flight Lieutenant Wright said.

"Urgent?"

"Not marked so, sir."

"Put it with the others." Durban made a vague motion towards his growing to-do pile, which was topped as usual with a noise complaint from Matlock's Farm.

Wright hesitated.

"Well? Put it there and bugger off, will you?"

The Operations Officer blanched.

"Oh, bloody hell," Durban said, rubbing his eyes. "I'm sorry, Bony."

"Rough night, sir?"

"Rough month. Rough war, if I'm honest."

"Have you heard anything from Sarah Lane, sir?"

"Squadron Officer Lane only contacts us when she needs to," Durban said firmly. "Which, if we're very lucky, will be never. What can I do for you?"

"Well, sir," Wright said, "a few weeks ago you remarked you were expecting something like this, and that I was to bring it straight to you if it arrived."

Durban frowned. Puzzled, he reached out and took the folded paper, flipping it open and angling it for better sunlight.

"It's a request for volunteers, sir," Bony said. "For service in the Far East."

"I can read," Durban snapped. He scanned it all the way to the end, repeated the process, marvelled that rereading did not make it any better. His gaze lingering on the paper, he handed it back. "The bastards. The absolute bastards."

"Sir?"

Anger flooded through him. Too much to remain polite. Too much to stay seated. The desk shook as he all but leapt to his feet, the wastepaper basket by his desk flying across the room, barely missing Bony before crashing against the metal of his filing cabinet. Balled up pieces of paper scattered across the cheap carpet, silent testament to days of failures to finish a single letter.

Outside in the corridor, two young airmen stood open-mouthed, almost trembling, their desire to be anywhere else plain on their faces. He should have felt embarrassment, Durban knew, at the loss of control itself, not just being caught in the act. Instead, he gave them a hard stare and slammed the office door. "Haven't they done enough?"

Bony's mouth twitched as he scrambled to find words. "Who, sir?"

"The boys," Durban grated. "Kittens. Barton. Even Finnegan, for Christ's sake." He motioned beyond the window. "There are men and women out there who have been doing this since 1939.

Most of the ones who started the war are already gone, buried over here if their families were lucky, scattered in bloody little pieces over Germany if they weren't. Did you ever do the maths, Bony?"

"I—"

"Four percent loss rates for Bomber Command. Thirty missions for a first tourist crew. That's a less than thirty percent chance of surviving if you only do one tour, but who does? You finish your tour, you go off to do an instructor tour teaching the next bunch of poor saps who are going to get butchered over Germany, and what happens?" He remembered it well. Sensed the sweat on his neck, felt his hands tremble the way they had then. "You feel the guilt. At first you think you've done your bit and you'll get over it, but it keeps gnawing away. Night after night. Gets so you can't sleep. You know they are going to want you to do a second tour soon enough, but it doesn't matter. You must go now. Because if it isn't you, it will be someone else taking it in the neck in your place."

Damn, he wanted a drink. Instead, he paced the length of the room. He left the door clear, giving Bony an out, knowing the younger man wouldn't dream of using it without permission. "You've already used up every bit of God-given fortune to survive one tour. Now they've brought you back for another. Second tour is twenty ops. Fifty total. Less than thirteen percent make it through two tours."

"You've done four tours, sir?"

"It's not about me," Durban said, angry at the interruption, yet glad for it. "I'm talking about everyone. Anyone who ever flew a sortie or dodged a German bullet. Because believe me, this war doesn't care how much time you've put in. I've seen incompetent pilots who made it through an entire tour without a scare, and I've seen brilliant aviators who bought it on their first trip over the Channel. This war has a thousand ways to kill you. Most of them you can't control, and you'll see none of them coming."

Bony lowered his eyes. "We've all lost friends."

Durban ran his hand through his hair, letting his fingers close so tightly that they tugged at the roots. The pain made his eyes water, but he welcomed it anyway. A reminder that he, at least, was still alive. Blinking, he pointed to the signal in Bony's hand. "How many copies do you have of that?"

"Three, sir," Bony said. "Including this one."

"Give it to me. And destroy the others."

"Sir, I'm not sure I'm allowed to do that."

"I just gave you a direct order to do so," Durban said. "Tell no one about this signal."

Bony nodded. He still hesitated, though, shifting his weight from one foot to the other, his face pale. "Sir, are you afraid there would be no volunteers?"

"Quite the opposite, Bony, not that it is any of your business. I'm afraid they would all volunteer. Because that's what they do. Well, they've done enough. If any more signals like this arrive, you bring them straight to me. Do I make myself clear?"

"Yes, sir."

"Get to it, then."

Durban waited for Bony's footsteps to fade down the corridor before locking his door. He placed the folded signal in the top drawer of his desk, then went a drawer lower for the whisky. He was supposed to fly later, but that could easily be changed. For once, he didn't want to fly. He hadn't really wanted to for days. Not without Grant.

He had poured too generously. The shaking of his hand sent some of the whisky sploshing onto his thumb and desk, and it was far too good to waste. He took a long swig and felt the delicious burn in his throat, pushed the unwritten letter aside before it could get wet, then used a discarded draft to mop up the spills. Outside, twin Merlins spooled up as a Mosquito raced down the runway and hauled itself into the sky for an air test.

Who was he kidding? It was still the most wonderful sound in the world.

He picked up the pen his father had given him, and with a sigh, pulled the letter in front of him. Maybe the last one he'd ever write. Stared at it. Saw the expanse of unsullied white, like virgin snow. Saw his neat handwriting at the top.

Date. Place. The words *Dear Mrs Durban*.

It would do for a start.

Chapter Thirty-Two

East Prussia, 12 April

It wasn't the smell of the crowded street that really shook Stahl, though it hung thick in his nostrils. Unwashed bodies and the smoke from burning buildings. The rancid stench of fear and human waste. The sickly undertone of rotting corpses, numerous enough to defy the efforts of the Baltic Sea breeze to clear the air. These, at least, lay mercifully unseen in narrow alleys or piled up under tarpaulins for burial by soldiers already reassigned to more pressing tasks. It wasn't the noise that bothered him, either. The front line still lay a few miles from the densely packed buildings of Pillau. Near enough to fill the air with a steady drumbeat of artillery fire, but too far to drown out the sobbing and whimpering and cursing of the surrounding throng.

Stahl had heard such sounds before, too many times, and six years of war had left the stink of panic and death irrelevant in its familiarity.

Alone against the tide of desperate humanity, he again tried to pick a path. Yet again, he failed. A shoulder struck hard against his. A middle-aged man with a girl aged three or four in his wake, screaming as she battled to keep her grip on his hand.

That was what shook Stahl. The sunken eyes in the gaunt, unshaven face didn't so much as blink at the contact. For eight years, his SS uniform would have been enough to part any crowd. No German would have dared to stand in his way, let alone jostle him in the street. In the space of fifty metres, it had happened three times. No one cared. No one even noticed him.

Stahl had long felt the war was lost. Now he knew it.

The man stumbled on with his oblivious gaze fixed solely on the small freighter that Stahl had disembarked from minutes earlier. Within seconds, both man and child vanished from sight as more people pressed up behind. The girl's screaming dissolved among a thousand other cries. The crew of the *MV Alberich* were trying their best to control the flow of refugees onto the vessel, with a small detachment of soldiers attempting to check identification, but they were already being overwhelmed by the sheer volume of panicked civilians. For some, this might be their only chance to escape in days. Maybe the last chance they would ever get.

Stahl fought his way to the front of a nearby shop, ignoring the motionless form huddled in the doorway in a filthy blanket and blood-soaked bandages. Straining to see over the crowd, he looked back across the docks. He easily spotted the U-Boat training facility a few hundred metres across the icy waters, the dark-grey shape of U-78 moored alongside with a dozen soldiers milling nearby. Beyond the *Alberich*, a Kriegsmarine corvette moved slowly across the bay, anti-aircraft guns trained on the smoke-filled sky. He could make out at least three waterfront warehouses from here, with sharp timbered roofs and loading cranes. He'd seen more from the ship as it inched into the port. Each of them able to hold enough *Götterdämmerung* to turn continental Europe into a mass grave.

It was almost enough to make him laugh. What had he really expected? With his fake papers to intimidate anyone he met, he'd taken an overnight troop train from Bavaria to Dresden, its carriages only half-filled with soldiers, all of them old men or children. From there, he'd bullied his way onto a Ju-52 flying into besieged Danzig. The exhausted aircrew had told him they normally carried ammunition into the city and brought the seriously wounded back. But there was no more ammunition to take, and Stahl sat alone in the cargo area except for the brown smudges of dried blood. Plenty of room, at least on the way in. They would pack the flight on the way out.

Finally, his papers had bought him a place on an overnight voyage on the darkened *Alberich* as it steamed its way from Gotenhafen across the Danziger Bucht, zigzagging to avoid the Soviet submarines that had claimed dozens of similar vessels. Yes, getting to Pillau had been the straightforward part. Finding the target building was going to be far more difficult.

He would need help. It was risky, but he was running out of options. And time.

Pulling the collar of his officers' overcoat up against the sea breeze, he plunged back into the crowd, head down, walking with purpose. It didn't reduce the jostling, but it helped keep the pace up. He saw a handful of regular army soldiers but ignored them. Instead, he scanned the crudely painted improvised road signs that he passed every hundred metres or so, until he found the right one and turned into a side street that left the wharves behind.

A soldier stood at the corner. Waffen SS. A rifle hung from his shoulder. The man's eyes flickered up as Stahl crossed the street towards him, then returned their focus to the cigarette in his trembling hands.

"You. I am looking for HQ 247th SS Transport Battalion. Show me."

The soldier stared blankly. For a moment, Stahl thought he didn't understand German. That was possible. Some units of the Waffen SS recruited solely from occupied or aligned nations. Three-hundred thousand Romanians, twenty thousand Estonians, nine thousand French. Even a handful of British. Half a million non-Germans all told, some conscripted, many volunteers. This man could be either.

But then the soldier shrugged and pointed further up the road. No words. No salute.

Stahl walked on. He passed between two bomb-gutted buildings, stepping over the rubble that their destruction had left in the street. To his right lay an open area where trees had probably once stood, before the siege and the frigid winter saw them stripped to the last splinter for firewood. Half a dozen trucks stood empty and abandoned beyond it. No sign of their drivers. He picked a path across the muddy field, past a water-filled shell crater, until he reached the sandbagged entrance to the bunker.

The SS flag flew outside on a crude wooden flagpole. Its flickering movement couldn't conceal the shrapnel holes torn through it. A few feet back, a single radio aerial rose from the mud.

A guard stepped out to bar his path. At least this one managed a salute.

"Where is your battalion commander?"

"Down the steps and straight ahead, sir. Have you brought reinforcements?"

"There are no reinforcements, boy," Stahl said sadly. "Just do your best. It will not be long now."

Pushing past, he saw that the lightbulbs in the corridor hung dormant and dark, but a sliver of flickering light emerged from a cracked door at the far end. The incongruous notes of classical violin drifted to him, and he followed them.

Two candles on a shelf sputtered in their last throes above the young man in the battalion commander's office. His jacket hung on the back of his chair, his booted feet resting on an ammunition crate. Eyes shut, fingers interlaced, he sat with a half-smile on his face while a phonograph played in the room's corner, a Walther pistol casually abandoned next to it.

"I said I did not want to be disturbed this week." The man didn't bother to open his eyes when he spoke. A junior officer, a mere SS-Sturmführer, a second lieutenant. Probably too young to have finished university.

Stahl nudged the crate with his toe. "Where is your battalion commander?"

"Dead. The second in command, too. And the operations officer. Even the quartermaster. I guess I am next in line." His eyes slowly opened. "Sir," he added, seeing Stahl's uniform. He did not stand. "Is there something you needed?"

Hot anger flushed through Stahl's body. That this was what SS discipline should come to. "Stand when I address you." It took effort to keep his voice calm.

The man made no such effort to conceal his smirk as he rose slowly to his feet. His shirt hung untucked. "My sincere apologies, Herr Obersturmbannführer."

"What is your name?"

"Schnellinger. Joachim Schnellinger." He peered myopically in the semi-darkness. "Yours?"

"My name is Plendl. And I advise you to take care you do not have cause to remember it. Why are the electric lights not working?"

Schnellinger sighed. "Fuel is short. The generator is thirsty."

"Yet you run it to power your music?"

"Herr Obersturmbannführer, we will all be dead in a few days. If I cannot listen to Brahms now, when can I?" The man laughed.

Laughed in Stahl's face.

Once, he would never have let such a slight pass. But there were more important things at stake now. He forced himself to relax. The mission was everything. Besides, the young fool was right. It hardly mattered if Stahl let him live. The Soviets would not.

"In March, the 2nd Company of this battalion made two trips to assist the movement of critical equipment from Königsberg to Pillau. Do you recall this movement?"

A shrug. "We move a lot of things. Have we met before?"

"No. This movement would be different, Schnellinger. A priority tasking. Highest security, with full authorisation for fuel. Your orders came directly from Berlin. Think carefully, Sturmführer. Serious mistakes occurred during this operation. I have come from the *Reichssicherheitshauptamt* to ensure they are corrected. It would be unfortunate for you if I found you to be the one at fault, yes?"

The smirk faded. "I remember, sir."

"Good. Where did you deliver these items?"

"The waterfront district."

"Obviously," Stahl snapped. "Where precisely?"

Schnellinger cocked his head to one side, staring at Stahl, then shrugged. "I would have to check."

"Do so, then. Quickly."

Crossing the room, Schnellinger ran his finger down the spine of several thick box files. "We lost a lot of our documents in the retreat from the Vistula," he said. "It seems we have been retreating since the day I enlisted."

Stahl nodded. "Have they given you a date for evacuation?"

The man snorted. "To where? It is not like Berlin is any safer. Besides, what is the alternative? Operation Hannibal? They must have put a million people on ships out of Prussia now, but the damned Soviets seem to move westward faster than our boats. You heard about the *General von Steuben*? The Navy packed five thousand people on her when she left here, including all that remained of 2nd Company, and a Russian submarine sent most of them down with her to the bottom of the Baltic. That is where we lost our operations officer. Though if you ask me, that fool was no loss at all." His finger halted its slow traverse. "This is it," he said, dropping the file on his desk. He paused, looking first at the book, then at Stahl. "Are you sure we have not met, Herr Obersturmbannführer? You look very familiar."

"I am certain of it," Stahl said. "I spend most of my time in Vienna."

"Must be nice," Schnellinger muttered. He leafed through the book, paused. Looked at Stahl again. "Damn. It is not written here. I blame the quartermaster, alas. Very lazy. Did not even bother to run from the shell that killed him."

"I do not punish the dead for their mistakes," Stahl said coldly. "Only the living."

Schnellinger swallowed. His face paled.

Finally, Stahl thought. Some respect. The thought brought back memories of other men, of fear in their eyes. For a moment only he revelled in it, until revulsion struck. He thought of Canaris, and buried that thought in an instant.

"I have an idea," Schnellinger croaked. "Please bear with me, sir. I think it is time my radioman did something useful besides relaying no retreat orders from Berlin. Müller!"

Stahl heard booted feet hurrying in the corridor. His fingers were already on the grip of his pistol before he caught himself, eyes flickering to Schnellinger, but the Sturmführer was busily scribbling a note and did not seem to notice.

"Take this to Weber," Schnellinger said, folding the note and passing it to the radioman as he appeared in the doorway. "Quickly." He watched the soldier go, then dabbed at a bead of sweat on his brow. "Scharführer Weber has been here longer than anyone. He will know where to find the information."

The phonograph fell silent, leaving only the sound of the guttering candles and the faint crump of shells in the distance.

"I only have this one record," Schnellinger said. "The Violin Concerto in D Major. Do you like Brahms?"

"Of course," Stahl said. "Though I prefer Wagner. *Götterdämmerung*."

"I've never heard it, sir," Schnellinger said. He seemed nervous, rubbing his hands on his trouser legs and glancing at the door behind Stahl. No more nervous than before, though. If he had heard of *Götterdämmerung*, he hid it well.

"The docks area," Stahl began as Schnellinger carefully restarted the record, "where you moved the items. Is it safe?"

"Safe? Have you looked outside, sir? Nowhere in Pillau is safe. Not unless you are already dead."

"But they have not moved the cargo on? Perhaps loaded it on a ship?"

"Not as far as I know." Schnellinger yawned. "God knows the ships are crowded enough already. Even with the bombing and the submarines, they are moving thirty thousand civilians a day back to Germany."

More heavy boots in the corridor outside. Multiple men. Müller, no doubt, returning with Weber. And at least one friend. Their footfall slowed as they approached.

Schnellinger looked with expectant eyes towards the doorway.

And Stahl suddenly knew with awful clarity exactly what the man had written on that note.

Yelling orders, the first soldier burst through the doorway, his machine pistol pointed at Stahl's face. Two more followed, Müller and the young guard from the front entrance, crowding Stahl. He kept his hands visible.

Schnellinger spat on the floor. "You are under arrest, Herr Obersturmbannführer."

"What is the meaning of this?" Fury swept through Stahl. At himself. At his overconfidence. He did not need to feign the anger in his voice, but he added indignation. "Soldier, you will lower your weapon now."

"Ignore him, Weber. I knew I recognised you, Stahl."

Stahl kept his eyes on the nearest threat, the man holding the weapon. Keep them off balance, he told himself. Make them think. "My name is Obersturmbannführer Plendl. I have my

253

papers." He reached for his coat, and for the pistol hidden beneath it.

"Don't move," Weber screamed, gobbets of phlegm arcing from his trembling lips.

Schnellinger shook his head. "Your picture was on the wall of the lecture theatre at the SS-Junkerschule Bad Tölz. I could not believe it when I saw the signal with the arrest order."

"Shut your filthy mouth, traitor." Stahl's mind moved quickly, considering options. He turned to stare at Schnellinger, using the movement as cover while he marked the positions of the soldiers. "Weber, your battalion commander is under arrest for colluding with the Soviets. My orders are to arrest him and any accomplices."

Doubt flickered in Weber's eyes.

"Pathetic," Schnellinger said. "To think we cadets dreamed of one day being like the legendary Jan Stahl. Müller, find rope. Bind his hands."

"Are you married, Weber?"

The Scharführer seemed abruptly to realise the enormity of what he was doing, pointing his weapon at a senior officer.

Stahl could sense the hesitation in the other two soldiers as well, but he focused purely on Weber. He kept his voice calm. It would help little to intimidate the man so badly that he pulled the trigger by mistake. "You are married? Children?"

"Yes, sir," Weber mumbled. "Twins." The muzzle barrel twitched but did not lower.

"Were you working with Schnellinger, too? With the Communists?"

The man's eyes bulged. He glanced at his officer.

"He's lying, Weber. His name is Jan Stahl. He is a wanted man, and Germany will honour us for his arrest."

"Weber, look at me. Think of your twins. Do you wish them to see your wife brought before a People's Court? The wife of a traitor?"

"I am loyal," Weber mumbled. But the weapon remained fixed.

"Damn it," Schnellinger snapped. "I'll do it myself." He turned towards the phonograph and the pistol next to it. Weber's eyes, as haunted and wild as a trapped animal, followed the movement.

Knocking the barrel aside, Stahl drove his forehead into Weber's nose. He heard it splinter, the adrenaline already deadening any sensation of pain.

The man grunted and stumbled back. Stahl spun and slammed the ridge of his hand into the stunned Müller's windpipe, but the third guard was on him now. Grabbing his coat. Pushing him back against the wall. Stronger than he looked.

Wrenching at the man's forearm with one hand, Stahl snaked the other free and reached for the guard's face.

His nails raked the man's cheek before he found the eye socket. He drove his thumb in behind the eyeball, feeling the wet warmth deep inside the skull. The guard squealed, his grip loosening. Stahl's elbow cracked across his jaw, a glancing blow, sending him stumbling back into the choking Müller while his eyeball lolled half proud of the socket.

Stahl's other hand closed on his pistol.

His finger hadn't reached the trigger when he felt the blow, the sudden impact of something against his shoulder that pushed him back.

Schnellinger shouted something, his own pistol raised in his hand. Stahl's ringing ears heard nothing but the fading roar of the gunshot. The words didn't matter, anyway. Stahl shot the officer through the base of the throat before he could repeat them.

Next, the guard. Stahl's bullet tore through the hand that was still trying clumsily to stuff the eye back in. Exited the back of the skull. Buried itself in the blood-flecked sandbagged wall.

Weber, his eyes wide, reached out a despairing hand. Stahl put two more rounds in his chest.

That left only Müller, on his knees, clutching his throat. Tears streamed down his reddened face.

Seven seconds to kill three men and cripple a fourth. Stahl grimaced. He was slowing with age.

He took a step forward. His legs gave, and he stumbled sideways into the wall. Pain shot through him, urgent and vicious. His overcoat was wet. Confused, he looked down at his left hand. It felt cold.

Across the upper sleeve and breast, a dark stain spread.

"Müller." It took him two attempts to get the word out. "Do you want to live?"

The man nodded, still trying to draw breath.

"Good," Stahl said. "That is good. You are the radioman, yes? Where is your radio?"

"Next room," Müller gasped.

"Is anyone else in this bunker right now?"

A shake of the head.

"Thank you, Müller," Stahl said, and pulled the trigger.

The echo faded, leaving the room silent but for Brahms and the steady dripping from the guard's shattered cranium.

Stahl shuffled across the room, keeping his breathing even to stop the darkness that wanted to encroach on his vision. Schnellinger's vacated chair looked comfortable and inviting, but Stahl knew that if he sat down now, he might not get up. Instead, he stayed standing. It did not take long to flick through the battalion file on the desk to the right page. *19 March. 1125 local. 4x truck Königsberg to loading area D3. 1345 local. 3x truck Königsberg to loading area D3.* His fingertip added bloody emphasis to the end of the record.

"Lying bastard," Stahl spat, and kicked the dead Schnellinger in the kidneys. The impact sent a fresh shock of pain down his left side. The room blurred, as if underwater.

Shock.

Breathe, he thought. Fast and shallow.

Wait for it to pass.

He left the music playing. More gunfire in the distance, and the low drone of aircraft. He felt a bass rumble through his bloody palm as he let the wall guide him back out of the room and down the fifty feet to where the dead Müller's radio waited. It took him minutes to get there. Too long. Longer still to get the radio working and find the right frequency, one handed only, his left arm already numb and useless.

"*Pesta* to *Huldra*," he said, and waited.

Nothing.

"*Pesta* calling *Huldra*, how do you read?"

Silence. Just a faint hissing of static.

He checked the radio settings. It should be right, but the words were already swimming in his head. Less than seventy-hours since he had left England. That didn't seem possible. The bullet in his shoulder was real. The smell of blood in his nostrils? Real. Everything else? Fading. Unreliable memories. Not to be trusted.

"*Pesta* to *Huldra*." More silence, both from the radio and within the empty halls of the bunker. Maybe the sounds of gunfire had gone unnoticed or lost in the din of the front line. Maybe not. Maybe others were already closing in to finish him.

He was going to die. The realisation didn't surprise him. Deep down, he had known when he boarded the Hudson at Tempsford. Earlier. Back in the cell at Flossenbürg with Canaris. They had both known. The Admiral had gone first, that was all.

It didn't matter. Only *Götterdämmerung* mattered.

He gripped the microphone again. Perhaps they could hear him in Stockholm, perhaps not, but someone was listening. They had to be.

"*Pesta* to *Huldra*. AFTERLIGHT. I say again, AFTERLIGHT..."

Chapter Thirty-Three

Norfolk, 13 April

She found him on the control tower balcony. He must have heard her approaching, met her footsteps with a slow turn of the head. No surprise, no change of expression. She couldn't read his eyes.

"Barton said you'd be here," Lane said. She shivered in the wind coming in off the North Sea. The day was still too young for the new sun to take the edge off the chill. "I brought you tea." She passed him the mug, then cupped both her hands gratefully around the warmth of her own.

"Thank you." He took it and went back to staring out over the airfield.

"What are we looking at?"

"Everything," Durban said. "Nothing. I wasn't sure I'd see you again."

"The operation isn't over yet."

The control tower wasn't very tall but still towered over the rest of the airfield. She counted thirteen Mosquitoes parked in their various states of maintenance. She knew Durban's wasn't among them. The Uelzen after-action reports had stated, in the emotionless tones of officialdom, that two had been struck off strength. Too badly damaged to salvage. Another moved to depot for repair work. Three wounded. No mention of courage, or terror, or pain.

She took up a position next to him, a few inches apart, resting her arms like his on the railing, feeling the cold metal through the sleeves of her uniform. "Have you seen Johnny?"

"He's still in the hospital. Lucky, really."

"Lucky? He almost died."

"I meant me. Lucky, that I didn't get him killed. We missed one, and instead of thinking it through, I went in like a damned trainee and got us shot to pieces." His gaze remained fixed on something in the distance. Perhaps a Mosquito. Perhaps something that only he could see. "I messed it up, Sarah. Nearly blew the whole bloody show."

"That's not what it says on the report," Lane said. "Textbook attack was the phrase used. Complete mission success. There is talk of another bar to your Distinguished Flying Cross."

"They can keep it."

"You know, Napoleon once said that a soldier will fight long and hard for a piece of coloured ribbon. Medals must mean something."

"Napoleon never flew low-level ops."

She laughed. The wind plucked at her hair. From the look of the Wing Commander's own locks, he had been out here far too long. The handful of RAF air traffic and operations personnel behind the tower's windows seemed much more comfortable. "Can we go somewhere a little less breezy?"

"I like it up here. I can think, without Bony or anyone else knocking on my office door. And we have three replacement kites due in; I want to get a look at them when they arrive. No word from Stahl?"

"Not since he jumped."

He looked at her sharply, and she realised he knew nothing of Stahl's mission. She turned away to hide the irritation that crossed her face, partly because once again she had told this man more than he needed to know, but more because she had to keep anything from him in the first place. She glanced at the window and doors behind her. Closed. No way they would hear her through the glass over the wind, but she still lowered her voice. "Stahl has returned to Germany to locate your final target.

We're monitoring every SS frequency we have, contacting every agent network left out there, listening for signs of *Götterdämmerung*. Nothing yet, but at least we haven't heard of his arrest. He'll find it."

At last, Durban turned to look at her. He looked older, the last few weeks putting years on his face. She wondered if the same was true of hers. "You believe that, don't you?"

"Of course," she lied. "Why, have you got something better to believe in?"

"I don't. Could you at least tell me what he's looking for?"

"You know I can't, Andy."

"Yeah, I know." There was bitterness in his voice, she noted. It had been there since he first saw her. She knew it had little to do with his level of security access, or her willingness to share it. "How long do you think Stahl has? To find the final target location?"

"I don't know," she admitted. "If he can track it down, and if he is still alive to get the message to us... well, I still can't say. We don't know what timescale the Nazis are working to. All we know is that they haven't moved it yet." Which was also a lie, though one based on hope. Yesterday's imagery of Pillau, taken from a high-flying P-38 photo-reconnaissance aircraft, showed the U-78 still alongside at the port. The consensus at the Joint Intelligence Committee was that the SS scientists would release the weapon only when they were ready to board the submarine and evacuate. For all their fine talk of the nation going down fighting, she doubted many of them planned to go down with it. Especially not the men with the perverted science to create *Götterdämmerung*, and who knew better than any what it was capable of.

But she couldn't know for sure that U-78 hadn't left since then, and the next PR flight wasn't scheduled for another four hours. If the docks showed empty, it would already be too late.

Durban sipped his tea. Grimaced. "It's sweet."

"Barton said that's how you take it," she protested.

"He knows it's not, the vindictive sod. Still, it's hot. That's something. How are you coping, Sarah?"

"I'm..." The abrupt change of subject caught her off guard. She sipped her tea to give her time to think. "I'm sorry."

"For what?"

"Leaving in the way I did. Not being in contact. Not checking on you after... after Uelzen."

"You had your reasons, I'm sure."

"I did. And you deserve to know them."

Lane took a deep breath. She knew that some of her hair had escaped her bun. It flicked against her face in the wind, and she absently brushed it aside, only for it to return immediately. Durban was waiting, watching. His expression showed patience but couldn't fully hide the curiosity in his eyes. Now that she'd promised to do so, she wished she hadn't. In three years, Durban was the only person she'd felt able to share anything with, that she'd come close to opening up to.

"I told you once that I personally sent one hundred and thirteen agents into Occupied Europe. That's true. Maybe I didn't sign the orders myself, and someone else would have sent them on their way if not me. But they were still mine, you know?"

"You feel responsible."

She nodded. "The men you've lost, under your command. Do you remember their names?"

"Most of them. The first time I lost someone, it nearly broke me. But I learned you need to move on. It's war, Sarah. You can't let it break you. The best way I can keep my men alive is by being strong. Being a leader."

"But don't you see, Andy? That's the difference. You lead your men into combat. I sent mine, but I didn't go with them. I stayed here, where it's safe."

"You did your job. You did it well."

"Did I?" Her eyes were damp. Doubtless, the stiff breeze. Damn Andy for wanting to stay up here when his office was warm and comfortable. "Of those one hundred and thirteen agents, eighty-five were men. Some were former military, others new to the game. They came to me fully formed from SOE, trained and ready to go. I picked the exact task, but I didn't pick them. I remember all their names, but I never knew them. The other twenty-eight were women, and I know all of them like they were my own sisters."

"I didn't know we sent so many women agents," Durban said.

"You weren't supposed to. No one was. Those were just the ones who went to Germany and Austria from my section. SOE sent far more to France. It caused a hell of a legal mess. You see, women can't be combatants, even though we were sending them out with pistols and explosives. A man, if arrested, might be lucky enough to be treated as a soldier, kept as a POW with rights under the Geneva Convention. The women? Spies. A spy has no rights."

She heard a noise in the distance. Aircraft engines. Over a distant treeline, she saw a Mosquito emerge from the early morning mist, heading their way. A spare arriving. The reason Durban was up here.

He didn't even glance at it. He kept his eyes on hers.

"One month ago," she said, "I thought I understood. I'd made mistakes. Who hasn't? But I'd done my job, to the best of my ability. In war, people die. I didn't kill them, and I knew who did."

"Stahl."

She nodded. "Just saying his name allowed me to absolve myself of so much of the blame. I told myself every night that their blood wasn't on my hands, but his." She rubbed at her eyes. She had risen early to drive to Norfolk, but she knew her exhaustion went much deeper than that. "And then the bastard ruins it. It wasn't his fault at all."

"He pulled the trigger, Sarah."

"Out of mercy. The ones he killed were the lucky ones. He saved them. Not me. I didn't do a damn thing to help them."

"Now wait a minute," Durban said. "What could you have done? Flown in yourself and been captured too? Fat lot of good that would have done for them. You once told me I wasn't to blame for Clive Lampeter's death, and maybe you're right, but do you think he would rest any easier knowing I bought it as well? No. Clive Lampeter volunteered. He fought for what he believed in. We all do. Whatever it takes. We all know the war can claim us at any time, but that doesn't mean we walk away from it. Your agents didn't walk away either. Don't cheapen their sacrifice by taking their choice from them."

Anger flared in her, then faded as quickly. She wanted to yell that he didn't know what it was like, what she was going through, but he knew. If anyone did, it was him. The difference was that he'd been able to bury Lampeter, or at least whatever was left of him. They denied her agents even that. She knew the fate of some. A bullet in the head, Stahl's finger pulling the trigger. The rest were dead too, most likely, and she could only hope that they had died so quickly and painlessly. She wasn't fool enough to believe it, though. She had read too many eyewitness accounts of what the Gestapo and the SS would do to the unfortunates they captured. If any were still alive, it was only because the Germans thought they still had information to share.

No, she thought, as the chilly wind pierced her uniform, it was probably too late to help them. But she could still find them.

He broke the silence first. Lane was grateful for that. "Do you want to know the real reason I'm up here, Sarah?"

She followed the direction of his pointed finger. "That farm?"

It seemed pretty enough, though no more so than a dozen other farms she had passed on her drive here.

He nodded. "Matlock Farm," he said. "The bane of my existence. You would think that after six years of war we'd all be pulling the same way, but not there. Every squadron commander who has ever served on this airfield knows them all too well. They cause us more problems than the Germans."

"How?"

"Noise complaints," he grimaced. "Our aircraft are too loud, apparently. Never mind that we are trying to fight a war. They are trying to sleep. A few weeks before I took over, the squadron had an aircraft come back badly damaged from a night raid and crash just short of the runway. The rescue crews hadn't finished cutting the bodies out of the burned-up wreckage before the complaint arrived from Matlock Farm that the explosion had woken them up."

She stared at the farm with a surge of contempt. The pretty buildings suddenly seemed less appealing. The unkempt surrounds and the wear and tear on the barn loomed large, casting a shadow over the whole. She muttered a Polish curse under her breath. It rang oddly in her ears, a word and a language left unfamiliar by years of disuse. "Can't you just ignore them?"

"I can, and do," Durban said. "But then they write to Group Headquarters, or to the parish, or to the local newspaper. Everyone is too polite to tell them what they should do with their letters, so they pass them on to me with an admonishment to *take more care*. Part of me wants to go over there and hurl curses in their faces, and sometimes when I am on final approach, I imagine my finger reaching for the trigger for my cannons and giving them something to really complain about. But what I truly want to do is even more shocking."

"What's that?"

"I want to buy the place."

She cocked her head. "Why? So you can burn it down in front of them?"

"I want to live there."

That took her by surprise. "I never really thought of you as the farming type, Andy."

He laughed. "I said to live, not work, though the place definitely needs more work than I'd like. I can't imagine raising cattle or harvesting, nor do I want to try. But there's something about that farmhouse. I see it every time I land here. Somehow, it feels like... safety. Like coming home. I can't imagine they will keep this airfield once the war is done. Once our Mosquitoes leave, Matlock Farm will go back to being quiet and isolated. That's the place I want. Away from all of this. Away from the memories."

"A place to be alone?"

"I didn't say alone." Again, his gaze pierced her with its intensity.

She swallowed. Stared back. Below them, the Mosquito cut its engines, the roar of its engines subsiding abruptly, leaving only the silent fields and the gentle rush of the breeze. "Andy, you know..."

He shook his head, cutting her off. "God knows I'm not asking for anything from you, Sarah." He looked away. His hands closed tight on the railings. Anger at himself, not her. "It's just a foolish dream."

She took a deep breath. Placed her hand on his. "It seems restful," she said. "You're not the only one who has foolish thoughts, you know. The Nazis destroyed my past life. The war denied me a new one. When it is all over, maybe I'll get to choose how my future looks."

He nodded, his eyes still on the farm, and she felt a sudden longing. She wasn't sure for what, but as the sunlight burned off the mist, so the farmhouse looked more inviting. The repairs needed wouldn't take long. Wildflowers shimmied in the breeze by the front door. For an instant, she imagined herself coming home to that place. Up the long driveway. Drawing her key from her purse. Andy opening the door to her before she could reach the lock.

The anger flooded back, vicious and sudden. Foolish? It was stupid. Worse, it was a betrayal. Beyond the ranks of familiar faces that flashed across her mind, already fading in death, she saw Durban wince as her grip tightened with crushing force around his fingers.

"The war doesn't end when Berlin falls and Hitler burns in Hell, Andy," she said. "Not for me. It ends when I find my missing agents."

Durban looked at her. Not shock. Not even surprise. Just a deep sigh and understanding eyes.

"Alive or dead," she told him, knowing which one it would be. "Wherever they are. Every single one."

"I know," he said. "I knew it the first time we spoke. That you'd see it through to the end." He looked away, back towards the distant farm. "And I will, too."

"Whatever it takes," she whispered. She let her grip relax, wishing the rest of her could do the same, just once. She didn't pull her hand away, though. Simply left it there. Until his fingers closed around hers and they stood, looking across the familiar green fields of England, in silence.

There was nothing left to say.

Chapter Thirty-Four

Norfolk, 15 April

Durban switched off the office lights and stopped with his hand in his pocket, fingers on the door key. "I'm leaving, Bony."

"We've received a note from SHAEF, sir."

"SHAEF?" Durban frowned. What could Supreme Headquarters Allied Expeditionary Force want with 465 Squadron? A transfer to a forward airfield on the continent, perhaps? Their sister squadron 464 had already received orders to move to Melsbroek in Belgium and would leave in two days, but those orders would come from 2nd Tactical Air Force HQ, not SHAEF.

It was probably some random supply question or other trivia. "Put it with the rest of the squadron admin traffic," he sighed. "I'll handle it in the morning. I want to get some dinner before they close for the night."

"It's not for the squadron, sir. It's for you, by name."

"Well, that makes no sense at all." He snatched the note and opened it. It was indeed addressed to him, sent less than two hours ago from the office of an Air Commodore in SHAEF's HQ in Versailles. He vaguely remembered meeting the man once. Possibly at the Palace ceremony for the third bar on his DFC. He felt his body relax. Probably personal, and not work-related, except for the SECRET marking.

A mobile Signal Intelligence unit intercepted the following on 12 Apr 45. Ack receipt and indicate significance, if any.

MESSAGE BEGINS // PESTA TO HULDRA. AFTERLIGHT. I SAY AGAIN, AFTERLIGHT. PRIORITY MESSAGE FOR SARAH LANE AND ANDREW DURBAN. TARGET LOCATED,

267

WATERFRONT DOCKS. PRECISE BUILDING UNKNOWN. TIMESCALE UNKNOWN. BOAT STILL PRESENT. IMMEDIATE STRIKE NEEDED. I WILL TRY TO LOCATE EXACT TARGET. SORRY. I AM HURT. I WILL TRY. IMMEDIATE STRIKE NEEDED. SAY AGAIN, IMMEDIATE // MESSAGE ENDS.

"Sorry, sir," Bony said, "but are you alright?"

"Jesus."

The Ops Officer stared in alarm at the paper as it violently fluttered in Durban's shaking hand.

"Jesus," Durban repeated. "This was three days ago."

"It just arrived, sir. I brought it straight to you."

"They sat on this for three days." Durban read the message again. And again, eyes drawn each time to the abrupt ending. Like someone had cut the broadcast off. Or Stahl could no longer speak. The words *I am hurt* sprang from the page as if typed in boldface.

Three days. *Götterdämmerung* could be halfway across Europe by now.

Bile burned in his throat, hot even as a paralysing chill spread across the rest of his body. He forced it back. No time for that. Too much time wasted already.

"Get the word out, Bony. I want the base sealed, understand? No one leaves. Call the SWO and have him send someone to Staverton. Check the pub, the hotel, the dance hall, anywhere we might have people. Cancel all leave passes. Any aircrew on leave are to be recalled right away. You understand? Immediately."

"Roger, sir." Bony turned and half-ran back towards the Ops Room. His face suggested he wasn't convinced, but Durban didn't need him to be convinced, only to act, and Bony was a damned good Ops Officer.

Durban threw open his door and dialled the number from memory, adrenaline bringing clarity of recall. Five rings, his anxiety mounting with each one until he heard her voice, surprised at how calm it made him.

"Sarah, it's Durban."

"Andy? Hi. Is everything ok? I was just heading home."

"Sarah, did you get the message from Stahl?"

A pause. "This line isn't cleared to discuss that." Cool approbation in her tone.

"Did you?"

Another pause. Longer still. "No."

Durban cursed. "He's made contact."

She didn't respond immediately, but he knew she was still there. More than the faint intake of breath. He could sense her tension and excitement through the receiver, even if she was too professional to let it seep into her voice. "When?"

"Seventy-two hours ago. How soon can you be here?"

"Four hours."

"Too long." His mind raced. "Do you know how to get to RAF Northolt?"

"Of course. But it's in the wrong direction."

"Trust me. Get there as soon as you can. Bring Anders." He hung up. There was so much more he wanted to say to her, but there was no time, and a dozen other things to be sent in motion.

Ninety long minutes passed before a roar of engines announced the landing of an Avro Anson, and barely ten minutes more before the doors of the Ops Room swung open.

"My wife is most put out with you, Andy," Air Vice Marshal Sir Basil Embry roared, startling the handful of ops staff Durban had pulled together this late at night. "I trust I wasn't lying to her when I said it must be very important?"

"No, sir," Durban said. "Thank you for coming."

Embry snorted. "I can't help thinking you have used me as a very expensive taxi service. As you'll see, I brought a couple of strays."

"I don't think you'll regret it, sir," Durban assured him. He nodded at Anders, then returned Sarah's half-smile. She looked tired, but her eyes glowed with excitement.

With a single barked order, he dismissed those staff without the proper clearances from the room, then offered seats to his guests. None took them, standing impatiently while they waited for the Ops Room doors to close, leaving the four of them alone.

"This is for you, Wing Commander," Sarah said, passing Durban a copy of the latest imagery. He placed it on the planning table while they crowded immediately around him, then read them the text of Stahl's signal.

"After I spoke to you, sir," Durban said, "I called SHAEF and got through to Air Commodore Ackland-Rowe, the man who contacted me. One of the tactical Signals Intelligence units intercepted the message, but it didn't seem to match any collection criteria. It got passed up the chain to a junior officer who was on a forty-eight hour leave pass in Paris. When he returned, he had no idea what to do with it, and it somehow ended up on the Air Commodore's desk. He recognised my name and sent it to me."

"By which time it had been gathering dust for seventy-two hours," Embry grated. "Someone needs to be sacked for this."

"Not sure that will help much, sir," Sarah said. She pointed to the image. "A Spitfire took this earlier today. The U-78 is here."

"Well, that's good news," Embry said.

"About the only good news, I'm afraid," Durban said. "Stahl said the weapon is in a waterfront warehouse. As you'll see, that doesn't narrow it down much. There are at least a dozen buildings here meeting that description."

"Twenty-two," Sarah corrected. "I see that damned town in my sleep. I've counted every warehouse, every German military outpost, and it doesn't help at all. We don't even know which side of the Spit that warehouse is on."

"Surely," Embry protested, "it will be the one closest to the submarine?"

"Why? Only the scientists will leave on the submarine. The *Götterdämmerung* won't be let loose in the crowd until they are safely gone. The U-78 is at the U-Boat training facility, where it always is. Pillau isn't that big. Wherever the scientists are, they can walk there easy enough. One last stroll, before they kill half of Europe."

"Then we destroy all the warehouses." Embry smiled grimly. "Air Marshal Harris can have six hundred heavies there tomorrow night. Obviously, there will be a lot of civilian casualties that way, but that's never stopped Bomber Harris. If we don't hit that warehouse before they release this stuff, all those civilians are going to die, anyway. It's just that a lot of us will die with them."

Lane sighed. Durban got the impression that she would rather Embry was a mere taxi driver, and that he'd left after dropping them off. "If you recall the JIC meeting, sir," she said, "heavy bombers won't work. Even if they hit the building..."

"Yes, yes, I know all that. We'll just crack the seal and release the bloody stuff early. Do you have a better idea, Squadron Officer Lane? Or do you propose we wait here until the U-78 leaves and then roll the dice?"

Silence descended. Hopeless. Durban felt the image on the table mocking them. So close, yet without that last piece of the puzzle, even levelling the entire city wouldn't be enough. He felt weariness press down on him. Crushing him. Six years of war, six years of exhaustion, all bearing down in a single moment. Across the table, the big Dane's eyes seemed transfixed by the image, as if willpower alone could deliver the answer. "Major? You're very quiet. You have any thoughts?"

"Just one. Stahl. He will get us the answer."

"Anders," Sarah said gently, "there's a good chance that Stahl is dead."

271

"Stahl is a hard man to kill. Many have tried. Including me." The Dane smiled. "It will take more than the SS to finish that snake." His tone made it clear that it was not an insult, but respect.

"I want to believe that," Sarah said. "I do. But why hasn't he got a sign to us by now?"

"Maybe he has." Anders shrugged. "Maybe it is sitting on someone's desk waiting to be passed to us like his last message. Or he's hiding. We know he's hurt. Perhaps he is waiting for a sign from us."

"Like what?"

In an instant, adrenaline rushed through Durban's veins, sweeping away even the memory of his tiredness. "Like a squadron of Mosquitoes overhead."

A moment of silence.

"By God, that might do it." Embry's blue eyes blazed with new enthusiasm. "Can you go tomorrow?"

"Yes, sir. The new aircraft need about twelve hours' work on them, but the napalm arrived this morning. With planning and preparations, we could be ready to go by lunchtime."

"Did you recall the squadron?"

"Manning is at ninety percent. We're rounding up the last few now. The crews will be ready."

Embry paused, weighing his next words. "Did you find a new navigator yet?"

Colour flushed Durban's cheeks. "Not yet, sir."

"Get a move on, then. Because if you aren't ready to lead this attack, Andy, I'll do it myself." His voice softened. "They will be waiting for you. Not just the Germans. The Soviets, too. They won't sit by and let you destroy *Götterdämmerung*, not while they still think they can get their hands on it. If Stahl doesn't get a signal to you, you'll be circling in the teeth of German flak while every fighter for three hundred miles tries to do you in. You know that, don't you?"

Durban knew. He'd known it the moment the signal had come in. The moment these same three people had walked into his office and used the word AFTERLIGHT. That it would come down to this. A target. Flak and fighters. His squadron around him. His navigator by his side.

One last chance for the war to take him like it had taken so many others.

He saw Sarah watching him.

He'd seen the hope in her eyes when Embry suggested he might take over the mission. She didn't want him to go, even though she knew he was the best chance they had of success.

Roll the dice, Embry had said, and Durban had rolled them so many times. Got lucky, so many times, even when others around him didn't. Johnny Grant. Clive Lampeter. Others before them, right back to the day this awful, wonderful war began.

Eventually, everyone's luck ran out.

"Sounds like fun, sir."

"Yes, it does." Jealousy shone in Embry's eyes, bright as moonlight. "You lucky bugger. They will talk about this for years."

"I hope not," Anders said, his own eyes twinkling with excitement. "It is still most secret, after all." Then he reached out and wordlessly squeezed Durban's shoulder before joining Embry, hurrying towards the telephones.

Until only Sarah Lane's eyes remained on him. And in her gaze, he could discern nothing at all.

Chapter Thirty-Five

Another morning in the hospital, another sunrise shining half-heartedly through the thin curtain, another visit from the doctor. Days and nights had long since blended into a grey smear of sleep and boredom. Grant had little idea what day it was anymore, and it sometimes seemed the doctor didn't care. Both going through the motions, waiting for the war to be over.

"I feel fine," Grant said. He'd become accustomed to beginning each day with a lie. I'm fine. No, the wounds don't hurt anymore. Yes, I am ready to fly again. The last one was partly true at least, even if he suspected it was his personal guilt talking and not his still recovering body.

"Good lad," Doctor Carpenter said absently. "I admire your spirit. But there's a big difference between lying in bed thinking you are recovered and being strong enough to spend all day on your feet. I'll do you a deal. Two more days here, and I'll discharge you."

"And clear me for flying?"

"Oh, Lord no," the doctor laughed, his gaze already drifting to the next name on his list. "You've got at least another two or three weeks before you even think about getting in a cockpit again. In the meantime, try getting more sleep, there's a good chap. Rest is nature's cure, you know." With that, he strolled away. He'd said the same thing every morning for a week. Grant wondered if the man even bothered to read his charts anymore.

After breakfast – two thin rashers of bacon, powdered eggs, four small and over salted mushrooms, same as yesterday – Grant conceded that the doctor might be right about one thing.

He could use more sleep. The nightmares had abated a little. Less terror, more guilt.

Guilt at laying in his bed while the squadron got on with the war. Guilt at leaving Durban alone, though he suspected that the Wing Commander had long since replaced him, and probably forgotten him too. Guilt at the self-pity and whining he constantly caught himself indulging in.

Most of all, guilt at the secret thrill of relief that washed over him every time the doctor marked him down as medically unfit. One more day before he had to go back to the skies. To the dangers that tainted their beauty.

Eyes closed, the warming morning sun playing on the lids, he let himself drift off.

"You've got to let one of them down eventually," he heard Nurse Anita say. She had a pleasant voice. Soothing.

"Do I?" That would be Nurse Claire. A lovely girl, but the opposite of soothing. Usually giggling, always too loud. If she knew that some of the more seriously wounded casualties on the ward were still sleeping, she didn't let it slow her down. "Why would I do that? It's nice being chased. Besides, we don't all have to settle for the first one who shows an interest, do we?"

"I'm not settling."

"I'm teasing, love," Claire said. "Are you serious that you'd go back to Australia with him? When he asks?"

Grant wondered if it would be too obvious if he pulled his thin pillow over his head to cover his ears.

"New Zealand, and yes. Of course. If he asks." Anita sighed. "I really thought last night was going to be it, you know? The dinner, and everything. He'd even got hold of a bottle of French red wine. It must have cost him a fortune."

"Let me guess," Claire interrupted, her tone lascivious. "The two of you got distracted and pretended you were already married."

"Hush. You'll make me blush. And no, that's not what

happened at all. We were still in the restaurant when a man came in, wearing uniform. From the base, but not a pilot. He comes over, salutes, and whispers something in Mark's ear. He goes proper pale. Scared the life out of me."

Pain shot through Grant. He realised he was sitting up, mind still racing to work out why.

"Then he kisses me on the cheek," Anita said, "and just like that, he's gone."

"Isn't that just like a pilot?" Claire shook her head. "All flash, no bang. That's why I only go for gunners."

Grant stood quickly. Too quickly. The blood rushed from his head. Not his blood, he thought vaguely. Half of it was borrowed. Transfusion after transfusion to make up what he'd left spattered about the Mosquito's cockpit.

He steadied himself with one hand and forced his dizziness from his face. "Nurse Anita?"

She started at the sight of him, so close. "You alright, Johnny? Doctor said you should—"

"Have you seen Kittens since last night, Ma'am? Or spoken to him?"

"No," she stammered. "I tried calling the squadron, but the exchange said all the lines were down."

Grant turned around, the movement almost enough to topple him. Placing one hand on the wall, he leaned carefully down to look beside his bed. "Where are my clothes?"

"Gone," Anita said. "We had to cut them off you when they brought you in."

"I'll need a new uniform, then." He plucked at the front of his cheap hospital pyjamas. "I can't leave wearing these," he added under his breath. He took a deep breath, warding off another wave of nausea, this one born not just of physical exertion and pain, but from new and certain knowledge. The abrupt end to Anita's date and the closure of the phone lines to Charney

276

Breach could only mean one thing. They had recalled 465 Squadron. The next stage of the operation was on.

"Johnny," Anita said hesitantly, "you're not cleared to leave yet."

Durban had replaced him, no doubt, but that didn't matter. He was still part of 465 Squadron.

"Get back into bed, love," Claire said. "I'll bring you a cup of tea. If you're lucky, maybe I'll tuck you in." She gave him a lascivious grin.

He could do that, he knew. Go back to bed. Watch the lazy passage of the clouds through his window, and not through the Perspex of the cockpit, wondering what else lurked up there. No one would think any less of him.

Well, almost no one.

"Get Doctor Carpenter," he said. Both nurses blanched slightly at the command. They weren't used to it. Not from him. They figured him all shy smiles and polite requests and had probably forgotten he was an officer.

He didn't hold it against them. He'd forgotten too. But that changed now.

Giving Claire his best smile, he added, "please." She blushed and glanced at Anita, waiting for her colleague's nod before hurrying away.

Anita shook her head. "Johnny, it won't matter. Look at the state of you. You can hardly stand. The doctor won't clear you to leave."

He believed her.

"You know," she said, "Mark thinks the world of you. He asked me to keep a close eye on you. Said you'd probably ask to get out of here early. I guess he was right."

"He's a good man," Grant said. Meaning it, even while he was simply stalling her while his mind fumbled through his nausea, trying to come up with a plan.

"He really is." She beamed.

"Hopefully, he likes me enough to invite me to the wedding."

"Of course," she said, then her cheeks coloured. "Well, he has to get around to asking first."

"He will," Grant said. "I reckon he's crazy about you. How could he not be?"

More colour, turning her cheeks an appealing shade of pink. Kittens was a lucky man, Grant thought. They would be happy together when the war was over.

But the war wasn't over. Not yet.

Grant sighed and let his body sag. "Sorry, Anita," he said. "I know you're right. I just got a little excited, that's all." He glanced at the bed. "Maybe I'll take a nap. Can you find Doctor Carpenter and tell him not to bother? I'd hate to waste his time."

"That's ok," she said brightly. "He understands. You're not his first patient to ask to leave before they are ready. He won't mind coming and chatting with you."

Grant stifled a curse as he glanced down the corridor. No sign of Claire and the doctor. Hopefully, she was struggling to find him or had got distracted on the way there. Either way, now he had a time limit.

He let Anita help him into the bed, exaggerating his exhaustion, hiding the fact that adrenaline had already won the battle with exhaustion, at least for a few moments. "I feel like I've just gone fifteen rounds for the championship," he said, truthfully. "Please, would you get me some more water?" He motioned to the half-empty jug by his bedside.

She looked at him. Eyes inscrutable. He blinked, letting his eyes half close. Pretending that sleep was close. She didn't look away.

She knew.

But she nodded anyway. "Fine," she said. "I'll be back in one minute."

He watched her walk away, telling himself that he must have imagined the emphasis she had placed on the last word, but sure he hadn't. Gaze glued to every slow step, he waited until she had turned the corner, jug in hand. Then he moved.

Sixty seconds, she had promised him.

He was up in less than two, ignoring the dizziness. He slid his feet into the hospital slippers, knowing they would give him almost no grip if he needed to run, not that he could run if he wanted to. Walking as fast as he dared, he headed the opposite way from the nurses, half-expecting to hear Claire or Doctor Carpenter's shouted challenge from behind him. It didn't come.

Fifty seconds. He kept his eyes firmly forward, refusing to meet those of the other patients. He sensed a couple of them watching him with quizzical expressions. Most ignored him, sleeping or lost in their own pain.

Forty seconds. He was in the hallway now. This was about as far as they'd let him come since he arrived at the hospital, short walks with a nurse by his side, just enough to prevent muscle atrophy and bed sores. His legs felt unsteady beneath him. Like they weren't his, but merely borrowed for the occasion. It wasn't too late to go back. This was a stupid idea.

He kept moving, letting his momentum drive him forward.

Ahead, two doctors he didn't recognise hurried towards him, shoulder to shoulder, talking to each other, their eyes on him. Grant's heartbeat pounded in his ears, drowning out anything they might be saying. He glanced left and right. No fire escapes.

No exits at all.

The doctors split now, forming a wider barrier ahead of him. An odd prickling sensation spread up his back and neck. Like they were closing the net on him from behind, too. He fought the urge to turn around. He didn't want to see the disappointment on Doctor Carpenter's face, or Claire's knowing look.

His hand curled into a fist. He looked at it, surprised at himself. Right now, he was in for a stern talking to, an admonishment for trying to leave the hospital without permission. He doubted it would be any more formal than that. Punch a doctor and that became a court martial, never mind the nobility of his reasons. That wasn't the major reason he forced the hand to relax and open, though. The doctors had their reasons, too, and Grant would not hit a good man for doing his job.

The two doctors were barely three yards from him now, still closing, and Grant smiled at the thought of punching anyone. If he was only half as weak as he felt, they wouldn't even notice the blow.

Splitting further, the doctors passed on either side of him. One ignored him completely, still talking about another patient, some other condition. The other doctor returned the smile that still hung on Grant's face. Then they were gone.

Grant turned and saw them hurrying on. There were no suspicious looks back. No Carpenter. No nurses.

Twenty seconds left.

He leaned against the wall, checking the lay of the land, allowing himself three deep breaths, just another recovering patient out for a recuperative stroll. This junction was the last bit of the hospital he recognised. The signs above told him everything he needed with cold, medical precision. Surgery. Wards 1-4. Wards 5-8. Burns. Cafeteria. The last two were side by side, like they belonged together. He forced away the foolish grin he felt at that. Delirious, he told himself. Ten seconds left.

Exit.

He ignored that one. Whether Nurse Anita was being helpful or merely gullible, it wouldn't be long before they would look for him, and the first thing they would seal off would be the front entrance. Instead, he turned left, letting the white-washed wall support his weight a little, careful that it wasn't too obvious. Sunlight poured through the windows on the other side of the corridor, revealing trees and fields rich with that distinctly vivid shade of green that only England seemed to possess. He glimpsed the roof of an ambulance, one floor down, static but poised in expectancy of the next call out. That made him think of the squadron again, the looming mission, and he felt a different kind of nausea at the thought of how many ambulances would be needed when the survivors made it home.

He reached the fire escape at the end of the corridor. He was out of time.

No shouts of alarm. Not yet. No wailing sirens. He wondered what they would sound like. He'd heard air raid warnings before. Something similar, he supposed. Maybe less strident, so as not to upset the patients who behaved and did as their doctors told them. Halfway down the cold and dimly lit staircase, his nostrils caught a whiff of cigarette smoke. He froze, then flinched as an orderly threw open the fire door below him with a crash of metal on brick. Their eyes met.

The orderly tossed a smouldering cigarette butt back out of the open door, muttered an apology, and ran past him up the stairs, taking them two at a time.

Last chance to turn around.

Catching the door before it closed, Grant stumbled out into the morning air. Nothing fresh about it. The whiff of cigarettes became almost a miasma.

Five men and a woman stood or sat around the entranceway, smoke rising from them, the pavement below their feet littered with dozens of abandoned cigarettes, all drawn down to the last gasp and beyond. Four were patients. The other two worked here – he vaguely recognised the nurse – but neither showed any more interest in him than the patients.

Forcing a smile of greeting that was politely ignored, Grant walked past, fumbling in the pocket of his pyjama shirt as if reaching for his own cigarettes. He leaned against the wall, tilting his body so that they wouldn't notice that his hands were empty, enjoying the support that the stones offered his exhausted frame. He took a deep breath. Slowly, feigning interest in something seen or heard, he walked around the corner of the building, out of their sight. No one called or followed. They probably hadn't even noticed he'd gone.

Now he blinked, looking straight towards the morning sun. He was on some sort of service access road by the back side of the hospital. Staff parking, rubbish bins placed neatly for pickup, two more ambulances waiting with their back doors flung open to reveal empty interiors. The scent of cooking drifted across the tarmac. His stomach grumbled in approval, not caring that the food smelt better than it had ever tasted. Ahead, a car passed by on the main road, and Grant saw a bus stop. Not an option, he knew, not in his hospital slippers and pyjamas. Besides, who knew how long the bus would take to arrive? He certainly couldn't risk tarrying in the open long enough to find out.

No sirens yet, he thought. Doctor Carpenter and his staff were obviously closing the net in silence, choosing not to warn him they were coming. Clever, he thought. They were probably already watching the bus stop.

Suddenly cold, he crossed the service road and tottered away from the bus stop, heading further towards the back of the hospital, where the fields pressed close. There had to be some sort of footpath, he thought, trying to remember his maps, how far it was from the little hospital symbol back to Charney Breach.

Nine miles. Maybe ten.

He could do that, he told himself. He used to walk that far to school every morning as a child, carrying his schoolbooks over one thin shoulder. Easy.

His legs buckled.

A car pulled up next to him. He hadn't heard it coming over his own gasping breaths. A Hillman Minx. Official looking. The passenger door opened, flung wide from within. A shadowy figure stared at him.

Well, Grant thought, at least they would let him sleep while he waited for the court martial.

"Are you getting in?" That voice. Familiar. "Or are you going to waste more of my time?"

Grant shook his head. It made no sense. "Sir?"

"Don't stand there gawping," Squadron Leader Barton snapped.

Numbly, Grant gripped the door frame for support and fell into the passenger seat. He pulled the door closed, marvelling at how sweaty his fingers felt. How the hands shook. "Sir, they called you?"

"Who?"

"The hospital staff." Grant saw the confusion on the Australian's face. "They are looking for me," he confided. "That's why I went out of the back. They sealed off the main entrance."

"Mate, I just came from the main entrance," Barton said. "No one has sealed off anything. I spoke to that nurse Kittens is seeing, the lucky bastard. She told me you'd wandered away from your bed, and I got bored waiting for you to come back. I thought I'd do one last lap of the hospital before I headed back. What the bloody hell were you planning to do? Walk back to the airfield? In those bloody slippers?"

"Of course not," Grant said, letting his head slump back against the window.

Barton gave him a long look. "You know what's going on?"

Grant nodded. It was all he could muster.

"I won't ask if they have cleared you to fly. Any fool can see they haven't. Question is, are you going to do it anyway?"

283

Not too late, Grant thought. Despite the cloud cover, the sky looked pretty from here. Safe. He should be in bed. He could be in bed. Resting. Healing. By the time the doctors cleared him to fly, the war would most likely be over. No more throwing up his guts as the fear tore through him. No more fighters or flak, no more of the countless other ways to die.

He thought of Durban. Finny. Kittens. The man next to him.

He knew what his mother would say. Listen to the doctors. Listen to your orders. He could already see the relief in her eyes.

But he wouldn't see it. Because if he said no now, he wouldn't be able to look her in the eyes ever again.

He took a deep breath. Saw Barton's approving nod even before he answered the question.

"Let's go."

Chapter Thirty-Six

Someone moaned in the darkness.

Stahl barely noticed. The dull background hum of human suffering never really faded in this place. Pain. Thirst. The agonized passing of a loved one in the embrace of helpless arms. Sometimes the noise disappeared beneath the crump of Russian artillery, falling in lethal sheets beyond the thick concrete walls of the overcrowded bomb shelter, but it never truly went away.

With great care, he tilted his wrist.

He didn't make the effort out of concern for disturbing the refugee who had lay slumped against his shoulder. He was pretty sure the man had died a few hours earlier, his soft snoring giving way to a single ragged gasp, then silence. Stahl figured there were probably five hundred people crammed into the shelter, huddled together for warmth or the simple companionship of shared suffering, and likely fifty or more of those were dead. The mourning period in this place was short. Pillau had become the worst place in the world. Heaven, Hell, or oblivion, at least the dead had gone somewhere else.

No, Stahl gave little thought to the surrounding others, but even slight movements could send paroxysms of pain shooting through his body.

In the dim light, his watch said half past ten. Morning. At night, the darkness pressed even closer. As for the date, that was beyond him to guess. Time had become a blur.

He had found a medic to attend the gunshot wound – young enough to be overawed by the SS uniform, too young to have the skills to do much more than stop the bleeding. If the wound didn't become infected, and that was a big if, Stahl was reasonably confident he would survive it. Not now. The shoulder was probably beyond saving, muscle and nerves destroyed by the bullet's impact. He would be a semi-cripple for life. The SS had made him a precision killing machine, and the SS had broken him. The symmetry of it did not displease him.

Crucially, the overworked young medic had no time to ask questions. If he had noticed that a German bullet and not the Russian shrapnel that Stahl had claimed had caused the wound, he had given no sign. Simply moved on to the next patient in a line that stretched halfway down the bomb-ravaged street. Stahl had thanked him and moved on, sticking to the shadows, avoiding soldiers and civilians alike until he had found his way into the Stygian embrace of this overstuffed bunker.

Twice, early on, SS patrols had come in, boots ringing on the steps, flashlights playing over the pale faces and lumpen shapes. Once, the light had passed right over him, and he had placed his hand on the pistol hidden beneath his clothes. Except they weren't really his clothes. The SS soldiers were looking for a disgraced Obersturmbannführer, not a civilian in filthy overalls dragged from the rotting corpse of their former owner.

There had been no patrols for two days or more. They probably thought him dead. Or there were simply no soldiers left to patrol, not when they had pushed every man able to hold a weapon to the collapsing front line, hoping to hold back the Russians long enough for a few more shiploads of civilians to escape.

The bunker shook, the sound of the shell's impact like a clap of distant thunder. Stahl felt the caress of concrete dust descending in flurries and thought again of the ships.

He had known from the start that his message to the UK had likely not got through. Even if someone had received it, what did it matter? The city was a ruin, a ravaged corpse crawled over by writhing maggots desperate to escape. Even if he hadn't ditched his uniform, he could not have used his rank and credentials to locate the warehouse where they kept the *Götterdämmerung*. They would shoot him on sight.

Loading Area D3, he remembered dimly from Schnellinger's records. Or maybe it was D4. It seemed like weeks ago now. It didn't matter. They didn't exactly signpost such things.

It didn't matter because his message hadn't got through.

It didn't matter because it had been days now, and *Götterdämmerung* was probably already loose.

It was funny, Stahl thought. When Schnellinger's bullet had struck him, he had been sure he would die, but that medic with the childlike face had done a better job than Stahl could ever have hoped. Right now, ships were still leaving Pillau. After Hildesheim, after Canaris, he had wanted to die, but staring death in the face had a certain ability to focus the mind.

He had never wanted to live as much as he did right now.

With a grunt of pain, he grasped the damp stone wall with his right hand and dragged himself to his feet. The ships. That was the first step. Schnellinger had said they were moving thirty thousand civilians a day. That wasn't enough to move everyone, but it would be enough to move him. His uniform and papers might be gone, but he was still Obersturmbannführer Jan Stahl. He still had his training. His instincts. The pistol tucked under his coat.

They would get him a place on a ship.

He picked his way across the room, eyes focused on the thin strip of light that marked the exit. Someone muttered a complaint as his boot brushed them. Another uttered no sound at all when he stepped full on them. He caught glimpses of upturned faces, bereft of hope. Resigned eyes. Waiting to die. Then he was at the staircase and heading up, his exhaustion forgotten in the sudden, brilliant clarity of a decision taken and ready to be executed.

Two children stood at the top of the steps, too small for their *Hitler-Jugend* uniforms, dwarfed by their ageing Kar-98 rifles. Perhaps they were supposed to be guarding the bunker, but their eyes were on the sea, just visible through the gaps in the warehouses ahead. Smoke rose above the rooftops, the whitish-grey from the smokestacks of a large freighter mixing with the darker, acrid clouds drifting up from burning buildings. The frigid breeze off the Baltic brought with it the clank of machinery and the low rumble of engines, mingled with more organic noises. The screams of gulls. Yelled curses and orders. Sobbing.

He followed the beckoning sound, keeping to the side of the road, always scanning ten or thirty or fifty metres ahead for patrols and a place to hide from them.

The streets seemed to have emptied during the days he had spent underground, except for the dead bodies. They lay at almost regular intervals, abandoned by the roadside or glimpsed as shapeless piles of clothing in alleyways. Only when he passed the burned-out wreckage of an SS half-track did he find the mass of people who had not given up, who had not simply lay down in shelters to wait for the end.

There were three steamers waiting at jetties. At the foot of the ramp, red-faced soldiers fought to slow down the rush of people trying to get onboard. The melee at the front quickly subsided to a larger, patient mass, and then to the silent thousands who sat packed together on the cold cobblestones. They knew what Stahl saw immediately, that there were far too many refugees for the ships. Two more freighters stood off at sea, waiting their turn, but it would take dozens more to clear the tens of thousands of desperate refugees.

Maybe a mile out into the harbour, a grey shape bobbed on the waves. Stahl took it for a fishing trawler until his eyes picked out the raised platforms at each end, towering over the deck, each topped with menacing black metal. Eighty-eight-millimetre anti-aircraft guns. Smaller guns, too, at regular intervals along the hull. *Vorpostenboot*. Flak ship. Dedicated to destroying enemy aircraft, and capable of putting thousands of lethal rounds into the sky every minute.

Perhaps it was better that 465 Squadron would never come.

Tearing his eyes from the crowd and the ships beyond, Stahl saw that the U-78 was still there. That was something, at least. The refugees filling every available square metre of the freighters would not be the ones to carry *Götterdämmerung* out into the world. Not yet. Perhaps they would make it far enough away to outrun the coming plague. Or at least to enjoy their new lives for a few weeks or months before it came to claim them.

Harsh shouts. A barked order. Stahl's hand flashed to the pistol as he saw four soldiers emerge from a building, but they weren't looking at him. Two were loading a heavy wooden ammunition crate into the back of a Magirus A3000 lorry with a shredded canvas cover, while a third carried several battered rifles cradled in his arms like firewood. The fourth, still yelling orders, pulled himself into the cab.

Stahl felt his adrenaline fading and slumped against a low stone wall.

A new life.

Returning to Germany was out of the question, of course. Even if he could bear to face the ravaged country again, there would be repercussions for anyone who had worn a black uniform. The SS would face its reckoning. He welcomed the idea, but that didn't mean he wanted to be part of it. Anders could probably put in a good word for him with London, but the British would want to clear their decks of any reminders of the war. America? Perhaps.

Gazing at the U-78 again, he thought of Argentina. He had only been there once, a short visit to Buenos Aires in the summer of 1941, just before the SS assigned him to spy on

Canaris. His mission was to carry well-wishes from Heydrich to Ramón Castillo, congratulating him on his accession to the Presidency and exhorting him to resist the efforts of many of his countrymen to join the Allied cause. The meeting with President Castillo had been dull, much like the man himself, but the Argentine weather, the scenery, and the food had all left their impression. Immigration in the nineteenth century had created a large and sympathetic German population in the country. Most of all, the word among higher-ranked SS officers was that Argentina, despite their sham declaration of war on Germany just a few weeks earlier, wouldn't ask too many questions of a man who arrived with a little money in his pocket and a few skills their government could use. There were rumours that an Austrian Cardinal by the name of Alois Hudal was already establishing ratlines through neutral Spain.

Maybe that was where the scientists would go, once they completed their filthy work and the U-78 slipped silently into the grey waters of the Baltic Sea.

Hope flared in his chest at the thought that the U-78 could be a way out of here. That same hope died in an instant. Even if he could somehow trick or finesse his way onboard, he could never remain undetected. Canaris had led him on a tour of a U-Boat once. Cramped. Austere. No place to hide.

Canaris.

I'm sorry, Wilhelm.

I tried.

A screeching whistle from the nearest steamship echoed across the dockyards. Sailors rushed to pull up the gangplank, wresting it from the hands of desperate refugees. One man clung on too long and it dragged him from the jetty into the grey water. The steamship threw its engines into reverse, foam churning as it pulled back, its hull slapping against the jetty with a hollow clunk. The refugee did not re-emerge from the waves.

The cargo truck's engine coughed and started as the soldiers loaded another ammo box, then disappeared back inside the warehouse for more.

Canaris...

Before he even knew what he was doing, Stahl was up and walking towards the truck.

Chapter Thirty-Seven

Norfolk, 16 April

Word must have spread fast. When Barton parked, half a dozen aircrew had already gathered. By the time they strode across the open ground towards the operations building, Grant struggling to keep up with the Australian's pace, it seemed half the squadron followed at their heels. Asking questions. Demanding answers.

"Piss off, boys," Barton bellowed, and threw open the doors to the building.

Durban's office door was open, the Wing Commander standing by his desk adjusting his tie, Squadron Officer Lane a few feet away from him talking to Flight Lieutenants Wright and Kittinger. Barton didn't knock.

"Where the hell have you been, Barton?" Durban's nostrils flared, then his eyes widened. "Johnny," he said, before colour flooded his cheeks and he turned his attention back to the Squadron Leader. "I ordered a strict lockdown. You were supposed to be assembling your flight crews and overseeing their prep."

"I've been telling you for two weeks that you need a navigator, boss." Barton kept his voice even, but Grant saw his eyes. The Australian wasn't a man to back down from a fight. "I brought you one. Merry Christmas."

"Do I look amused to you, Barton? You disobeyed my direct orders. Worse than that, you left your men alone to get ready."

"My men have been ready for the last three hours. I issued all the orders they needed as soon as I heard Embry arriving last night."

"Don't talk back. I would court martial you, except this squadron needs all the experience it can get."

"Your squadron," Barton sneered, "needs you to lead. You need a navigator."

"Preferably one who is fit to fly." Durban's voice shook with suppressed rage, but its volume never changed. "As for you," he added, turning to Grant, "I've spoken to Doctor Carpenter..."

"Every day," Lane said.

"...and I know you are a damned long way from being healthy enough for a local training flight, let alone ops. What do you think you're playing at?"

Grant didn't blink. "My job, sir."

"Your job is to obey orders." Durban motioned to Barton. "Much like his. They did not discharge you from the hospital. Right now, you are absent without leave. Give me one reason I shouldn't have you arrested right now."

"I can't be AWOL, sir," Grant said. "I'm on duty, and in your office."

Durban stared.

"Technically, that's probably true, sir," Bony Wright said. "Although you might charge him under the King's Regulations for being out of uniform on duty." He frowned. "Unless those are hospital-issued pyjamas, in which case..." He tailed off at the look on Durban's face.

"Andy," Lane said softly.

She said nothing more. Durban met her gaze for several seconds, then muttered something below his breath. He stared at his watch for longer than he could ever need to check the time. Grant was sure he could hear the damned thing ticking.

"Squadron Leader Barton, Flight Lieutenant Kittinger," Durban said, "convene your flights. There will be a full briefing at 1000. Flight Lieutenant Wright, please prepare the room and all required briefing materials." He paused. "Dismissed."

The three men walked from the room, Kittens slowing long enough to squeeze Grant's shoulder. "It's good to have you back, Johnny."

"Good to be here," Grant said, turning to follow.

"Not you, Grant," Wing Commander said. "You stay. Shut the door."

Kittens gave him a sympathetic smile, and Grant pushed the door closed, leaving just the three of them. The click of the lock resounded in the small office.

"Look me in the eye," Durban said, stepping closer. Grant had three inches of height on him, but he felt like he had to look up to meet the Wing Commander's gaze. "This will be brutal. We're going a long way. Hours in the cockpit, high altitude and low. There will probably be fighters. There will be flak." He paused as if to wait for a reaction to that. Grant made sure he didn't see one. "I admire you for coming, I really do, but you might yet regret it. Tell me the truth. Are you well enough to fly this mission?"

Grant sensed Sarah Lane watching him. Inscrutable. She was a professional, and she hadn't stopped appraising him since he entered the room. Surely, she could see the way he held himself, favouring the side of his body with the fewest stitches, the way his legs trembled under his weight, the way his jaw ached from keeping the pain from showing on his face.

"Yes, sir," he said.

It was the truth.

He hoped.

Durban took a breath. "Go get some proper clothes on. I'll see you in the briefing room. Twenty minutes."

"Yes, sir." He turned to the door.

"Johnny?"

"Yes, sir?"

"Kittinger is right. It is good to have you back."

Grant smiled. "I wouldn't miss this for the world, sir." Opening the door, he walked into the corridor and headed for his room, hoping you could believe anything if you repeated it to yourself often enough.

Chapter Thirty-Eight

Norfolk, 16 April

Expectancy hung heavy in the crowded briefing room, as thick as the cigarette smoke that drifted up from two dozen nervous hands. They must have known, Durban thought, even without the sight of AVM Embry lurking at the edge of the stage, next to Major Anders in his commando uniform. Whatever else happened with the war in Europe, whether it was days or weeks, this would likely be the last significant mission they flew as a squadron. For some, it would be the last time they ever flew at all. Durban let his eyes play over the assembled crews, wondering how many of those anxious faces he would see again, certain they did the same when they looked at him.

Barton stood, a dozen others doing the same, too keyed up to relax. Grant wasn't one of them. He sat near the front, slumped a little in his chair. Durban hoped it was because he was exhausted from all the claps on the back and hearty handshakes brought on by the young man's unexpected return. That had been satisfying to see, but it wasn't the reason. Durban figured he was as much a fool as the next man, but he wasn't foolish enough to believe that Grant was healed.

It didn't matter. He needed Grant. Watching the young man walk into his office, seeing him for the first time since they'd stretchered him away from their damaged Mosquito, had almost been enough to derail his anger at Barton. Like it had lifted a great weight from him, allowing him to breathe again. Almost enough to remove his fear of the mission ahead.

But not quite.

He checked his watch. Sarah, standing alongside the

unusually quiet and pensive Embry, gave him a reassuring nod. He quickly looked away.

Time.

He cleared his throat, both hands gripping his pointer stick. "Ten hundred hours, gentlemen," he said. "I won't waste your time with pre-amble or platitudes. Every one of you will have guessed that what we have been doing these last few weeks is more than just a random selection of missions. Today marks the final stage of Operation AFTERLIGHT. Squadron Officer Lane?"

"Thank you, sir."

She took the stage. Like she owned it. Tall, confident, powerful. An amazing woman, Durban thought. How much better things might have gone if she had been in charge from the start instead of him.

"Operation AFTERLIGHT," she repeated. "You've all heard of the V1, the V2, the German jet fighter programs. Hitler has known he is losing the war for years, and he has turned to what the Prime Minister once called perverted science to turn the tide. It hasn't worked. Yet. But there's still time. The Nazis have developed a weapon that far surpasses all of those, both in impact and lethality. The nature of that weapon must remain a secret for now, and if you succeed today, it will remain a secret until your grandchildren grow old. Fail today, and I fear there will be no grandchildren. Anywhere."

She already had their full attention, but every man in the room seemed to find an extra level of focus at that.

Sarah nodded to Bony, and he brought up the first projected image. "There are three parts to Operation AFTERLIGHT. You may remember this location, a buried facility near Hildesheim. Destroyed, as you can see. Damned fine work, gentlemen. That was part one, to remove their ability to develop any more of the weapon." She looked at Bony, and the image changed. "Part two, destroy the modified delivery aircraft for the weapon. Accomplished at Uelzen."

A sudden wave of nausea welled up inside Durban. He looked at Grant. The young man's face stayed utterly impassive.

The image changed again. "Part three. Obliterate the remaining stocks of the weapon before they can use it." Sarah looked at Durban. Her mouth twitched, as if she wanted to say his name but couldn't.

"The city of Pillau," he said, swapping places with her on stage, declining to meet her gaze yet letting his fingers brush hers as they passed. "On the Baltic coast of East Prussia." He ignored the hiss of breath from several navigators, the ones who knew their maps and therefore knew they were in trouble. "Just reaching the target will be a job. To avoid enemy defences, we'll be crossing neutral Sweden. Before you ask, the answer is no. We don't have permission. We should be too high and fast for them to shoot us down, and hopefully they won't try. But don't doubt that if you have an emergency and have to land in Sweden, you will be arrested and interred until the war is over."

Holding out the pointer, hoping its shaking wasn't too obvious, he tapped the projected map.

"German air defences aren't as good as they used to be, but there are long-range air surveillance sites on their north coast here that will see us almost as soon as we clear Swedish airspace. That would be bad news; we don't want the entire Luftwaffe waiting for us. That's why we'll descend as we reach the Swedish coast. This narrow island is Oland. By the time we clear it, we'll be at fifty feet over the waves. We'll stay there until we reach the target. At that height, even cruising with low revs with our props set at maximum coarse pitch, we'll be burning a lot of fuel. You'll carry a hundred gallon drop tank under each wing, but fuel will still be a major consideration for the way home. Navigators?

Factor that into your planning now, so you don't have to do it in a dogfight later."

Grant, he noted with satisfaction, was already taking notes.

"Now," he said, motioning Bony to move to the next image, "this is the target area itself."

"Oh, bloody hell," a pilot muttered.

"Indeed." Durban tapped the pointer against a circle, hand-drawn on the image to highlight a flak position. Then another. He stopped at five. "We've counted at least twenty emplacements around the city and on the peninsula. You can see the big eighty-eight-millimetre guns clustered along the shoreline here, facing our approach route. The rest are mostly twenty-millimetre, with a couple of thirty-seven millimetres to keep us honest."

"Sir," Kittinger said, raising his hand, "is that a flak ship?"

"Two of them. The *Hela*, out to sea here, and the *Siegfried*, right in the protected harbour. I don't need to tell you that between them and the eighty-eights, they have the approaches to Pillau well sewn up."

"My apologies, sir," Kittens said, "but can't we go around them? Approach the city overland?"

"A good question, Kittens, which brings us to the next problem. Even if fuel wasn't a consideration, German fighters are on high alert at several airfields in the north. Because of the short notice and the daylight attack, there will be no diversionary raids to draw off the Luftwaffe. We're on our own. The Red Army has cut off Pillau. You see how the city is almost an island, with the peninsula linked to the mainland by this very narrow isthmus to the north? Well, the narrowness of the land there is the only thing holding the Soviets back. They now control everything except the city itself. That's a lot of flak and a lot of itchy trigger fingers. The Soviet Air Force has also been very active in the area. You may think that is a good thing. It's not." He saw the confusion on their faces. "Forget any notions that Uncle Joe is still our friend. I can't guarantee that the Soviets will attack us, but they have a vested interest in seeing that we fail. If you see a Soviet fighter, do not shoot unless fired upon... but be very ready to shoot. Understood? Good."

Bony brought up the last image, and Durban took in every black and white square inch of it, glad the audience focused on the picture and not the concern in his eyes. It was a blown-up shot of the dockyards. Rows of warehouses, both on the edge of the city and on the wide jetties that spread like fingers downward into the Vistula Lagoon. More flak positions. The thin grey smear that was the U-78. "This submarine is our secondary target if we have weapons left after the initial strike. The primary target..." He stopped, swallowing.

His eyes met Embry's. They had discussed this. Bounced ideas between them half the night until exhaustion and crew rest regulations sent them stumbling away to grab a few hours' rest. From the look of him, Embry had been no more successful at finding sleep than Durban had. And for all their ideas and discussions, they had found precisely zero answers.

"The primary target," he repeated, "is one of these warehouses."

A low moan of disapproval.

"We don't know which one is the target?" Barton shook his head. "What are we supposed to do? Try to damage them all?"

"No," Durban said, sharper than intended. "We can't afford to damage anything. We target the right building and eradicate it, down to the last brick, or the mission fails."

"How?"

"Six of us will carry two five-hundred-pound high explosive bombs, the rest napalm. HE cracks open the building, then we burn it up from the inside. The destruction must be complete."

Silence descended, the silence of professional experts

conducting their calculations, and not liking the answers they found.

"I meant," Barton said, "how do we target the right building?"

Durban forced back the urge to shout at him. "We have a man on the ground," he said. "When the time comes, I am hoping he can give us a signal."

"Hoping?"

"I'll circle over the city," Durban said, ignoring the interruption. "If we receive the signal, I'll direct your target runs. If I don't, I'll make an estimate and we'll do what we can." He refused to meet the eyes of either Embry or Sarah. It was difficult enough to sound confident; he didn't need to see the stifling hopelessness that clutched at him mirrored in their eyes.

Barton sighed. "You know that's a long shot at best, sir?"

"Of course," Durban snapped. He saw Embry half-rise from his chair, concerned. He composed himself. It wasn't easy. "This is 465 Squadron, Don," he said, ramming levity into his voice, smearing a fake smile over his face. "The long shot is what we do, isn't it? If it was easy, they'd give it to someone else."

There were a few chuckles. A touch forced, but at least there were no tears.

Durban relinquished the floor to Bony and stood off to the side next to Sarah while the Ops Officer ran through all the minutiae of the raid; weapon loads, radio frequencies, callsigns, timings, diversionary airfields. Durban tried to listen, but his mind was a whirl. The raid, Stahl, and most of all Sarah Lane, all tumbled through his thoughts together, his brain too tired after years of war to find the space for all of them.

Bony described the codewords they would send back to HQ as the raid progressed. Embry's orders, but not his idea. The idea had come from higher up. Joint Intelligence Committee. Probably higher.

WALLABY. Target area reached.

301

JAEGER. German fighters engaging.

COMRADE. Soviet fighters engaging.

DINGO. Primary target unlocated.

DISMAL. Mission aborted.

TRIGGER TWO. Secondary target located.

TRIGGER ONE. Primary target located.

BATHTUB. Secondary target destroyed.

AFTERLIGHT. Primary target destroyed.

Durban's hands shook again, and he gripped them together behind his back. Thank God for Grant, taking page after page of notes with a steady pen, only the occasional twitch of his cheek revealing the pain he must be in.

He hadn't lied. It was good to have Johnny back.

Bony wrapped up with the weather forecast for the North Sea – breezy, overcast, much like Charney Breach – and Embry rose from his chair next to Sarah. "Might I add a few words, Andy?"

"Of course, sir."

"It's been a long fight to get here, chaps," Embry said, "and I'd like to thank Wing Commander Durban and Squadron Officer Lane for their efforts. The rest is up to you now. Take off is in two hours. We're in the fifteenth round and the world is on the line. Legally, I can't tell you why this mission is so important, but please assume I'm not lying when I say this is the most critical day in all our lives. To quote the Holy Bible," – he paused – "don't bugger it up."

That got a proper laugh.

Embry waited for the collective release of tension to subside before continuing. "I'll be remaining in your ops room for the raid," he said, "along with my colleagues here. I'd much rather be flying with you, of course, but the Prime Minister himself will expect updates as quickly as possible. Any last questions for me or your squadron commander? No? Splendid. I'll buy the beers when you return. Good luck."

As suddenly as that, the briefing was over.

All stood to attention while the AVM turned to go. Embry hadn't even cleared the stage before Durban followed. He heard Sarah say his name, felt her fingers brush at his sleeve, and ignored both, just as he ignored the sensation of her hurt eyes watching him go. He didn't slow his pace until he reached his office and locked the door behind him.

Writing the note didn't take long. He'd composed it in his mind days ago, mentally editing and tweaking it a hundred times since, yet not knowing for sure whether he would need it at all. Now he knew. Her presence in the briefing had just confirmed what he already suspected. He couldn't say what he needed to say. Not face to face. He didn't have the words.

And he certainly didn't have the time.

He scribbled the note, slid it into an envelope, and wrote her name on it. Squadron Officer S. Lane. He didn't know her middle name. It was, like so much of her, a mystery. One that he would most likely never get to solve.

By the time he had conferred with his two flight commanders and Bony one last time, Durban was almost the last to reach dispersal. Embry, as he'd expected, was waiting there in the noon sun, shaking hands with every pilot and navigator he could before they reached their aircraft. The AVM smiled as he saw him approach.

"Good luck, Andy," he said. "Remember what I said."

"Don't bugger it up, sir?"

"Well, that is rather important. But I wanted to thank you again. That we've got even half a chance to pull this off is down to you and Sarah."

"And Stahl, sir. If he doesn't come through for us, none of it will matter."

Embry grimaced. "Does it worry you that the fate of Europe comes down to yet another bloody German?"

"It's less than ideal, sir."

"Still, if he manages it, I'll happily buy him a beer, too. What's this?" He looked down at the envelope in Durban's hand.

"For Squadron Officer Lane, sir."

"I'm not a bloody postman, Andy," Embry said. "Why didn't you give it to her yourself?" He sighed. "Oh. I see. When do you want me to...?"

"You'll know when, sir."

Embry nodded. "Yes, I suppose I will. I think you'd best get going, don't you?"

Durban came to attention, accepted the offered handshake, and headed to his aircraft.

He did a quick walk around inspection to make sure everything looked okay. Every combat scar on the fuselage, every scratch and sanded-down patch of battle damage repairs stood out in the morning light. He ran his fingertips along the wood. Around him, a handful of ground crew scurried to ensure the battery cart was in position and that all their checks were complete. Next to Grant, the crew chief waited with a clipboard.

Durban gave the young navigator a smile, then took the clipboard. "How's it looking?"

The crew chief passed him a pen. "You've got two five-hundred bombs, sir, as well as a full load of fuel and ammunition and your two drop tanks. You'll be right at the edge of your maximum take-off weight."

Durban thanked him, signed the form, and turned towards the ladder that led up into the snug cockpit. Clambering up, he squeezed through the narrow doorway into his seat on the port side, scanning the controls in front of him while he slipped on his flame-retardant black leather flying gloves. He heard a clumsy scrambling on the ladder as Grant followed him in, his Mae West life preserver snagging on the doorway. The navigator seemed a little out of breath.

"Last chance to change your mind, Johnny." Durban secured himself in his seat, pulling two straps over his shoulders and two up from the sides of his seat. He locked them together with the brass pin.

Fidgeting in his own seat, mounted a fraction lower and behind to Durban's right, Grant did the same. With his jaw set, he leaned down to check the small map box by his right knee.

To their left, Kittinger's engines burst into life. The New Zealander waved. Durban gave him a nod, then shot the crew chief a thumbs up. The cockpit door slammed shut. The latch clicked home, turned from the outside, leaving them alone in the cold silence of the cockpit. Durban plugged in his intercom and opened the small panel in the Perspex next to him. "Contact," he yelled through the gap. The man at the battery cart returned the call.

Durban pressed hard on the start button for the port engine.

The prop turned twice, then the engine roared. A second later and he pressed the button for the starboard engine. It misfired once before catching. Hopefully not a bad omen.

Edging the throttles forward, he requested permission to taxi. Thoughts of Sarah Lane and even *Götterdämmerung* melted in the familiar mechanics of piloting his aircraft. The ground crew pulled the chocks away. The crew chief signalled to them, beckoning them to pull out onto the taxi strip. Within less than a minute, they were at the end of the runway and ready to go. Durban made sure the brakes were on and then inched the throttles further forward until the revolutions per minute reached three thousand. The wooden frame of the Mosquito shuddered with suppressed power.

"Colt Leader, you're cleared for take-off."

Durban released the brakes. The aircraft lurched into motion. He glimpsed Barton's Mosquito taxiing alongside, and then he shot forward, the other aircraft left behind.

The tail came up as they roared past the control tower. As they passed one hundred and fifty miles an hour, he pulled back on the controls. The Mosquito lifted, notably more sluggish with the extra weight, and he kept her low to build up more speed before the throbbing power of the twin Merlins took them soaring over the twisted trees at the end of the runway. Yanking up on the undercarriage lever, he willed himself to remain professional, to keep all his focus on their steady climb over Matlock Farm to the assembly point where the rest of the squadron waited.

He couldn't do it, though. Couldn't stop from twisting in his seat to look back at the Control Tower, to the figure standing alone on the balcony where just a few days earlier they had stood together, her face upturned to the sky as she watched them go.

She hadn't waved goodbye.

Chapter Thirty-Nine

The Baltic Sea, 16 April

At fifty feet, the icy waters of the Baltic seemed to pulse with malignant intent.

Every rippling wave became a new attempt to catch an unwary crew, to pull them down into its fatal, suffocating embrace. Even from the navigator's seat, Grant could feel the extra weight and drag of the drop tanks coating the normally graceful Mosquito with a sluggish veneer. Durban's face was a mask of intense concentration, his gloved hands tight on the controls, making a dozen minor corrections every second.

The worst thing was the quiet. Not the radio silence, which was only to be expected, both to avoid an international incident as they had violated Swedish neutrality and to avoid tipping off both Germans and Soviets that they were coming. Rather, it was Durban's silence that made Grant's skin crawl. Even on the intercom, he had spoken only a dozen clipped words since they had taken off. Since he'd seen Squadron Officer Lane at the Control Tower.

Grant didn't know what was going on between those two, and he doubted they did either. It was none of his business, anyway. His business was navigation, and it kept him busy. Over the sea, at this altitude, there wasn't a single landmark to check his plots against. That meant regular references to the hand-drawn lines on his maps, estimates of wind speed and drift, constant checks of the gyro and magnetic compasses and the Mk IX airspeed indicator, all to keep their position accurate. Even a mile or two off-course would force them to climb over a coastline teeming with German fighters or Soviet troops.

Though that might still be better than getting it right and reaching the city of Pillau with its dense flak and a target that they hadn't even identified.

Behind them, the other Mosquitoes kept pace a few feet above or below, fifteen thoroughbred killing machines streaking towards an unsuspecting enemy. More than once, Grant saw the surface of a wave ripple as spinning props passed over it, dangerously low. Wresting his attention from the aircraft and the churning fear in his stomach that props and waves would meet, he scanned the sky above. No fighters. The sky was clear to six thousand feet and the thick band of waiting grey-white cloud.

Ahead, he saw a thin, dark smudge on the horizon. It could have been a shadow from the clouds above. He knew it wasn't.

"Enemy coast ahead," he said into the intercom.

Durban nodded. He didn't pass the message on to the rest of the formation; they would already have seen it by now. With the Mosquitoes racing towards it at over three-hundred miles an hour, the smudge rapidly thickened. Part of it, lighter than the rest, broke away, took shape, became a layer of smoke. A city in flames.

"Pillau," he said.

"Good navigation," Durban said. Emotionless.

Grant checked the sky one more time, then directed all his focus forward. Looking ahead hurt much less than twisting in his seat. More smoke in the distance, this time from the stacks of ships. Individual funnels became visible. One was a larger passenger vessel, probably ferrying refugees. The other had a single smokestack, mounted far back on a deck dotted with thinner structures.

He went cold. That ship should have been three miles east of their path, not directly ahead. He turned, but the pilot was already ahead of him.

"Flak ship," Durban called sharply. That was something worth breaking radio silence. Not that there was much they could do now.

Flashes rippled along the length of the low grey vessel. Tracers, bright enough to be visible even in full daylight, whipped across the sea's surface towards them. Grant saw one lurch upwards and disappear over their heads. A ricochet off a wave top, a dry and professional part of his mind noted. The rest of his brain focused only on the ones that still came their way.

At this altitude, any sharp attempt to change course could be disastrous, while climbing to give themselves room to manoeuvre would just bleed airspeed and make them even more vulnerable. Speed and a low profile were their best defence. It should have been enough. Even with all its firepower, the *Hela* was too far off and their targets too difficult for the gunners on the flak ship to do more than cross their fingers and hope for a lucky shot.

With enough rolls of the dice, though, anyone could turn up double sixes.

Grant didn't think it was a direct hit that got Colt Bravo Four. Probably a near miss from an 88mm, the sky briefly marred by an expanding inky flower of smoke above the top of the Mosquito. Perhaps it was the shrapnel, accelerated in misshapen lumps at bullet-like speeds in all directions. More likely, the simple expansion of gases was enough to nudge the speeding aircraft down a few feet. To where the waves waited.

Either way, the radio burst into life for a single panicked scream, cut short. A few pieces of wreckage sailed through the air, and then Bravo Four was gone, and the *Hela* was behind their port wingtips and dwindling into the distance, still sending ineffectual rounds streaming into the sky, hoping lightning could strike twice.

Durban kept his focus purely on his controls. "Did you see who it was?"

"Chapple and Elmore."

The Wing Commander nodded. Said nothing. A slight tightening of the lips, perhaps, but no more. The coast loomed ahead, a single forbidding mass except where the Pillau harbour channel forged a single valley-like break. Grant saw the rooftops of buildings, their brickwork as grey and cold as the water beneath them. In the bay ahead, the flak ship *Siegfried* waited, its guns silent for now.

Waiting until we're higher, Grant thought.

Durban thumbed his R/T switch. "I'm climbing now," he said. "Flight leads, follow me. All other callsigns loiter here at one thousand feet and await my signal."

"Roger, Colt Leader." Kittens, his voice warm and respectful.

"Got it." Barton, his voice neither.

Durban pulled back on his controls, and Grant felt gravity press him back in his seat as the Mosquito clawed its way into the sky. A wave of nausea rippled through him.

The Wing Commander didn't wait long to turn, just time enough for his wing tips to be free of any risk of clipping the sea. Then he was banking to port, trying to put some room between the Mosquito and the *Siegfried*. Kittens followed in his wake. Barton went to starboard instead. Probably to put some doubt into the minds of the *Siegfried*'s gunners and force them to split their firepower, Grant thought, though pure truculence seemed just as likely. The result was the same. The gunners made their decision, and a stream of rounds rose in a seemingly leisurely climb into the sky before hurtling by either side of the Australian.

A barrage of foul epithets filled Grant's headphones.

"Keep this network clear, please," Durban said calmly.

Alpha One disappeared behind a greasy pall as two 88mm shells exploded, then re-emerged, somehow unmarked. Enjoying every drop of the luck that had deserted Bravo Four.

"Colt Leader to Alpha One, are you hit?"

"We're fine. Permission to engage the bastard?"

"Negative, Alpha One," Durban said. "Hold above the city. Kittens, do you see anything?"

"There's heavy incoming fire to the north, Colt Leader. Multiple impacts, possible 105mm artillery. Looks like the Russians are making a push down the isthmus towards the city."

Or what remained of it. Even though Grant was looking down from three thousand feet and still climbing, the patchy smoke from ships, burning buildings and exploding flak couldn't obscure the destruction. Too many gutted structures to count, their once impressive edifices now rendered skeletal. Artillery had reduced entire city blocks to rubble. Burned and abandoned vehicles dotted the debris-choked streets.

He wished they could climb further, through the clouds, up to the clear air of high altitude where the Earth became just a blur of colour below. Anything to make the scene beneath them seem less real.

"Roger," Durban said. "Any sign of a signal?"

A long pause. Shells from the distant *Siegfried* still pumped into the sky, barely in range now and dwindling, but that still left more flak positions below. One by one, they were joining the fray.

"Negative, Colt Leader," Kittens said. "Lots of smoke, but nothing that stands out."

"Keep looking." Durban glanced at Grant. The face was impassive, but the eyes betrayed his true thoughts.

There was no signal.

Chapter Forty

Stahl had long since become inured to the sounds of Russian artillery. What was another shell among hundreds that fell every day? This was different, though. A sharp crack, rather than the dull thud of a bomb. Then more. A staccato rhythm echoing across the bay. Sirens wailed, and more guns joined in.

He looked to the south first, where the air raids normally came from, covering his eyes against the sunlight trying to break through the cloud. Nothing there. No Russian bombers, nor any flak bursts.

The hum of aero engines drifted on the breeze, struggling to be heard over the roar of the guns. Getting louder now, as he turned to face the sea.

Now he saw them. Small dots, almost like insects or motes of dust on the western horizon, except for two that grew larger as he watched, climbing. Then a third, heading off to the side, drawing the fire from the flak ship in the harbour. A little way down the waterfront from where Stahl sheltered behind a wrecked staff car, another heavy anti-aircraft gun joined in, adding its own lethal contribution to the hail of steel reaching towards the intruders. The gun position must have been a few hundred metres away at least, but the roar as it belched its first huge shell upwards was near-deafening.

Mosquitoes.

His heart gave a sudden jolt, and he felt a small twinge in his cheek muscles as they broke into an unfamiliar smile.

They had got his message.

He heard shouts and dropped to one knee behind the long

bonnet of the Mercedes. The red pennant on the front snapped in the breeze despite the jagged shrapnel rent ripped through the centre of the Swastika. Three more soldiers emerged from the warehouse to join the two already on sentry duty. He chanced a longer look to confirm their weapons and uniforms. It was a risk, but not much of one. They were too busy watching the pair of Mosquitoes banking a few thousand feet above them to notice the dirt-smeared face watching them from the waterfront.

The four men loading their truck could not tell him where Loading Area D23 was. Nor did they much care, even after he persuaded them that a senior officer had tasked him to carry a message. The best they could do was to make a vague and sullen gesture to where the peninsula curved around to form the eastern end of Pillau's great harbour. Stahl had thanked them and left before they could grow any more suspicious. He must have passed twenty warehouses, most with soldiers outside, all of them more than large enough to accommodate a few dozen scientists and their unholy work.

Until he had reached this one and stopped. The soldiers who emerged from inside to gawp up at the circling aircraft merely confirmed what he had suspected straight away. Like their colleagues on sentry duty, they wore Waffen-SS fatigues and insignia. Slung across their chests, they carried the latest model Sturmgewehr 44 assault rifle. These weren't the unshaven reservists or beardless children that half-heartedly stood watch at the other buildings.

This was it. This was where *Götterdämmerung* waited.

A few hundred metres away, the gentle waves of the protected Vistula Lagoon caressed the dark grey hull of the U-78. She bobbed gently at what looked like an electricity supply pier. Several crew members stood on her deck. Some wore the overalls of mechanics. Final sea checks, Stahl thought. Two others, standing by the 20mm anti-aircraft gun on the deck with their heads bowed in conversation, wore the smart coats and hats of officers. They, too, were looking up at the sky, where the Mosquitoes flew higher now, drifting in and out of sight among the lower tendrils of cloud.

The U-78's diesel engine was running. Which meant it was preparing to depart.

Two soldiers laughed and disappeared back into the building. Maybe they took the visitors for reconnaissance aircraft. Whatever they were doing up there, they certainly seemed to pose no threat. It appeared the various flak crews around the harbour area agreed, for the anti-aircraft fire became noticeably less intense, almost desultory. Three soldiers remained outside the warehouse now, watching the sky, talking in low voices. Stahl strained to make out the words but couldn't, not above the still wailing sirens and the intermittent shell fire.

He should probably get clear, he thought. In his excitement at locating the building, he had forgotten the danger he was in. And yet still the Mosquitoes remained aloof, their engines a constant hum, but the aircraft themselves only occasionally visible in the overcast above the Lagoon. Remaining out of range.

To the west, over the Baltic Sea, he saw the rest of the attack force circling above the horizon. Waiting.

Waiting for what? The warehouse had to be struck now, with *Götterdämmerung* possibly only minutes from release, the U-78 standing by, ready to take the scientists to safety.

The target was right there.

And they didn't know it.

Chapter Forty-One

Above Pillau, 16 April

"Colt Leader to Control. DINGO."

Durban let his thumb slide off the R/T switch. Three times he had spoken the word into the radio, to be relayed via the British Embassy in Sweden. He didn't expect a reply, but he could imagine what they would make of it back at Charney Breach.

All this way for nothing. Maybe less than nothing. The target remained unlocated. Bravo Four was gone. Barton and Finny had almost joined them. Clear daylight showed through a gash in Durban's own left wing where a long-range flak shot had almost pegged their range. No damage to their flight controls, thank God, but the next cloud of shrapnel might do more than scuff the woodwork.

The city lay off his wingtip, engulfed in carnage. Columns of smoke rose from the harbour to the northern suburbs, where it became a single roiling mass of burning buildings and exploding artillery. German ships had laid down a smoke screen to hide their positions, concealing large swathes of the harbour and reducing the waiting flak ship *Siegfried* to a lurking dark shadow. Only the warehouses near the docks seemed miraculously, mockingly intact. Durban could make out at least twenty likely locations, most untouched since the last photo-reconnaissance pass. Two or perhaps three showed signs of damage severe enough to rule them out as safe locations for the SS to use, and therefore knock them off the target list. Seventeen left, then. More than he had aircraft, even if he wasn't looking at a minimum of two aircraft for a successful strike. One to break it apart with HE, a second to incinerate the contents with napalm. Preferably three or four, to be sure.

That meant they could strike a maximum of six targets from the seventeen, assuming perfect accuracy from both lead and trail aircraft.

Durban grimaced. Five targets. Bravo Four had been one of the six HE-equipped aircraft.

The radio crackled. Barton's voice. "Where the hell is the signal?"

"We've only been here six minutes." It seemed like so much longer. "We have to give him more time."

"Bandits," Kittens said. "Due east. Angels eight and descending."

Durban turned the nose, stared, methodically scanning the sky from eight thousand feet downwards.

"I see them, sir," Grant said, pointing.

"Tally two," Durban confirmed. A pair, dropping from the clouds in close formation. Small. Single-engined. He'd hoped it might be merely a bombing raid, not that the city needed any more chaos right now. "Likely Soviet fighters," he said. "Remember, they are supposed to be our allies. Don't start shooting until they do."

"Should we jettison drop tanks, boss?"

"Go ahead, Kittinger. All callsigns, follow suit once you reach a safe height to do so." Grant had already transferred the fuel under air pressure from the unwieldy drop tanks into the outer wing tanks, and ditching their weight and drag would restore some of the Mosquito's manoeuvrability. Durban had no illusions that they could out turn a modern Russian fighter, though.

The shapes came closer. Durban turned towards them. "Kittinger, Barton, stay here and watch for that signal."

"You're going out to meet them?" Grant's voice seemed a little high.

"Let's find out their intentions."

At a mile away, he turned north, keeping the Mosquito level at three-thousand feet. The fighters, still descending, turned to an intercept course. Not dropping behind, he saw, but trying to get directly alongside. They didn't know who he was yet. He could be friendly. Whatever that word meant.

He waggled his wings, almost inviting them to come closer, not trying to evade but keeping the Mosquito in a gentle turn. The fighters were only a few hundred yards away now. "What are they, Grant?"

"Yaks, sir. Yak-3, I think."

"Damn." He'd held on to some hope they might be one of the older models, or even a ground attack aircraft like the IL-2 Sturmovik. The Yak-3 was about the best fighter the Soviets had. Well-armed and powerful. A pure dogfighter. The certainty of German technological superiority had long ago died on the Eastern Front, and the Yak-3 had been the final nail in that casket.

It looked a lot like a Spitfire at three hundred yards, Durban thought, except for the huge red star on the tail. He had heard stories from pilots who had flown both. Some said the Soviet aircraft was the superior.

The lead Yak drifted even closer, following the Mosquito's gentle turn to port. The pilot looked hardly young enough to shave, let alone fly a high-performance fighter. Durban could see the puzzled expression on his face, the way he looked at the Mosquito's British markings in disbelief.

"Give him a wave, Johnny."

Grant raised one hand. After a few seconds, the Yak pilot did the same, his mouth hanging open.

"I think he's a friend," Grant said.

"Where is his wingman?"

Grant twisted in his seat. "Above and behind. Four hundred yards."

A perfect firing position.

The young Yak pilot's face went cold, and he broke sharply to starboard.

Clearing the way.

"Jettison tanks," Durban yelled.

He flung the Mosquito to starboard, following the lead Yak. A ripping sound drowned out the engines, like a chainsaw in his ears, but the sudden turn had caught out the trailing pilot. Instead of hitting a helpless Mosquito, his two Berezin autocannons sent streams of 20mm cannon shells into empty airspace. Grant, straining against his straps, sought to keep sight of the lethal fighter behind them. Durban fumbled for the wing tank jettison button, and the Mosquito gave a pleasing upward lurch as the dead weight of the drop tanks fell away. The controls felt a little lighter as he brought the nose swinging around until the lead Yak-3 hung in the centre of his armoured windscreen, four hundred yards ahead.

Good aircraft, Durban thought. Poor pilot. Probably expected his wingman to have already taken care of us. Too inexperienced to watch his six. His mistake.

He fired.

For an instant it seemed, ludicrously, like the drop tanks had dragged themselves back onto the wings, such was the braking power of the recoil from his four cannon and four machine guns. The Yak-3 broke apart, the same lightweight construction that made it so manoeuvrable now nothing more than flimsy. Wings and tail section spun away to the sides. The nose kept in a straight line, the weight of the engine taking it on an arcing path towards the waiting Vistula Lagoon with what remained of the pilot still strapped in behind it.

"Second Yak is on our tail," Grant called.

Durban had already pulled hard on the controls, tipping the Mosquito into a banking shallow dive. It was too much to hope that both Yak pilots were fools, and they weren't. The Yak followed, smaller and faster, already on them, like a shark harrying a whale.

A killer whale, Durban thought grimly, but that wouldn't help at all if they couldn't get the bastard off their tail. Tracers whipped through the air. Too high again. That error would soon be corrected.

"COMRADE," he said into the radio. As if HQ needed more bad news.

"Two more bandits to the east," Grant said. "Three miles."

Durban took his word for it. The Yak three hundred yards behind him deserved all his attention. "All callsigns," he called, "watch your sixes. Barton, take A Flight up to ten thousand feet and hold off the Soviets."

"Roger," Barton said.

More tracers. Compared to the Yak, the Mosquito was a big aircraft, and Durban suddenly felt every square foot and every pound of its mass. Not that their size would help much if they were hit. A single HE shell in the right spot would effortlessly spread them across the Lagoon that now waited only three hundred feet below.

He kept descending, twisting in his seat, watching the Yak as much as he did the looming waves, knowing they were going to die. There was an inevitability about it. The revelation did not surprise him.

It had always been inevitable. He had just hoped he could complete the mission first.

"Kittinger," he said calmly, "keep watching for that signal. Take over the strike if I'm hit."

A strangled groan burst from Grant's lips.

Fifty feet now, heading towards the city again. No room left to manoeuvre. Just like the approach, the mission ending the same way it had started. He turned for one last look at the Yak.

It had gone.

Just a cloud of water hanging in the air in their wake.

"Splash one," Barton said. The Australian didn't conceal the smugness in his voice. "You're welcome."

"Thank you, Don," Durban said. "Now get to ten thousand feet, like I ordered."

"Yes, sir." Alpha One pulled up into a tight climb, following the distant shapes of seven other Mosquitoes towards the clouds and the incoming Soviets.

A sound like air escaping from a punctured tyre hissed from Grant's lips.

"You ok, Johnny?"

The young man nodded. The forced confidence of a man about to vomit.

"Bravo One to Colt Leader. Nothing seen yet."

"DINGO," Durban acknowledged, sending the message to London. Wondering if he sounded as hopeless as he felt. Climbing, he looked once again towards the warehouses. Too many to strike.

"There's good visibility up here," Barton said, sounding disappointed, "but the second pair of bandits appear to have turned and run. I guess they didn't like the odds."

"They will like them more when they come back with their friends," Durban said. "Keep your eyes peeled."

"Obviously," Barton grumbled, and fell silent.

A Flight's Mosquitoes had mostly vanished above the clouds, with just a single aircraft dimly visible through one of the scattered gaps in the grey coverage. Out to sea, Durban could make out the rest of B Flight, circling while they waited for a word that would never come. Bravo One remained loyally over the city, constantly changing altitude and heading, heedless of the occasional flak burst or stream of tracers that sought to end his vigil.

And still the warehouses waited. Pristine. Nondescript. There might as well have been a thousand of them. "I don't suppose you see anything, Johnny?"

They had been lucky so far. Only one lost aircraft, just two letters to write. Right now, they could make it home, clear the target before more Soviet fighters arrived. If they ditched their bombs in the sea, they should have plenty of fuel.

"No, sir," Grant said. A pause. "There's not going to be a signal, is there?"

They could head home. All it would take was one word, aborting the mission, sending them all on their way back to England. No one else needed to die.

At least, not until *Götterdämmerung* did its work. But, he knew now with awful certainty, there was nothing 465 Squadron could do to prevent that.

"No," Durban murmured, "I don't believe there is."

Chapter Forty-Two

Norfolk, 16 April

Sarah Lane shoved her doubts aside and slipped through the Operations Room door.

Somehow, she had expected the room to be a blur of movement and noise, dozens of RAF personnel running around, supporting 465 Squadron's mission. That seemed proper. Regardless of how few people might ever be allowed to know it, AFTERLIGHT was the most important job not just of her career, but of the war. Succeed, and it would be just a footnote in an archive somewhere, possibly to be puzzled over by future historians when the statutory period was up and the millions of classified records this war had created opened to the public. Succeed, and the war would meander to its inevitable conclusion, the Nazis already consigned to history as a new war began, pitting the democratic Allied nations of the West against the Soviets and their subjugated satellites. Succeed, and AFTERLIGHT would be blissfully forgotten.

Fail, and countless millions would die.

It occurred to her that the occasion deserved more than this. The big Operations Room stood mostly empty. Bony Wright paced with his hands behind his back. A handful of WAAFs stood monitoring a situation board, with fifteen light blue placards displayed on the left and one on the right. Air Vice Marshal Embry and Major Anders sat at a table next to another WAAF wearing headphones, an intent look on her face as she stared at her large radio set.

No crowds of expectant viewers. No sound at all.

Lane took a deep breath.

Anders saw her coming. Pushing his chair out for her to take,

322

he strode off across the room in search of a replacement. Embry looked up at her approach. He didn't smile. Exhaustion hung on his pale face.

She hesitated for a moment. "Dare I ask, sir?"

He motioned for her to sit. "They reached the target about ten minutes ago, Sarah. They lost an aircraft on the approach."

She swallowed. "Who?"

"Bravo Four," he said. "Flying Officer Dickie Chapple and Flight Sergeant Sam Elmore."

Relief washed over her, replaced in an instant by guilt. She didn't know the two men she had doomed when she brought them this mission. She only knew that neither was Andrew Durban.

"Stahl?"

Embry shook his head. "DINGO. Three times so far. We also have COMRADE. The Soviets have intervened."

"We knew they would. They want it too much to let us destroy it."

He nodded. "I don't suppose it would help if we told them how close it is to being released?"

"It's too late either way, sir."

"You're probably right," he said. Anders pulled up a chair, and the three of them sat in silence.

Lane felt her eyes drift to the board where the WAAFs stood, as helpless as the rest of them. Each placard showed the names of a crew, Durban/Grant at the top. So far, only the placard marked for the unfortunate Chapple/Elmore had shifted to the column marked *lost*, but there would be more. It was only a matter of time. Was it worth it? How many of those placards would she be prepared to move to the right-hand side of the board if it guaranteed success? Thirty-two lives, against millions. A simple decision for the politicians. The greater good. The big picture. All part of the ultimate blueprint for victory.

She saw Andy's face in her mind and gave silent thanks that the burden of choice wasn't hers.

"Are you okay, Sarah?"

Maybe she had shuddered. Or spoken aloud without realising it. All she knew was that she had given something away, and that Embry was staring at her. It wasn't her eyes, at least. They remained dry. So many tears she had cried in this war; she never let anyone see them. "Not really, sir," she admitted. "You?"

"I'd hoped for better news," he said. He looked at his watch. "Their time is up. Durban should have aborted by now."

"He'll hold on for as long as there is a chance, no matter how slim. If there is a way, Andy will find it."

The WAAF looked up from her radio, face intent. Lane knew before she spoke what the radio operator would say. The slump of her face said it all. "DINGO, sir."

Embry nodded. "Stahl must be dead. I'm sorry, Major Anders."

The Dane said nothing.

"I think that might be it, I'm afraid," Embry added. "Durban has no choice but to abort now."

Lane stared at the utter hopelessness in the AVM's eyes. "Would you, sir?"

"What?"

"Abort."

He sighed. "I suppose not. Damn, I wish I was leading this, to make that call myself."

"What do you mean?"

Embry ran one hand over his face. "It's not what you think," he sighed. "I love to fly, but I'm not a fool who seeks danger for its own sake. I don't envy Durban the peril he is in, nor do I think I could do a better job than him. But this is torture, Sarah. I would rather risk my neck a thousand times than listen to someone else face the threat instead."

324

Lane nodded. She felt a surge of respect. The AVM wasn't lying. Not even close. No wonder good men like Andy Durban admired him so much. "If it's any consolation, sir, I think Andy would say the same thing if he was here in your place."

"Of course," Embry agreed. "He's proven himself to have that quality. As have you, Sarah."

"Sir?"

Embry hesitated. "Major, give us a minute, would you?"

Anders stood, his face expressionless, and walked away.

"I received your request," Embry said. "You may work for SOE, but you wear an RAF uniform, and the RAF pays your wages. I know you have requested a special assignment to the British Occupation Zone in Germany. And I know why."

"Did you approve my orders?"

"Of course. And you should know I will rescind them the moment you ask."

"I won't."

"Look, Sarah, I understand why you feel you need to go. There are thousands of RAF prisoners of war still held in Germany, and I feel a responsibility to every one of them. But there is a whole machine ready to find them, just as they stand ready to find your missing agents. You don't have to do it alone. The war is nearly over. As much as any man in Britain, you deserve the peace."

"So do my agents, sir."

His mouth opened, but no words followed. Neither spoke the obvious, that if Andy couldn't destroy *Götterdämmerung*, the peace would be worse than the war.

The WAAF stirred again. They turned to her.

"DISMAL," she intoned.

Mission aborted.

It was over.

Everything was over.

Chapter Forty-Three

He got to within four feet before the guards finally tore their eyes from the dogfight above.

Close enough.

Stahl drove the tip of his SS honour dagger into the man's throat, then spun towards the second guard, too late to stop the warning shout but soon enough to prevent the man bringing his rifle to bear. He slammed the dagger into the man's side, between the ribs and into the lungs, his hand a blur as he plunged it in, over and over. The soldier wrestled with him, trying to grab his wrist hand, and Stahl lunged, all his body weight through the point of his useless left shoulder. As the man stumbled back, Stahl thrust the steel blade down into his clavicle. One last twist and pull, and the second soldier dropped, leaving Stahl's hand slick with bright arterial blood.

The first sentry writhed, both hands clutching desperately at his ruined windpipe.

Stahl dropped into a crouch, watching the front doors, alert for any sign that the second guard's shout had been heard over the cacophony of engines and flak. The doors remained closed. The gurgling moans of the first sentry had no chance to be heard, and they fell silent soon enough.

He wiped the blood off the knife on the dying man's uniform, revealing the words *Meine Ehre heißt Treue* etched longwise on the blade. *My honour is loyalty.* Stahl could have laughed as he sheathed the weapon. He stepped over the man's fallen StG 44. The five-kilogram automatic weapon would have been useful inside, but with his left arm hanging limp at his side, it might as well have weighed thirty tons.

With his one good hand, he edged open the heavy front door, peeked inside, and drew his Walther P38.

The warehouse was mostly a single space, twenty metres wide and perhaps fifty long with a high, flattish ceiling. Towards the far end, metal steps rose to a platform with a line of offices and a ladder that seemed to lead to the roof. Three SS soldiers in respirators leaned against the railing of the platform, watching over the men standing on either side of the long line of white tables that ran the length of the building. Most of these men wore white scientific robes with matching white surgical facemasks. The only exception wore a black leather trench coat. That one's white mask seemed comically incongruent below his black-peaked cap with its familiar Death's Head insignia.

Along the length of the table, Stahl saw thick glass vessels, like clear water flasks, each with a steel screw cap. The liquid inside was colourless. Two larger vessels stood on horizontal mounts, each with a tap concealed inside a clear plastic sheath. They reminded him of black, burnished metal wine casks. As he watched, a scientist very carefully placed his hands and an empty bottle through the sheath, turned the tap, filled the vessel and screwed the top. Then he put the newly filled vessel with the others.

There must have been two hundred of them. Maybe more.

"Fifteen minutes, *meine Herren*," the SS officer announced. "Leave the rest or remain with it." He motioned to the masked soldiers. "Is the dispenser truck ready?"

"*Jawohl*, Herr Standartenführer."

A full colonel, then. Stahl had expected no less. The SS wouldn't have entrusted this final, critical mission to just anyone. There was too much at stake.

"*Ausgezeichnet*," the Standartenführer said. "Bring it to the

327

loading doors and summon the driver. Do not let him see what he will be carrying."

One soldier threw out a stiff-armed salute and took the steps down two at a time before vanishing through some unseen rear entrance.

Behind Stahl, the door slammed shut. With reactions honed by years of SS training and deadly field experience, he took two steps into the shadows of a doorway marked Toiletten. The wind, he realised, closing the door after he had failed to do so. He had been lucky. No raised voices. No sign they had spotted him. Just the steady thud of anti-aircraft artillery. Beneath his feet, through boots and concrete alike, he could feel the distant shuddering of Soviet rounds hammering against the thin grey line of exhausted German defenders.

With deliberate care, Stahl ghosted his way through the assorted crates and shelves that filled every inch of space between the open central area and the right-hand wall. A scientist, grey-haired and slightly stooped, said something to the officer. Stahl heard neither the comment nor the reply. His heartbeat pounded in his ears. Far too fast.

Adrenaline had reduced the pain in his ruined left shoulder to a dull ache. He refused to think what harm slamming it into the guard had done, or what other damage lurked inside him. He scanned the wall. His gaze lingered on a first aid kit, for all the good it could do him. He was looking for something more important and found it just a few feet further along. An emergency distress kit, with a flare gun and several refills inside a hard plastic shell. He took it, though simply lifting its weight brought a wave of exhaustion, and then edged back towards the exit with the plastic case hanging from his hooked and nerveless left hand.

Footsteps behind him. He spun around.

The grey-haired scientist, reaching for the toilet door, stared at him in surprise.

Their eyes met. Held the stare for a long second.

The scientist frowned and opened his mouth, and Stahl shot him between the teeth.

He was moving before the body hit the floor, out onto the central floor. He sent four rounds towards the guards on the platform, hitting one in the gut while the other scrambled for safety, clutching at his head. The officer ran for the back door, yelling for help, and Stahl loosed off two quick shots. Too quick. One missed. The other hit the man in the hip instead of the spine, sending him sprawling onto the concrete floor, squealing in pain.

The scientists stood dumbstruck until Stahl shot another in the head. Then the rest scattered, wailing and tumbling over each other in their haste to escape, leaving hundreds of clear flasks forgotten on the table.

With the eight-round magazine exhausted, the top slide on Stahl's Walther had remained in the locked back position. He put down the distress kit and fumbled for the second magazine in his pocket, glancing up at the platform above.

It saved his life.

The second soldier had ripped off his mask to breathe better. Blood poured down the side of his face from a shallow gouge. He must have only clipped the man, Stahl thought idly, then threw himself desperately towards the cover of the shelves.

The soldier yelled in anger as he pulled the trigger of his MP-40 in a poorly aimed spray. 9mm rounds skipped off the concrete floor, and a metallic screech rang out as one nicked the metal upright of the shelving unit and spun away into the far wall. The ricochet could just as easily have hit the metal table and its delicate cargo. Stahl spat. If he had dived for the closer shelter of the table instead of the shelves and crates, they would all be breathing *Götterdämmerung* already.

The soldier kept yelling, incoherent with rage, but with

enough self-control to avoid wasting all his ammunition. Peering through a narrow gap, Stahl saw the soldier watching the shelves even as curses continued to spill from his mouth.

The officer, unseen on the ground beyond the table, yelled something. The soldier shouted back a reply, his gaze flickering away from the shelves towards his commander. A momentary lapse in concentration, and a last one.

Stahl shot him in the eye, spreading a thin film of blood over the unbroken office window behind the man. A lucky shot, for sure, but hadn't luck always been on his side when it came to killing?

The officer gave a low moan of despair.

Stahl ignored him. Even if the Standartenführer didn't bleed out, he would die soon enough when Durban's Mosquito finished the job. Picking up the emergency kit once more, he turned to the door.

Outside, the pace of anti-aircraft fire slackened for a second, and Stahl heard engines. Not aircraft. Trucks. Behind him, beyond the rear doors, shouts and hurled commands echoed into the warehouse.

He heard the officer laugh. The noise descended into a wracking cough.

No way out to the front. Nor the rear. That left upwards.

Stahl didn't hesitate. He took the steps as fast as he could, his lungs heaving with the effort, then stepped over the two soldiers on the balcony. One was still alive, his hands clutching the glistening distended mass that had been his stomach. His eyes pleaded with Stahl. He looked so young. Nodding, Stahl shot him in the head, then slipped the Walther into his pocket and reached for the ladder.

The emergency case was the problem. He could hardly hold it when standing, let alone halfway up a ladder. With hands that were sticky with drying blood, he unlatched the case and dumped most of the contents onto the platform with a hollow clang. He kept only the flare gun, which he tucked into his belt, and four flares.

The shouts from below were louder now. Questioning. The Standartenführer croaked out a response.

One step at a time, he told himself, pulling himself onto the ladder. Above him, the roof hatch waited, looking impossibly heavy. His breath came in ragged gasps as he forced the useless left side of his body close to the ladder, keeping as much of his bodyweight on his legs as he could, leaving the right hand to guide his progress, always in contact with a rung or at least the thick uprights.

Halfway up, the front door swung open and slammed into the wall with a thunderous bang. Men spilled through, their uniforms a mix of SS and Wehrmacht. Some paused at the bizarre sight of the apparatus that covered the table. It bought Stahl half a second, and he scrambled for the hatch above. Pushed it. It barely yielded before dropping shut again.

A soldier yelled.

The movement had given him away.

One of them fired. Bullets smashed into the wall around Stahl. Fragments of steel and stone sliced into his left knee. Instinctively, his leg sought safety in flinching away, and his left boot slipped free of the ladder. He hung suspended above the platform for one long breath, only the fingertips of his right hand and the tip of his right boot between him and a leg-shattering fall to be followed shortly after by more gunfire and death. His body swung against the ladder, and he felt something snag.

Dragged free from his pocket, the Walther P38 spun end over end and shattered on the warehouse floor, two flare cartridges descending almost apologetically in its wake.

The soldier fired again, and Stahl's ears filled with the painful crash of bullets on steel. With a roar of anger and pain, he lunged up again. Driving his good hand against the hatch, he shoved his arm through the narrow gap he had created. Keeping his feet churning on the ladder, he forced first his head and then his shoulders through the hatch's heavy steel embrace. Excruciating pain flared as metal ripped skin and scraps of flesh from his ear. Almost whimpering, he flailed his feet for purchase and wriggled his body up, waiting for the agony of a bullet or the hatch itself taking off a leg.

It didn't come. The hatch fell shut behind him. He was on the roof, eyes screwed shut, sobbing with pain. His good hand fumbled at his clothes. Not seeking wounds. They didn't matter.

His questing fingers found his belt empty, then fell on the flare gun's grip, miraculously clinging to his belt until it finally came free as he wriggled to safety. Muttering a silent prayer to a God he had long since disavowed, he hugged the flare gun close, then checked for the two remaining cartridges in his pocket and opened his eyes.

One flare, one spare. After that...

Above, he saw two Mosquitoes, out of strike range. A thin column of smoke hung over the Vistula Lagoon, already breaking apart in the breeze. He had no way of knowing which side's dying aircraft had caused it.

It hardly mattered, anyway, so long as there were enough of them left to do what must be done.

Bolting the hatch shut, Stahl slipped the first cartridge into the flare gun and raised it to the sky.

Chapter Forty-Four

"Flare!"

Durban heard the excitement in Barton's voice, the single syllable drenched in the exuberance that only puppies and Aussies seemed capable of. They were heading away from the city over the Baltic, the order to abort given barely a minute earlier, already forgotten as Durban flung the aircraft back into a maximum rate turn, the wooden airframe straining as he peered up through the Perspex at smoke shrouded Pillau. "Johnny, do you see it?"

"Not yet, boss."

"Bravo One, what about you?"

"I'm not sure, sir," Kittinger said. "There's so much smoke."

"East end of the docks," Barton said confidently. "Close to that bloody submarine. Want me to come down and show you?"

"Negative, Alpha One. Stay up there and provide cover. I don't think we've seen the last of those fighters. I'm going in for a closer look. Kittinger, keep an eye out in case I miss anything."

Or get shot down.

Levelling out at one hundred feet, Durban pushed the throttles fully open and raced back towards the city. The *Siegfried*, given an unexpected second chance against the Mosquitoes that had hung maddeningly out of range, opened fire with everything it had. Around them, the air turned an ominous shade of oily grey. The Mosquito shook, buffeted by fifty localised changes in air pressure. Then they were through, passing low over the navigation channel between the old Prussian forts that guarded the approaches, zipping through the belching smoke of two freighters below the height of their funnels. Ahead, he saw the U-78, their secondary target but hardly worth the risk of attacking if the primary wasn't already destroyed.

"See anything, Johnny?"

He didn't need an answer.

Arcing raggedly up, ahead and above their nose, a second flare dispelled smoke and gloom with equal ease.

"Got him!" Grant's triumphant yell almost deafened him. "Third warehouse from the end. There's a man on the roof."

"Stahl," Durban said, turning the nose towards the warehouse, climbing and reducing power. The Mosquito slowed, and Durban stood it on his wingtip, hanging against his straps. He waved as he passed barely two hundred feet above the lone figure on the rooftop. Dressed in ragged civilian clothing, his face a mass of blood, the man was almost unrecognisable as the cold, ascetic German that Durban had known in England.

It made no difference, though. It was Stahl. Right there. Waving one hand only. That same hand then dropping to point urgently at the floor below his feet.

Showing them the target.

"TRIGGER ONE," he said calmly into the radio, then switched back to the squadron communications net. "All Bravo callsigns, maintain your position and prepare to attack on my signal. Bravo One, form up on me."

"Roger, Colt Leader."

The flak intensified as Durban swung out over the Vistula Lagoon again. The gunners didn't need an invitation, and Durban's return made it abundantly clear this wasn't merely some drawn out photo-reconnaissance run. Grant muttered a curse as a line of 20mm tracers tore through the sky ahead of them.

"Bravo One to Colt Leader."

"What is it, Kittinger?"

"Permission to send Bravo Two and Six against that flak ship?"

Durban looked at Grant. He knew what the young man would say. The *Siegfried* had almost got them twice already, and it would make any south to north bombing run against the target an extremely dangerous affair. But... "Bravo Two and Six both carry HE," he told Grant. "If they use them on the *Siegfried*, that will leave only two more attempts at that building if you miss."

"Sir," Grant said, grinning, "I will not miss."

Durban nodded. "Roger, Kittinger. Send them. I'm going back in for another look at the warehouse. Your boys should have a clear run while we draw the flak ship's attention."

Grant's grin vanished when he heard that.

Trying to ignore the myriad flashes from the deck of the *Siegfried*, Durban opened the throttles and raced across the harbour from the south, getting the line of his target run right even as he kept the aircraft far too low for bomb release. He had to count the warehouses from the right to be sure of his target, but in navigational terms it was an easy run to the target. The only thing that made it difficult was the lethal flak pouring up from all angles.

"Alpha One to Colt Leader, bandits."

And the fighters.

"Roger, Don. How many?"

"At least a dozen. Permission to ditch our bombloads to increase air-to-air performance?"

"Not until the target is destroyed."

"Roger, Colt Leader," Barton said. "Get on with it, will you?"

Ahead, the details of the warehouse became clearer. The vehicles parked out front, swarming with soldiers. Its long, corrugated sides. The single man on the rooftop.

He yanked back on the throttles and put out the air brakes.

The Mosquito groaned as it slowed, sending the nose lurching up in outrage.

"Stahl is still there," Grant said. "Why is he still there?"

"Because he's a bloody fool." Frantically gesturing him away, Durban passed overhead. Saw the man point at something.

Still, Stahl didn't move.

What was he waiting for?

Chapter Forty-Five

Pillau, 16 April

Stahl watched as the Mosquito came around for a second run. The flak ship in the harbour looked almost ablaze, every gun flashing and leaving a haze of smoke in the air as it turned its full attention on the incoming aircraft. Tracers reached up towards it, a storm of lead and high explosive so intense that Stahl could see no plausible end to it but for the Mosquito fragmenting to fall into the cold harbour below. He wondered how Andrew Durban could stand it. The man had to see the explosions and tracers around him, and yet he kept on coming. Stahl couldn't help but admire the man as he waited for the Mosquito's bomb doors to open.

They didn't.

Beyond the onrushing aircraft, he saw a line of familiar figures in white running along the stone wharf towards the distant U-78. One stumbled and fell, reaching out to his colleagues for help, only to be ignored. No soldiers accompanied the scientists, nor tried to stop them. Stahl could tell from the yells and the steady banging of an unseen rifle butt on the locked roof hatch that the soldiers were all busy elsewhere.

Willing Durban to understand his meaning, Stahl stabbed his one functional hand towards the fleeing scientists.

The Mosquito's engine note changed, with a reduction in volume so sudden that Stahl thought for a moment flak must have struck it at last. The nose lifted, and once again Durban tilted the aircraft so that their eyes met for a fleeting moment. Now the British pilot was gesturing too – a frantic pushing motion, away from the rooftop and the harbour, towards the city.

Then the aircraft was over him and climbing away again, turning back towards the Vistula Lagoon, beneath the dark spots of distant fighters moving slowly across the sky.

Durban wanted him to clear the target.

To escape.

Stahl almost smiled. The thought had not even occurred to him. Certainly not since the soldiers had arrived to surround the building. Probably not since he had shot the scientist and turned the laboratory below into a charnel house.

Earlier, he thought. He had known so much earlier than that.

He had known when he saw Canaris at Flossenbürg.

Known this could end in only one way.

Durban surely had to realise it, too. Even if Stahl could somehow evade the soldiers below, slide off the roof into the alleyways behind them, he could never escape the blast radius of the bombs and the napalm. Not on foot, wounded. Not in time.

The Mosquito was completing its turn now. He could barely make out the figures in the cockpit, the roar of the engines already fading with distance. He had no radio. No more flares. No way to signal them. Except one.

Carefully, grunting with the pain, he sat down.

The roof was cold, but so was he, warmth and sensation fleeing his body together. The stone felt damp beneath him. He realised it lay drenched in the blood running down his left arm and dripping from nerveless fingers.

He closed his eyes.

Out across the bay, something exploded with a dull crump. It didn't seem to matter.

The breeze off the sea stank of smoke and cordite. He ignored those odours and concentrated on its feel on his face. The way it had felt rolling down off the Alps and across the clear waters of the Forggensee. He heard his sister's voice, calling him the way she would when they were children. Persistent, almost plaintive, yet resonating with her love for him.

He thought of Sarah Lane, watching as he left the barn at RAF Tempsford, and of Admiral Wilhelm Canaris, showing him the truth. Canaris, who had died first, and who now waited for him with his sister and her children.

Stahl heard the Mosquito's engine note grow louder again, and was at peace.

Chapter Forty-Six

Above Pillau, 16 April

A tremendous flash lit up the sky to their west, and someone gave a triumphant yell into the radio. Around them, Grant felt the air settle. No more tracers. No more explosions.

"Well played, Bravo Two," Durban said.

"Great shot, Desveaux." Kittinger's voice betrayed his pride in his men.

The *Siegfried* was gone, at least as a coherent piece of military machinery. Where it had once floated were two shattered pieces of metal, their angles all wrong as they sank inexorably beneath a flame-tinged cloud of greasy smoke. Bravo Two and Bravo Six climbed away, no longer worried about any threat of defensive fire from their victim. With its back broken by direct hits from one or more five hundred-pound bombs, and with its crew scurrying to abandon their posts, it was no longer a threat to anyone.

The shore gunners saw it too and redoubled their efforts. The sky around the two climbing Bravo callsigns became a suffocating mass of flak bursts.

"Bravo Six is hit," an Australian voice said calmly. Johnson, Grant thought as small pieces of wing tumbled from the climbing Mosquito. The venomous fast bowler who had turned out to be a nice guy in the pub after the game.

Durban thumbed his R/T. "Is it bad?"

"No," Johnson said. "I think I can hold her together."

The damaged wing came apart with sudden fury. The Mosquito tipped on its axis and plunged into the harbour. Gone.

Johnson hadn't said another word.

"All Bravo callsigns," Durban said, "attack. Form up in my trail and prepare to attack in a single column, three thousand foot spacing, speed three-fifty, three hundred feet. Bravo One, you'll be straight after me. Drop your napalm on my impact point."

"Wilco, Colt Leader," Kittens said.

Grant felt bile in his throat. Both men had spoken without emotion, like they were safely in an office discussing some trivial matter and hadn't just witnessed the sudden, brutal death of two friends and colleagues. A death that could come as easily for all of them. He looked out across the harbour. The sea had already settled, no trace left of Johnson and Gillespie except a few fragments of wood bobbing on the surface. Beyond it, the bow of the *Siegfried* was sliding down from sight. The stern had already disappeared. Leaking diesel from the flak ship's ruptured tanks had coated the surface. Now it burned fiercely. A single crewman clung desperately to the metal of the bow as it sank, at least until his flailing legs met the rising flames. Grant knew it was impossible for him to hear the man's screams over the roar of the Merlins. That didn't stop them echoing in his ears.

"Alpha One to Colt Leader." Barton's voice. Grant looked up through the Perspex towards the clouds above. Something flared like a comet as it fell through the clouds.

"I read you, Alpha One."

"We've got quite the party going on up here, boss. There are Soviet and German fighters now. We've shot down three so far, but there are more coming."

JAEGER.

Durban circled wide out over the bay, other Mosquitoes dropping into line behind them at intervals. "Roger, Alpha One. Casualties?"

"Alpha Seven is gone."

Craig and Keane, Grant thought. A likeable crew, an Englishman and their only Irishman. His eyes fell on the smoke trail left by the falling wreck. That could have been theirs, but so could several others. Columns of smoke dotted the Vistula Lagoon, each a funeral marker for its crew. No way to tell if they were British or Australian, German or Russian.

"Keep them busy for a few more minutes, Don. We're attacking now." He switched to his intercom. "Johnny, open the bomb doors."

"Sir?"

"What?"

More bile. Grant swallowed. It burned on the way down. "Stahl is still on the target."

Durban kept his eyes straight ahead. "The bomb doors, Johnny."

Grant realised his hand was already reaching for the bomb door lever below the central instrument panel. His mind hesitated but his fingers didn't. Training kicked in as he lifted the safety cover, moved the weapon switch to the lower position, and opened the curved Perspex that shielded the bomb selector panel. A quick check of the fuse settings, then he dropped the bomb door lever down. The Mosquito shuddered as the doors fell into the slipstream, protesting their high speed.

An orange light blinked on. Bomb doors fully open and ready.

His eyes went back to the distant target, still too far away to see if Stahl had gone. He knew he hadn't.

"You saw him sit down," Durban said.

"Yes, sir."

"You know why."

"Yes, sir."

"I'll drop them. Just tell me when." A pause. "You're better at this than me, Johnny. I need you."

For a moment only, Grant was tempted to stay silent, as if that might somehow wash his hands clean of what they were about to do. But the training had already taken over. He wouldn't fight it anymore. "Yes, sir."

Durban nodded and brought the Mosquito's nose around, head on to the target, throttling forward to compensate for the drag of the bomb doors. "Three hundred feet," he confirmed. "Airspeed three fifty."

"Three-fifty," Grant intoned. He was already calculating. Three hundred and fifty miles per hour of airspeed meant five hundred feet of ground passing beneath them every second. The arithmetic was simple enough. Knowing the altitude and the type of bomb he planned to drop allowed him to calculate the time that bomb would take to reach the ground. Multiplying that by the airspeed produced the range. Some bomber variants of the Mosquito carried the Mark III bombsight to do the angular velocity calculation for the crew. Grant felt oddly pleased that their aircraft did not have it. The calculations consumed his mind. They left no room for Stahl.

At first, the building ahead didn't seem to get any closer. An optical illusion, Grant knew. Soon it would race towards them, faster and faster, until it vanished beneath them. When it did, it would already be too late to release. The aircraft's momentum would transfer to the bombs and take them sailing over the target. No good. The time to drop was before that, when the target still seemed to move slowly and yet was speeding up.

He'd done all this in training. Topped his class in medium level bombing. All that had changed was the altitude. And the speed. And the margin of error.

"Five seconds," he murmured.

Flak burst around them. Grant ignored it. Ignored the way his stomach roiled, the bubbling of vomit in his throat, the sharp metallic ring as a piece of shrapnel struck the armour at the back of his seat. Ignored everything, except the maths. To hit within fifty feet of the centre of the building? Accurate enough to be sure that the bomb would punch through the roof, the fuse delay settings holding back the explosion until it was within the walls, where the overpressure could crack it open and expose the insides to the napalm of the rest of the squadron? The margin of error was next to nothing. One-tenth of a second. No room for hesitation.

"Three seconds."

The building filled the windscreen ahead. Grant saw the long roof looming over the horrified faces of soldiers on the quayside as they fired their rifles towards the onrushing aircraft. He saw the man sitting on the rooftop, eyes closed, one hand still outstretched and pointing.

"Now!"

Durban pressed the bomb release.

No hesitation.

Freed in an instant of a thousand pounds of weight, the Mosquito bounced up as it roared over the city beyond. Half a second later, it shook as a wave of violent air overtook it, but Durban's grip remained tight on the controls. Grant pulled the bomb door lever again and felt them slam shut beneath him.

Only when the dull thud of the explosion caught up with them did Grant allow his eyes to close.

He felt his body loll back in the seat. His straps struggled to contain his sideways slide as Durban threw them into a climbing turn.

"Direct hit, boss," Kittinger yelled. "Bombs gone."

Even through the protective shade of his closed lids, the flare of the napalm stung.

"Bravo Three, dropping."

"Bravo Five, bombs away."

He opened his eyes.

The ground beneath them was already a mass of incandescent

light, so hot that it seemed to draw in smoke as it sucked the air in from all around it. One by one, Mosquitoes passed over the dockside and added their napalm canisters to the inferno. At the very heart of the fiery maelstrom, nothing remained of the building. It was simply gone.

Stahl was gone.

Grant felt the vomit come again, hot and urgent, and this time it didn't stop.

Chapter Forty-Seven

Above Pillau, 16 April

"AFTERLIGHT," Durban said. "I say again, AFTERLIGHT."

He kept his voice calm. There was no doubt in his mind. An eighteen-hundred Fahrenheit inferno of gasoline, magnesium and sodium nitrate consumed everything in its path. The building. The unfortunate soldiers outside. *Götterdämmerung*.

No doubt. And no time to waste.

"Bravo One, take all Bravo callsigns. Get clear over the sea and then climb for home."

"Roger, Colt Leader." Kittinger needed no second invitation. His Mosquito peeled away and raced south, skirting the smoke-shrouded city, heading for England with the survivors of B Flight in his wake.

Durban kept his attention on the clouds above. With the bombs gone, the full power of twin Merlins powered them upwards. There were more smoke trails now. "Alpha One, what's your status?"

"Not good," Barton said. "Alpha Five bought it."

Durban took a deep, shuddering breath. Another one lost. They had achieved success, but they hadn't finished paying the price for it. "All Alpha callsigns, you are cleared to jettison your bombloads."

"Already done, boss," Barton said. "I gave the order the moment you called AFTERLIGHT." There was an edge to his voice. Too late for Claiborne and Ball.

"Roger," Durban said. "Disengage and head for home."

"Not an option right now. They're all over us up here."

The radio net exploded in Durban's ears. Loss, pain and

absolute terror mingled into a single deafening shriek. It filled his ears, drowning out the sound of his straining engines.

"Get your bloody finger off the transmit button," Barton yelled. The radio net fell silent.

Above them, the clouds parted. A burning mass of wood and metal rushed towards them. Durban tugged on the controls, ready to evade, but the Mosquito was already past them. The flames had already turned the wings and rear fuselage into a ball of flame. Now they had reached the cockpit, the men inside responding to Barton's cry for discipline, even in their dying agony.

"Machin and Tucker are gone," Barton said.

To Durban's right, Grant flinched. His face looked drawn with exhaustion and pain, the front of his overalls spattered with watery vomit, eyes welling with tears. But he kept his gaze not on the plummeting wreckage but on the sky, gaze roaming, searching for fighters. Good lad.

Visibility shrank to nothing as they passed through the clouds, raindrops briefly plastering the windscreen before being carried away in the rushing air. Then they were through and into the blue sky above. Durban blinked against the sudden sunlight.

Utter carnage awaited.

All was confusion. Aircraft of three air forces darted about the sky at full pace, weaving and diving as the dogfight spread out to cover several thousand feet of altitude. In less than five seconds, Durban counted twenty aircraft. The four remaining twin-engine Mosquitoes were obvious, bigger than their enemies but just as fast and deadly.

Less than two thousand yards ahead, a Yak dropped onto the tail of a Mosquito, but before Durban could even radio a warning the grey, square wing tipped shape of a Messerschmitt Bf-109G closed in its turn on the Yak, sending lines of tracers smashing into the Russian's tail and cockpit. The Yak rolled over

347

and dropped towards the waiting clouds, a single thin stream of oil hanging wormlike behind it.

"Barton, get your people below the cloud and head for home," Durban said, turning behind the 109G. "I'll cover for you."

The German pilot had made the fatal error common to so many new pilots, flying straight and level to admire his success rather than immediately evading in case of pursuit. At max power, Durban needed only a second to judge the lead on the 109 and fire a brief burst. The Mosquito's heavy shells did the rest, breaking the 109 in half behind the wings.

He didn't make the same mistake as the German. Instead, he already had the Mosquito in a tight turn without waiting to see, or even caring, if the enemy pilot wrestled his way out of his stricken aircraft. Instantly spotting a Yak turning away from them, he fired again. The Gods of War clearly had his back. At least one of his speculative shots dinged the underbelly of the Soviet fighter. A puff of smoke hung in the air behind the Yak as it flew on. Then, with startling ferocity, flames engulfed it from nose to tail.

Behind them, a dark shape dropped into place. He twisted to get a better look at it and saw relief on Grant's face. "Looks like we picked up a shadow, sir," he said.

"Ready when you are, Colt Leader," Barton said, his Mosquito falling into place on their wing.

"Johnny, plot us a course for home," Durban said. "Alpha One, we're going home. Try to keep up."

They dived at full speed for the cover of the clouds. A mile ahead and two thousand feet below, the three other surviving Mosquitoes of A Flight were already well on their way to the coast, avoiding the stricken city of Pillau while they headed for the sun that was rapidly sliding towards the Baltic Sea.

His neck ached from all the twisting, and Durban winced as he checked behind them. "Looks like our German and Soviet friends are too busy killing each other to think about chasing us," he said, feeling a surge of satisfaction. The guilt would come later, when he sat down to write the letters to families. Five aircraft, ten good men. A heavy price. "How's that course coming, Johnny?"

Grant said nothing.

"Johnny?"

The navigator jumped as if suddenly woken. "Sorry, sir. I was thinking about Stahl."

Eleven men, Durban reminded himself. Eleven good men had died today. "I know, Johnny," he said. "But I need that course."

"He was just sitting there."

"He chose this, Johnny. He knew what he was doing."

"I don't, sir. What was he pointing at?"

Durban remembered the peaceful composure on Stahl's face as the bombs fell. He could have been sleeping, but for the outstretched arm. Pointing the way across the bay, towards the waiting grey shape...

"The bloody U-78," he said, cursing himself. In the exultation of striking the primary and the urgent need to support the beleaguered A Flight, he had forgotten it. Bloody fool. Too busy congratulating himself to realise the mission was not over. "How is our fuel state?"

"Not great," Grant said. "We used a lot in the climb and dogfight."

"Can we make it home?"

"Yes, sir. But only if we go now."

Something about Grant's voice made him think of another navigator, another night.

I'm sorry, Clive.

Durban looked down at the instruments, at the controls in his hands, at the burning city of Pillau already slipping past them beyond their starboard wingtip. Ahead lay the Baltic Sea and the way home. A gentle climb, cruise power at maximum altitude, and they could slip unmolested across the top of Denmark, protected by their speed and the darkness of the approaching night.

But only if they had the fuel.

"Understood," Durban said. "Give me the course."

"Sir?"

"What?"

"We can't leave yet. Not without the U-78." He paused. "That's what Stahl would have wanted."

Durban wanted to shout at him that Stahl was dead, just like Clive Lampeter. That he didn't want to write any letters to the family of John Grant in Barbados. That he'd already killed one navigator by fighting when he should have run, and he would not kill another. But a stronger emotion overwhelmed his anger.

"Thank you, Johnny," he said, and hurled the Mosquito into a turn to the north.

Barton followed. "Where are you off to, boss?"

"The submarine," Durban said. "Head for home, Don."

The Australian's Mosquito kept pace with them. "Not a chance. You don't have any bombs."

"Neither do you. I ordered you to jettison them."

"You ordered A Flight to jettison them. Me? I never trust a Pom to do an Aussie's job."

Bloody Australians. "Fine," Durban snapped. "We don't have the fuel left to mess around, so we're going to do this fast and first time. I'll go first and see if I can draw off some of the flak for you."

"Wait," Grant said, "what?"

"You sink the thing and we'll go home. Got it?"

"Piece of cake," Barton said.

The flak crews had every reason to believe that the raid was over. Perhaps that was why it took them several seconds to man their weapons again. Durban pulled out of his dive two hundred feet above the water and was already halfway to the target before the first gun opened fire. In an instant, all other guns followed suit, and the sky ahead vanished in a blur of smoke and tracer, almost blotting out the sight of the submarine, no longer at the dock where they had left it but heading across the harbour towards the deep access channel out to the sea.

"They're diving," Grant said.

Durban's teeth clenched painfully. The navigator was right. Already the body of the submarine was below the surface, with only the sleek shape of the conning tower left to betray it. Another minute and they would be gone, concealed within the protective depths of the sea, off to South America or wherever men who had just perpetrated the greatest evil in human history would retire.

465 Squadron had already stopped the evil. One last task to be accomplished.

Ignoring the flak and the sound of shrapnel peppering the airframe, Durban lined up his sights and fired. Shells stitched a line across the water's surface, then converged on the tower. He saw the sparks of metal on metal.

The submarine kept descending, the conning tower seeming to melt into a bubbling white froth.

"Hold on," he shouted, banking low across the water, his wingtip barely above the surface, so that he could see how every gun in the harbour followed them. All their focus was on him.

None was on Barton.

As Durban watched, the second Mosquito released its two bombs. They plunged into the water, straddling the submarine.

For a heartbeat, nothing happened. Then the water exploded up in two columns as hundreds of pounds of Amatol detonated. Trapped between the hydraulic shock of both blasts, the U-78 stood little chance. Intensified by the weight of the water, the expanding shockwave struck the hull. It didn't collapse it – they were too close to the surface for that, and the water pressure not enough – but something towards the rear must have given way. Not by much. Not enough to let a human being swim to safety. Just enough to let tens of tons of sea water break in.

As the Mosquitoes climbed to safety, already leaving behind the swarm of shells that followed them like enraged wasps, Durban managed a last glance back at the submarine. The conning tower lurched backwards, the bow breaking the surface again as water flooded into the rear compartment, bubbling the surface with escaping air. Then fuel, spreading in a dark smear.

The U-78 disappeared into the ice-cold water of Pillau harbour, a fitting tomb for the terrified scientists drowning within her unyielding shell.

"BATHTUB," Durban said into his radio, unable to hold back the smile that crossed his face. They turned west, still climbing. "How about that course, Johnny?"

Grant stared at the fuel gauge. Then, slowly, he turned to Durban and shook his head.

Durban sighed. "Understood." He thumbed his R/T switch. "Barton, it seems I've left us a little short of juice. Why don't you head home and run the debrief for me?"

"Ah, Kittens will handle it," the Australian said. "He isn't too bad at his job, for a Kiwi. Besides, Finny here just told me we don't have enough fuel to get back either. What's that, Finny? You liar. You'll never believe this, boss, but my rotten bloody navigator claims he told me that ten minutes ago. Fancy swapping? I'll trade him for Grant."

"No chance," Durban said, looking at Grant. The youngster seemed barely awake now. Durban kept the R/T open. "You okay, Johnny?"

"Yeah, sir. Just a little tired."

"I'll bet." With a gentle nudge of the controls, he turned them northwest. He didn't need a map for that. "Don't worry. You'll get plenty of sleep in Sweden."

"Sweden?"

Barton's laugh filled their headphones. "I always wanted to go to Sweden. I hear it's lovely this time of year."

"Let's find out," Durban said, reaching out to squeeze Grant's shoulder.

Behind them, in the onrushing gloom of the coming night, the still blazing funeral pyre of *Götterdämmerung* cast a pale glow over the still waters of the harbour.

Epilogue

Staverton St Mary, 8 May 1945

Someone was torturing the piano, filling the room with a discordant sound that could only be loosely described as music, but no one seemed to mind. The King's Ransom was full, Germany had surrendered, and the party was in full flow.

Kittens met them at the door, shaking their hands. Anita gave Grant a hug, kissing him on the cheek before showing him the engagement ring on her hand and bursting into tears. That seemed only to draw the attention of everyone else, and with it a bombardment of cheers and handshakes and enough slaps on the back that they propelled Grant to the bar whether he liked it or not.

"Johnny Grant," May shouted, abandoning a pint mid-pour to bustle over to him. She leaned over the bar, clasped her chilly hands around his face and kissed him full on the lips. "Don't get any ideas, young man," she admonished him. "I'm greeting everyone like that tonight."

"I promised I'd come, May," Grant said, struggling to raise his voice above the tumult. "I promised I'd come the night the war ended."

"And you're late," she said. "Where have you been until now?"

"Sweden."

"In Wiltshire?"

He didn't know quite how to answer that, but suddenly Finny was there with his arm around Grant's shoulders, Barton watching on with an avuncular grin.

"Oi, May," Finny demanded, "where's my kiss?"

"In your dreams, David Finnegan. What can I get you, lads?"

"Four beers please, May," Grant said.

"Better make it eight, Johnny," Barton said. "By the looks of it, we're playing catchup."

As if to prove the point, Hick appeared, drenched in spilt beer. With a gleeful roar, the huge Rhodesian swept Grant up in a big bear hug, then dropped him and repeated the same feat for the startled Finny. He might have gone for the hat-trick, but Barton simply stared at him. "Squadron Leader Barton, sir," Hick mumbled, and stumbled off into the crowd.

Barton shook his head. "Where's Andy got to?"

Grant picked up two pints and scanned the pub. Durban had been with them when they came through the door. He'd been a different man in Sweden, confident and carefree, first overawing the soldiers who had arrested them at Stockholm-Bromma Flygplats and then charming the nurses who had given them their medical examinations. Only as they left the DC-3 that had brought them home and drove through the Norfolk countryside from RAF Northolt had he become withdrawn.

He could guess why.

"I'm not sure, sir," he lied.

"Well, go find him, mate," Barton said, reaching out to tousle Grant's hair. "Before his beer gets warm."

Edging his way between half a dozen aircrew and locals, Grant passed through the archway towards the common room at the back, where the piano lurked. No sign of Durban, but Danny Bramante bore the guilt for the brutalising of the piano; his navigator, Gardiner, was doing his best to drown out the music with a falsetto rendition of some or other Vera Lynn song. Plenty seemed to enjoy it enough to join in. Nurse Claire, her cheeks flushed with joy and eyes glistening with tears, broke off her singing long enough to embrace Johnny. She gave him a friendly wet kiss on each cheek, followed it up with a more than friendly squeeze of the backside, then instantly forgot him as Bramante began a new tune.

Grant looked down at his uniform, flown out especially by the crew of the DC-3. It was damp with spilt beer. He doubted he was the only one.

A thin hand took his and shook it, and Grant looked up into the face of Bony Wright. They didn't quite see eye to eye. Bony's eyes were far too blurred and off focus for that. "Welcome back, Johnny, welcome back," Bony said.

"Thanks," Grant said. "Have you seen the Wing Commander?"

Bony burped. "He's outside, I think. Look, would you be a chap and give him this?" He clumsily pushed a folded piece of paper into Johnny's shirt pocket. "I was supposed to give it to him myself, but..." He lowered his voice to a conspiratorial whisper. "I've had a drink, Johnny."

"No worries, Bony," Grant said. "I'll handle it."

Bony shook his head, blinking. "Handle what?" Eyes almost rolling into the back of his head, he reeled off towards the piano.

Grant reached the double doors that led outside into the beer garden.

Durban was there, a cigarette in his hand. He was not alone.

"Sorry, Ma'am," Grant said. "I wasn't expecting you."

"That's ok, Johnny," Sarah Lane said with a smile. "It's good to see you, too."

"Here's your pint, sir."

"You should be thrilled to see her," Durban said, taking the glass. "Without her pulling some strings at SOE, we'd still be waiting to be repatriated with the other internees."

"That was you, Ma'am?"

"It wasn't as hard as you'd think," she said. "We've worked with Swedish Intelligence on and off for years. Between their newfound fear of the Soviets and Prime Minister Hansson's desire to ingratiate himself with the victorious Allies, neutral Sweden is far less neutral than it might appear."

"Johnny," Durban said, "would you mind giving us a minute?"

"Of course, sir." Grant paused. "It was good to see you, Ma'am."

She smiled again. "Take care of yourself, Johnny."

With a respectful nod to the Wing Commander, he pushed open the doors. The party hadn't subsided a jot. It was louder and more crowded than ever. Half the squadron clustered around the piano now. Barton had shoved Bramante aside and was proving to be a far, far better player. Kittens and Anita stood arm-in-arm, her head on his shoulder, watching Claire with amusement as she exchanged a passionate kiss with Finny. The New Zealander saw Grant and gave him a fond smile.

Grant finally took a sip of what little of his beer wasn't already plastered over him. It was terrible, like every other pint he'd had in Britain. It brought thoughts of Barbados, and that new Red Stripe beer that had become popular in Jamaica, and of sipping lager on white sand while the sun set over the Caribbean. The war was over. No more freezing nights. No more training, no more long hours in the cockpit, no more skies blackened with flak and the hunting shapes of enemy fighters.

Barbados was calling. Home.

He realised he was staring out of the rear window, watching Durban and Lane. They had been talking. Now they stood in silence, inches away from each other. Tentatively, her hands reached out and took his. Grant felt like a voyeur, but couldn't move. He remembered Bony's letter in his pocket. Now was not the time to deliver it.

Sarah Lane leaned forward, kissed Durban on the forehead, and walked away, towards the back gate of the beer garden and the waiting darkness.

She did not look back.

Grant pulled the folded paper from his pocket. It fell open in his hand.

By the time Grant pushed apart the double doors again,

Durban had lit another cigarette and sat on a wooden bench, staring at the sky. Like he already missed it, Grant thought.

"You should be inside, Johnny, enjoying the party."

"So should you, sir."

"I will. Soon." He took a deep draw, blowing out a smoke ring. It rose towards the distant stars, then faded to nothing.

"Bony... pardon me, Flight Lieutenant Wright... asked me to give you this, sir."

Durban's eyes flickered to the letter, then returned to silent contemplation of the heavens. "You read it?"

"Yes, sir. I didn't mean to."

"Relax, Johnny. Have a seat."

Grant slid onto the bench opposite. He felt horribly sober. A drunken roar of delight came from within the bar as Finny read out Churchill's address to the crowds in Whitehall. "God bless you all," the Australian shouted. "This is your victory. In our long history, we have never seen a greater day than this. Everyone, man or woman, has done their best."

The cheers seemed a long way from here.

"Is Squadron Officer Lane coming back, sir?"

Durban sighed. "I hope so. One day. When her work is finished." For the first time, he seemed to notice his untouched pint glass and raised it to his lips. Just that. He didn't so much as sip it.

Grant pushed the unfolded letter across the table. *Wing Commander Durban. Your request for voluntary service in the Far East has been accepted. You are to report to...*

"Why, sir?"

"Someone has to," Durban said calmly.

"But not you, sir. You've done your bit. The war is over."

"Tell that to the Japanese Empire, Johnny. God knows they won't listen to the rest of us."

There was no self-pity in Durban's tone, Grant realised. No

self-aggrandisement, either. Merely a rational acceptance that there was a job to be done. He thought again of Barbados, of the joy on his Murr's face when she saw him safely home, of the pride he would feel in his RAF uniform even as he campaigned for an independent Barbados.

A job well done.

"Understood, sir," he said. "I'll put my request in tomorrow."

Durban shook his head. "No, you won't. First, you'll nurse the same hangover as everyone else. Then you'll start planning how to become Prime Minister of Barbados."

"Sir?"

"I'm still your squadron commander, Flying Officer Grant," Durban said, the hint of a smile crossing his face. "Consider it an order, if you prefer." He rose to his feet and offered his hand. "It's been an honour, Johnny."

"Thank you, sir." Grant took the rock-steady hand and shook it.

The double doors creaked open. May poked her head out. "You gentlemen want another drink?"

"The next round for everyone is on me, May," Durban said. "I think it's about time I pulled my weight in the bar. Maybe showed those Philistines how to play that piano properly."

"Right you are, Wing Commander," May said. "I suppose I'd best go get them warmed up for you." She disappeared back inside and was promptly greeted by a string of wolf whistles.

"How about it then, Johnny? Should we drink enough to regret it in the morning?" Durban turned for the door.

"Sir?"

"Yes?"

"Do you think people will remember Jan Stahl? What he did for the world?"

Durban stood and looked up at the sky again for a long time, the cigarette forgotten in his hand. Somewhere in the darkness, aero engines rumbled unseen. Transports, not bombers or night fighters. The loud bangs and flashes that rippled across the sky were fireworks, not flak.

Car horns beeped. Songs rang out. A nation and a continent celebrated.

"No," Durban said finally. "I don't believe they will. And I think that's the way Stahl would have wanted it."

He held the door for Grant, and they walked inside to the biggest cheer of the night.

Acknowledgments

This book began life as a love letter to the wartime RAF. Even as it expanded to include SOE, the German resistance and other elements, that desire to pay some measure of tribute, however small and inadequate, to the aircrew and others who fought the Second World War never changed. My own eighteen years in the RAF saw a lot of changes in the Service, but with each one of those years, my admiration for the men and women who served from 1939 to 1945 only grew.

Beyond wishing to celebrate the wider RAF, several particular individuals inspired my main characters, to a greater or lesser degree.

Wing Commander Andrew Durban is my tribute to Guy Gibson, particularly when it comes to personal bravery and the hidden costs of combat stress, but with elements of Group Captain Leonard Cheshire, a later commander of the legendary "Dambusters" of 617 Squadron and perhaps the only other RAF pilot of the war who could compete with Gibson for fame or decorations.

Squadron Officer Sarah Lane of SOE's 'X' Section (and Women's Auxiliary Air Force) is based heavily on the less-known but equally impressive Squadron Officer Vera Atkins WAAF of 'F' Section.

Johnny Grant is an amalgam of several of the roughly five hundred young men from the Caribbean who volunteered to fly in the wartime RAF; more than a third would die in action. The closest direct model for Grant is probably Flight Lieutenant John Ebanks from Jamaica, a Mosquito navigator, but I also felt compelled to include major elements of Flying Officer Errol Barrow, who would later become the first Prime Minister of the independent Barbados. Of the eleven other men who enlisted with Barrow as the "Barbados Second Contingent", six were killed.

Of the POV characters, only Obersturmbannführer Jan Stahl has no historical antecedent. Nevertheless, he represents the brave (if ultimately failed) sacrifice of those who fought against Nazism from the inside, including trying to overthrow Hitler. Their motivations varied, from the moral to the practical, but almost all paid a deadly price for daring to oppose the Führer.

Stahl's biggest influence appears in his own right in the book – the doomed Admiral Wilhelm Canaris. Similarly, I have done almost nothing to change the larger-than-life character of Air Vice Marshal Sir Basil Embry who, believing that he should order no one to do anything he wouldn't do himself, did indeed disguise himself as Wing Commander Smith to fly on some of the most dangerous and challenging missions his aircrew undertook. I must also spare a word for the legendary Danish SBS officer Anders Lassen. Not content with stealing Lassen's name for my author pseudonym, I could not resist including the heavily-fictionalised but, I hope, suitably similar "Major Anders".

Producing any novel is quite an undertaking. The actual writing can and must be a very solitary process, but getting it over the line is something of a team sport – especially when you are trying to produce fiction with as much historical accuracy as possible. A huge thank you goes to my publisher, Humfrey Hunter of Silvertail Books, who has shown such faith in me – I hope this is the first of many projects together. Similarly, my gratitude to Rowland White for his friendship, support, and for his peerless *Mosquito*. I could not begin to list all the books and resources I used for this novel, but three books stand out as particularly critical and I cannot recommend any of them too highly. James Holland (*Dam Busters*), Sarah Helm (*Vera*

Atkins: A Life in Secrets) and Mark Johnson (*Caribbean Volunteers at War*) – I owe each of you a pint. If my book is accurate, the credit is mostly yours. Any epic fails are my own.

Of course, few true fans of the de Havilland Mosquito will be unfamiliar with Frederick E. Smith and *633 Squadron* – I picked up the first sequel, *Operation Rhine Maiden*, at a school fair when I was twelve, and it simultaneously filled me with a love for the Mosquito, a desire to join the RAF, and an urge to write novels for a living. Given that I later served in the RAF and have now written two novels heavily based around the Mosquito, it would not be a stretch to call it the single most influential book I've ever read.

Personal thanks go to Maxwell Alexander Drake for his sage advice (I hope you're pleased at the relative lack of passive voice), and to my long-time critique circle – Genghis, Rob O, Will M, Lori L, Michael G, Dan B, Benno, Rob H., Barto, Mitch, Peter R, Tim C, Dezling and many others – you've all made me a better writer.

To my wonderful wife Brie (the long-haired Air Vice Marshal in my life) and to my brilliant children Aidan and Charlie – I hope it was worth all the time I spent hiding from you, rattling away at my keyboard. All royalties will, of course, be spent on you!

And finally, to bring it back to where we started, to all the men and women of the Royal Air Force, past and present, I hope this book will not displease you.

Per Ardua ad Astra, my friends.

Robert Lassen, Germany, 2024